Pel and the Nickname Game

PEL AND THE NICKNAME GAME

Juliet Hebden

Constable • London

First published in Great Britain 2002
by Constable, an imprint of Constable & Robinson Ltd
3 The Lanchesters, 162 Fulham Palace Road
London W6 9ER
www.constablerobinson.com

ISBN 1–84119–520–0

Printed and bound in Great Britain

A CIP catalogue record for this book
is available from the British Library

Though the city in these pages does exist
it is however intended to be fictitious,
as are the characters.
Any resemblance to any actual living
person is purely coincidental.

Pour

L'Ours
La Jambe
La Tronche
Les Fesses
Snodgrass
Billy Boy
Bouba
Bozo
Maxou
Lala

Chapter One

Commissaire Evariste Clovis Désiré Pel didn't have a nickname
– well, except Difficult Little Bugger but that didn't count
because the only man who dared call him a DLB to his face was
the ex-Chief of Police and he'd retired a long time ago. Pel could
have been called Four Eyes due to his thick specs. Or *Clochard*;
his shoes never shone and his suits were permanently crumpled
as if he'd slept in them. Or *Pendu*, thanks to the length of silk
round his neck that looked more like a hangman's noose than a
tie. Or, contrarily, *Poilu*; he had very little hair left on his head.
Even *le Grand* might have raised a smile, seeing as he was one of
the smallest members of the Hôtel de Police, measuring a mere
1m 80. But no. Perhaps it was because he had a sharp mind that
worked in overdrive, a voice that could compete with Luciano
Pavarotti – for decibels, not beauty – and an undeniable respect
from all his men, that Pel had remained plain Pel. Pel didn't
have a nickname.

Nearly everyone else did. Lambert, due to the thick white
thatch that topped his imposing 1m 92, was known as the Snow-
Capped Mountain for instance. Then there were Napoléon, de
Troq', *l'Arab*, the Prize Idiot, *le 'Ulk*, the Puppy, *le Punk, Sac à
Puces, Haricot Vert*, and Fingers. And that was just Pel's team.
Until recently there'd also been Prince Charming and the Lion of
Belfort, but Prince Charming had disappeared for ever, mur-
dered by a terrorist, and the Lion of Belfort had disappeared to
have the Arab's baby.

Beyond their own offices, to while away the time, because the
city's criminal detectives had lots of time to while away in
between chasing arsonists, burglars, gangsters, hooligans, muggers, murderers, pushers, racketeers, rapists, slashers, smashers
and all the other sweet-natured citizens of Burgundy, they'd also
attributed nicknames to certain outsiders. The two pathologists
were understandably known as Blood and Guts. Leguyder, the

long-winded forensic expert, was known as Larousse, not because he was effeminate in any way, or red-haired for that matter; Larousse was the publisher of a famous encyclopedia, and everyone was convinced he spent his evenings reading it so he could confuse the ignorant police force with twenty-five-letter words the next morning. Marteau, the commanding officer at the gendarmerie, had acquired the name *Clou*, for obvious reasons; the *procureur*, *le Boss*; and the Ministre de l'Intérieur, *le Big Boss*. Plus a certain Lt. Col. Pierre Lapeyre from la Division Nationale Anti-Terroriste was called all sorts of things, most often *le Salopard de Paris*, in other words, That Bloody Man From Paris.

Jeudi, le 16 décembre
Ste Alice's day. That's to say, all the girls, women and old crones called Alice hoped – no, expected – to be wished a *bonne fête*, some of them would be given flowers to mark the occasion. First thing that morning, the florists checked their calendars and changed the name hanging in their shop windows, hoping to do another twelve hours' roaring trade – a different saint was celebrated almost every day of the year and female saints were good for business. France is strong on saints' days, being a Roman Catholic country. The average Frenchman, though outwardly perhaps not very different from an Englishman or an American, is proud – immensely proud – of his origins, considering himself to be part of an exuberant and romantic race. The average Frenchman snaps up any occasion to celebrate and linger a little longer in the bar after work with an extra drink – after remembering to buy his particular Alice a floral peace offering of course.

As the wintry sun rose to streak the pale grey sky with golden slashes, the radio announced, 'Washington DC: George Bush *est presque Président!'*

Most French citizens at this point crunched merrily into their early morning *biscottes* and chewed noisily, either that or they went to clean their teeth. No one was worried about missing the rest of the commentary on this world-shattering piece of news. The American elections had gone on far too long, boring Europe into a yawning apathy.

They were listening again in time to learn that in Auxerre, capital of l'Yonne, Monsieur Emile Louis, now over sixty years old, had been brought into custody after the police discovered girls' clothing at his home. He was suspected of murdering seven mentally handicapped girls who'd been living in the same centre – basically a state orphanage or, if you prefer, home for unwanted children – in the care of the DDASS – Direction Départementale Assistance Services Sociaux – and had disappeared between 1977 and 1979. Their bodies were never found. Louis had always been the prime suspect, having been the girls' bus driver at the time of their disappearance, but he didn't waver from his claim of innocence and, in the absence of admissible evidence, hadn't been charged. Yet.

And in Paris, the Prime Minister, Lionel Jospin (left-wing) marked time – and tried not to look too pleased – after accusations of *détournement de fonds* were made against President Jacques Chirac's government (right-wing).

Those were the headlines. The weather forecast was just as predictable: rain all day.

The sun streamed – anyone can make a mistake – through the dusty windscreen, making Nosjean sneeze, the sun always had that effect on him in a car. Not that he was allergic to the sun, far from it. He decided it was probably the dust and mites, warming in the sun's rays, that made him sneeze. He *was* allergic to mites and in a car from the police pool it stood to reason there'd be plenty knocking about in or under the upholstery. Gilbert, for instance, would certainly have spent some time in Nosjean's seat. Gilbert had been recently transferred from the CRS, la Compagnie Républicaine de Sécurité – basically a riot squad – to join the plain-clothes section of la Police Judiciaire. Jean-Louis Gilbert was also the most vulgar member of the Hôtel de Police who, if he had nothing better to do, would pick at his fingernails, his teeth or his nose, or, when he was really on form, scratch any part of his body that took his fancy. Gilbert scratched like a stray mongrel with fleas; comprehensively, vigorously and without inhibition, hence his nickname, *Sac à Puces*. Therefore it was reasonable for Nosjean to suspect there may be mites knocking about in the car in which he was being driven by young Morrison, an even newer member of the team.

It was another bright sunny day, incredibly warm for December – for the four or five hours after the sun broke through a chilling early morning mist and before it began sinking behind a darkening horizon – and, if it hadn't been for the urgent call from a young girl claiming someone had died in the room upstairs, Nosjean would've been a relatively happy man. His divorce was a pain in the arse, but that was to be expected, divorces usually are. His wife Mijo – real name, Marie-Josephine

– was demanding a startlingly large settlement, the custody of their small daughter, Erika, plus massive monthly payments to take care of her. On the other hand, things were going well with Anna, the nurse who looked like Julia Roberts, and with whom he spent his weekends off. He'd started laughing again, something he hadn't done in a long time, and after the final frigid months before Mijo left, he was also thoroughly enjoying a reinstated sex life – all the better for Anna's enthusiasm and imagination – when he got the chance; weekends off weren't frequent when you were part of la Police Judiciaire, particularly with a commanding officer like Pel.

Nosjean looked across at Morrison; his habit of blushing whenever addressed had endeared him to Nosjean. He'd had the same problem when he was younger. His marriage, his daughter's birth, the divorce and his best friend's death – shot by a terrorist – all had something to do with the maturity he now felt. However, Nosjean was a sensitive man, and he still remembered his acute nervousness when first meeting Pel, and he also recalled Pel saying he looked like the Young Napoleon on the Bridge at Lodi; he'd had to look that one up and when he did, he'd agreed there was a vague resemblance. Not many people made reference to it nowadays. It may have had something to do with his promotion to second-in-command. It may have been that 'Nosjean' was simpler. Not that that made any difference really; Morrison's nickname was more complicated. It should have been Carrot-top in recognition of his orange hair, but for some reason, perversity perhaps, as was often the case, or perhaps because he was long, thin and professionally still very green, it was *Haricot Vert*.

'The pathologist's on his way,' Nosjean said. 'He should arrive at about the same time as us.'

Morrison turned pink, making Nosjean smile, he'd known he would. 'Yes, sir.'

'Nosjean'll do, the only person you have to call "sir" is Chief Lambert.'

Morrison turned scarlet. 'Right . . . Nosjean.'

'The landlady's been told to stand by with the keys, she'll open the door. If there *is* a dead body, you keep your eyes open, your mouth shut and your hands in your pockets, okay?'

Morrison was doing an impression of a beetroot. 'Okay.'

Nosjean grinned and looked out at the passing buildings to hide his amusement.

*   *   *

10

The landlady fiddled with her keys. 'Don't know what all the fuss is about,' she complained. 'These girls . . . I don't know. Mind you, the smell is something 'orrible. I'll put that Théodora out if she's been up to something she shouldn't 'ave.'

Oh, but she had been up to something she shouldn't have.

The stench surged out as soon as the door was opened, a sweet putrid stink, thick and sickening, and Nosjean, an experienced criminal detective, knew only too well what it was.

'Thank you, madame, you can go downstairs now. Please stay in the building, I'll need to talk to you later.'

'Well, yes, all right, and you can tell that young scallywag she's looking for new digs.'

The young scallywag wouldn't be looking for anything ever again.

Nosjean glanced at Boudet. He was already pulling on his latex gloves, frowning as he did so, then fitting a sterile mask over his mouth, hooking the elastic tapes round his ears. As he pushed the door further into the room, Nosjean followed him in.

The bloated corpse lay on its back on the floor, the swollen black lips open, vomit caked but dry in the shoulder-length hair. The girl's legs were straight, slightly apart, and, as she'd slipped from the edge of the bed, her short skirt had been pushed up untidily round her hips, revealing laddered tights and soiled black briefs. Nosjean wondered if she'd been attractive when she'd been alive, it was difficult to tell. She was hideous lying on the rumpled rug and, as often happened, she'd evacuated her bowels – death does that. Suicides believe that taking a handful of sleeping pills and arranging themselves prettily on a bed will make a poignant scene when they're found. Not so, the human body empties itself before giving up its struggle for life; in the last few moments, during the death throes, so to speak, it rejects any unwanted matter, trying to rid itself of the alien substance. Hence, instead of a delicate picture of sadness and desperation, the police, or whoever finds the cadaver, are faced with a charming mixture of vomit, urine and shit. And, of course, the smell, which is bad enough even if the victim is discovered before advanced putrefaction sets in.

This one hadn't been.

After a week, the other inhabitants of the house had noticed rather a lot of flies on the landing where Théo – easier than Théodora – had her room. It was unusual for the middle of December but it had been a very mild start to the winter with no

11

frosts, so when the sun came streaming through the grubby windows, warming the corridors and everyone's hearts, no one questioned the constant buzzing, irritating though it was. They'd also smelt something unpleasant, commenting casually, 'Someone's forgotten to take their rubbish out.' One or two girls had said it was enough to put them off their food, and anything else they might be doing in their digs. But no one bothered to investigate until Fleur – baptised Marguerite, but she'd never liked it, she said only cows were called Buttercup or Daisy – found a small dark damp stain on her carpet and discovered something dripping through her ceiling. She'd bolted up the stairs and hammered on Théo's door. 'What are you doing in there! Chemical experiments?'

A reasonable accusation, Théo was a student of chemistry. 'Hey! Open up! *Ça schleng!*' But of course there'd been no reply and Fleur went out for supper suspecting that fun-loving Théo was expertly concocting a handful of stink bombs for the coming festivities. It had been hilarious in June when she dropped one in the Students' Union, it had been empty for days.

After supper, Fleur spent the night in her boyfriend's bed and didn't give another thought to Théo until she came back from a hard day's work at the city's university the following evening.

The stain had grown into a puddle, the smell made her retch, and she finally decided to do something about it. After hammering once more on Théo's door, and again receiving no reply, Fleur called her boyfriend, a fourth year student of medicine, and he, having some knowledge of these matters, told her to call the bloody police, and quick.

Which was why Nosjean, Morrison, no longer blushing, if anything he was slightly green, and Boudet – the police's appointed medical examiner and the city's assistant pathologist – along with two uniformed representatives from the local gendarmerie who were automatically informed if anything exciting was happening on their patch, were all now involved.

'Phone for a meat wagon, Morrison,' Nosjean said calmly. 'Tell the gendarmes to temporarily seal off this floor, and inform Pel, he'll have to let the Chief and the *procureur* know. Then get on to the SPST,' (short for Service de Police Scientifique et Technique) 'we'll need it all on film; Forensic and Fingerprints, in case there's suspicion of foul play, and don't forget the *juge d'instruction*, Brisard needs to see this before anything's moved.'

Théodora Roussillon, a discreet though fun-loving girl, had

never before attracted so much attention, not even with her well-placed stink bombs. Over fifty-six people – if you included the lab assistants and secretaries who'd type up the reports – would be informed and involved in her death, and that wasn't counting her family, still ignorant of her departure.

Counting the phone calls he had to make on his fingers, Morrison disappeared gratefully, still holding his breath, and, as he ran down the stairs, he pulled a handkerchief from his pocket to gag the bile rising towards his mouth.

While Boudet crouched cautiously over the corpse, Nosjean's eyes swung round the room. It was an ordinary student's bedsit with a washbasin and mirror in one corner displaying a large range of spot creams and a small selection of make-up; a work surface over two cupboards; a microwave; an electric coffee maker alongside which sat two mugs with spoons in them, an open box of sugar cubes, and a dirty plate containing a knife and fork. The walls were covered in posters; the bed was unmade; the bedside light was on, which seemed to indicate she'd died during the hours of darkness. There were clothes discarded haphazardly over a wooden chair and overflowing on to the floor, but the desk was neat, papers and books arranged ready for study. The shutters were open, the window was closed.

And on the floor the bloated rotting body.

'Suicide?' he asked.

'Take a look at her arms,' Boudet replied. 'She was an addict. Are overdoses suicides? Or accidents? Or indirect murder? You tell me.'

Nosjean peered at the puncture marks on the left arm which lay across the girl's stomach, her claw-like discoloured hand clutching the air, as if in pain. The other arm was thrown outwards, reaching for something, and beside the lifeless, almost formless fingers were an empty syringe, a metal ashtray, a lighter, a short piece of cord and, oddly, a crucifix.

'Overdose,' Nosjean repeated. 'Any idea what?'

'She's too far gone to hazard a guess, you'll have to wait until I get her in the lab for tests.'

'Anything else to add at this stage?'

'Yes.'

'I'm listening,' Nosjean said seriously.

'Thank God body-bags are waterproof; this one would drip all the way down the stairs.'

13

St Gael's day. You don't buy flowers for men, not macho Frenchmen, romantic though they may be. The Gaels of our proud Republic simply looked forward to an extra pair of beers – or pastis, whisky, *coups de rouge*, whatever their tipple was – in the bar, on their way home, as usual, that evening.

In Auxerre, Emile Louis had finally admitted murdering the seven mentally handicapped girls.

In L'Herault, an ex-Air France pilot, Philippe Narré, and his wife, Aimée, had been murdered. The cleaning woman called the gendarmerie after finding their home in disarray that morning. Shortly after the boys in blue arrived, the bodies were discovered in the garden shed; Philippe strangled, Aimée suffocated. A member of the family or close friend was being sought to help the investigating team with their enquiries.

In Nevers (Nièvre), La Pharmacie Tahoo was broken into. It was another in a long and worrying series of chemists' burglaries. A police spokesman said that addicts and illicit drug users were very probably responsible.

And in Paris, Jospin waited impatiently for Chirac's televised reply to the accusation of his government's illegal use of party funds. Chirac was also waiting impatiently for his reply; he told the men who were writing it to jolly well hurry up.

Contrary to the weather forecast of clear skies, it rained on and off all day, the charcoal clouds rolling in from the north-west, gathering ominously until, as the twilight thickened, the real deluge began.

Outside, the city was changing her robes, clothing herself in sophisticated black, adorned with glittering gems of diamond light, preparing for the night. The streets were quieter now, just a few cars, their tyres hissing on the wet tarmac. The gutters ran, water hurrying, rushing, turning and cascading into its channelled caverns underground; it was raining cats and dogs – why cats and dogs? – or as the French say, *'il pleuvait comme une vache qui pisse,'* a useful little expression which adequately described the downpour that was drenching the streets and pedestrians alike.

Inside, the Bar Transvaal was crowded and noisy, the windows had misted over long ago and the atmosphere was thick with smoke. It was 1845 on a Friday evening. For most people the working week was over and they could look forward to two days away from the rush and bustle of their offices, enjoying instead the rush and bustle of their homes and families. Among the men and women partaking of their well-earned refreshment were a magistrate, a handful of lawyers, a doctor, a couple of ambulancemen, one or two witnesses who'd been called in to make a statement and, dotted about in the crowd, there were also a number of secretaries and messengers. All of them were pleased to celebrate Friday evening – except the group of taxi drivers at one end of the bar; they were grumbling they'd be working the weekend even if the other buggers weren't, and receiving very little sympathy. Inevitably, because the bar was opposite the Hôtel de Police, there were also a lot of policemen present, no longer in uniform of course, and the members of the Police Judiciaire de la République de France. Seven at the bar, fingering their glasses or calling for a refill, and pockets of plain-clothes detectives sat in the booths down one side discussing the cases they'd dealt with that day, and would continue to deal with until they were brought to a satisfactory conclusion, or not. Some of them had Saturday and Sunday off, some of them didn't, it depended on the duty roster, so carefully filled in and signed by their superior officers; a minimum of eight hours a day or night, five days a week, forty-six weeks a year, year in year out whether they liked it or not, regardless of what their long-suffering wives said, regardless of their kids' birthdays, regardless of Bank Holidays, New Year and Christmas. 'A mini-mum' was a joke; unlike the office and factory workers, the lawyers and the secretaries, the insurance agents and tax inspec-tors, these men couldn't look at their watches and say, 'Goody, knocking off time,' not when they were chasing a screaming car through the back streets, or negotiating the release of a woman and her three kids, held at gunpoint by a drunken husband, or interviewing the weeping victim of violent robbery or rape, or, for that matter, waiting for the medics, the scientists, the examin-ing magistrate and any other official person required by law to be present when a corpse was discovered. *Eh non, con,* they just had to see it all through to the end – and report for duty at the allotted time the following morning.

The television in the corner was chattering inanely, the good-looking newscaster on FR2, Rachid Arab – a good name for a bloke from Morocco – was announcing, 'It's official; George Bush is President.' At last. No one was listening, who gave a damn after so long?

Certainly not Commissaire Pel. He was sitting hunched in a booth not far from the door talking to Nosjean and the Baron de

Troquereau de Turenne, an aristocrat by birth, but paupered – relatively speaking – by the Germans' confiscation of art treasures in 1943 from his family's château (they also confiscated most of his ancestors' lives), the French economic climate after the war and finally his father's untimely death due to a hunting accident, obliging his only son and heir, Charles Victor, to accept the fact he was going to have to work bloody hard to earn his living. He'd accepted it without comment, had done well at school then university, and subsequently at Saint-Cyr's police academy and the Canet-Cluse School for inspectors, and much to the consternation of his mother – Madame la Baronne, in spite of everything, she was still a very grand lady – was finally proud to be a member of Pel's team. De Troq', as he was known at the Hôtel de Police, spoke French, English and Spanish, a smattering of German, and could get by in Occitan, and, while he was an excellent officer to have on the team, Pel, occasionally, wanted to wring his ruddy neck; he always looked like a ruddy aristocrat, polished and well pressed, something Pel would never be.

'Boudet confirmed death due to a drugs overdose,' Nosjean told him. 'He found 0.27 grams of heroin in her blood, 0.07 grams more than she needed to kill herself.'

'Anything else?'

Nosjean looked down at his notes. 'Traces of benzodiazepine.'

'What's that?'

'Apparently she suffered from petit mal, the benzodiazepine kept it under control.'

'You've checked?'

'Spoke to her family GP earlier today, he confirmed prescribing it before term started in October.'

Pel raised an eyebrow. 'And she had enough of the stuff to keep taking it until now?'

'The petit mal was mild. She had periods when the fits struck, he prescribed it as a precaution against the stress she'd be under with end-of-term exams.'

'Did he know she was injecting heroin?'

'When he examined her in September, he found no evidence of it. Her blood test was normal, her urine too, therefore he felt it was safe to prescribe for the petit mal.'

'So the addiction started afterwards.'

'She had plenty of time. You only need a couple of weeks to

progress from experimental sniffing through skin popping to mainlining.'

'What side effect does this benzopine have?'

'A benzodiazepine can cause amnesia and sometimes aggressive behaviour, alcohol exaggerates these conditions and should be avoided. More usually though it's thought of as a tranquillizer.'

'Had she been drinking?'

Nosjean shook his head.

'But it could've helped her forget she'd already injected herself?'

'Boudet seems to think not. She'd've been enjoying the usual state of euphoria while it lasted. Once high, she wouldn't have worried about the next fix.'

'Could someone have done it for her?'

'The door was locked from the inside, there were only her prints on the syringe.'

'So you want to close the case.'

'I can't see any point in keeping it open. It's pretty clear, isn't it? The kid was an addict, she OD'd.'

'I'm inclined to agree.' Pel took a gulp at his beer and looked over his shoulder towards two large men at the counter; their shoulders were rounded in relaxation, their heads confidentially close, and alongside, pretending interest in their conversation, was a tall lanky youngster. He knew the three of them very well, they were part of his own *équipe*. Timothé Morrison, the youngster, was blushing as usual, his pale complexion turning from pink to scarlet to crimson, and clashing with his orange hair. Beside him was Josephe Misset, the man with his brain stuck in neutral, considered by Pel to be a prize idiot, and he told him so often, although, he had to admit, Misset had the uncanny knack of coming up trumps just when it counted. The one doing the talking was Gilbert; *his* brain rarely deviated from the subject of sex and he possessed an extensive vocabulary to illustrate his opinions that made them all cringe. But, in between scratching himself like a stray mongrel with fleas, or picking his nose, he managed to play his part in the team fairly efficiently, although he still distributed lewd magazines throughout the Hôtel de Police, causing occasional disturbance at Chief Lambert's lengthy procedural meetings.

'I wonder what those two buffoons are planning,' Pel said idly, turning back and stubbing out his smouldering Gauloise.

17

Nosjean and de Troq' glanced towards them. 'Probably discussing the barmaid's cleavage,' Nosjean suggested.

De Troq' smiled. 'You have to admit she's asking for it, her accoutrements are very well fitting.'

'Accoutrements? Where the hell did you find that word?' Pel retorted. 'Why don't you just say her jumper's bloody tight?'

'His upbringing, *patron*,' Nosjean answered, grinning. 'Talking posh comes natural.'

Pel put his beer down and licked his lips. 'And I'm a plain proletarian policeman, bugger the long words. It's bad enough with Leguyder's thousand-page forensic reports and Rigal's ruddy computer print-outs, not to mention Boudet when he gets going on an autopsy – don't you start, for God's sake!'

'Since Gilbert joined us, the vocabulary in the office has taken a turn for the worse,' de Troq' replied without apology. 'I'm simply trying to keep a balance. You have to admit he does have one or two particularly repulsive expressions.'

Pel shrugged. 'At least I understand him. I wonder what they *are* up to?'

'Whatever it is, it's enough to turn Morrison the same colour as a decent claret.'

Gilbert was in fact trying to persuade Misset to join him at a club he'd visited during the week. There'd been a fight there, not much more than a scuffle really, but one of those involved had whipped out an Opinel pocket knife, so witnesses said, and, after a great deal of trying, had finally managed to do some damage with it, before scarpering into the street and disappearing into the darkness. One customer and the club's bouncer had had to be stitched up – the customer's forearm and the bouncer's right hand – hence the police were pursuing their enquiries as well as the unknown escapee for whom they had the usual useless description; 'you know, ordinary-looking really' – they'd been watching the knife's cutting edge not the bloke's accoutrements or physical attributions – and Gilbert wanted to do what he called 'a bit of private surveillance'.

'The dancers are incredibly well stacked, never seen knockers like that before in me life, like bloody great balloons filled with water. Nice arses, too, the sort you can get your teeth into. Hardly a stitch on either, nothing left to the imagination. What do you say ? We introduce ourselves to the doorman, surreptitiously allowing him to see our identification, slip into the crowd and Bob's your uncle. I'd like to bet they'll give us free booze too, after all, we're only doing our duty, keeping an eye on the Bilboquet's clients.'

Misset shook his head.

'Oh come on,' Gilbert insisted. 'It'll make a change from sitting in front of the telly. You know what Attila the Hun's like on a Friday night, all she wants to watch is that crappy game show.'

'My mother-in-law's going to do as she's told tonight. If necessary I'll gag her and lock her in her room.'

'So what's so special about tonight? The wife's promised you a quickie?'

'My daughter's coming for the weekend.'

'I didn't know you had one.'

'Well, she's not really my daughter. She's my niece, but I think of her as a daughter now. We've taken care of her since the wife's brother was killed in a car crash. Her mum died of cancer a couple of years before that. She had no one left, so we kind of adopted her. Lovely girl. I tell you when you've got three sons like the ones I've got, a niece who flings her arms round your neck whenever she sees you and tells you you're the kindest, most wonderful man in the world, is pretty bloody special. And she's clever. All my boys have ever done was their bit in the army and fondle their girlfriends' tits while moaning about what isn't in their pay packets. Sandrine's different, she's a student at the university. Wants to be a teacher and I'm going to do every sodding thing I can to help her.'

'Pretty, is she?'

'Very, which is why I don't talk about her much. I don't want any of you lot getting your filthy hands on her. She's a good girl and that's the way I want her to stay.'

'Okay, keep your hair on. When's she getting in?'

'Tomorrow morning.'

'So tonight's free. How about it, Misset?'

'Nope, I'm whacked, been on my feet since six this morning. All I want is a decent meal and a good night's kip.' He swallowed the last of his drink and winked, a grin spreading across his face. 'And there is the wife's quickie to attend to.'

'Bollocks, it won't be any fun on my own. Unless . . .' He swung round abruptly. 'It's time you lost your virgin's blush, Morrison. How about it?'

19

Samedi, le 18 décembre

St Gatien. Various newspapers carried various headlines. Among them were:

'*L'Algérie à l'heure de la barbarie*. Suspected members of the GIA assassinated 16 teenagers yesterday evening. Will the killing ever end?'

'George W. Bush takes office as the 43rd President of the United States. Will it make any difference to Europe?' Considering the farcical way he acquired his presidency, the general consensus of opinion was, what the hell?

'Nantes beats Toulouse 5–2.' Nice one.

And on the back page, the inevitable, 'Widespread rain forecast throughout France.' In the Côte d'Or, Nièvre, Saône et Loire and Yonne – the four *départements* that make up the *région* of Burgundy – it was dry all day.

Colin Cuquel, twenty-one years old and in his final year studying for a history degree, woke as the grey dawn crept through his half-open shutters. For a moment, he lay in the comfortable warmth of his bed, enjoying the laziness of the first day of his weekend. No classes today; a couple of hours of revision, then he'd shower and shave, and clean his teeth particularly carefully – nothing worse than bad breath when you're whispering sweet nothings to the girl you love – in preparation for an afternoon with Sandrine. She'd called the night before to tell him there was something important in the post and that it should arrive the following morning – this morning – and he couldn't help the childish excitement he felt when he thought of something important coming through the post from Sandrine.

On Wednesday, the last time they'd met, he'd finally plucked up the courage to ask her to marry him; he was an old-fashioned boy and, being French, naturally romantic with it. She'd looked suitably surprised, a little confused and finally delighted as her fingertips touched his cheek and she leant forward to add a brief but delicious kiss to his lips. Now she'd sent him something important through the post – her reply? A written reply to his question? It was an old-fashioned and romantic way to accept his proposal, but being an old-fashioned and romantic young man, the idea appealed to him. He was looking forward to making his happy announcement to his parents.

Sandrine woke about half an hour later than Colin and rolled over, blinking into the dim light of her room. Then, as so often happens, the events of that week came swimming back through

20

the receding somnolence, and she smiled; her life was about to change for ever.

Pushing back the covers, she struggled wearily out of bed and shuffled across to the cupboard in the corner. Lifting down the suitcase she'd so carefully stored on top at the beginning of term, she placed it on the floor, clicked open the catches and slowly began packing. She'd call Uncle Jo later, when everything was fixed. She had to let him know why she was moving. Dear Uncle Jo, she hoped he wouldn't be disappointed.

Colin and Sandrine lived within walking distance of one another, just a couple of kilometres from door to door, in two of the many student houses divided into acceptably comfortable but unacceptably expensive digs, filling the maze of small streets to the west of the Centre Universitaire – situated just to the south of the Centre Hospitalier, le Centre Anti-Cancereux Georges François Leclerc, le Faculté de Médecine et de Pharmacie, l'Ecole de Formation d'Educateurs Spécialistes, l'Institut National de la Recherche Agronomique, la Faculté des Sciences and l'Institut Pédagogique: that part of town was known as la Cité des Sciences. The whole university complex, with all its many other institutes, schools and laboratories, was to be found on the eastern side of the north–south railway line, approximately five kilometres as the crow flies from the city centre and also from the Cité des Flics – a name which was a bit unfair, there were also modern-fronted shops with old-fashioned flats above in the area, together with the inevitable bars and brasseries, one or two insurance offices, a funeral parlour, a florist's, a couple of chemists, and so on and so forth. However, Fuzz Town it was.

You only had to walk down that wide tree-lined avenue to know why.

First, if you were coming from the Place de la République, you passed in front of the Préfecture, huge and square and always busy. That's where, if you had a pressing appointment with the Préfet, or you'd recently bought a vehicle, lost your identity card, or you'd recklessly applied for French nationality and were now being investigated financially, you'd stop. If you didn't, you'd arrive at the gendarmerie, the military section of the police. The gendarmes had their offices and their homes here; they and their families alike were housed in the out-of-date apartments behind the *caserne*.

If you walked a little further, you'd find, diagonally opposite and on the other side of the street, the Hôtel de Police, where the Police Judiciaire and the Police Municipale had their offices.

Attached to the front of this building – elderly, square and with ominous bars at all the windows – was a permanently lit, red white and blue neon sign with the word 'POLICE' written in large black letters. Behind the austere façade were the many offices inhabited by another posse of our proud Republic's law enforcers, uniformed and plain clothes. Standing in the entrance hall – painted beige with dull brown tiles underfoot – you would be excused if you thought you'd walked into a public lavatory, thanks to the city's architects' dubious expertise when deciding on how to redecorate. However, on noticing the dozens of posters and official notices, you'd quickly realize this was not the place for relieving a pressing need. Directly opposite the double swing doors leading from the pavement was *Acceuil*; a wide desk behind which sat a duty sergeant and his assistant. To the left, and marked clearly on a carefully painted wooden plaque, was the Police Municipale, responsible for all things to do with traffic, order on the streets and generally making their presence known; reassuring little old ladies and small children that help and protection was at hand. To the right was an electronically operated door which led to the Police Judiciaire.

In Paris, the capital of France, the Police Judiciaire is divided into the Brigade des Mineurs (kids), Brigade des Mœurs (sex), Brigade Criminelle (blood), Brigade des Stupéfiants (drugs), Brigade des Cambriolages (theft), Brigade Financière (money), Brigade du Crime Organisé (work it out), Brigade Aéroport, Brigade de Sécurité, and finally the Brigade des Enquêtes Générales (for anything else not already covered). Here, however, in the capital of Burgundy, the numerous activities came under one heading: le Commissariat. Of the seven Commissaires working within the Commissariat, there were only two – and their under officers in certain circumstances – with the required training and experience giving them the right to present themselves as Brigade Criminelle: Pel and Klein.

Klein's team were catching the calls. Pel and his nine active agents were inactive and happily relaxed for the first time in more than a month. The Butcher, who'd hacked a woman's body into more manageable pieces and lobbed them into the river, had at last been arrested and charged; the second murder that they'd first thought was a companion case, but which turned out not to be, had also been closed, its perpetrator satisfactorily behind bars. There were still hundreds of enquiries to be followed up – like the knifing at the Bilboquet as well as a string of irritating car thefts, and a startling rise in robberies – but that was understandable just before Christmas. Then there was the twelve-year-old kid who'd been arrested in possession of a kilo of cannabis – where the hell had he got that much?; the fourteen-year-old who'd been raped in the back row of the cinema – hey, that's what she claimed; Madame Delgas who'd poisoned the next-door dog because it crapped on her front door step every day and Madame Valras who'd tearfully buried her precious pooch then picked up a poker and had gone round to deal with the murdering Madame Delgas. Seeing her coming, Delgas had grabbed a rolling pin and both women were now in hospital and refusing to answer questions, which wouldn't be too bad if the pair of them, while trying to scratch each other's eyes out or do other bodily damage to their persons, hadn't ended up outside on the pavement where they'd comprehensively smashed the windscreen of Monsieur Barret's brand new four-wheel drive Suzuki. He was definitely bringing charges against 'those two vicious old bags'.

Not forgetting of course the usual assaults, frauds, muggers, pushers, racketeers, suicides – not that the season had really started yet – swindlers, threats, vandals, etc, etc. Always something to keep you busy when you're a policeman.

But all that could wait until Monday. In the meantime Nosjean was on his way to a dirty weekend with his nurse. Cheriff Kader Kamel – he looked more like an Arab prince than a policeman, but he was French, born and brought up in the heart of Burgundy, and as Pel pointed out, you can't get much Frencher than that – and ex-Lieutenant Annie Saxe were cooing over their newborn son, Daniel. Bardolle, the team's very own hulk, slept late, ate well, snoozed for an hour then went to train his village soccer team. Misset was supposed to be enjoying his niece's visit but wasn't. Morrison helped his mum do the shopping and his dad wash the car. Pujol put on his specs, licked his lips and plugged himself into his personal computer to surf the World Wide Web, before finishing a very interesting, and very lengthy, biography on the life and loves of Louis Quatorze. De Troq' and the only remaining woman on the team, Alexandra Jourdain, renamed The Punk because of her short spiky blonde thatch –

well, actually, no one knew where they were . . . And Gilbert; no one cared what he did as long as he did it out of sight.

St Urbain. The morning light was dull, the sky was slate grey and although it wasn't actually raining – not the way it had on Friday – the air was damp with a constant and irritating drizzle. The thermometers read 14 degrees, still very mild for the middle of December.

Pel pushed his front door closed and went into the sitting room to read the paper. Nothing like a Sunday morning for reading the paper in peace.

'I hope you wiped your feet, you mucky man!'

He scowled; had his wife been home, his housekeeper wouldn't have dared speak to him like that. But, it being the last full weekend before Christmas, his dear Geneviève had her work cut out, filling her cash register with silver and gold, and banknotes, at Nanette's, the most expensive hair salon and beauty parlour in town, not forgetting the cash registers in her two equally expensive, and successful, boutiques. It was very reassuring having a wealthy wife. An astute and intelligent one too. And damned attractive. And she still seemed to love him. He couldn't think how it had happened; he wouldn't have given himself house room.

It wasn't at all reassuring being at home alone with the housekeeper, Madame Routy. What was the old witch doing up so early?

'What are you up to in there?'

'Preparing a very special cassoulet for this evening, it needs a lot of simmering!'

'Old toad cassoulet boiled to inedibility in your ruddy cauldron, no doubt?'

'What else? I'm having a bit of trouble skinning the bats' wings, the sea hag heads were easy! You wouldn't give me a hand, would you?'

'I wouldn't venture into your cavern to give you a hand for a million dollars! You might chop it off and roast it for lunch. Any coffee going?'

'Only the dregs you left from breakfast!'

'What about tea?'

'You don't like tea!'

'I like it more than that foul infusion of iron filings you try and pass off as coffee. Consider yourself sacked!'

With the normal pleasantries over, the housekeeper contentedly continued her cooking and Pel settled comfortably into his favourite armchair, sighing as he sat. Cleaning his specs on the end of his tie, he put them carefully back on his nose and began reading:

'L'Herault: Cédric, 19, a known addict, admitted murdering the ex-Air France pilot, Philippe Narré, and his wife, Aimée. The son of Narré's ex-mistress visited the couple often. On the evening of the murder, he and another young person demanded money to buy drugs. The pilot refused, provoking a violent reaction and his subsequent death.'

'L'Yonne: Human remains have been uncovered after Emile Louis, suspected of killing 7 mentally handicapped girls, indicated the location.'

'Chirac's vote of confidence: 70% of French citizens believe the President was telling the truth yesterday evening when he made his public declaration of "not knowing" about the illegally used Party finances. 51% of the 70%, however, are not convinced he knew nothing.' Confusing, *n'est-ce pas*?

'Prime Minister Lionel Jospin opened a debate on the French electoral calendar for 2002.'

Pel sniffed. 'We're getting as bad as the ruddy Americans, we haven't finished with the year 2000 yet. Is that all the buggers have got to do all day?' he muttered, mostly to himself. 'I was definitely misdirected at school, I should have been a politician, far less tiring than being a detective.'

'You wouldn't've got a single vote.' Madame Routy banged down a mug of tea. 'Certainly not mine.'

Pel studied the steaming mug; the tea bag was still floating in it and its thin string hung over the side soggily. 'What's that? A mouse you poisoned?'

'Only thing I could find,' and she marched off humming.

But apart from the usual warring between Pel and his housekeeper, it was, to all intents and purposes, another peaceful day in Burgundy. Well, peaceful as far as Pel's team was concerned. Only Misset and Bardolle were fed up, in fact both of them were confused and not a little upset. Misset had reached the stage of contemplating buying his mother-in-law a one-way ticket to the salt mines in Siberia to stop her interfering, and Bardolle was close to tears; the boys he'd trained so proudly the day before had just been beaten, 4–0.

Colin was feeling beaten as he paced back and forth in his room; metaphorically speaking, his room wasn't large and with the furniture needed for one male student to eat, sleep and study – bathroom and WC down the hall – it left little space for pacing. Perhaps it would be more accurate to say *il tournait en rond*. When that 'something important in the post' had arrived on Saturday morning, he'd torn open the envelope full of old-fashioned and romantic feelings. He'd unfolded the single sheet of paper, recognizing Sandrine's handwriting, and started reading. As he read, his happy heart thumped more apprehensively in his chest, a frown creased his young brow and after a while, he noticed his hands were shaking, making the paper rattle between his fingers. He screwed it into a ball and sat down heavily on his bed to weep. The 'something important' wasn't what he'd expected, it had left him feeling bereft and confused. Now he was wondering, why? Why had Sandrine led him to believe his feelings of deep and enduring love were reciprocated, only to tell him three days later – and in writing no less – she never wanted to see him again? He couldn't understand what had gone wrong. He couldn't accept her decision was final.

He fished the crumpled letter out of his waste-paper basket and smoothed it out on his desk, sending a cup of cold coffee flying and swearing as it hit the floor, spilling its contents in a black puddle across the lino. He stared angrily at it for a moment then ignored it, rereading the hurtful words.

'. . . our childish affair is over . . .', '. . . seriously involved with someone much more mature . . .', '. . . I'm moving out, please don't come looking for me . . .', '. . . I'm very fond of you but . . .', '. . . definitely don't want to see you again . . .'

Tears welled up in his eyes; how could she! Then, with the unshakeable certainty of youth, he decided there and then that it *wasn't* over. He *would* see her again, he'd find out where she'd moved to, and talk her out of her commitment to the older man, whoever he was. He wanted her to love him again – not suspecting for a moment that she'd possibly never loved him in the first place.

While Misset wondered what to do about his niece, and Bardolle uncharacteristically snapped at his wife, the rest of the team sighed with satisfaction and resisted thinking about the following week. And Colin, sorrowfully but determinedly, picked up the small Adidas sports bag he carried his essentials around in – a wallet containing some money, his identity card, student card, university canteen card and library card; his mobile phone, electronic diary cum address book, tobacco, papers and lighter – pushed Sandrine's letter in and set off in search of her.

And twenty-five kilometres south of the city centre, Angel – silly name for a bloke, but there you go, that was *his* nickname – waited for the returning phone call. When his mother, Maria, registered his birth twenty-seven years previously, she declared her son would be called Angelo after her own father – which would've been fine if they still lived in Italy, there are millions of Angelos in Italy, rather like Pierres in France. Pierre Malfaite became Angelo's stepfather when he married Maria and insisted the five-year-old boy took his name if he was going to be paying for the little bastard from now on. 'Malfaite' means 'badly made', and when school started that September the teasing started with it. At first, this made little Angelo cry but he learnt very quickly how to defend himself with his fists. He acquired a reputation for being aggressive. When his mother died three days after his fifteenth birthday, angry at his loss, he told his stepfather he could stuff his rotten surname, from now on he was reverting back to Dinero. He still got teased, translated Angelo Dinero means black angel – or thereabouts – but he didn't mind that; the Black Angel was a good label for a daring adolescent to have, he thought it went well with his developing personality. In retaliation, his stepfather kicked him out, and not knowing where else to go, he demanded to be taken in by an elderly uncle and aunt in Burgundy, a long way from the scruffy suburb of Paris where he'd lived until then. To his surprise, they accepted him with pleasure, having never been blessed with children themselves. Unfortunately, they had no idea how to handle the tearaway teenager and, believing money bought happiness – like a lot of people – they bribed him to behave. He pocketed the money, making his promises and, instead of behaving, he bought cigarettes and booze, strengthening the image he was busy creating, and generally carried on as before. Once puberty was over, and the initial outbreak of acne under control, he very soon discovered that his dark Italian eyes with their long black lashes appealed to the girls, and quite quickly Angel had a new reputation as an aggressive and sometimes cruel lover.

When the old couple died, Angel inherited the farm. It sat behind a wall of trees, hidden from view from any passing stranger, which was very convenient considering what went on there. Outside in the thickening dusk, the farmyard was empty; the poultry – chicken, ducks and guinea fowl – had been locked up, away from the marauding night-time scavengers. The rows of covered cages, housing a motley collection of rabbits, were quiet and dark. Only the dogs, two large Alsatians, roamed the perimeter of the enclosure, looking for something to eat. They'd stay hungry until dawn, that's when Angelo fed them. He liked his dogs to be alert at night, to warn him of any approaching intruder, he didn't like surprises, and he didn't encourage visitors.

The farm had changed considerably; it still looked like an average run-of-the-mill peasant smallholding with its ram-shackle buildings and house – all the doors and shutters needed a lick of paint, the high chain link fencing was rusty as were the corrugated iron roofs on the many pigsties. That's what his relations had reared, good healthy pigs, for transportation to the abattoirs to be turned into *charcuterie* and sealed into plastic packs and sold in the supermarkets. It was one of the reasons for the farm's isolation; no one likes living next to pigs, they have a tendency to smell rather strong. The other was that the old boy, who'd finally dropped dead at the ripe old age of eighty-two, had been a particularly unpleasant peasant; over the years he'd lost every friend he'd ever had, and that hadn't been many. Angelo had made it clear in the village seven kilometres away that as the sole descendant he intended carrying on the tradition in his own way. No one argued with him, no one went to his uncle's funeral, the local community kept well away from troublemakers, they had enough troubles of their own without worrying about a loud-mouthed show-off from Paris.

Sitting with his feet up in front of the well-stacked log fire, nursing a glass of whisky and Coke, he was feeling satisfied. Things were going well, very well. Better than he'd expected. Just one little problem but that, he hoped, would soon be resolved. He'd already made his phone call and was waiting for Goldy to call back to discuss it.

As the mobile started bleeping beside him, he reached out and answered. *'Oui.'*

'Goldstein here, *qu'est-ce qu'il y a*?'

'Gina the Gypsy won't co-operate.'

'You told me she was begging to join the business.'

'She was, now she's changed her mind.'

'Then get rid of her.'

'I just needed confirmation.'

'You've got it.'

'I'll organize the usual farewell present.'

There was a short silence, then, 'No, perhaps the usual fare-well present isn't enough. Angel . . .'

'Yeah?'

'I'll send someone over for her. I'd like her dismissal to be noticed, a little imagination is needed for that. You know, I invest a lot of money in these girls, when one drops out it's a consider-able financial loss to the firm. Yes, I think I'd rather handle it myself.'

Chapter Two

Lundi, le 20 décembre
St Abraham.

Nanterre: Magali Guillemont, serving fifteen years' imprisonment for the death of her two-month-old son, Lubin, was released awaiting appeal – odd that the behaviour of the baby's father, who was present when Lubin died from mistreatment, wasn't considered suspect.

Toulouse: The giant Franco/Anglais A380 aeroplane was given the go ahead. The Americans don't approve of the project – they wouldn't!

Paris: Politicians continued arguing over the electoral calendar for 2002 – filling another day with exhausting discussion, trying to reach a decision that the taxpayers, indirectly their employers, didn't give a damn about.

Auxerre: A second site was being explored for the sordid remains of Emile Louis' victims.

Dijon: Commissaire Klein – known to his team as *le Belge* for obvious reasons – heaved a sigh of relief and checked out of the Hôtel de Police. Behind him, he could hear phones ringing enthusiastically. He smiled – over to Pel – pulled up his coat collar against the driving rain, and walked away.

Pel studied the duty roster, then Nosjean. 'You've forgotten de Troq' and Jourdain.'

'On leave, *patron*.'

'What, both of them?'

'You signed the request forms.'

'I must've been mad! Two officers absent at the same time, we'll have worn our legs down to stumps by the end of the week.'

'But they volunteered for duty over the Christmas weekend, as back-up to Klein's men.'

'Hmm, I suppose that's fair enough then.' Pel added his

signature to the bottom of the chart, kept a copy and handed the other three back. 'Everyone in?'

'Yup, even Misset. He's got a nasty glint in his eye.'

'If a light's burning behind his eyeballs it only means he's plugged his brain in, nothing to worry about.'

'It's been happening regularly recently.'

'We'll have to watch him then, he might blow a fuse.'

Misset looked as if he might blow a fuse. He'd just tripped over Morrison's long legs for the third time in the space of half an hour, and this time, in trying to save himself, had collided with a filing cabinet. Its corners were sharp, sharp enough to have opened his eyebrow which had dripped on to his clean white shirt. He stared furiously at the spotting blood then at Morrison whose face was rapidly changing colour.

'Sorry,' he said, standing up and banging his head on the overhanging metal light-shade which swung drunkenly, rather like the lantern of a ship on a stormy sea.

Misset turned on him. 'Why can't you keep your bleeding appendages to yourself?'

'Look, I said I'm sorry.' Morrison was doing his impression of a beetroot again. 'But maybe you could look where you're going.'

'Maybe you should put those things somewhere else! Unscrew them, for instance, you long-legged lout, bung them in a cupboard and lock the bleeding door!'

Surprisingly diplomatically, Gilbert stepped between them. 'Here's your coffee,' he said to Misset, holding out his own.

'Look at my sodding shirt, covered in blood.'

'I've got a spare in my locker.'

'Next time,' Misset said over his shoulder, 'I'll belt you one.'

'Next time,' Gilbert soothed, 'you won't be in such a bleeding awful mood. What's got into you?'

'Nothing.'

'Yes, it has. Row with the wife, is it? Didn't get your oats?'

'Fuck off, Gilbert.'

Misset went to his desk, slammed a drawer shut and bent over the report open in front of him, all the time muttering obscenities. He only stopped when the door crashed open and Pel entered, followed closely by Nosjean.

'Morning meeting!' But before it got under way, as often happened, the phone rang at the back of the room and Pujol lifted the receiver, scribbled on his notepad, said, *'D'accord'* and replaced it. Pel raised an eyebrow, waiting for the young officer to lick his lips. If he did, they'd be galloping off into the city on a new investigation, or an old investigation with new information; if he didn't, Pel would be sitting in boring Chief Lambert's office listening to another lecture on protocol and police procedure. Fortunately for Pel, Pujol's tongue darted out, did its work and disappeared.

'Let's have it,' he said.

'A body's just been fished out of the river, *patron*. It was caught in the weir downstream at Citeaux.'

'The Christmas suicides have got under way early this year,' Pel commented.

'Boudet doesn't think this was a suicide.'

'Strangled, stabbed, shot?'

'No.'

'He'll let us have the post-mortem report in due course, if there's any hint of foul play he'll tell us.'

Pujol licked his lips again.

Pel frowned. 'Spit it out, what's the problem?'

'It was a nun.'

By midday, they had a few more details. It was suggested that she was very probably from the Sacré Cœur in rue du Château d'Eau, in the south-eastern part of the city. Sœur Julienne confirmed that one of her sisters hadn't arrived for work and that the body found trapped in the weir may be her. She agreed to go to the morgue for a possible identification.

It was positive, so now they knew.

The dead nun's name was Sœur Agathe, she was forty-three years old and a qualified nurse. She'd left the convent on her bicycle at approximately 0630 to go down the hill, cross the narrow bridge over the river and pedal up to the hospital on the other side where she worked from seven o'clock until three in the afternoon. At seven thirty the hospital telephoned to say she hadn't arrived. The question was, how the hell had she ended up in the river wrapped round part of the weir?

Cheriff picked round the subject carefully, not wanting to distress a woman of God – he may have been brought up by Muslim parents but, being an intelligent man, he respected all religions, whatever denomination, and anyway, Annie was Catholic, consequently their son hadn't yet been declared as either yet, which caused antagonism between the two families. If any-one could, he understood the need for cultural tolerance. 'Her bicycle has been found,' he said, 'parked neatly against a lamp-post at the end of the bridge's parapet. Can you suggest why she would have left it there?'

Sister Julienne couldn't.

'Would she have stopped to talk to someone?'

'The streets are fairly empty at six thirty.'

'Perhaps someone who needed help?'

'At that time in the morning the only people about are in their cars, hurrying to their places of work, they don't stop to talk to the likes of us.'

'I know this is a ridiculous question, but I've got to ask it; did she have any enemies? Anyone you can think of that would wish her, or any of your sisters, harm?'

Sister Julienne shook her head. 'We are a curiosity to most, we're thought of as archaic and old-fashioned, some even con-sider us stupid, but generally we are allowed to live in peace. There have been no threats.'

Boudet's autopsy report didn't help much either. 'She drowned,' he said when Pel asked him.

'It can't be suicide,' Pel muttered as he put the phone down. 'Nuns don't.'

'Nineteen-year-old students of history don't just disappear,' Misset said, leaning heavily against the bar and stifling a belch. He and Gilbert had just finished eating *le plat du jour*, a rather heavy plate of pork and beans; digestion had begun, indigestion would follow.

'Maybe she's got a boyfriend?' Gilbert suggested. 'You know what kids are like nowadays, the university's nothing but an intellectual knocking shop.'

Misset's eyes flashed. 'Make one more comment like that, mate, and I'll knock you straight through the plate glass window.'

Gilbert ordered coffee and a brandy for his colleague. 'Calm down, okay?' He went on, 'But it's possible, isn't it?'

'Not her, she's a good girl. And she said she'd be home for the weekend.'

'Yeah, I know and she didn't turn up.' Gilbert had listened to Misset's grievances on and off all morning. 'Maybe she forgot.'

'My niece does not forget to come home if she says she will.'

'So put out an *avis de recherche.*'

'She's not a bleeding criminal.'

'Missing persons?'

'And have the whole police force know what she looks like? No thanks, they'd be queuing up outside the door. Anyway, she's over eighteen,' Misset said miserably, 'I can't force her to come and see us if she doesn't want to.'

'Then belt up and sink your drink.'

Colin was drinking whisky. He'd asked for a beer, but the man beside him, the one doing the talking, insisted the order was changed to whisky, to celebrate. Since this man had just told Colin something he dearly wanted to hear, he'd accepted and was now rapidly swallowing the bracing amber liquid. After twenty-seven hours – only eight of them in his own room, mostly asleep – chasing round the university complex, the maze of streets where the majority of the students lived and the numerous dives, cafés, bistros and clubs they frequented after dark, he'd finally found someone who knew where Sandrine was. All those hours he'd spent hassling anyone and everyone he came across, had at last turned out to be worth it. As he'd walked into the Cáfe des Sports, the barman had pointed and a stranger had introduced himself, saying, 'Looking for someone?' or words to that effect. Colin had at once, and once more, pulled his wallet from the Adidas bag to show the stranger a photograph he kept amongst the canteen card, the student card and all the other cards any self-respecting student carried. As he handed it over, he explained he and the girl in the photo had been going out together, and how much he loved her, and the stranger studied the picture, smiling a knowing smile. He patted Colin's arm in a friendly way and offered to take him to her new address. He said she was having second thoughts and wasn't convinced she'd made the right decision about her relationship with an older man. He said she was regretting losing the boy she was going out with before but felt trapped because of a misplaced pride; she wouldn't, couldn't, bring herself to tell him herself. Colin, anticipating a tearful but very loving reunion, was overjoyed and that was probably the main reason he was hurrying his way through the contents of the small glass. A further reason was that his new friend had just paid for it and was waiting to leave. The whisky seemed to be the only thing keeping Colin and Sandrine apart. He tipped the remains into his mouth, grinned and followed the man out to his car.

Mardi, le 21 décembre

Winter officially started. It was enough; no self-respecting saint would want to share his or her special day with the beginning of winter.

It might have been officially the first day of winter but nature wasn't listening. The *météomen* predicted it would be cloudy but warm for the time of year; 9 degrees min, 16 max, and sunny.

Paris: After great deliberation, the proposed election calendar for 2002 was adopted, a slim three hundred votes ended the argument. Many politicians, however, continued to show a deep discontent – and waste more time.

Ajaccio: the FNLC *'a revendiqué trois attentats . . . mais réservait le droit de frapper.'* The Free Corsicans hadn't finished their bombing yet.

Nîmes: One policeman was killed, *'une balle en pleine tête'*, by suspected drugs dealers. A second was taken to hospital by helicopter after being hit by the getaway car. He was not expected to survive. The incident occurred at Roquemaure (Gard) at the motorway's pay area, after a tip-off of a *'transaction de stupéfiants'*.

A police spokesman expressed sadness at his colleague's death and continuing concern over the increasing use of illicit drugs. 'We're not talking about just heroin here. More and more often we come across youngsters misusing anti-depressants and tranquillizers. In 1992 there was a sharp increase; well over 65,000 drug offences were recorded and the figures have been steadily rising since then. We estimate that when the statistics for this year are published, more than 25% of crime in this country will be linked to drugs. Recently we've seen a number of chemists being broken into, the tills were emptied but packs of pills were stolen too. It is a very worrying situation.'

And in *La Dépêche* (Côte d'Or Supplement, separate from the national and international section), the main story was the mysterious drowning of a nun.

Monsieur Robert Bordarios, an electrician employed by Ets Ubaldi, looked up from the early morning newspaper at the clock and hurried off to work on the building site in rue Pierre

Joseph Antoine. He thought about what he'd read all morning; it bothered him that he'd perhaps done something he shouldn't, that he'd interfered with an investigation concerning the death of a nun. A nun for God's sake!

When the *conducteur des travaux eléctriques* gave him the nod at midday, he stopped fiddling with the maze of wires under the floorboards, put his tools away, then shrugged himself out of his overalls and into his jacket, and made his way down the stairs as quickly as possible; it was a long way to the Hôtel de Police and he didn't have a car. By the time he arrived, his hair was plastered to his forehead and his trousers were drenched – so much for the warm and sunny forecast. He shook himself as he went through the door, leaving a trail of droplets behind him as he crossed to the counter.

'Mornin', mate,' he said.

The sergeant on duty looked up. 'Good afternoon, monsieur.'

'Oh sorry, haven't had me lunch yet.'

'*Bon appétit* for later. Can I help you?'

'You know that nun they found in the river?'

'I don't know her personally but I've certainly heard of her.'

'Well, I think I know something about it. I'm not really sure. But I do know I did something I shouldn't have. Well, I think so. Maybe not. See?'

The sergeant didn't. 'You've got information relating to the incident?'

'I might do.'

'Give me your name and address, monsieur. I'll call the detective dealing with it.'

'Robert Bordarios, 15 Chemin des Petites Roches. I'm an electrician,' he added unnecessarily.

'Take a seat, please. Someone will be down to see you in a minute.'

Cheriff accompanied Bordarios through the electronically operated security door – not to keep the employees in, you understand, more to keep the curious out, as well as the dangerous until they were at least handcuffed securely – and led him up the stairs to his office, one that he shared with the whole team plus a few others besides. The reinforced glass panel door had a newly painted sign attached to it: '*Centre des enquêtes (I) – Inspecteurs.*'

A number of desks were still occupied, Misset was sulking in the corner, telephones were ringing and being answered, and somewhere down the corridor, Pel was bellowing. All perfectly normal, although Bordarios found it fascinating, it was the first time he'd been behind the scenes at the Hôtel de Police. He walked slowly, his head swinging from side to side, taking it all in, ready to tell his mates at the bar that evening. Closing the door quietly behind them, Cheriff reduced the disturbance slightly and offered Bordarios one of the two chairs in his allotted space. Cheriff went round his desk and sat down on the other, picking up a biro as he did so, then pulled a notepad towards him.

'Well, it's like this, see,' Bordarios began.

'Excuse me, monsieur, perhaps we could start with your name and address?'

'I did that downstairs.'

'For my records, upstairs.'

Bordarios sighed but complied.

'Phone number?'

'I'll give you me shoe size if you like, but it won't help you catch the *salaud* that did for the nun.'

Cheriff's pen came to a halt, he glanced up at the electrician.

'*Eh bé oui*, that's what I reckon. I reckon she was knocked off her bike. Not that I actually saw it.'

'Just tell me what you know.'

'It's a bit difficult really, but I was walking towards the Pont Vieux –'

'East or west side?'

Bordarios shrugged. 'I don't know, I was on the same side as the hospital. It was raining, right pissing down, and I sees this nun on her bike, see.'

'The nun left the convent at 0630, it was dark.'

'There are street lights on the way down to that old bridge, I saw her all right, she looked like Batman wearing a bib, didn't she? And I thinks to meself, poor old devil, well, excuse me but that's what I thought, just like me out in all weathers. You'd think they'd give her a car or something, well, some nuns drive, don't they?'

'She didn't.'

'No, well, anyway, behind her, quite a long way behind, there was a pair of headlights. And, well, then this flippin' great lorry belts past and I can't see nothing 'cept a tidal wave coming in my direction, drenched me it did, the bugger. I shook me fist and me coat tails, if you know what I mean, and carried on walking, still had three kilometres to do and time was getting on. I usually stop for breakfast at Marc's bar around seven, read the papers, warm meself up and get meself sorted before going on to the site. Quite a few of us do that, it's quite jolly in there in the morning. Better than my old lady any day, all she does is moan and complain, permanently ill she is. If it isn't one thing it's another.'

'Could we revert to you walking towards the bridge?'

'Where'd I got to?'

'The tidal wave.'

'Ah yes. Well, off I go again. Then the headlights, the ones that'd been following the nun, comes past and I turn my back, didn't want another drenching, did I?'

'I can understand that. Did you see what sort of car it was?'

'It was a red Kangoo, you know, one of them new Renault vans.'

'You're very observant, monsieur.'

'Well, I'm interested in cars and things. Anyway, once there was no danger of being drenched, I had a good look at it. You know, if I ever have enough money to set meself up in business, that's what I'll buy, smashing looker, and plenty of room in the back for me equipment, see. Electricians need a lot, you know.'

'You're sure?'

'*Putain, oui*. Think about it, drills, bits, pliers, light switches, sockets, rolls of coloured cable –'

'I meant you're sure the van was red?'

'The bridge is well lit, I told you, because of being narrow, I suppose. I saw it was red. Don't like red vans, white's better, smarter if you know what I mean, more professional.'

'I'm sure you're right.'

'Anyway, as I turn back again, I thinks to meself, the little nun'll be coming round the corner any minute, maybe I'll say good morning to her, give her a smile. Well, you've got to be charitable, haven't you? Anyway, I reckoned our paths would cross somewhere on the bridge. But I didn't see her at all. She'd disappeared. Probably turned off, I thought. I gets to the other side and that's where I come across the bike.'

'The bike.'

'The nun's bike, well that's what I reckoned – mind you, one bike looks much like another to me. It was lying in the road, sort of half leaning against the wall of the bridge, just at the beginning of it, it's low there, see, and I said to meself if it stays like that some bugger'll clip it with his wing and bend the thing, specially with everyone in a hurry to get to work. So I picks it up, and wheels it to the next lamppost where I left it, nice and neat out of the way. Which I shouldn't have done because now she's dead, and I thought, blimey, they'll find me fingerprints on the thing and come looking for me. I didn't touch her, you know. Just the bike. If it was hers.'

'Do you have a police record?'

'Me? Not likely, straight I am, never no trouble. Not even a parking ticket, well, I haven't got a car, but . . . why?'

'Because, monsieur, if you haven't got a police record, your fingerprints won't be on our computer.'

'Blimey, all that for nothing.'

But it wasn't for nothing. Although Bordarios hadn't been able to add anything more to his statement, which Cheriff typed carefully and printed out in triplicate for the witness to sign, he had given the police one small element which might help them solve the conundrum of the dead nun: a red Renault Kangoo which had been following her and which crossed the bridge, soaking Bordarios for the second time, but ahead of the now deceased sister. It was possible, as the electrician had suggested, that the vehicle, while overtaking the nun, had touched the bike and hence knocked her flying over the parapet to fall 15 metres into the cold and swollen river below. Not a nice way to go.

Cheriff escorted him downstairs, thanked him for his help and let him out into the entrance hall. Two minutes later, he was back at his desk dialling the number for the Préfecture. 'L'Inspecteur Kamel,' he announced to the receptionist – his actual rank after succeeding in an annual push for promotion was Capitaine but, until they reached Commissaire, most officers preferred the ambiguous title of Inspector – '*de la Brigade Criminelle. Cartes grises, s'il vous plaît.*' A few clicks and buzzes and another voice came on the line. He announced himself again then asked for a list of all Renault Kangoos they'd got on file.

'Do you know how many there are?' came the incredulous reply. There was a background noise of newspaper pages being turned. 'All vehicles are registered here, regardless of whether they've been logged elsewhere in the county.'

'I am aware of that but I still need the names and addresses of every single owner.'

The woman sighed impatiently. 'We'll post it to you as soon as possible.'

Cheriff could have sworn he could hear coffee being poured and stirred. 'Madame, this is urgent, I need the information immediately.'

'But that's impossible.'

'How long will it take?'

'It could take days.' The speaker swallowed hurriedly and clinked her cup into its saucer.

'How about if I come round and give you a hand while you finish your lunch?'

'That's not allowed! Only authorized personnel are allowed in this office. You'll just have to be patient.' Something was rasping quietly by the phone now.

'And while I'm being patient and you're filing your nails, madame, we've got a murderer on the loose . . .' – a gross exaggeration but often very effective – '. . . and thanks to your lack of co-operation he may stay that way. That's fine, but don't call me when you meet him on a dark night just round the corner from where you live, you'll just have to be patient while I decide if I've got time to help.'

Silence.

Then, 'I'll do my best.'

'It'd better be good, I'll be round in half an hour to collect.'

With the list finally in front of him – thirty-nine Kangoos in the Côte d'Or, twenty-three in Nièvre, sixteen in Saône et Loire and another thirty-one in Yonne, surprising really, they'd only been on the market for a matter of months – he searched the telephone directories for the relevant phone numbers and started ringing round. Working on the supposition that the red Kangoo hurtling across one of the city's bridges between 0630 and 0700 was logically a local, either on his way to work, or returning from a night shift, he reasonably started his calls with those numbers listed for the Côte d'Or. 'Good afternoon, I believe you placed an advert in *La Dépêche* selling your red Renault Kangoo?'

Most of the replies were something like, 'Oh no, you must be mistaken, we're not selling and anyway ours is white.' Or green, or whatever it happened to be, although white was the prevalent colour. The rest of the replies were recorded: 'Sorry, there's no one in at the moment, please leave your name and number, and we'll call back later.' He didn't bother.

Much as he would have liked to concentrate on one case at a time, it was impossible, other things kept cropping up and he spent most of his afternoon chasing round the city and surrounding countryside gradually gaining information which might, one day, lead to an arrest of a mugger, rapist, thief, or some other delightful criminal that made Burgundy such a beautiful place to live.

By six, he was weary but not ready to give up and, after a rejuvenating though foul cup of coffee from the machine in the corridor, he continued his phone calls. With the 'no replies', and the repetitive *répondeurs*, he sighed, underlined the numbers and waited another forty minutes when, he hoped, the city's workers would at last be drifting home.

While he was waiting, Forensic confirmed that the nun's bike was undamaged, it definitely hadn't been hit by a car, white, red or sky blue with pink spots for that matter. However, Cheriff, while he'd been out and about, had now visited the exact spot where Bordarios had found the bike. He'd measured the width of the bridge and done a few calculations relating to speed, swing, braking time and so on, and he wasn't willing to give up the hypothesis that the Kangoo had been responsible for Sister Agathe's demise. He still reckoned he was on to something.

By seven forty-five that evening, he'd tracked down eight red Kangoos, none of which were for sale, and a white one which might be for sale if he was seriously interested.

With Pujol in tow, who was the only one prepared to add another couple of hours to his day, Cheriff went out to the addresses of the eight red Kangoos, dotted inconveniently on all sides of town. This time he presented his police identification and asked to see the vehicle.

Having believed he was on to something earlier in the day, by nine thirty that night he was beginning to think maybe he'd made a mistake. All eight had near perfect paintwork, not one of them had a scratch on the near-side front wing, which one of them should have had: there was red paint – still to be analysed by Leyguder in the labs – on the lamppost just beyond where the bike had been found 'sort of leaning' against the parapet and he was sure it came from the ruddy van Bordarios had seen. By the time he arrived home just after ten, he was tired, hungry and fed up to the back teeth of Kangoos.

'Ridiculous name for a car, anyway,' he said to Annie, stifling a yawn and trying to smile at the same time. 'How's Danny?'

Annie laughed at his comical expression. 'He's fine. He'll be up for a feed in an hour. Which do you want first, violating or feeding?'

Cheriff grinned. 'Keep the dirty talk for later. I brought Pujol home for supper, the violation'll have to wait. He helped me out this evening, I reckon I owed him one, is that okay?'

'It's fine by me,' Annie teased, 'but you might regret it later when Danny's bawling his head off and I'm about to clamp him to my breast.'

'No more talk about breasts, you'll embarrass Pujol.'

The door whispered open as Pujol stepped across the threshold, and he tiptoed in.

Annie smiled affectionately, he reminded her of Pel. Admittedly he was considerably younger but he had the same sort of unloved scruffiness about him; his clothes never seemed to fit properly and his shoes never shone, but behind the thick specs his eyes were bright with intelligence. 'What's the creeping for, Pujol?'

'I didn't want to wake the baby.'

'Babies have to learn to sleep through ordinary household noises, otherwise our life would be a misery. Anyway, his door's closed.'

'How will you hear him if he cries?'

'An intercom clipped to my belt, I'm a modern mum and well equipped. How about a drink? I opened a bottle of Bordeaux Moelleux if it's of any interest.'

'Don't tell Pel, Bourgogne is the only white wine fit to drink, Moelleux or not. And surely you shouldn't, not if you're feeding.'

'Pujol! There is life after birth and I intend to enjoy it. One glass won't pickle the baby.'

'It might give him colic.'

'How come you know so much about it?'

'I read a lot.'

Mercredi, le 22 décembre

Ste Françoise Xavière. The headlines hardly showed much of the hoped-for Christmas spirit.

'A gendarme (35) died last night after being hit in the head by a bullet. The incident occurred at Pont-Saint-Esprit (Gard), the 2 gunmen escaped on foot. Robert Fine and Guy Fraco, wanted by the police for "*grand banditisme*", and in connection with the death of a police officer and wounding of another at Roque-maure the night before, are still free.'

'Jean-François Mitterand, son of the Republic's ex-President, and the author, Paul-Loup Soulitzer, spent the night in a Paris prison. They are suspected of being involved in the sale of arms between France and Africa.'

'3 men arrested at the beginning of the week in connection with the assassination of Jean-François Filippi were released last night in Bastia. A total of 6 men were helping the police with their enquiries, one had already been set free. The remaining 2 men have been transferred to Paris into the hands of La Division Nationale Anti-Terroriste.'

'Auxerre: A new enquiry has been opened into the past of Emile Louis. No further remains have been found of the seven handicapped girls he admitted murdering but the police continue their search.'

As the dawn spread, filling the countryside with dull grey light, Burgundians looked up at the heavy charcoal clouds rolling in menacingly overhead. The *météomen* had said more rain was on its way. For the moment, however, it was warm and windy.

A large proportion of France's citizens slept later than usual: it was the first day of the school holidays.

Sandrine woke feeling bad. Her head ached, her skin prickled with perspiration and she knew she was going to be sick. She'd drunk a lot of wine the night before, now she was regretting it.

Colin woke feeling bad too. His head ached and his skin prickled with perspiration. But he was also feeling confused and more than a little frightened. This wasn't what he'd expected at all.

They were both a long way from home and wondering how to get out of a difficult situation they'd walked into perfectly willingly, even enthusiastically. You know what they say: fools rush in where angels fear to tread. Neither of them was a fool but their particular guardian angels were rather self-centred and hadn't rung the warning bells loud enough, in fact hadn't given any warning at all. The two young lovers had been scooped up and dropped in a whole load of trouble. Serious trouble. And worse was to come.

During the morning meeting, Cheriff explained his campaign to find the offending Kangoo and, with Pel's blessing, he and Pujol began ringing every one of the seventy-eight car paint shops in or around the city, wanting to know if anyone had brought in a red Kangoo to have a scratch on the near-side front wing touched up. He was determined to exhaust all possibilities for the Kangoos from the Côte d'Or before being forced to move on to Nièvre, Yonne and Saône et Loire.

They started their phone calls at 0835 and, much to their surprise, at 1120 Cheriff struck gold. 'Nah, not a touch-up job, mate, a full paint job. Seemed daft to me, the rest of the coachwork was in good nick. Still, the customer's always right and I did what he said.'

'What colour is it now?' Cheriff asked.

'White.'

Cheriff sighed. There were dozens of white Kangoos – the prevalent colour, remember. 'What was the customer's name, monsieur?'

'Dunno, he didn't say.'

'When did he bring the vehicle in?'

There was a certain hesitation on the line. 'Well, I'm not sure I should say . . . see, I don't usually work on Mondays.'

'He brought it in on Monday?'

'Well, yes. He rang me at home first thing, said it was real urgent, that it was booked in to have the name of his company stuck on the side on Tuesday and his boss was creating a stink because the thing was red and not white like the rest of the fleet. Said he'd be in real trouble if he didn't get it done in time. So I said if he paid me cash I'd do it for him immediate like. So he brought it round and I got to work. He came back the same evening to collect and hand over the folding.'

'Not a cheque?'

'Nope, that's what I told him, cash or no deal.'

'What did he look like?'

'Well, ordinary really.'

'What colour was his hair?'

'Dark, sort of black, I think.'

'And his eyes?'

'I don't know, brown maybe.'

'Tall, short?'

'Average.'

'How old?'

'Couldn't say. Older than me but younger than me dad.'

'How old are you?'

'Thirty-six.'

'And your dad?'

'Sixty-one.'

Well, it narrowed it down slightly. 'Glasses, moustache, scars, anything out of the ordinary?'

'Nope, just like any other bloke really.'

'As it was a cash job, I don't suppose you logged it in your accounts?'

'Here, you're not from the tax office, are you?'

'No, I'm a humble policeman. If you fiddle the books that's your affair.'

'I don't fiddle the books!'

'But you don't declare all your earnings, do you?'

'You are from the tax office!'

'The reason I'm asking, monsieur, is that if you'd logged the entry, you'd have a record of the registration number, which could be a great help to me.'

'Oh, I see. Then no, I didn't.'

'I don't suppose you remember it?'

'It was covered with tape so I didn't get paint all over it.'

'Who covered it?'

'Well, actually he did, I don't live on the premises, I got there after him and he was just finishing off and starting on the wing mirrors when I arrived, said it would save me time. I wasn't complaining.'

'What about when he collected?'

'I'd uncovered them by then.'

'And?'

'He was local, the last number was 21 like everyone else round here, I'd've noticed if it'd been different. I'd've noticed that. But search me for the rest, I just ripped the tape off and didn't bother. I get so many cars through here . . . hang on . . . now you mention it, the letters were RT, same initials as my kid brother. Funny that was, because two of the numbers made his age too; 27. Well, bugger me! It's amazing what you can remember if you put your mind to it, isn't it?'

Cheriff agreed it was, thanked him and rang off. 'Pujol! We're now looking for a white Kangoo, more importantly the registration number includes 27 and ends with RT 21.'

Five minutes later they had the details in front of them; 1275 RT 21, the van that might be for sale if they were seriously interested. Owner: Jean-Philippe Gaffié, 7 rue Algers, Longvic. 'See him in the lunch hour?' Pujol suggested.

'Pray he comes home to eat.'
'I'm not religious.'
'Sensible chap.'

RÉPUBLIQUE FRANÇAISE

MINISTERE DE L'INTERIEUR

DIRECTION
de la
POLICE JUDICIAIRE

SERVICE :

DIJON

PROCES-VERBAL

Ref :

94745112

L'an deux mille 00

le 22 DECEMBRE

à 14 heures 21

KAMEL CHERIFF MOHAMMED KADER

Officier de Police Judiciaire

TRASCRIPTION OF
RECORDED
INTERVIEW :
GAFFIE JEAN-
PHILIPPE

7 RUE ALGERS
21140 LONGVIC

- Go ahead.
- I didn't touch the woman.
- Tell me about your movements on the morning of Monday, 20th December.
- I came home.
- Most people were on their way to work.
- I'd been out, it was the wife's birthday. Well, the day before, Sunday. I don't work on Mondays, so we decided to celebrate on Sunday.
- Where did you go?
- L'Amazone, after we'd eaten. We had dinner with friends in a restaurant and went on after, round about midnight.
- And you stayed until 0630.
- I don't know what time it was, mate, it was still dark. Our friends left before us. My wife was tired so I drove. After a bit, she started singing and I joined in. We'd had a really good night out. I wasn't worried, there was hardly anyone about, all I had to do was get across town and into the country, we only live five kilometres out.
- The most direct route is the Chemin des Saverneys, avenue Maréchal Joffre, rue St Martin, Pont Vieux, rue St Jean and onto the N71.
- If you say so. I can't remember.
- One too many?
- Trying to catch me out aren't you? I wasn't drunk. I'd watched it all evening. I know what you lot are like.
- Continue telling me about your journey.
- Well, we were trundling along nice and happy, not too fast, not too slow - there was no one about. No-one. Parked the car in our drive and went inside to bed.
- That's not quite how it happened though, is it?
- It ruddy is.
- Tell me about crossing the Pont Vieux. You must've changed gear a couple of times, the corner's tight, the bridge's narrow.
- So I changed gear and slowed down. So the bridge's narrow. I've crossed it hundreds of times. I know how to drive!
- You clipped a lamppost when you swerved away from the cyclist.   .../...

REPUBLIQUE FRANCAISE

MINISTERE DE L'INTERIEUR

DIRECTION
de la
POLICE JUDICIAIRE

SERVICE :

DIJON

PROCES-VERBAL

Ref :

94745112

TRANSCRIPTION OF
RECORDED
INTERVIEW :
GAFFIE JEAN-
PHILIPPE

7 RUE ALGERS
21140 LONGVIC

L'an deux mille 00

le 22 DECEMBRE

à   14 heures 21

KAMEL CHERIFF MOHAMMED KADER

Officier de Police Judiciaire

.../...
- I didn't swerve, and I didn't see a cyclist. There wasn't one.
-    There was, it was a nun.
-    I didn't see her.
-    Driving while under the influence of alcohol is an offence.
- I wasn't drunk!
- So you must've seen the cyclist.
- I didn't overtake any ruddy cyclist.
- We have a witness who can testify you were following her on your approach to the bridge but arrived on it ahead of her.
- So what?
- As you came level with her, you didn't notice her wobble, topple or fall?
- Look, mate, when I'm driving, I keep my eyes on the road in front.
- You never look in the rear view mirror?
- Course I do, there was nothing behind me.
- Nothing?
- That's right, nothing.
- You're sure.
-    The road was as empty as my ruddy mother-in-law's head.
-    You're absolutely certain.
-    Yes, I'm bloody certain. Cross my heart and all that jazz.
- There should have been a nun on her bike, remember?
- Merde. I'm not answering any more of your questions mate. I know my rights. I want to make a phone call.

GAFFIE JEAN-PHILIPPE

page   02

Signé L'O.P.J.

'Well,' Pel said when he'd finished reading the statement, 'for once we've managed to wrap something up quickly. Good work, Cheriff. The Chief'll be pleased, another successful statistic to add to his self-importance.'

'*Patron* . . .' Pujol shuffled inside his clothes. 'What will Gaffié be charged with?'

'We'll leave that to the *juge d'instruction*. Admittedly murder seems rather harsh, but the nun drowned and Gaffié is indirectly responsible. No doubt Brisard'll throw the book at him: driving without due care and attention, causing an accident with loss of life, not giving assistance to a person in danger. The list will fill pages and no doubt Brisard will thoroughly enjoy doing it.'

Jeudi, le 23 décembre

St Armand.

Nanterre: Two men were sentenced to eighteen years for the murder of a Japanese architect. His body was found in a freezer in 1998.

St Nazaire: A twenty-year-old was killed by a seventeen-year-old after forcing his way into the teenager's flat and starting to break the place up. The younger man drew a knife.

Besançon: A man's arrest saved his life. He was transporting heroin in his stomach when he attempted to cross the frontier at Villiers-le-lac (Doubs). One of the bags burst inside him, endangering his life from a massive overdose. He is recovering in hospital.

Bobigny: The son of a deceased and horribly mutilated Beninoise woman confessed to the crime. The out-of-work son said his mother suffocated him.

Rain had been forecast; it was warm and windy.

Sandrine was in pain, crying for someone to come and help her, weeping for her dear old Oncle Jo. He was a funny old stick, her Oncle Jo, always pretending to be a severe and hard-hearted bully, but he had a way of looking at her when she asked for something, folding a corner of his newspaper down, and peeping from behind it with one eyebrow raised, that told her she wouldn't be refused. In the early days, just after her father was killed in a car crash, she'd felt so utterly alone; it was worse than her mother's death, which had been almost a relief after the weeks of watching her suffer. Then suddenly she had no one left to lean on, no one left to love her, to rely on, it had been an aching loneliness that consumed every minute of every day. Gradually, Oncle Jo had changed that. He'd given her a reason for carrying on, given her hope for the future, he'd given something back to her that her parents' death seemed to have snatched away. When he came home in the evening, even though it was very late, he'd tap gently on her bedroom door and creep in to kiss her goodnight. Sometimes, when she was half asleep, his lips lightly brushing her forehead were just part of a pleasant dream. It made her feel like a little girl again. On other occasions, often during a sudden sharp moment of despairing bereavement, he'd been there, sitting on the edge of her bed, pulling a crumpled handkerchief from his pocket for her tears, listening to her saying . . . saying mostly nothing, waiting for a hug. He'd told her once he needed her hugs to keep him sane. He was like that, her Oncle Jo. Oncle Jo and Tante Hortense. *Tonton et Tatti* who'd taken her in. She wished they didn't squabble so much, it was boring, that and the old bag rabbiting on like a stuck record in the background, it was one of the reasons she'd left to live in digs. Oncle Jo had looked heartbroken when she made her announcement, but when she explained it would be easier to study, closer to the libraries and lectures, he'd given her one of his special hugs and said he understood. He understood about Colin too. Told her that true love wasn't simply wanting to live with someone, but knowing you couldn't live without them; romantic old Oncle Jo. Then he'd added that if she wanted to break it off with Colin, the best thing to do was say so, honestly and without any frills attached, not beat about the bush, that sort of thing, he'd said, only ended in misunderstandings and tears.

She was in tears now. She was ashamed and hurting, wishing she was home, wishing she'd never left, regretting her cruel letter to Colin. While she wept, she began to realize how sweet he'd always been, that Oncle Jo would like him. Sandrine wanted Oncle Jo to like her boyfriend. And now he was an ex-boyfriend. Perhaps she could put that right, go and see him, explain about the awful mistake she'd made. If only she wasn't so ill . . . sometimes she felt as if she'd rather die than carry on with the treatment. Another spasm doubled her up, folding her into a tight knot of screaming pain. When it at last subsided, she flopped back on the bed, exhausted, and started crying again, for Oncle Jo and Colin, calling their names softly into the sweat-drenched pillow.

But good old Oncle Jo couldn't hear her.

Neither could Colin.

They were both miles away.

*   *   *

After a great deal of discussion, it was decided to charge Gaffié with non-intentional homicide. Under the New Penal Code, 1994, Article 111–1, crimes – not misdemeanours or violations; crimes – were classified into 'attacks against persons', 'attacks against property' and 'attacks against public security'. 'Attacks against persons' included intentional homicide (murder, assassination and infanticide), intentional violence (non-intentional death, harm resulting in a permanent injury), non-intentional violence (the same as above, except the perpetrator really didn't mean to kill or maim) and rape (we all know what that means). Hence Gaffié's case came under the heading of non-intentional violence causing non-intentional death to a second party.

The second charge was dropped: 'non-assistance of a person in danger' (which, if this non-assistance resulted in death, could be considered as non-intentional homicide and carry a prison sentence of up to five years, although more usually it was three for such incidents). Gaffié was still claiming he'd never seen the ruddy nun, and his lawyer – a clever clod with plenty of experience – protested that as his client did not know of the victim's existence, he certainly couldn't have known she was in danger.

As for the drunken driving, the police could not prove Gaffié had been drinking heavily (a blood test would be pointless three days after the event and the friends with whom Gaffié had eaten and danced weren't willing to testify against him, nor was the barman at the Amazone – he couldn't remember seeing Gaffié and his wife, which wasn't really surprising, you needed a miner's lamp to see anyone in the night-club).

Brisard, his usual pompous self, signed the single charge sheet and was present, along with the clever clod lawyer, plus Pujol, when Cheriff formally read it all to Gaffié before escorting him down to the waiting gendarmerie van which would take him to 72 rue d'Auxonne, as the local prison was lovingly known, where he would spend an uncomfortable afternoon, evening and night before being committed for trial the following morning, and be released in time to enjoy Christmas with his wife and family. The trial would be set for sometime in January, or, taking into account the silly season, maybe February. During this time, eight weeks maximum, Gaffié would be required to present himself at his local police station once a day. When the magistrates and lawyers had done their stuff – and if he was lucky – his driving licence would be confiscated for one year, which wouldn't matter much because it was very likely he'd be doing porridge for that year if not a couple more. However, in view of the fact it was his first offence, and anticipating his good behaviour, Cheriff estimated he'd be out of prison within eighteen months. Somehow it didn't seem enough for the death of an innocent hard-working woman of God who'd drowned in the ice-cold waters of a swollen river, but that's justice for you.

As Cheriff and Pujol rejoined their colleagues in the main office, Nosjean was questioning a good-looking young man, early twenties, dressed from head to foot in white, sporting a rather snazzy haircut and an unusually bright suntan – perhaps he'd been skiing? He smoothed his dark hair over his ears. 'She's been chasing me for ages, I live across the road from her. She's always hanging about waiting for me to come out. Trying to talk to me. This time it was my car, a convertible VW Golf, said it was smashing, something like that.'

'So you offered her a ride and raped her.'

'I didn't! At least, I did offer to take her for a spin.'

'Where did you go?'

'On to the bypass, you know, do a quick tour at top speed. Thought it would impress her.'

'Did it?'

'It seemed to.'

'Then what?'

'Then I asked her if she'd like a drink. She said no, she'd like to go somewhere quiet. I suggested the cinema.'

'Hardly quiet.'

'I knew what she was after. I couldn't take her home for a grope, Mum was cooking for Christmas.'

'So you took her to the cinema.'

'That's right.'

'And that's where you raped her.'

'No! We watched the first film, it was rubbish. I bought her an ice-cream in the interval, then the lights went down again and she leapt on me.'

'Leapt on you, monsieur?'

'Yeah, she was all over me, there weren't many people in there at that time of day, you know, in the middle of the afternoon, and most of them were further down, closer to the screen.'

'Convenient.'

'Look, she had her hand inside my trousers and was whispering she had no knickers on. She was willing.'

'For how long?'

'All the time. I didn't force her.'

'Are you aware that rape of a minor under the age of fifteen is a serious crime? Punishable by up to ten years in prison.'

'She told me she was seventeen!'

'And you believed her?'

'Course I did. Look, when a bird's panting for a poke, a bloke doesn't mess about asking for her bloody birth certificate!'

'It would've saved you a lot of trouble if you had.'

The young man studied his bitten fingernails for a moment. Then, he looked up sharply, beseeching Nosjean to understand his mistake. 'Have you actually seen her?'

'I interviewed her, yes.'

'So how old do *you* reckon she looks?'

Nosjean had thought she was the fourteen-year-old victim's well endowed eighteen-year-old sister.

As the twilight thickened through the city and turned into darkness, the shopkeepers secured their doors and pulled down their shutters, the bars and restaurants prepared for the evening, the streets emptied and grew quieter. The garlands of seasonal decorations blinked brightly among the more stark neon announcements and a chilling wind rustled the branches of the hundreds of Christmas trees attached to the shop fronts; millions of metallic paper bows rattled one against the other as they were disturbed by the gusts. Gradually, the city went quiet, two days before *Noël* and most people were busy in their own homes. It was Thursday evening, not a night to be out on the town. Thursday evening; a night to settle down in front of the television to watch *Thalassa* – if you liked that sort of thing – or La Gaff's game show if you didn't.

And, in between scratching private places, fortunately concealed under his clothes, Gilbert was doing voluntary overtime.

Having spent a great many hours lounging about in the Bilboquet after dark, doing his own bit of 'private surveillance' as he put it, he'd now built up a good description of the knifer who'd slashed a customer and a bouncer. And having compared the details with the mug shots on Rigal's computer, in the room labelled 'CID (I)' – *Centre d'Information et de Documentation* – he'd managed to put a name to the face, plus an address.

After visiting a large number of second-hand jewellers, searching for the possessions of an unfortunate couple in Talant, on the off-chance their burglar was daft enough to hock them right there in the city – he wasn't – he'd driven, with Misset constantly complaining beside him, to the suspected knifer's address and parked underneath the block of flats, hoping that he'd be back from work soon.

Misset might have been complaining but he was in a better mood; Sandrine had phoned the previous evening to tearfully apologize for her absence and say she hoped to be home at the end of the week. 'See, I told you she was a good girl. She's been ill, poor little thing, flu or something, and didn't want to pass it on to us.'

Gilbert wasn't listening, he was staring through the wind-screen, concentrating hard.

'That's him,' he said and stepped out on to the pavement.

Misset followed, crossing the road at an ungainly gallop. After a short scuffle, the man resisting arrest was handcuffed and bundled into the back of the car where the child security locks prevented escape – a wise invention, child security locks, they made life a little easier for the police as well as prudent parents. Slightly out of breath, Misset picked up the microphone and was patched through to Pel. 'We've got the Bilboquet knifer, *patron*! He had the Opinel on him, says he uses it for eating – among other things. He's got a record. Bringing him back to base now.'

Pel looked up at Nosjean as he replaced the phone. 'Seems like Gilbert and Misset are on the point of closing this one,' he said, pushing a file across the desk between them.

Nosjean shook a cigarette from the packet in front of him. 'Three cases wrapped up in as many days, the Chief'll be ecstatic. All we've got to do now is wrap up our presents and have a happy Christmas.'

'Sir can be anything he wants to be as long as he doesn't give me another "end of the statistical year" lecture and stop me getting away on time. And there's still all the paperwork to complete.'

'No problem, we've got all day tomorrow for that. You know, it'll be nice to have a real Christmas with no hassles. I was dreading it all on my own; Mijo's being a bitch, she won't let me see little Erika until the divorce is final. But Anna's come up trumps and invited me to her father's house for the day. He really pushes the boat out and apparently the housekeeper and farm workers eat in the dining room – he serves them.'

'I thought he was a judge.'

'He is, but he inherited the family farm and employs a man-ager to run it.'

'You wouldn't catch me serving anything to our employee, Madame Routy, except the sack.'

'You do that every day.'

'Mm, I know and she's still there.'

'It's Christmas, *patron*, make an effort. You know, the season of good will towards men – and housekeepers.'

'I must confess,' Pel agreed cautiously, 'it'll be nice to have a few days off without some foul puzzle hanging over our heads, threatening to spoil everything.' He even managed a smile; it made him look more like a gargoyle with dyspepsia but it was a rare and truly contented smile.

Ho ho ho, Commissaire Pel, just wait and see what Santa's got in his bag of goodies for you!

Chapter Three

Vendredi, le 24 décembre

Ste Adèle.

'St Chamas (Bouche du Rhône): 3 young women died early this morning when their car hit an electric pylon. 2 young men, also in their 20s, were seriously injured.'

'Paris: A dozen people and 4 firemen were slightly injured during a fire in a Montmartre block of flats.'

'Toulouse (Haute Garonne): One of Air France's A310s bound for Libreville was rerouted to Toulouse after a man on board threatened the 173 passengers and crew. He was arrested on arrival.'

'Gentilly (Val de Marne): 2 armed individuals held up Intermarché cashiers and escaped with 36,000 francs.'

'Vichy (Allier): 3 young travellers (17–19) were arrested for the murder of a pensioner who died in hospital after being attacked in the park.'

It was cloudy but warm. The *météomen* had announced – or guessed – at rain; not a drop had fallen in Burgundy when dusk descended on the countryside.

Monsieur and Madame Cuquel put the finishing touches to their tiny Christmas tree, they wouldn't have bothered for themselves but what with their Colin coming home, well, you had to make an effort. They were proud parents of a very humble background and with little formal education. Their families had been poor and, when they reached legal school-leaving age, they'd done just that, going to the ANPE – *Agence National Pour l'Emploi* – to find a job. Klébert Cuquel was taken on as an apprentice builder and had worked hard during the first two years, hoping his employer would sign him on indefinitely. He did, and for the next five years he'd scaled scaffolding, hammered and chipped, shovelled cement and sand into the cement mixer, strained his muscles pulling on ropes and bent his back pushing heavy wheelbarrows back and forth across building sites, always either battered by the freezing wind and rain of winter, or baked and sweating under the unrelenting sun of summer. The palms of his hands and the underside of his fingers grew hard, thick pads of callous skin to protect him from the pain of the broken blisters he'd suffered during his apprenticeship. When he was twenty-three, and anticipating a secure future as the builder's mate, he met Edith, working in the local grocer's shop. She'd given him a brilliant smile as she said, *'Voilà, monsieur,'* and he'd dropped the bag of beans she was passing him over the counter. As it hit the tiled floor, the brown paper had split and his evening's greens had scattered far and wide, making him feel a fool rather than the polite young man he'd hoped to seem. While he was gathering the haricots up, she'd started laughing and, embarrassed and confused, he'd told her rather stiffly that bruised beans weren't very appetizing, particularly at the price he'd just paid. Apologizing, Edith had offered to cook them for him, adding that even beaten beans were good with fresh cream, a small jug of which she happened to have, and she'd gone on cooking for him every night for the last forty years. His labourer's pay didn't go far but they'd scrimped and saved to build their own two-bedroom bungalow on the outskirts of town and prayed every day for a child; it was the one thing they felt that would complete their happiness. But no child came. They adopted Colin when Klébert was forty-three and Edith thirty-nine, and loved him more than they loved even each other. When Colin got his baccalaureate and secured his place at the university, they were the proudest parents in the whole of Burgundy. They believed their son would achieve everything Klébert and Edith hadn't had the chance of dreaming about.

Now they were waiting for him to come home for Christmas, the way he always did, bringing with him his stories of the students, of his studies and his life that was so different from their own. By three o'clock that afternoon everything was ready; the colourfully wrapped presents sat invitingly under the blinking lights of the tree, an extra one, bought in haste, slipped in at the last minute. Colin had said he was specially looking forward to this year's celebrations as he'd something very wonderful to tell them. Knowing their son so well, they suspected he might be ready to announce his forthcoming marriage, he'd hinted at it often enough. Although they'd not met young Sandrine, they were confident she'd be a delightful girl if their Colin loved her.

The idea of his wedding made them very happy, they'd already started making plans for the occasion. As Edith added the silvery Christmas wreath to the nail Klébert had just hammered into the front door, they couldn't help exchanging a knowing smile.

The sergeant on duty couldn't help smiling ruefully to himself. The main entrance hall of the Hôtel de Police was packed with drunks, vagrants and layabouts, all trying to be arrested for a minor misdemeanour. Once a year, the homeless and unloved misfits – those of them who hadn't already managed to gently fall flat on their faces, or pass out in a public place, and be carted off to a centrally heated hospital for observation – clamoured at the doors in the hope of being sent to prison for Christmas. Twenty-four hours in the warm; twenty-four hours of decent food served to them by cheerful – well, fairly cheerful – warders. A whole night and day of comfort and joy. Not many of them would make it but every one of them was trying hard. The sergeant on duty was resisting well but couldn't help being amused by their ingenuity as the insults flew every time an officer came through the door.

Upstairs the paperwork was almost finished, together with the childish paper chains looping across the ceiling over the detectives' heads; Morrison, blushing as always, had to walk about with his knees permanently bent for fear of strangling himself. Someone had had the bright idea of bringing a radio into the office and had tuned it in to a concert of Christmas carols, giving added atmosphere to the almost party spirit of Pel's team. It was definitely the season of good will towards men – housekeepers and policemen alike.

By six thirty, Pel was shrugging himself into his heavy overcoat and preparing to leave with a calm satisfaction that a good day's work had been done and peace was with the world – the small corner he was concerned with anyway. Klein's men were catching the calls over the weekend, which meant, possibly for the first time in his marriage, the first time in eleven years, he'd be sharing a glass of Piper Hiedsieck with his wife on time and joining her for dinner before going with her to Midnight Mass. He wasn't a religious man but he felt it was the least he could do considering he was for once available.

Across the corridor, he could hear happy raised voices. De Troq' and Alex Jourdain had made it back in time for the celebrations, bringing with them a couple of bottles of Mousseux – a tradition on 24th December – and the team were contentedly emptying them, toasting each other and generally making merry. The only one who'd been missing when Pel had swallowed his half glass was big Bardolle; built like a sideboard with fists like sledgehammers, he was a gentle giant, and he'd been called out an hour earlier to a very private meeting with a local pickpocket who occasionally sold information. The pickpocket's *carte d'identité* showed LACOMBE, Pierre André Stanislav, which surprised even Bardolle when he found out, he'd always known him as Pierre La Poche.

Now normally, when a minor villain made contact late on Christmas Eve, Pel and his men might just tell him to go and boil his head. They might, if they felt inclined, wish him a *Joyeux Noël* and add, 'now sod off' for good measure. Or they might ask him to wait a minute and leave the phone off the hook as they slipped silently out of the office for a much needed two-day uninterrupted holiday. However, after he'd whispered his greetings followed by his message, Bardolle, who knew him well, agreed to the meet and off he went. It was the only thing preventing Pel from loading his pockets with Gauloises and beating a hasty retreat.

There was a knock at the door. '*Entrez!*'

Nosjean entered. In his hand was a half-finished paper cup of sparkling wine together with the inevitable smouldering cigarette. On his face was a worried frown. '*Patron*, I'd like you to hear what Bardolle's got to say, he's just arrived back.'

'Wheel him in.'

Nosjean glanced over his shoulder and nodded. The big man squeezed through the door frame. 'Robbery,' he said. 'La Poche gave me the tip-off. He told me where, he told me when. He also told me the three men doing it would be heavily armed and willing to use their shooters.'

Pel sat heavily in his chair and lit a cigarette. 'Where?'

'Tabac du Centre.'

'When?'

'0730, the day after tomorrow.'

Pel sighed, exhaling a stream of blue smoke. 'That's buggered Christmas then. Instead of relaxing in an armchair, we'll be putting our lives on the line.'

'I've told everyone to hang on for a possible emergency meeting,' Nosjean said.

'What about Lambert? We'll need Sir's blessing before setting anything up.'

'Already left for a cocktail party with the Mayor.'

Pel sighed for a second time. 'Send someone to bring him back, tie and gag him if necessary, he's got to be informed.'

Samedi, le 25 décembre
Noël. Merry Christmas!

'Versailles: A married couple will appear in court accused of cruelty, having made their 11-year-old daughter stand nude in the rain as a punishment for tearing up paper serviettes.'

'Troyes: Just before midnight last night, 3 adults and 5 children, aged between 1 and 12 years old, died in a fire at their home in Essoyes (Aube).'

'Créteil: Taking advantage of the late night shopping, a hold-up was thwarted at the supermarket, Leclerc du Kremlin-Bicêtre. The robbers escaped empty handed.'

'Nanterre (Haute de Seine): A 38-year-old man was taken to hospital by helicopter, he was suffering from 3 stab wounds and his condition is said to be critical.'

'Mètz (Moselle): 3 girls and 2 boys (13–15 years old) are suspected of being responsible for the wave of thefts in the area.'

'Bobigny (Seine-St Denis): Armed robbery in a toy shop yesterday morning. 2 men escaped with the contents of the till. It is not yet known how much they got away with.'

'The weather: cold at first, brightening later, warm and sunny.'

Monsieur and Madame Cuquel woke early. They were both disappointed not to have shared the previous evening with Colin. He should've arrived well before Midnight Mass, but being understanding parents, they'd winked at each other as they walked into church saying, perhaps he was with his fiancée, well, it was only natural, wasn't it? He'll be along later or tomorrow morning.

Tomorrow was now – today. Edith left their bed, crossed to open the window and pushed the shutters back against the wall. They thumped gently, wood on brick. Edith didn't notice the noise, she was staring down into the drive; Colin's little car wasn't parked outside.

She frowned. 'It's not normal,' she said. 'Something's happened. Do you think we should call the police?'

'Don't be daft, woman,' her husband replied from the pillow. 'He's probably having a whale of a time with that little girl of his.'

'Sandrine? No, he said she was going home for Christmas. It's not normal, he would've rung.'

'He's switched his phone off, we found that out last night when you tried to ring him. You know how it is when you're young and in love, she must've changed her mind about going home and they don't want to be disturbed.'

'That's all very well, but it's disturbing me. I'm worried.'

'What time's lunch?'

'Not for hours yet!'

'Then close that flaming window and come back to bed. If he's cooped up with young Sandrine, I don't see why we shouldn't take a leaf out of their book and have a bit of fun ourselves.'

In the city centre, the streets were alive with last-minute shoppers, hustling and bustling to find a solution to that forgotten present. The market stalls offered oysters, crabs, prawns and smoked salmon; chestnuts, walnuts, peanuts and almonds; pralines, nougats, caramels and chocolates – ready to be exchanged for a handful of coins and bring a smile to your face.

Pel wasn't smiling; the frown creasing his forehead was even deeper than normal. Changing down, he touched the brake pedal with his right foot, flicked on the indicator, and drew out of the main stream of traffic. Letting the engine idle, he peered across the road at the Tabac du Centre. The shop was crowded, everyone anxious to stock up for the day, buying more cigarettes than usual and treating themselves to a seasonal cigar or two. They were also doing a roaring trade with the odds and ends on display in the well-stocked window – lighters, cheap jewellery, watches and clocks, hideous pottery ornaments and a rather revolting selection of painted dolls, all overpriced specially for Christmas. The owner, with his young assistant, was cheerfully tapping numbers into the cash register and folding notes into the drawer every time it opened. So far, he knew nothing about the proposed armed robbery. That would come later, once he'd shut up shop and counted the morning's takings – estimated by the police computer to be in the region of 50,000 francs. Not a lot really, when three men were about to break the law, if not their own necks, in their attempt to relieve him of it but, as had been pointed out the evening before, the robbery was probably only a beginning. It was suspected that the cash was simply for financing something far bigger.

The morning meeting took place at midday. The whole team was present, plus Marteau from the gendarmerie with a dozen uniformed men and a handful of marksmen, and of course Chief Lambert, pink in the face and glowing like a glass wassail ball under his snowy white hair. He'd already been informed the night before and had insisted on personal involvement – albeit from his comfortable leather chair behind his desk. Unlike the rest of them, he didn't have a wife and children waiting impatiently at home.

'*Joyeux Noël,*' Pel said unenthusiastically as the men took their places in front of him. 'Unfortunately, criminals are an inconsiderate lot and don't give a fig for religious festivals, all they're interested in is getting their hands on someone else's money, therefore our peaceful weekend has been disturbed to decide how we can stop them.' He pointed to a red circle marked on the street plan behind him. 'This is the location, Tabac du Centre. The owner will be brought in and briefed later this afternoon. He will be asked to open tomorrow as usual, to take delivery of the bundles of newspapers, push his stands out on to the pavement and generally get himself seen as he always is. After returning to the inside of his shop, he'll start sorting the papers, the phone will ring and, with the phone in his hand, he'll get safely out of sight. One of you will take over the distribution of news items to the shelves in front of the counter, and serve any members of the public wishing to do business. Morrison, I hope you'll volunteer. Since your ankle is still rather weak from the break at the beginning of the month, I don't want to risk it letting you down if there's a scuffle. Also, as youngest and newest member of the team, you'd be better off out of the way just observing. That way, although you'll be faced with three armed robbers . . .'

'Heavily armed,' Chief Lambert interjected.

Pel ignored him. '. . . you will not be involved in the arrest as they leave the shop, which could be dangerous.'

Grateful to be let off the hook from a possibly violent confrontation, Morrison blushed scarlet before answering. 'Yes, *patron*, certainly, *patron*.'

'In the meantime, two men will be behind the shop in the alley, just in case – there is a back door; two more standing on the pavement to the left by the entrance to the bread shop, chatting and sharing a cigarette or something; two of you in the bar to the right, drinking coffee and watching through the window; de

Troq' and Jourdain, you'll be across the road in a car, simulating an argument. I'll be directly opposite in the square, inside the stationary communications vehicle, our pizza van, liaising with the lot of you. You will act on my orders not on your initiative; there may be innocent people around and I want no shooting, if it can be avoided. Once the robbery is in progress, you'll be alerted. Once it's completed and they are on the way out, you will move in. We must expect a getaway car to drop them off and wait for them; de Troq' and Jourdain, when I give you the word, you'll deal with that, quietly. At the same moment, the rest of you will surround the targets, disarm them and get them on the ground, hands on their heads and we can all go home. I repeat, I want no shooting unless life is being endangered.'

'They'll be heavily armed,' Lambert repeated. 'And, we've been told, intending to use what they have. We must be ready to fire if necessary.'

'With all due respect, sir, I think my men can handle themselves correctly. There will be plenty of handguns out front, two more in the back alleyway, plus a covering from the gendarmerie. Four marksmen will have the targets in their sights from the moment they arrive to the moment the arrest is made.'

Marteau nodded. 'I'll also have two units waiting in the side streets, under cover. It should be enough to keep control of the sensation seekers once it's over.'

'Gentlemen, you now have the basic plan. Let's have your comments and suggestions, before we get down to details. This looks like being a long afternoon, so I'd appreciate it if you'd be succinct, we've got a lot to organize and an early start tomorrow morning.'

Dimanche, le 26 décembre
Ste Etienne.

'Here is the national news: In Essoye, the fire that claimed eight lives started in the chimney. The two survivors say the danger wasn't taken seriously at first.

'In Valence, the five occupants of a car that skidded off the road into a field walked back to the road to get help. As they arrived, a twenty-five-year-old woman lost control of her car and hit the group, killing a retired couple and wounding the three others.

'In Créteil, eight people were treated in hospital after inhaling the contents of a festive *bombe à paillettes.*

'In Evry, an eighteen-year-old was badly hurt by one of three hooded men carrying a firearm.

'In Orleans, a thirty-year-old man was killed by three bullets from a .22 rifle. A neighbour is helping the police with their enquiries.

'Now for the weather: Frost at first, warming later . . .'

Not that many people were listening at 0430.

Klébert and Edith Cuquel weren't listening, although Edith was awake. Klébert had tried hard to persuade his wife that their Colin was in his own little love nest having himself a whale of a time with young Sandrine, but when night fell and once again they switched the bedside light out, both of them were worried. Even so, they had at last fallen asleep. Every so often, Edith would wake abruptly, open her eyes and listen, then sigh unhappily, pull the covers up and try to settle. Now, she lay silently beside her husband and wished with all her heart that he'd reassure her. Stretching out a hand, she let it rest on his arm; it was covered in soft hair, warm and comforting. She gave it a squeeze, only gently, needing to feel his strength under her fingers. As the minutes passed, the caress became more urgent, until Klébert, finally roused, rolled over towards her, pulling her close. She turned her back, fitting her buttocks and spine into the curves of his body, and he held her tenderly against him, breathing in the pleasant and familiar smell of the woman he'd loved so dearly and for so long. He frowned, curious; her legs were still, her shoulders and stomach were trembling, gently but jerkily, and, tightening his embrace, he tried to calm her, still not understanding. His mind remained clouded with sleep, then as it slowly surfaced, he realized she was silently crying.

'If he doesn't turn up this morning,' she sniffed, 'I'm going to ring the police, whatever you say.'

While the rest of the city slept off their hangovers, Pel, his team, Marteau and his men watched the Chief strutting up and down importantly giving last-minute instructions.

'No chances are to be taken,' Lambert insisted. 'I want this to be a neat operation to show the hoods of our town that the law is not to be ignored. Either they behave or we take them out.'

Pel sighed, covering his impatience by bending over a lighter and touching it to the end of a Gauloise. He straightened up. 'Out to the cemetery is rather permanent, sir. We're police officers in the Republic of France, not gangsters in New York City.'

'Must I stress again that the tip-off is three *heavily* armed men, Commissaire? We have an obligation to protect ourselves as well as the innocent inhabitants of our city against any eventual mishap; if they look dangerous, you will all be ready to react. Darcy died last summer because a terrorist shot first, I don't want another unnecessary death on my patch.'

Someone at the back of the room coughed uncomfortably. Pel made no comment, he knew damn well how one of his best officers had died, he didn't need reminding.

Half an hour of listening to Lambert was enough to give them all the fidgets and by the time they were climbing into bullet-proof vests and overcoats and checking weapons, every one of them was itching to be off, guns loaded and almost cocked, ready to fire.

Pel noticed the restlessness: it spelt danger. He glanced at his watch. 'Okay, we've still got a few minutes. For the last time before we move out, let's have your positions, calmly and quietly talk me through your roles, giving the exact orders needed before moving in and tackling the targets.'

As the men went through their instructions, final cigarettes were lit, nerves were soothed, voices became less excited. The ripple of fear had been temporarily eliminated. Pel knew it would be back again once contact was made, but that was different, it was the rush of adrenaline they felt in a tricky situation that could save lives: that sort of fear was acceptable, inevitable, and mostly useful.

'Ninety seconds after I give the order to move in, it should be over, with no more than a quick scuffle on the pavement.'

Famous last words.

Chapter Four

The vehicles moved quietly out of the forecourt; the gendarmerie vans went the long way round, approaching the site from behind, stopping and concealing themselves in convenient and already emptied garages. The men inside sat and waited.

The unmarked cars used by Pel's team and the marksmen took different routes, arriving in the well-lit square within a few minutes of each other, but parking haphazardly it seemed, where there was a space available. The snipers, dressed casually and carrying a suitcase, holdall or gaily wrapped packages, made their way up the inside of the buildings to the rooftops and started assembling their Herstal BAR 7.62 mm calibre rifles, carefully clipping the telescopic night-sights into place on the barrel.

Young Morrison, only slightly pink – the chilly wind may have been responsible – was dropped off round the corner and walked smartly but anxiously towards the tobacconist's, and tapped on the door.

Inside the radio van, Pel watched the owner opening up and allowing him inside. It was 0640.

0645: Misset and Pujol called in to confirm their position had been established in the back alley where the shop had its dustbins.

0649: Nosjean pulled his car up with two wheels on the pavement, extinguished his headlights, got out and went into the bar for a cup of coffee. Gilbert joined him a few moments later on foot.

0653: Big Bardolle bought a baguette from the bread shop and, coming out, bumped into Cheriff Kamel. They stopped to talk.

0658: De Troq' and Jourdain parked neatly alongside the kerb opposite and proceeded with staging a lovers' tiff, gesticulating gently and pulling faces.

0701: An orange and white striped van drew up outside the

shop and stopped on the double yellow lines. LA DÉPÊCHE was clearly marked in blue on its side, which meant it was either the normal delivery of newspapers, or the gunmen's getaway car in disguise. With a few brief words, Pel informed his men – except young Morrison, who'd been cut off temporarily and deliberately. If it *was* the armed robbery in progress, they certainly didn't want the men holding the guns to know the police knew by broadcasting the fact through a pair of highly sensitive headphones hanging round Morrison's neck, looking like part of a Walkman.

Morrison could be seen advancing towards the door with the owner of the shop, the Walkman clipped to his belt, its lead disappearing under his jumper and apparently reappearing at his neck. What couldn't be seen of course was the network of wires taped to his chest to receive and emit messages.

Without dousing his lights, the driver of LA DÉPÊCHE got out, walked round to the back and opened the van's double back doors. He lifted out a bundle of newsprint, walked towards the shop and dumped it on the pavement.

No one moved a muscle.

The driver returned to the van and repeated the process. Another bundle was dropped on the pavement, followed by a third and a fourth. The delivery completed, the driver slammed the doors closed, climbed back into LA DÉPÊCHE, indicated, looked rapidly in his wing mirror and pulled out into the street, accelerating away noisily.

Pel breathed out. 'Relax. It was legitimate.'

0705: Morrison was helping heave the bundles of newsprint inside, then cutting the string and placing them in neat piles along the front of the counter.

0706: Pel told the communications technician beside him to call through to the portable phone. A moment later, the shop's owner picked up his instrument, nodded at his instructions and with the phone still clasped to his ear retreated to the back of his premises. He disappeared to the left into the safety of the stockroom and locked the door.

0707: A few cars had appeared in the road, their headlights cutting fuzzy tunnels in the darkness. One or two stopped to buy bread. One man, pulling up the hood of his duffel coat before leaving his car in which three other silhouettes could be seen, went into the tobacconist's and asked for a packet of Winfield Bleu.

'Stand by.'

He paid and left.

'Relax, false alarm.'

0708: Two youngsters in identical parkas and leather boots came out of the bread shop. They halted in front of the shop – 'Stand by' – broke off a piece of baguette each, started chewing and walked on. 'Relax.'

0709: A young woman wandered into sight. At least they assumed it was a woman, she was wearing the same sort of boots as the youngsters and an anorak, but by the curve of her jean-clad buttocks it was unlikely to have been a bloke. Plus the fact that, while her anorak's hood was tied tightly round her face, concealing most of it, a long lock of dark curling hair had escaped, and added to that, she was busy adjusting an Indian-style scarf that was wrapped round her neck, plus an open shoulder bag with long trailing tassels. All in all, it was reasonable to assume it was a young woman.

She hesitated in front of the shop, looked across the street as if searching for someone, shrugged and went inside, still pulling at her scarf.

Morrison, not quite knowing what to do with himself, was standing behind the counter reading a magazine – or at least pretending to. He'd only been with the team a matter of weeks and his inexperience in handling deadly criminals was making him jumpy. All he had to do was exactly as he was told; faced with the gunmen, he followed their instructions to the letter then got out of sight, if they hadn't already told him to hit the deck. Nothing easier. Trouble was, young Morrison, tall and thin and professionally very green, was a bag of nerves.

Pel wasn't, but he was becoming impatient. Outwardly he was calm, watching and waiting, idly following the girl through the door and her approach to the counter. The only sign of the tension he was inevitably feeling was his consumption of Gauloises; he was smoking ferociously. Suddenly he sat up, concentrating. 'I don't believe it! It's going down now! One armed person, female, I think. Repeat, probably one armed woman. Prepare to move in as soon as target exits.' Then, muttering to no one in particular, 'Why only one, we were tipped for three?'

'Coincidence,' the officer alongside replied, waving away a new cloud of smoke and adjusting his headphones. 'Two groups decide to do the same place, it's happened before.'

'But the same day, the same time?'

'Unlikely admittedly, but possible.'

67

Pel spoke to the waiting team. 'Steady, wait for confirmation – there is some doubt – Morrison's backing into a corner – yes, she's definitely got a gun, in right hand – left hand now, right hand on the till – inside – extracting the drawer – bringing out the bank bag – this is it. Prepare to take over as target exits front – she's on the move, waving the shooter at Morrison – he's gone down behind the counter – don't move yet – mission accomplished, exiting any moment – wait for my order.'

The communications officer was peering through the side of the van. 'Where's the fucking pick-up? There's no one outside for her, she arrived on foot.'

Pel glanced rapidly along the pavement. 'Looks like she'll be leaving that way too.'

'That's crazy, she can't be alone.'

'If she is, we could block her inside, avoid a public display on the pavement . . . Change of direction! Hold everything – she's not coming out – going back towards Morrison – past his estimated position towards alley exit – through the back door – Misset, plug your brain in! Pujol, lick your lips quick – the single target is yours – Morrison's still on the deck.'

When the girl entered the shop, her Indian scarf was effectively concealing the rest of her face, leaving only her eyes visible. Morrison had briefly thought her wrapping against the weather was rather excessive; the wind was chilly outside, but not ruddy arctic. He'd smiled at her, thinking maybe she had a mum like his, who fussed continually about her health. He was ready to make friendly conversation, reassure her; she looked bewildered, slightly fearful. When she pulled a gun out of her bag, he dropped the magazine he was holding with a clatter. He couldn't take his eyes off the Smith & Wesson pointing first at his nose, then at his genitals and although he couldn't take his eyes off it, he didn't notice something he should have.

Her words were muffled as she went round behind the counter to join him. 'Where's the bank bag? Don't go for it, just tell me, or you won't be a man much longer.'

Morrison backed away and stuttered out his reply, pointing to the till. He watched impotently as the girl tapped a two-figure number into the cash register, added two zeros to represent the centimes and out came the drawer. She removed the tray, placed it carefully on the counter, lifted out the flat canvas bag, and told Morrison to lie down. He rapped his knuckles on the counter on the way down, stumbled, caught the headphones, untangled them, and finally lay flat on the floor, terrified he was about to receive a bullet in the back of his head. He could hear his heartbeat pounding in his temples. Then he heard her footsteps; they seemed to be moving to the right, they stopped, and moved back towards him. He started sweating. Wanted to look up, didn't dare. Wanted to say something intelligent, couldn't find his voice. The footsteps hesitated, went past then continued to his left, going to the back of the shop. He listened as the back door came open and closed with a click. He breathed a long sigh of relief, he was alone again. That's when he started feeling humiliated. He lay there for a moment, hoping for radioed instructions but none came; the wires had been dislodged, and although Pel was being patched through at precisely that moment, Morrison didn't hear a word he said.

As the girl stepped out into the alley, Misset and Pujol saw her, highlighted by the single light bulb over the exit as she moved towards them. She walked quite slowly, concentrating on stuffing the money into her tasselled shoulder bag, the gun in her left hand.

Pujol stepped out of the shadows. 'Police! Don't move!'

Her head snapped up.

She dropped the money.

The gun changed hands and her right arm whipped up to point shakily towards Pujol.

He was staring into the barrel of the Smith & Wesson, staring at his own funeral. It wasn't the first time and he still hated the sensation. For a split second, he felt panic welling up from his guts, an acid tingling pricking his skin from inside. He breathed in and, unlike the younger inexperienced policeman stumbling to his feet behind the counter, Pujol got the fear under control as the image of the handgun imprinted itself on his brain. He looked up in surprise at the girl, he'd noticed what Morrison hadn't. He lowered his own *semi-automatique MAS-G1*.

'Drop the gun, love,' Misset said kindly, coming out from behind the huge plastic dustbins.

Her startled eyes swivelled round on to Misset. They widened in horror. She took two paces back, three forward.

'Do as he says, love, we won't hurt you.'

The barrel of the gun swung back and forth between the two men as she advanced. 'I'll blow you away first.' Her voice was shaky, the words trembling in the half light, as if she wasn't convinced by what she was saying.

'Whatever you do,' Pujol hissed at his partner, 'don't shoot, she won't do any real damage.'

Now Misset noticed too; he nearly smiled as he visibly relaxed. 'Come on, love, give it up, there's no way you can escape, and anyway the whole thing's been filmed. Relax and we'll have a chat, okay?'

At that moment, the back exit banged open, and Morrison, ashamed of his gnawing fear faced with a gun, appeared. His pink face was shining with perspiration, his hands holding his own handgun extended and aiming, tense, ready to fire.

The girl was confused, seeing a third armed policeman behind her. Her eyes flicked from one to the other in alarm, then fixed on Pujol again. 'Get out of my way or I'll fucking shoot the lot of you!'

Pujol saw Morrison's expression tighten, his eyes narrow. 'Morrison, don't . . .!'

Too late.

Morrison squeezed the trigger.

Small bloody explosions spat from the girl's body, twirling her round, lifting her off her feet, and dropping her like a rag doll into a twisted mess of torn clothes through which livid crimson stains were spreading steadily. Morrison was still shooting.

'Cease fire! For Christ's sake, stop! That's enough!'

Panting, exhausted, horrified, staring, he stopped. He straightened up, opening his fingers as he rose and dropped the gun in disgust. 'I had to! She was going to kill you . . .' He started retching.

In the sudden silence, Pujol's voice was clear. 'It's over, *patron*, target down.'

'An ambulance is on its way. Stay where you are, I want photographs and measurements.'

For a moment, no one moved, the alley was filled with the acrid smell of cordite. Then Misset apprehensively stepped forward. He put an arm round the snivelling Morrison. 'Oh shit,' he said.

In the aftermath of the shooting, Pujol stripped off his jacket and laid it over the corpse's head and shoulders. Morrison was puking up his breakfast and Misset continued his efforts to console him.

A trickle of blood had oozed from the body on to the pale concrete path. It shone in the electric light, giving it a dark brown colour, almost black. It was an ugly epitaph.

Pel climbed out of the pizza van, ran across the road and

marched straight through the shop. He banged open the back door and came to a halt. 'What the hell . . .?'

'The target is dead, *patron*.'

Unsure of what had happened, Pel lifted his radio. 'Nosjean, seal off the front entrance immediately! Marteau, get your men in position, no one's to get through, I repeat no one!'

Within seconds, the area was cordoned off while the experts from the SPST were called in to do their stuff. Particular attention was needed from Forensic, and Fingerprints; strangely, the young woman wasn't wearing gloves. Plus a police cameraman was required to film the scene, every detail had to be carefully and precisely recorded.

The ambulance arrived together with two men and a qualified doctor. As they made their presence known, Pel was standing staring unhappily at what had been, until a few minutes ago, a human being. He'd already checked for a pulse, not that he needed to, it was pretty obvious the target was indeed dead.

The death was quickly confirmed. 'I can't do anything for her,' the medic said. 'I don't know why you called us, she needs the morgue not the hospital. Do you want me to organize it? The ambulance is ready and waiting after all.'

'Once the *juge d'instruction* has been, seen and made his comments. It's definitely a girl then?'

'I'd say so, look at her hands, those are female. Was there some doubt?'

'Briefly, yes.'

'There's one way to be sure,' and the doctor squatted down once more. He lifted Pujol's jacket off and began tenderly unwinding the bloody Indian scarf, undoing the anorak hood and peeling it back. 'What a waste,' he sighed. 'She was pretty.'

The police looking down at her were silent, they'd witnessed death before, no longer shocked, no longer sickened, but it was still saddening. And the medic was right, she had been pretty; very dark brown hair, in tumbling waves, in need of a wash, but even so – she could have been beautiful.

Morrison was still choking over his breakfast and Misset, watching his colleague vomit, was beginning to feel queasy. He decided his soothing words were falling on deaf ears and, out of honest curiosity, he wandered towards the corpse. He glanced down at its uncovered face, gasped and looked more closely, his fist rushing to his mouth. A second later, he was attacking Morrison with the savagery of a wounded animal, clawing at his face, pounding his fists into his head, screaming like a banshee.

Knocked senseless, the younger man collapsed. Misset went down with him, still hammering at his skull. It took three strong men to haul him off. Pel studied him and noticed in his eyes something he'd never seen before; bright, white, undiluted hatred. He slapped his face viciously to bring him to his senses.

Misset shook his head and focused on his senior officer. Then he looked away, down at the dead girl. His eyes filled with tears, his knees folded and he sank to the ground. He was sobbing, weeping uncontrollably. Then, lifting his head, he let out a long tortured howl of pain.

When the journalists arrived, almost immediately, they mistakenly, and fortunately as it turned out, thought the shooting had taken place inside the shop and clamoured to see in through the front window. While a large number of figures were moving about within, a temporary screen had been erected half-way to the back door to allow a certain amount of privacy for the police and scientists. The screen was also strategically placed so that no member of the public – in particular the journalists – could see through the open back door to the disturbing scene beyond. One bright spark, however, worked out what was going on. Breaking away from the group, he walked casually round the buildings, dodged the gendarmes on duty, climbed a couple of fences and finally dropped into the alley.

Seeing Misset in distress, seeing Morrison laid out, seeing the body, now covered with a hospital blanket, the ambulancemen smoking in a corner, the confused faces, and Pel's expression, he left his camera in its case and approached with caution. While Pel and Sarrazin had agreed to dislike each other years ago, there was a strong respect between the two men for their professionalism, and the journalist knew when it was best to be discreet. He stood quietly taking it all in, headlines and possible following phrases flashing like lights in his mind.

Pel noticed and walked wearily towards him. 'You were quick.'

'Had a tip about a girl robber.'

'No photos, okay? I don't want any of this spread across the front page yet.'

'Is he dead too?' Sarrazin pointed at the prostrate Morrison.

'Just temporarily unconscious.'

'What happened?'

'It's not yet fully clear.' Pel stopped abruptly. 'Are you recording?'

'I'm not, I'm asking as a colleague and friend.'

'No journalist is a friend of mine.'

'Maybe not but at least you know you can trust me.'

Pel studied the man. It was a fair enough comment for him to make; when he'd been asked for discretion or even the omission of certain facts from his articles, Sarrazin had always co-operated. 'As far as I saw,' he said quietly, taking the journalist's arm and walking slowly away, 'from my position in the square, an unknown person entered the shop and held a police officer at gunpoint while emptying the till. Instead of exiting to the front as expected, and into our carefully prepared welcome, the attacker disappeared through the back door. We had two officers ready for that eventuality, so I wasn't particularly worried. I then saw the first officer get up from where he'd been on the floor inside, take his own automatic from under the counter and follow. Almost immediately afterwards, I heard a series of shots. That's all I know for certain.'

Pel came to a halt and lit up, offering the packet to Sarrazin.

'Thanks. As I see it, you anticipated a robbery and reacted in the only way you could, hoping for an arrest.'

'We were anticipating three heavily armed men.'

'So you armed your officers, that's simply a matter of police procedure.'

'And now we have a corpse.'

Sarrazin looked back over his shoulder. 'Plus one policeman unconscious and another crying. Who shot first?'

'I don't know.'

'Who shot her?'

'The one that's spreadeagled on the ground.'

'So why's Misset sobbing his heart out?'

'He hasn't been able to tell us yet.'

The pathologists, Cham and Boudet, were roaring with laughter. They had a macabre sense of humour; their work in the path lab was such that they had to have a good sense of humour. Dissecting dead bodies was hardly the same as selling washing machines; you had to have a strong stomach, and the ability to laugh faced with death, or worse.

The phone rang, interrupting their joke. Cham answered, listened and replaced the receiver. 'There's a body on its way,' he said. 'Shall we start straight away or leave it for after lunch?'

'After. I'm having *Tripes à la mode de Caen*,' Boudet smiled, 'my wife's speciality, she was preparing it as I left the house this morning. Come and share it with us if you like?'

'I shan't say no. On the other hand, we'd better do the autopsy before. I'm supposed to be helping my wife take the grand-children to *Holiday on Ice* this evening, I promised to be home early – it starts at seven.'

'What information have we got on the deceased?'

'Only that it's Pel in charge of the investigation.'

'Aha! Now I see why you want to start on it now. His bodies have a nasty habit of being tricky. Maybe I should call the wife and tell her to put the *Tripes* on hold for supper.'

'Let's see what we've got first.'

'Who is it? Do we know?'

'The driver didn't say, just a silly bugger that got too close to a bullet or two.'

A knock on the door announced the arrival of the silly bugger. The ambulancemen rolled the stretcher in, the corpse still covered by the bloodstained blanket – unusual since body-bags had been invented. 'They were in a hurry to get it off the streets,' one of them explained.

Everyone shook hands, Cham and Boudet lifted the body from the stretcher and placed it on one of the twin metal tables, then, handing Boudet an envelope, the ambulancemen nodded and left.

Cham swivelled on his heel and took the corner of the blanket in his hand. 'And now for the unveiling. God bless this cadaver and all who sail in him . . . I beg your pardon, mademoiselle . . . her.'

The blanket slipped to the floor and folded into an untidy pile to reveal the girl; her dark eyes were open, staring blindly at the ceiling, dried blood was caked round colourless lips. Her clothes were twisted and torn, covered in leaves, dust and mud. Paper-white hands. A bag of rags and flesh and bone.

Neither man flinched, they'd seen it all before. They'd seen more gruesome sights – they'd seen a man who'd been attacked with an axe. And their old friend, Darcy, with most of his entrails hanging out in bloody loops – although that had made them

74

gulp and hesitate briefly. They'd dealt with the remains of a woman who'd been jointed with poultry shears and another who'd been sliced with a Stanley knife. Murderers were an imaginative bunch. More recently, and probably the most sickening: a tiny bruised baby covered in cigarette burns. But whoever it was, it was all in a day's work.

Cham switched on the tape recorder. 'Name? Age? Address? What's in the envelope?'

Boudet pulled it from his pocket and immediately recognized Pel's untidy scrawl. He ripped it open and drew out a single sheet of paper. '*Eh merde, quelle tristesse,*' he said slowly. 'This is going to be a *very* tricky one.'

Cham crossed to his colleague and read the instructions for himself. 'Mm, I see what you mean,' he replied quietly. 'Well, the sooner we begin the better.'

While Cham removed the girl's boots, Boudet opened the anorak and, picking up a pair of tailor's scissors, he started cutting gently up the right leg of the girl's jeans, through that side of her pretty briefs, and on through the thick waistband. The same for the left leg. Now for the jumper and T-shirt, wool and cotton, more supple, but the sharp blades snipped and advanced, severing a lacy bra as the scissors made their way to her throat. The pathologists peeled the clothes off the pale tortured body, lifting each limb and other pressure points – the head, shoulders, buttocks and heels – in turn to release the garments, and dropped them into a large plastic box, finally clipping the lid into place and writing the case number in large felt tip on the label, ready for Forensic. With the toe of a white rubber boot, Cham pushed the case towards the door, poked his head out and called for a collection. Within seconds it swung open, an arm appeared, clutched the handle and withdrew the case.

'I don't think our new messenger enjoys his job,' Boudet said as they scrubbed up.

'Probably gives him nightmares,' Cham grinned, soaping himself to the elbows.

They tied each other's gowns and pulled on sterile latex gloves, before preparing the necessary instruments – scalpels, saws, surgical tweezers, clamps, probes, plastic containers of varying depths and diameters. Each instrument was unwrapped and placed it in its correct position on the trolleys.

Boudet checked their equipment. 'Don't forget to make a wish.' He made light of the task they had ahead of them. The dissection didn't bother him in the least – fiddling about under a flap of skin for a particle of grit, or sorting through the half-digested contents of a stomach, or digging deep through lifeless flesh and shattered bone to retrieve a bullet, even sawing his way into a skull to remove a brain didn't bother him, but the first incision oddly gave him goose bumps. He'd decided after the first few weeks of assisting Cham that, to his mind, the first incision of an autopsy was verging on violence, and he didn't like violence.

Cham picked up a scalpel and frowned. 'I wish intelligent kids like her didn't end up like this,' he said and clicked on the tape recorder.

Chapter Five

St Jean. The weather forecast was for more rain. The day started with a sparkling frost after which the sun appeared in a bright blue sky. For once, however, the inhabitants of Burgundy, country and town folk alike, weren't discussing the weathermen's inability to get it right. They were talking in animated voices about the headlines. They were deliberately large and, equally deliberately, shocking:

'BURGUNDY GIRL GUNNED DOWN BY POLICE'
'POLICE SHOOT GIRL STUDENT TO DEATH'
'GIRL SLAIN IN BRUTAL POLICE GUN BATTLE'
'TRAGIC END TO POLICE STAKE-OUT'

Goldstein read through the articles quickly, occasionally pausing to lift the bowl of coffee at his side to drink. When he'd finished, he called the maid to take his breakfast tray away and moved towards the wide window at the front of his apartment. Not far off, the Saône ribboned between the busy road and the buildings on the other side. He smiled to himself, he liked to watch the river, it reminded him of his own personality; silent and strong, never deviating from its destination. It had an air of calm, of tranquillity; a deceptive force. Once in a while it was provoked by external elements and rose up, its immensity sweeping away all in its path, crushing any obstacle that remained. Yes, he thought with satisfaction, very like me.

Directly beneath the block of flats, the small square was bright with colour, the parasols like absurd extravagant flowers sprouting from the paving stones, the striped awnings flapping lazily, caught in a dusty current of air as a heavy goods vehicle swept past. It was market day and the stall holders had spread their wares on long stands between the leafless plane trees. Each week, people from the surrounding hamlets and valleys gathered in animated groups to discuss their various problems; the same problems as last week, the same as next week, it was usually a question of weather, drought or flood, burn or freeze – unless of course there'd been a disaster, like a policeman killing a young girl.

A stream of elderly black berets edged towards a bar as they left their women to gossip and buy their provisions, pushing large handfuls of vegetables efficiently into their battered baskets. Goldstein watched and was glad to be above it all, avoiding the sickening smell of African spices, the dirty gypsies' sweets, the peasants' hot breath coming in clouds, billowing into the sharp morning air and laced with stale garlic, and the inevitable sweat on unwashed bodies that had been at work since dawn. He was well out of it, cushioned from the unpleasantness of life, pleased by his own perspicacity; supply and demand, a successful business was as simple as that. Together with, of course, prompt payment, but he'd never had any problems with that. Just the merchandise going bad once in a while necessitating rapid removal.

He lifted the mobile from the small leather pocket in his chair and tapped in five two-figure numbers.

'*Oui.*'

'Have you seen the news?'

'Yeah, the pig police have done it again.'

Goldstein chuckled. 'Indeed they have. Step up the programme, will you. I've a new client, they need delivery within the next few weeks.'

'I'd better send Luzanne out recruiting then.'

'Not in the same area, Angel, try the factories this time, and further afield. You know what they say; variety is the spice of life.'

'But he's got someone already interested. Someone who didn't go home for Christmas because she had nowhere to go.'

'Use your brain! The kid that was killed was a student, right? The police will be all over the campus for a few days.'

'Oh, right!'

Pel looked at the headlines and groaned. The sensationalism had been inevitable, it sold newspapers, which made money for the owners – and, as the song goes, money makes the world go round. Sarrazin's article was at least toned down, stating the facts as he'd been given them and no suggestive suppositions. The dead girl was, as requested, referred to as an unidentified person. The addition of the editor's comment, however, made what little hair he had left on his head stand on end, with its implication that the French police were armed to the teeth and far too fast on the draw. 'Is anyone safe on our streets when even officers of the law are so trigger happy?' None of it would do Morrison any good.

None of it would do any of them any good. Lambert was already raising merry hell, demanding to know the full story which, so far, Pel was unable to give. The picture was becoming clearer but there were still a number of details he wanted to check before going to the Chief with his report to have it analysed and criticized. The whole team would be interviewed individually and no doubt demoralized, and Pel would have another strip torn off him, if not being totally torn to pieces, in front of the *procureur*, who was also on the warpath. No one appreciated the police using firearms and killing someone – even if that someone was in the process of attempting to resist arrest after an armed robbery and making threats into the bargain. The big problem was that their 'someone' was an attractive nineteen-year-old girl who'd been doing well at the city's university.

Fortunately, the identification of the corpse had taken place in the back alley, and subsequently the name had been silenced; no one but her immediate family knew who she was. And of course the pathologists and the police present at the time. Pel's heart had missed a beat when he heard Misset's whispered explanation and instead of reprimanding him for misconduct towards a fellow officer, for trying to beat Morrison's brains to a pulp, he'd said nothing, not wanting to believe what he'd heard, and allowed Misset to weep a little longer. Then he'd radioed for de Troq' and Jourdain to bring their car round and take him away. As he left, Misset turned, his eyes red and beseeching as he asked Pel, 'How am I going to tell my wife?' Pel hadn't been able to answer. How does a man tell his wife that a colleague has just killed their adopted daughter?

Sandrine's body had been removed and taken to the morgue to undergo the necessary post-mortem. Necessary because although they knew how she'd died, who'd killed her, and why, it wasn't enough. Scientific fact was required to back it up, to prove cause and effect before the coroner released the body for burial.

Pel lit a cigarette and inhaled, sucking the nicotine deep into his lungs; another tragic funeral in his beloved Burgundy.

Not long ago, he'd buried Darcy; a brave officer and good

friend, a family man. Now it was another officer's family. Misset could be sluggish and lazy but, when he chose to, he could behave with remarkable intelligence. How would he behave when he returned to work? The likelihood was that he'd resign. Funnily enough, although he regularly accused him of being a prize idiot, Pel hoped he wouldn't. He also hoped Pujol had got his message, bellowed into the phone to Gilbert, who'd replied, 'Keep yer 'air on, guv', I'll give 'im the goods.' Such an erudite man.

Pujol knocked and entered Pel's office, adjusting his specs as he crossed the thin carpet. He wasn't particularly smart, he wasn't good-looking, in fact to be honest when he'd first joined the team most of them thought he was a bit thick. He'd acquired the nickname 'the Puppy' because of the slight whimper he emitted when faced with Pel's bellowed demands. Time and experience had proved, however, that Pujol was brighter than most – in fact, Pel believed he would, one day, be an exceptional policeman, he noticed details the others sometimes missed. This was why his second verbal report was so important – possibly more important than the first – now he'd had time to recover from the shock. Whatever their qualifications and training, it was still a shock to witness violent death, and shock sometimes obliterated or distorted the memory.

'Sit down, Pujol.' Pel opened the file in front of him. 'Tell me again, exactly what happened.'

He started slowly, confirming his position in the alley opposite Misset, both tucked out of sight. Pel listened carefully, checking it corresponded exactly with the facts already on paper.

Pujol repeated what he'd heard: the delivery van's arrival and departure then the two false alarms. He confirmed hearing the robbery was in progress, the doubt and the confirmation, then Pel's alert when the target moved towards the exit, changed direction and opened the back door of the shop. He confirmed his own first sighting and what he'd said. Then he licked his lips. 'It was at that moment,' he went on quietly, his face creasing into a frown, 'when I glanced at the firearm before regaining eye-to-eye contact, that I realized it could be a hoax.'

Pel looked up. Pujol had finally deviated from his original story.

'You didn't mention this yesterday.'

'No.' Pujol's frown grew deeper. 'It all happened so quickly . . .'

'Go on. You looked down at the girl's hand . . .'

'The target pointed the gun at me and I looked at it, not her hand . . . I was frightened, *patron* . . .'

'Under the circumstances, it's understandable.'

'I very nearly shot her myself . . . I wanted to . . . she had this crazy look in her eyes.'

'Drugs?'

'Surely Misset's niece wouldn't . . .'

'Forget who it was, you didn't know at the time. Concentrate on what you remember. Did her eyes suggest drugs?'

'Could've been. She seemed unstable, unpredictable, desperate. Then Misset appeared and I told him not to shoot, that she wasn't dangerous . . . no, I said she wouldn't do any real damage.'

'Correct, it's on file.'

'He lowered his gun too and for a moment we just stood there looking at her, it was so absurd.'

'What was absurd?'

'All that fuss Lambert made, and everyone wearing bullet-proof vests; our three heavily armed men was a defenceless girl.'

'*Quoi?*'

Pujol's tongue darted out and whipped quickly across his lips. 'The gun she was holding, *patron*, it was a toy. One of those replicas that fire plastic pellets. For a moment, I was looking straight down the barrel, the exit wasn't wide enough to fire anything else.'

Pel listened even more attentively to the rest of Pujol's verbal, acknowledged its content – which coincided with the transcript of the recordings and what Pujol had personally written the day before – and dismissed him. Then, pressing three buttons on his phone, he called Nosjean in and told him what he'd just learnt.

'Hell's teeth,' Nosjean replied, 'that's all we bloody needed. Wait till the press gets hold of that.'

'And unfortunately, they will, we can't withhold this sort of information. The only mitigating circumstances are that she had just forcibly emptied the till brandishing what *looked* like a real gun, we've got that on film.'

'And she dropped the money bag the moment she was challenged.'

Pel referred to his notes. 'By mistake, she was trying to stuff it into her own bag before making her escape.'

'That's not the way it'll seem when the follow-up story goes to press.'

'No, it'll be suggested in no uncertain terms, I'm sure, that she'd voluntarily abandoned her ill-gotten gains in the hope of remaining unharmed.'

'And was shot in the back.'

'Several times.'

'Conveniently forgetting, of course, that at the time she was shrieking murderous threats at the two challenging officers.'

'Holding a toy gun.'

Pel lit up and tossed the packet irritably across to Nosjean. 'What a way to spend Christmas. I've a nasty feeling this is going to be a long winter.'

No longer than usual, Commissaire Pel. Winter would still end officially on 20th March, but he certainly wasn't going to enjoy much of it.

He didn't enjoy his brief conversation with Lambert when he was called into the Chief's office at midday. Le Commissaire Principale was combing his thick white hair in front of a mirror in preparation for a private lunch. Without thinking, Pel's hand touched his own sparse growth, just to check he had a little fuzz left on top.

'That wasn't much of a salute, Commissaire!'

'It wasn't a salute at all.'

Lambert put down his comb with a click. 'It wasn't a salute at all, sir!'

'Well, at least we've agreed on something for once.'

Lambert adjusted his tie and, satisfied with his appearance, turned round, his hands on his hips. 'You're getting sloppy, Commissaire, your behaviour as well as your appearance. Look at you.'

Pel glanced down at his crumpled jacket, twisted tie and creased trousers; normal enough.

'You should take more pride in yourself, I don't know how you manage to look so scruffy.'

Pel shrugged. 'It's an art.'

'And it's reflected in your team; I note a particular lack of efficiency, Pel. The unfortunate incidents of yesterday appear to be handicapping operations rather longer than necessary. Where's your report? What's the hold-up?'

'The hold–up was a fiasco. The journalists . . .'

'. . . a fiasco, sir!'

'. . . a fiasco, sir. The journalists of this city were told correctly about a single girl robber. We were misinformed. As a result Sandrine Da Costa is dead and Morrison's been suspended. My team is undermanned and under increasing pressure. Sir.'

'Aren't we all, Commissaire? I've just had the *procureur* on the phone, he wants to know exactly what went wrong.'

'We're still collating information. It's clearer now but my own report cannot be completed until I have *all* the details. Sir.'

'Hurry it up, Pel. Twenty-four hours is long enough, your conclusions are overdue. I've promised the *procureur* a full explanation by 1800 hours this evening. The press are hammering at the door, they suspect we are withholding certain facts to cover up for Morrison. I sincerely hope this is not so. If we don't give them what they need for their deadline tonight they'll start guessing and that's not good for my police force.'

'I cannot complete my report until the pathologist has let me have his. Sir.'

'Then chase him up. How long does an autopsy take?'

'The actual dissection probably only takes a couple of hours at the most but the subsequent analysis of body fluids, blood, stomach contents –'

Lambert interrupted, impatiently glancing at his watch. 'And the informant who assured us it would be three armed men, where's he got to? Surely you'd like to know how he received his misinformation? Surely you want to know why we were deliberately misled? Or doesn't that bother you, Commissaire?'

'Bardolle's been out looking for him since dawn. Sir.'

Bardolle was knocking at yet another door. He'd been to the usual dubious joints that Pierre La Poche frequented only to find he'd apparently disappeared off the face of the earth; no one had seen the pickpocket since he'd been stuffing his face with a plate of cassoulet at the Poulet d'Or, early on the evening of the twenty-fourth. And Bardolle knew all about that, he'd paid for the meal at the same time as paying for the misinformation.

The door opened; a girl of about twelve poked her head out of the flat.

'Hello, love. Your mum in?'

'No.'

'Dad?'

'No.'

'What about your Uncle Pierre?'

'Mum said I wasn't to let him in even if he begged me.'

'When was that then?'

'Yonks ago. Rotten really, I quite liked Pierre. He gave me a Walkman a while back.'

'When did you last see him?'

'Months ago. He hasn't been round since the summer. Hasn't phoned neither.'

Bardolle thanked the girl and went slowly down the concrete steps to the ground floor. He was cold and cursing. Where the hell had the little blighter got to? He had to be in the city somewhere; Pierre La Poche didn't have a car and he only had the 200 franc note Bardolle gave him – if he hadn't already eaten or, more likely, drunk it. He couldn't be far away, for God's sake.

Pierre La Poche wasn't far away at all and he was scared. The money Bardolle had so generously given him was spent – some food but mostly booze – and now he was wondering what to do. He shouldn't have spoken to the *flic* personally. It was the twisting fist in his empty stomach that had driven him to it, he was sick of being hungry and he'd been sure good old Bardolle would buy him a meal. That meal seemed a long time ago and he daren't demand payment for the message he'd delivered because to do that he'd have to go out on to the streets and leave his own message together with a suggested meeting place. That's what was frightening him. After the girl had been killed, he was sure Bardolle would be looking for him, wanting to know why he'd said 'three heavily armed men' and if he replied that that was what he was told – which was the truth – he'd want to know who told him and why a different message had been given to *La Dépêche* and the other papers. And he didn't know the answer to that. And once the police found him, he'd be taken in for questioning and if that happened the consequences were terrifying. Luzanne would know he hadn't followed his specific instructions about how to deliver the tip-off and that could turn nasty. Luzanne was an evil bugger; he might even push La Poche in the canal, he'd threatened to once before, and Pierre couldn't swim. It was his own fault; he should've thought about that before meeting Bardolle. He shouldn't have been so damn hungry – but he had been and now he was scared.

* * *

Boudet rapped smartly on Pel's door. It was well after six and he was feeling tired. Sandrine Da Costa's post-mortem had been finished the day before in time for both pathologists to enjoy a late lunch of *Tripes à la mode de Caen*. Their analysis of the autopsy, however, had taken a lot longer. After Cham left at five for his evening with the grandchildren and *Holiday on Ice*, Boudet went on working until after nine, checking, rechecking, setting and resetting the intricate and complicated tests needed to draw a conclusion from their examination. Twelve hours later, eight of them spent asleep, when he returned to the lab, he'd noted the changes and progressions, giving him the desired results, and translated them into understandable words and figures, again, checking and rechecking, before settling down to write the report. That took the whole afternoon; it necessitated reference to a number of medical volumes to understand what he'd discovered. He still wasn't completely satisfied.

'*Entrez!*'

Closing the door behind him, Boudet crossed to the thick cloud of smoke through which he glimpsed the glint of a pair of glasses. 'You in there somewhere, Pel?'

'Just lighting a precautionary gasper in preparation for your visit. Talking to you starts my nerves jangling and my stomach doing somersaults.'

'Sorry about that.'

'Not your fault. Only doing your job. What can you tell me – apart from the fact that she died from multiple gunshot wounds?'

'Well,' Boudet sat down and opened the file, 'for a start she was using heroin. There were three puncture marks on her left arm, two on her right, another two inside her lower eyelids, the eighth in her groin. Her internal organs confirmed regular use over a short period – say a week, perhaps more. Enough to be well and truly hooked.'

Pel's door opened; Nosjean came in. 'No Pierre La Poche yet,' he said. He shook hands with the pathologist then took the third chair.

'Heroin,' Pel informed him, 'recent.'

Nosjean nodded. 'Robbery to pay for a new habit.'

'Mm.' Boudet frowned. 'There were other substances present in her bloodstream too: scopolamine and phenothiazine.'

'Translate.'

'Scopolamine: derived from the plant belladonna, it's an anticholinergic, which prevents one's nerves functioning properly.

Used as a sedative before anaesthetic, also used to treat Parkinson's Disease and, funnily enough, to reduce the secretion of sweat glands. It was used in conjunction with morphine to produce what was known as the "twilight sleep" for painless childbirth. Now more commonly known, surprisingly, for its suppression of travel sickness.'

'In other words a tranquillizer?'

'"Tranquillizer" covers a hell of a lot of different drugs with just as many different effects.'

'D'accord. What about the other one, the pheno thing?'

'Phenothiazine's a neuroleptic drug and, as its name may suggest, is used to treat epilepsy. Also psychiatric and geriatric patients. Its milder form, thioridazine, is being researched for its possible advantages in overcoming antibiotic-resistance – a modern phenomenon.'

'Another tranquillizer?' Nosjean asked.

'More an anti-depressant.'

'So we've got a tranquillizer, cancelled out by an anti-depressant?'

'No,' Boudet said firmly. 'That's not the way it works at all. Individually, if administered correctly, they're relatively harmless. Mixed, the results are astonishing.'

'Go on.'

'The consumer can be persuaded into participating in some act he or she previously refused, plus, the subsequent loss of memory guarantees the participant will have no recollection of having done so.'

'Explain.'

'I had to do some research before putting this in my report, they're substances I haven't dealt with often, and certainly not mixed, but apparently there have been cases when it was administered to a person over whom another wishes to gain control; it removes resistance.'

'What are you implying?'

'I'm not implying anything, Pel. Those are the facts; either she was suffering from depressive seasickness and BO, and the treating GP prescribed scopolamine and phenothiazine, which is unlikely, there are clear warnings in le Vidal –'

Nosjean frowned. 'What the hell's that?'

'The dictionary of drugs and medication. Or she was being treated for over-active sweat glands with scopolamine, then subsequently changed doctors and didn't inform or forgot to inform the new one, and he prescribed phenothiazine for symptoms of agitated depression or epilepsy, unwittingly completing the cocktail.'

'Or,' Pel said thoughtfully, 'someone with medical knowledge fed both to her, making her co-operate fully with his plans. How are they administered?'

'Individually, by injection, or orally, either in tablet or capsule form. Mixed, by capsule or as drops diluted in water.'

'What about these drops? What do they look like?'

'Colourless, odourless and tasteless.'

'If told to, would the consumer be capable of doing *anything*?'

'As far as I've been able to find out, it was used on unwilling, or underage, prostitutes, before Gamma OH and Roofies were discovered.'

'Gamma what?'

'O, H. *Hydroxybutyrate de sodium*. It's an injectable narcotic. In conjunction with an analgesic and a neuroleptic, it's used as an anaesthetic for childbirth, caesarean section; in fact surgery in general.'

'And Roofies?'

'Rohypnol, it's a benzodiazepine, more commonly known as the rape drug.'

'So *would* the consumer of your particular cocktail be capable of doing anything?'

'I would've thought armed robbery is stretching a point rather far.'

'But possible?'

'I can't answer in the affirmative. However, I'd be misleading you if I answered in the negative. I don't know. But if you're interested in hypnotic drugs, you ought to take a look at barbiturates as well.'

'Who'd be using them, medically speaking?'

'Epileptics again, insomniacs, the over-anxious.'

'Are they often prescribed?'

'General practitioners try to avoid them, but yes, they have to sometimes. The alternatives don't always give satisfactory results.'

'What alternatives?'

'The non-barbiturates; benzodiazepine with or without phenothiazine and meprobamate with phenothiazine.' Boudet paused to take a breath and turned to the next page in his notes. 'As far as neuroleptic drugs are concerned, you need to look at butyrophenones, thiozanthenes and the benzamide substitutes as well as phenothiazine.'

'How the hell do you spell that lot?'

'Here, I made you a list.'

Pel took the sheet of paper and studied the confusing names. 'All these have a hypnotic effect?'

'A hypnotic drug regulates antisocial or distressing behaviour, often inducing sleep. If you look at the headings of my list, you'll see the barbiturates and non-barbiturates are described as hypnotic drugs, as they are in le Vidal, the others are neuroleptics. And they are sub-headings under the section *Neurologie and Psychisme*. Once you know what sort of drug is required, the specific brand names are listed. Rivotril, for example, is manufactured by Roche and is a member of the benzodiazepine family, a non-barbiturate hypnotic. It's a sedative, although in certain cases can be used as a muscular relaxant. It can be injected, taken orally in tablet form or in peach-flavoured drop form, undetectable in orange juice. I prescribed it to a chap with severe and prolonged pain due to a trapped nerve, he weighed around 120 kilos so I increased the dose accordingly. His wife called me after two days, she was frightened; normally a bit of a bully, he'd become as quiet as a lamb, doing exactly as he was told. He was sleeping unusually long hours too; she'd called him for lunch, he'd replied from the sitting-room sofa, then slept for three hours, missing his meal; that's what got her worried. When I arrived, he didn't know what day it was and couldn't remember a thing about the previous forty-eight hours. I stopped the treatment immediately and he was back bellowing at the kids – they've got rather a lot – the following day.'

'Benzodiazepine,' Pel muttered, staring at the list. 'I've heard of that one.'

'Rohypnol, the rape drug.'

'No, somewhere else, another case.' Pel lifted his head, eyes half closed, a thread of smoke curling from the end of his cigarette. Snatching the Gauloise from his mouth, he leant forward. 'The overdose just before Christmas.'

'Théodora Roussillon.'

'She was definitely prescribed the medication by her family doctor, for petit mal,' Nosjean pointed out.

'Do you think the two cases are connected?'

'Pel, I don't know. All I can give you are medical facts.'

'What happens when you mix one or more of these drugs with heroin?'

'Unfortunately, the effects are apparently being experimented with by the black market dealers. A new tablet has appeared recently, a mixture of amphetamine –'

'Which is normally used for?'

'Giving back the energy a sedative removes.'

'You mean first you prescribe a drug to make the patient sleep, then you feed him another to wake him up?'

'Sometimes it's necessary. Amphetamines were also used in the slimming drug, it decreases your appetite, but that was withdrawn from the market.'

'Okay, so what was the mixture you were on about?'

'Amphetamine and heroin, and the users pay between 100 and 200 francs for it.'

'For how many tablets?'

'One.'

'Jesus.'

'The consumption of alcohol exaggerates these drugs' effects, the patient can become highly aggressive.'

'Had Sandrine been drinking?'

'No, she hadn't.'

'Neither had Théodora Roussillon,' Nosjean commented.

'But they were both addicts.'

'The difference being that Roussillon died alone locked in her room, Sandrine was attempting armed robbery.'

Pel sat back, taking a long suck at his cigarette before stubbing it out. 'If she couldn't pay for or wasn't able to reach her supplier . . .'

'She'd be suffering withdrawal symptoms; abdominal pain, shivering, sickness . . .' Boudet pointed out.

'. . . or if she was deliberately denied access . . .'

'. . . and willing to do anything for a fix . . .' Nosjean was following Pel's train of thought.

'. . . if she was offered the benzodiazepine as a substitute . . .'

'It would calm the craving.'

'. . . and she'd become the desired puppet for armed robbery.'

'But Pel,' Boudet concluded, 'that's an awful lot of "ifs".'

Chapter Six

That evening, Pel mulled the day's information over while Madame Routy crashed pots and pans about the kitchen in her usual harmonious way. He'd already sacked her and was therefore able to relax – as far as Pel ever relaxed – in his favourite armchair with a finger of his favourite whisky poured over two ice cubes, listening vaguely to the comforting tick of his wife's grandfather clock. As it chimed eight from the corner of the room, he flicked the television on for the weather and news.

The serving hatch slammed open. 'Turn it up will you, I can't hear!'

'You're supposed to be cooking supper, you evil woman, go back to your cauldron!' He turned it up all the same. But not for long. Once the adverts were finally finished and the predicted weather was safely out of the way – rain, minimum temperature 1, maximum 7, snow above 1,200 metres – and three more minutes of raucous, incomprehensible adverts, the national and international news announced itself. The first report concerned the gendarme who'd died in the Gard whilst attempting to arrest a drugs dealer; it was now being said that he was most likely killed after being hit by a stray bullet from another police officer's gun. This was followed by a three-minute debate on the safety of an armed police force, before neatly running into the revelation that the girl robber in Burgundy, who'd been slain by the police – the newscaster paused briefly to make his point – had only been holding a replica pistol that shot harmless plastic pellets. After that Pel listened to the story of Guy Georges' thwarted attempt to escape from La Prison de la Santé. Georges was suspected of killing seven women between 1991 and 1997, but no one was congratulating the police on keeping him off the streets.

'No doubt we'll be told he murdered the women because his mother never loved him and he's a victim of an unhappy home,'

Pel muttered, switching off in disgust and going back to his own private thoughts. The police were bullies and thugs, shooting each other and innocent bystanders just for the hell of it; the one-sided journalism made him angry. Did anyone ever think about the dangers they faced, the stomach-churning fear you felt when confronted by a desperate criminal? That deep, skin-prickling fear that turned your saliva acid, that produced an unavoidable spontaneous behaviour pattern: one of self-preservation. It was perfectly normal, apparently, for a young addict to strangle or suffocate an innocent couple to gain money for the drugs he needed, or for a man to shoot his next-door neighbour to end an argument about parking rights in a public street, or for a band of kids to stab an old age pensioner to death for kicks or a few coins, but for the police to defend themselves . . .

Which is what Morrison believed he'd been doing in that moment of panic as he came out into the alley behind Sandrine Da Costa.

Misset's niece; heroin, a mixture of pills or deadly drops, and a toy gun, why? he asked himself. Why? Who was behind it? Had some bastard set her up? And again he asked himself, why?

Mardi, le 28 décembre
Saints Innocents.

'It's six o'clock, Tuesday, 28th December. Good morning to those who've just joined us. Here is the news. "*Omar m'a tué*", the inscription written in blood on the locked door of a utility room where Ghislaine Marchal died in June 1991, led to the arrest of Omar Raddad. He was released after serving seven of his eighteen years sentence thanks to a presidential pardon, and is prepared to co-operate in a DNA comparison, allowing his innocence, his lawyer said, to be established once and for all.

'Ex-President Mitterand's son, Jean-Christophe, accused of arms dealing with Angola, had his demand for bail refused. A further demand will be made between 2nd and 5th January.

'The gun carried by a nineteen-year-old girl during an armed robbery in Burgundy on 26th December was only a sophisticated toy. It was loaded with harmless plastic pellets. Confronted by two police officers, she dropped the stolen money, which may have been a gesture of surrender, and was shot dead by a third. He has been suspended from duty.

'Cloudy with short spells of sun, minimum temperature 2,

maximum 7, with winds of up to 80 km an hour, and more rain on the way.'

Klébert and Edith Cuquel were on their way to the village gendarmerie, and as soon as it opened its shutters at seven, Klébert leant on the bell beside the locked iron gates to the courtyard. A few moments later, he and his wife were standing erect in front of a young uniformed gendarme, asking quietly for news of their son. There was none. An *avis de recherche de personne disparue* had been sent out with his description to every one of France's 4,250 gendarmeries. It had also been sent to the Centre d'Information et de Documentation to be passed on to all civil Commissariats – as opposed to Naval, Army or Air Force – but there was still no news.

Edith placed a photograph of Colin on the counter between them. It had been taken only last summer when he was smiling and happy, sitting on the edge of their terrace with the old dog, Nono. She'd had it framed and placed it on the dresser in the kitchen; it helped her feel that while Colin was absent at university, he was still present in their home. It made her smile as she cooked and cleaned, washed and ironed, and watched television with her husband. She had a silly habit of putting her fingers to her lips and blowing the photograph a silent kiss before she went up to bed. It was a lovely picture. It was her favourite. Now she was numbly staring at it sitting on the counter of the gendarmerie, hoping it would help. There'd been too many stories in the newspapers about children being victims of evil adults, or taking drugs and becoming evil themselves. She'd found the articles terribly disturbing, what with Colin still missing and everything.

Goldstein found the newspaper article about Gina the Gypsy very amusing, although why her name hadn't been released . . . ah, but she was an orphan, poor child, no one to identify her. He reread the paragraph about the toy gun. That had been a stroke of genius, it would create a blinding smoke screen and cause enormous upset in the police force; it was brilliant! Goldstein lit a small cigar to celebrate; he'd be able to carry on business as usual, importing and exporting, without irritating interruptions. He picked up the phone and dialled Angelo.

'You can pay the pickpocket now. I think we can call the case closed, for us at least, the fuzz must be wetting itself.'

'He'll be paid when we find him.'

'Problems?'

'No,' the Angel lied, 'we've been busy, haven't had time.'

'Busy training the new recruits?'

'Yeah.'

'When will the next one qualify?'

'Soon, I hope.'

'Good, I don't like to keep my clients waiting.'

Angelo put the phone down, tapped his fingers lightly on the plastic apparatus then looked up at Luzanne. 'Say that again.'

'La Poche had supper with a *flic*.'

'Goldy's instructions were an anonymous phone call.'

'That's what I told La Poche but he was seen eating at the Poulet d'Or with a detective from la Brigade. And now he's disappeared.'

'Then what are you doing standing there whining to me? You suggested La Poche, go and find him.'

'I was out all fucking day yesterday, tramping about asking questions. I'm tired, Angel, my feet are killing me this morning.'

'Something else'll be killing you if you don't find him. He's the only link back to you and me, and through us, Goldstein. He doesn't like being compromised and if the police pick him up before you do, we're in trouble.'

'How about giving me a hand?'

'You know I can't, there are two new girls and I'm the only one who can handle them.'

'I could manage.'

'Don't talk daft, they need my persuasive powers. My tender loving care to keep them co-operating. You'd just walk in and belt them one, and damaged goods don't appeal to the customers. Anyway, you know your way around the backstreets, that's your speciality.'

'I still say it's not fair, I'm always the one who has to do the dirty work.'

'But you do it so well, don't you? And there are advantages to your work. By the way, keep your hands off the kid in the kitchen, she's not for general consumption.'

'She's willing.'

'Use one of the others, she's earmarked for someone special, I don't want her spoiled. Look, for the moment let's finalize our problems with the pickpocket, so far Goldy's pleased with us, let's keep it that way, okay?'

*   *   *

93

Lambert, on the other hand, wasn't pleased at all, the *procureur* even less so. He'd telephoned Lambert at his house first thing that morning demanding to know if the alleged 'gun' really had been a replica and Lambert had been forced to agree that it had.

'Can you imagine what this'll do to our reputation, Lambert? One of your men killed a child holding a toy gun! You as Chief of Police are responsible for your men's actions.'

'With all due respect, Monsieur Le Procureur, Pel was in charge of the operation. Morrison took his orders directly from him, I wasn't in the vicinity of the Tabac du Centre –'

'Then perhaps you damn well should've been. If you can't control your men, Lambert, you shouldn't be Chief of Police!'

'I was present at the final briefing, indeed was most careful to point out . . .' but the line had gone dead. Lambert stared at it for a moment and felt his blood pressure rise; he wasn't responsible for the girl's death! Someone was going to have to pay for his dressing down and he knew exactly who; he'd have Pel's guts for garters. In fact, he thought more calmly, perhaps this was the golden opportunity he'd been waiting for: with a carefully planned strategy he might just finally manage to put the noose round Pel's neck.

Pel felt as if he was being strangled. As he prepared to leave his home, he'd added a thick scarf before climbing inside his overcoat and buttoning it up carefully. The *météomen* had almost got it right; they'd predicted temperatures as low as 2 degrees, the thermometer outside his front door read zero, and the heater in the car Pel's garage had lent him – after he'd all but destroyed his brand new and very expensive Peugeot, using it as a battering ram on a workshop door to save a woman from being sawn into small pieces – was on the blink. The slightly fraught journey into the city, constantly changing gear and narrowly avoiding the kamikaze pedestrians and cyclists who insisted on virtually throwing themselves under his wheels, then the final difficult manipulation of the unfamiliar vehicle into a parking place only just large enough, had tightened the scarf to such an extent that he felt as if any minute his head might just pop off and roll under the steering wheel. Dragging the offending garment from under his ears and throwing it on to the back seat, he stepped out into the biting wind, locked the driver's door and strode towards the Hôtel de Police, saluting vaguely as necessary at the ever enthusiastic uniforms coming and going along the 50 metres of pavement he had to walk. By the time he pushed his way through the swing doors, his ears were aching with cold and he was regretting the absence of his woollen muffler. Crossing the entrance hall and taking the stairs two at a time, he arrived in his over-heated office, where his ears immediately turned purple and felt as if they'd explode any minute.

Flinging his overcoat at the peg and missing, Pel bent down, picked it up and tried again. This time it caught, lopsidedly hanging like a bag of unwanted laundry from the coat-rack. He remembered he'd left his packet of Gauloises in the pocket and had to rummage between the thick folds to retrieve it. Then, with a cigarette smouldering comfortingly between his lips, he took two short steps and settled behind his desk, sighing as he did so.

The French press had gone to town on the story of the toy gun; the insinuations and accusations of police brutality were even more depressing than the day before. It hadn't helped that someone had inadvertently let slip Morrison's name and address, and, when a posse of officers from l'Inspection Générale de la Police Nationale – otherwise known as la Police de la Police – had turned up to take him in for questioning, they'd had to fight their way through the clustering journalists of whom there were dozens. It seemed every paper in France had been represented. It had been a very messy affair, and well recorded for everyone to see, prompting comments about police inefficiency: 'Can't even arrest one of their own men without a fuss'.

Pel pushed the newspapers to one side and picked up the printout of a message from Paris. The request for two temporary replacements to fill Morrison's and Misset's desks – whatever happened, neither of them would be allowed to continue on the case – had been noted. *Noted*, that was all. They'd probably have to wait for a day or two, a week or two – Pel exhaled noisily – or a month, perhaps more, most likely until the enquiry was as old and decrepit as Pel himself, either that or finally closed, one way or another. In the meantime, they had a hell of a lot of legwork to do, trying to find out where Sandrine had been during the days prior to her attempted robbery, and an enormous amount of research into her background; her friends, her enemies – if she had any, her teachers, her habits, her flatmates, her boyfriends, as well as her family – did any of Misset's three sons smoke, sniff, swallow or inject themselves? Plus the inevitable and sordid enquiry into Misset himself; did *he* have anything to hide? Was he being blackmailed, and was Sandrine the result of a refusal to pay? Was he or had he ever been a user? What contacts had he had with users and/or dealers? Who had he arrested in the last twelve months? What were they charged with? Had they gone to trial? Were they sentenced? Still inside or released? Did they bear a grudge? La Police de la Police were doing their own in-depth enquiry but Pel liked to be one jump ahead, prepared for any eventualities; he wanted to know what they'd find.

That plus all the other files in his pending tray, waiting for follow-ups, information, research, witnesses, facts and figures, was enough to give a bloke a headache.

Pel had one already.

He took the bubble pack of paracetamol out of the drawer, eased two into the palm of his hand and swallowed them with a mouthful of water from the bottle on the floor. Wiping his mouth on a handkerchief, he switched on the computer in front of him, inhaled and drummed his fingertips while the thing came alive, doing its little jingle as the screen cleared and turned into his virtual filing cabinet.

Opening the morning mail, he discovered the pathologists' lengthy post-mortem report on Sandrine, now logged officially in the electronic memory, and the forensic report on her clothes which was twice as long. However, Leguyder, who had worked in the lab ever since Pel could remember, and who, being a fastidious man, never let the slightest detail pass, knew Pel didn't read his explicit and scientifically phrased reports; he was only a dim policeman. Instead, the dim policeman usually rang and demanded a résumé, making Leguyder sigh with impatience. Either that, or he turned up in person with his foul-smelling cigarettes and caused complete chaos in the 'No Smoking' zone of the city's laboratories while demanding the same thing. To avoid this, Leguyder, who didn't like Pel much (the feeling was mutual), had added in his own words a short conclusion. 'The attached document suggests Sandrine Da Costa visited a farm sometime prior to her death on the 26th; I have been able to identify domestic ornithological excreta; chicken, duck or guinea fowl. The shoe did, however, reveal a coating of dust consistent with samples taken from the pavements near and around the scene of the crime. Between the treads there were a number of pale blue fibres. These are from a deep pile wool and acrylic carpet.'

Silently thanking Leguyder for his understanding of all dim

policemen, he now noticed there was also reports from Finger-prints – nothing unexpected – and Ballistics.

They'd been dealing with all weapons carried/and or used before and during the tragedy, including the replica gun. He moved down the page and read:

'1/1 real scale metal and plastic Smith & Wesson, weighing about 900 grams, 185 mm long. A high grade heavyweight gas type air gun, adjustable sight, magazine loading of 12 × 6 mm plastic bullets, on sale in specialist shops; *armureries, pêche et chasse, coutellerie, modélisme, jouets et jeux vidéo.* It retails at about 400 francs. This sort of air gun is advertised widely in many magazines mostly aimed at adolescents and men.'

Ballistics had sent him virtual copies of the documentation delivered with the purchase of such a gun. The 'instruction manual' was written in English with no translation and began, 'This product is developed for the user more than 14 years old and enjoying sports shooting. Be well aware of gun character and instruction, you can have a joyful and safe experience of sports shooting.' The whole manual, as they called it, was printed on a single sheet of A5 white paper.

They'd also sent him a virtual copy of the safety warning issued by the manufacturer. It was another small piece of paper with a number of childish drawings, each carrying a short explanation:

1. Always put on safety glasses to protect your eyes.
2. Never point the gun at anyone or any animal, though the magazine is pellet empty.
3. Never shoot as joking, always look before shoot, the careless use may cause injure and be punished.
4. Never pull the trigger even you think it is empty of maga-zine. It is dangerous, there maybe pellets remain in the magazine.
5. Never put your finger on the trigger unless you are prepared to fire.
6. Never look into the barrel of the gun.
7. Always keeps the gun to safe direction.
8. Do not carryout in public place, put into the bag for carrying.
9. Never dissemble the gun by yourself, which will cause the trouble and dangerous.
10. Keep out of the reach of children.
11. Always put on the safety cap.

Pel sighed. 'Pathetic,' he muttered sadly, 'and I speak a bit of English.'

The last and final virtual copy was in colour. It was the manufacturer's brochure – 44 pages – with photographs of their 106 products including a range of sub-machine-guns. The prices ranged from 99 francs to 3,195 francs.

He scanned through the pages; COLT (Legends Never Die), SMITH & WESSON (The American Tradition), TAURUS, DESERT EAGLE, WALTHER (*Eine Deutsche Legende*), UZI (*La Téchnologie Israeliénne au service du soft air*), FAMAS G2, SIG SAUER (*Quand la fiabilité germanique rime avec 'réplique'*), SPRINGFIELD (*Le plus ancien nom des armes à feu américaines*), and finally BERETTA. Every one of them looked like the real thing. Any one of them would leave a hell of a bruise if you got caught by a plastic pellet. It could certainly blind an eye if aimed accidentally or maliciously at the right place. But the gun Sandrine had been holding was still only a replica, or in Pujol's words, a toy.

Some toy.

Closing the documents, he scowled; an addition had been made to '*Reception Messages*'. Timed at 0800, it was from Chief Lambert: 'When you decide you've got a moment I wish to see you in my office IMMEDIATELY VERY URGENT and don't fob me off with you haven't come in yet I saw you arrive five minutes ago.'

Damn the man, he didn't have time to waste listening to the Snow-Capped Mountain, rambling on about police procedure and discipline. For God's sake, they had a huge problem to sort out, not to mention the hundreds of other niggling little things to do, like the series of car thefts which had got under their skin at the beginning of December and which they were still no nearer solving than the first day. However, duty called, and if Lambert saw fit to indulge in useless lectures, he'd have to grin and bear it. Well, bear it at least. Grinning wasn't part of Pel's personality.

Blonde Alex Jourdain knocked and entered with his early morning coffee. 'Bonjour, *patron*. Sleep well?' She placed the small mug on his desk and collected the papers from his out tray.

'Hardly slept at all.'

'Understandable. How long will Morrison be kept under lock and key? I had his mother on the phone a second ago, she was in tears, I didn't know what to say.'

'No doubt he'll be charged today. He may be released to await trial, he may not. She'll just have to be patient.'

'Oh, and the Chief wants to see you urgently.'

Pel drained his mug, regretted it bitterly as it burned the back of his throat and gathered together his cigarettes and lighter. 'Any clues as to why?'

'No, he's being very secretive.'

'Not for the first time. Okay, thanks, Alex.'

The pale young woman with spiky hair turned and left; she'd been very subdued, none of the usual cheerful banter he'd come to expect from the Punk. Heaving himself out of his chair, he plodded into the corridor, turned left and pressed the newly installed button on Lambert's door frame. A moment later, the small red light extinguished, a green one lit up, and he pushed his way in.

'Ah, Pel, at last.' Lambert wasn't alone. Judge Brisard was sipping a cup of coffee, his wide hips wedged into a wooden chair.

Pel touched his *briquet* to the end of another cigarette impatiently. One pompous ass was bad enough. Two was intolerable.

'Sit, Pel.' Lambert's eyes were glinting dangerously under the wavy white hair. 'I've had instructions from the *procureur*; a duplicate file on the Morrison fiasco has been forwarded to Paris, Maître Brisard here has been appointed to oversee the enquiry and requires your full co-operation. Anything and everything relating to this case is to be relayed to his office immediately. He in turn will send it on to Paris.'

'Wouldn't it be quicker if I sent two copies out, one to each destination?'

'That,' Brisard said, clinking his cup into its saucer, 'is not the way the police administration works. You are a police officer, I am a *juge d'instruction* with the authority and responsibility that affords me, i.e. overseeing your actions. Therefore you'll do as you're told. It isn't looking good for Morrison, Paris feels there must be no whitewashing and is hinting at charging him with intentional homicide. Personally, I feel that is inappropriate, we have our reputation to consider here; Morrison had been held, he believed, at gunpoint, and, if I understand correctly, fired only when the girl threatened to shoot Pujol.'

'With a piece of plastic!' Lambert pointed out. 'Tell me, Pel, why didn't you stop Morrison?'

'I told him to stay out of sight, that with the confrontation she may come back.'

'He deliberately disobeyed an order.'

'When we checked his wiring, we found the receiver had become disconnected, it was wrenched out.'

'When?'

'I don't know but I'm inclined to think it was when he went down on the floor inside the shop.'

'Inclined to think? Are you attempting to defend the misconduct of one of your men or of yourself ? Either he disobeyed an order or you didn't give it.'

'Morrison's young and inexperienced, I doubt very much that he'd have deliberately disobeyed. And I'm ancient and very experienced, I know I told him to stay where he was. If you don't believe me, I'll play you the tape, the whole bloody thing was recorded. Sir.'

'There's no need for bad language.'

Brisard stretched. 'Indeed there isn't. And if I may interrupt this interesting but irrelevant argument, I'd like to point out that we are talking about a qualified and well-trained police officer, young and inexperienced though he may be, who may stand trial for intentional homicide. Surely, we should be debating the possibility of having that charge reduced to non-intentional homicide.'

'I don't see how,' Lambert replied. 'It's hardly non-intentional when a detective draws his gun and fires repeatedly at a target. He aimed to kill. As his senior officer, in charge of the operation, Pel must be held responsible for his actions. It's the only way Morrison stands a chance.'

'That's cheered me up enormously.' Pel's sarcasm was delivered in a grim monotone. 'A mistake is made, and I'm the one with his head on the block. Perfectly normal. Tell me, if I'm responsible for Morrison's actions, who's responsible for mine? Surely as my Chief of Police, you are?'

'Trying to pass the buck won't help you, Pel. I was naturally involved in the planning of the operation, but I was not actively playing a part, therefore, and I quote, "the responsibility for all agents' behaviour remains with the senior officer at the scene of the incident." I will, of course, give you and Morrison all the support I can.'

'Oh thanks, that's all we needed.'

After a long half-hour, Pel left them to discuss his own and Morrison's fate and wandered disconsolately along the corridor to his team's communal office where the morning meeting was already in progress.

Nosjean was giving instructions for the day ahead, having listened to developments on the dozens of cases they were juggling. The room seemed sadly empty; no Misset slouching alongside Gilbert, tittering with him over a pair of outsize mammary glands plastered across the centre page of one of their favourite magazines. No pink Morrison, his long legs stuck out in front of him ready to trip them all up as they came and went. But someone else was missing; *le 'Ulk*, no wonder the place looked empty. He interrupted. 'Where's big Bardolle?'

'Tracking Pierre La Poche, hoping to catch him before he's properly awake and on the move.'

'If he's worried the tip-off he gave us was wrong, he'll have gone to ground. Have we got an up-to-date picture?'

'Rigal's computer came up with one taken eighteen months ago.'

'Get copies printed, make sure you all have one, ask around while you're out and about, we need to know Pierre La Poche's source. He seems to be a key figure in the fiasco.'

'What about Morrison, guv?' Gilbert asked. 'He's up Shit Creek without a paddle. I reckon he could use a spit of help.'

'Then get with it and get out on the streets asking questions.'

Pel was asking himself a lot of questions as he sat behind his desk going through the statements, photographs and recordings of 26th December. Apart from all the obvious questions that had inevitably been asked about every moment of the stake-out from the initial planning to the tragic end, Pel still couldn't help wondering why? Why, for the love of God, would a sensible and intelligent girl like Sandrine Da Costa take to crime? Why the heroin? It didn't make sense; she was Misset's niece, like a daughter to him, well and truly up to date with the horror stories of addicts and armed robbery . . . Okay, Commissaire, stop asking why, concentrate on who? Someone could have set her up, used her and thrown her away. Her supplier? A boyfriend with bad connections . . .?

He could hear voices seeping through the thin wall dividing him from Lambert's office. Who was the Snow-Capped Mountain boring now? He glanced at his watch; it was nearly midday. Already?

Addicts and armed robbery . . .

The door banged open. 'Pel! In my office now!'

Try as he might, the train of thought had been snuffed out like a candle. Pel scowled after Lambert's disappearing shadow. 'Damn, blast and buggeration,' he said under his breath and rose to follow.

The Chief's door was open, therefore Pel knocked briefly, entered and slammed it behind him, making the windows rattle in their frames.

'At last,' Lambert said unnecessarily. 'I'd like to introduce you to Lieutenant Capelle,' he added as the figure sitting to attention in front of his desk stood up.

He was a bearded man wearing military fatigues – or at least that's what they looked like. Pel gave him the once-over as they shook hands, suspicious of Lambert's tone of voice; he'd seemed very pleased with himself, which always meant trouble for Pel. Capelle had too much hair for a start, it seemed to be sprouting from every available place, even the backs of his hands were fuzzy in places. And his heavy leather boots were polished to such a shine, he could almost see his reflection in them. Pel glanced down at his own suede affairs, scuffed and sitting apologetically on his feet, and decided Capelle was bad news.

A noise behind him made him turn and it was only then he noticed a second stranger standing by the wall map with his back to the room; neatly combed blond hair not quite touching a stiff white collar under a smart grey suit, the trousers with well-pressed creases – unlike Pel's, his looked as if he'd slept in them.

'And this is, as I'm sure you'll remember . . .'

The smart suit spun round, his face as hard as granite, there wasn't a hint of a smile. A signet ring large enough to carry his lunch around in caught the light as he raised his outstretched hand for shaking. Pel recognized the Parisian with whom he'd been forced to work when Burgundy was being terrorized by a series of lethal bombs – and Darcy died. 'Lapeyre,' he said slowly. 'I told you I never wanted to see you again.'

Lambert opened his mouth to remonstrate; respect for senior personnel was something he demanded, particularly someone as important as a Lieutenant Colonel of La Division Nationale Anti-Terroriste.

But Lapeyre replied before he got a word out. 'The feeling's mutual, Commissaire, don't think I wanted to come back.'

'I presume your presence is official?'

'Correct.'

'If I needed interference from your lot, I'd have asked for it.'

'Pel,' Lambert finally managed to impose his own voice on the conversation, 'I insist on complete co-operation. Sit down and I'll brief you as to why the Colonel is here.'

Again Lapeyre interrupted. 'I can do that myself. No need to waste any more of your valuable time, Lambert, I'm sure you've got more important things to do than listen to me repeat myself. We'll have our meeting in Pel's office; leave you in peace. Capelle!'

The bearded soldier saluted Lambert and marched smartly to the door. As Lapeyre went out, he looked back at the Chief. 'Thank you for the advice but don't worry, I know how to handle Pel if he starts being awkward.'

As Pel's door swung closed behind them, he couldn't help allowing himself a slight smile; Lapeyre had successfully interrupted Lambert twice and finally shut him up completely. He turned to face the Colonel, Capelle standing stiffly by his side. 'Come to stir up trouble again?'

'Damn right! We need someone who knows how to handle themselves when disaster strikes. And you will co-operate or you'll be straight back in Lambert's office for a long lecture on discipline.'

Pel's mouth twitched. 'Oh God forbid; a fate worse than birth.'

As the two men chuckled, the soldier's eyes flicked from one to another; he, like Lambert, had been led to believe they loathed each other's guts.

'At ease, Capelle,' Lapeyre snapped. 'And for crying out loud relax; this is the Brigade Criminelle, Burgundy, not the Kosovo Peace Corps.'

'Sir!'

Pel shook out another cigarette and offered it to Lapeyre. He hesitated before accepting. 'I'm out of training,' he said as he lit up and coughed richly. '*Oh con*! I'd forgotten about *la Regie Française*.'

'You'll get used to it again.'

'I sincerely hope not, I don't intend staying that long.'

Pel offered the packet to Capelle who replied, 'Don't smoke, sir!'

'Never mind.' Pel withdrew the cigarettes and dropped them on the desk. 'We can't all be perfect.'

The three men settled into chairs and looked at each other. 'Over to you. Why are you here?'

Lapeyre exhaled noisily and coughed again. 'We've been interested in this guy.' He pulled a black and white photo from his briefcase and pushed it across to Pel. The face staring back was of a young man with close-cropped curly black hair. He had no beard but the dark shadow where it should have been suggested the need for frequent shaving. His eyes were set a little too close together. His nose was long and straight. His mouth was no more than a thin line. 'Jean-Paul Goldstein, believed to have changed his name to John Paul Dalton,' Lapeyre continued. '1 metre 78, slightly overweight at 85 kilos, expelled from Nancy university in 1975 for practising illegal abortions on his fellow students.'

'Medical student?'

'In his fifth year. Did eighteen months inside and was released early for good behaviour. Three years later he lost control of his Carrera . . .'

'That's an expensive car.'

Lapeyre nodded. 'Particularly when he didn't finish his studies and had never been officially employed. When he left hospital, Goldstein was supposed to be in a wheelchair, paralysed from the waist down, but he may have had surgery since, we don't know. He dropped out of sight completely, although Dalton kept cropping up in his place. To begin with, we thought they were two different men; now I'm convinced they're one and the same. He's fifty-one years old now, his appearance must've changed dramatically, although I can't confirm this. All we've got is our grapevine's suspicion that he's moved into your area, we're not quite sure why. The whisper is he's supplying the pill poppers, or possibly prostitution. We work pretty closely with the Brigade des Stupéfiants; terrorists often recruit amongst users. Usually, most of what we pick up is passed on to them for the follow-up, we only "see and tell", keeping the information on file for future use. In return, they keep us up to date. The same thing with the Brigade des Mœurs, prostitution's always been an effective way of making money to buy arms.' Lapeyre paused, took a drag on the smouldering Gauloise, exhaled and continued. 'On November 13th, purely by chance, we picked up on the tail-end of a conversation between a man calling himself Dalton and another called Luzanne.'

'How do you know it was the same Dalton?'

'Because in the Paris phone books there are precisely five

Daltons – it's not terribly French, is it? One of them's a burger takeaway, named after Lucky Luke's adversaries; the second's a bar, Dalton's Dive, named for the same reason; the third is an American teaching French to his compatriots . . .'

'An American teaching French?'

Lapeyre nodded. 'And you ought to hear his accent. And the other two listings are British, a middle-aged couple and their thirty-five-year-old son and family. The Dalton my man was listening to spoke an educated French, he's a native.'

'What was the subject under discussion?'

'Very little was heard. There was a lot of interference, we were tuning into someone else, however . . .' Lapeyre flicked through the pages of a fat file. 'Here it is: ". . . okay, Luzanne, there's a place for you in Burgundy, just do as you're told and you'll be well paid . . . thanks Monsieur Dalton . . . down here it's . . ."' Lapeyre looked up. 'That's all we got.'

'Luzanne – it doesn't ring a bell.'

'It wouldn't. He was dealing soft drugs in Paris for a Barbès gang but disappeared after witnessing the knifing of a certain Ahmed Abeddaa three months ago. 1 metre 83, 115 kilos, a big bloke and all muscle. Light brown hair, blue/grey eyes, and a diamond ear-ring in his left ear. We started tracking him, without much luck – until his photo turned up on a chemist's surveillance camera in Vézelay.'

'Casing the place?'

'I doubt it, he's too ham-fisted to be a burglar. A few days later, he turned up on a bank's security film here in Dijon.'

'A bank? Ham-fisted thugs get away with that sort of robbery; they shoot anyone who gets in their way.'

'Nothing like that. He was standing beside an attractive history student while she withdrew 300 francs from her account.'

Pel frowned, his brain turning over recent events. 'Sandrine Da Costa?'

'C'est exacte. For the ten days before she died, she stopped going to university, failed to return to her digs and had to all intents and purposes vanished. We searched and failed to find her. We found Luzanne though, on another surveillance film, standing beside another girl in another bank on the 23rd. We watched her like a hawk but her habits haven't changed, and no further contact has been made by him. We have to assume the relationship, if that's what it was, came to an abrupt end. On the 26th, however, Sandrine reappeared and we all know what happened. First problem: why steal? She had money in her account, not a lot but enough for the month's expenditure, we've got her bank statements until the day she died. She hadn't made a deposit or a withdrawal since she was filmed with Luzanne on 18th December. Two: why the hell was she brandishing a toy gun? Three: why the tip-offs? You were told to expect three heavily armed men, the press were told "single girl robber", they too were ready and waiting. Four: did the conflicting information come from the same source? And again why?'

'The press received an anonymous phone call from a male, thought to be reasonably mature, certainly not a youngster. Our sneak, not the same man, made contact with one of my team and organized a meet. Since then he's disappeared. He's well known and we've tried every one of his usual haunts. So far, zero.'

'I know. But let me finish. Dalton is a crafty sod, we've heard of his movements, not seen him. As I said earlier, we don't know what he looks like any more, but he seems to slip in and out of the country when and as he feels like it. We have evidence of purchases being made with a credit card in his name, drawn on a Paris bank account, all over Europe, but the descriptions we've put together from those places are all different.'

'What address do his bank have?'

'Post Office box numbers that change often. They think he's a travelling rep. He's appeared in our files with monotonous irregularity. It was thought, and I still think, he's one of the main sources of illicit barbiturates in north-eastern France. It has also been suggested that he's an arms dealer. I'm not convinced, it doesn't fit his past. It's more likely to be a tactical story he's put about to make his competitors wary of him, although he may be.'

'You think he was involved with Sandrine?'

'She was seen with Luzanne, he's connected to Dalton, therefore an indirect contact is a possibility I have to consider. I want Dalton and am prepared to backtrack from her to get him.'

'Have you had access to the post-mortem?'

'Not yet, I believe it was only logged this morning.'

'Boudet brought a paper copy in last night.'

'And?'

'Ever heard of scopolamine and phenothiazine?'

'Not that I recall.'

'I have.'

Pel and Lapeyre turned their attention to Capelle, still sitting to attention between them. 'Came across it in Southern Africa, otherwise known as burundanga. It induces total obedience, a sort of hypnosis. Not as easy as GBH.'

'Grievous bodily harm?'

'A nickname for Gamma OH.'

Pel rifled through his notes. 'The pathologist mentioned it.'

'One of the rape drugs,' Capelle continued. 'Victim doesn't remember a thing afterwards. We used burundanga to get an hysterical American research scientist across rebel lines. Nearly didn't make it, started wearing off before he was out of danger.'

'Its effects are short term?'

'Couple of hours, it doesn't do to hang around.'

'What if the dose is increased?'

'The dose depends on body weight; too little, you've got a non-cooperational situation; too much, you've got a corpse. Just right, you've still only got a couple of hours.'

Pel eyed the soldier. 'Is that the only time you've come across it?'

'Personally, yes, but I've heard of other cases.'

'Where?'

'North America, Thailand, Britain.'

'Britain?'

'A young sergeant was hit by a car crossing Piccadilly. Our chaps claimed her body, it was returned to Paris. They did a second autopsy, didn't want to accept the civilians' conclusions, they were English. There were traces.'

'And Dalton is a failed medical student with, apparently, criminal intent.' Pel lifted the phone, tapped in three numbers and put the handset to his ear. 'Rigal? Pel *à l'appareil*. Take this word down; B-U-R-U-N-D-A-N-G-A. Got it? Good, I want anything and everything you can find on it . . . *Quoi*? No, it's not a place, it's an evil mixture of scopolamine and phenothiazine. And while you're at it, have a look at Gamma OH, or GBH, plus barbiturates and benzodiazepine. Give me all the information you've got, plus all cases in which they appeared, were suspected, or were mentioned in passing . . . Urgent? Of course it's urgent, you ass, I need it by midday.' He crashed the phone down.

'It's nearly one o'clock already,' Lapeyre pointed out.

'Then he'll have to hurry.'

'What about background info on Sandrine?'

'We're working on it – in between a million other things. It's a slow process and wasn't, until now, particularly urgent. A full quota of men would help, we're working minus two at the moment.'

'What about Capelle here? I think you'll find he's worth a trial, he's well trained and needs very little sleep and, as you've heard, retains information like a ruddy encyclopedia. You probably don't recognize him but he was the bloke on the barbed wire when we were waging war on the Burgundy Bombers.'

Pel remembered the third man to be put down, he remembered him very well; coming from the copse, he'd stopped by the two looping strands of barbed wire barring his passage. As he lifted his leg to step over, something smacked him in the shoulder, twisting him round and throwing him at an angle on to the vicious barbs. His clothes caught and, although he was still alive, he was unable to free himself immediately. Another bullet thudded into his thigh, Pel had seen the spatter of blood, a chilling crimson, so clear, so colourful; the man yelled and struggled, making the situation worse. Then, after a few more agonizing moments, he went limp, hanging from the wire like discarded washing, an inert bundle of clothes. Pel had thought he was dead. He'd been informed later that the bloke on the barbed wire had survived, and, Lapeyre had added confidently, he'd be back at work in the autumn.

He nodded in recognition of Capelle's bravery, he must have been in agony hanging there while the rest of them went on fighting. 'I'm glad you made it,' he said, feeling it wasn't enough.

'As you see,' Lapeyre continued, 'he survived but is no longer a hundred per cent physically fit, I've had to dismiss him from special services. Various proposals were put forward, none of them suited, he still wants to be part of some action, although he is a little slower on his feet. In the end, I asked him what he'd choose from the limited possibilities available. Know what he said?'

'No idea, but I've a feeling I'm going to find out. And by the look on your face, I suspect I'm not going to like it.'

'Capelle, repeat your request.'

'Sir?'

'Word for word. If you don't get it right, I will.'

'Sir! I said: Sir, if I couldn't work for Lapeyre any more, I wouldn't mind working for the ugly little bugger, all bald and specs, in Burgundy.'

Pel stared at the deadly serious soldier, he hadn't smirked once. He looked at Lapeyre; his face had split into a wide amused smile, waiting for a reaction. Turning back, Pel said, 'You deserve a good thumping, Capelle, but as you're a great deal bigger than me, welcome to the team.'

'Thank you, sir.'

'Just one thing, don't call me sir. That's Lambert's name. And another thing, don't ever appear under my command wearing that God-awful uniform again. Report back for duty as soon as you look human. And perhaps you'd be kind enough to get your beard under control.'

'For the time being, he'll be working under cover; he keeps the beard, that and the long hair are appropriate. Which brings us back to Pierre La Poche; Bardolle has been searching for him unsuccessfully, and he's an important element. Without him, tracing the tip-offs' source is a dead loss, and I'm convinced Dalton is involved somewhere along the line. I want Capelle to try the doss houses and tramps' campsites. If you're in agreement, I'd like him to become one of them. Bardolle was born and brought up in Burgundy; even if he doesn't show his police identification, he's immediately recognized for what he is – *un putain de flic*. Tramps and addicts don't talk easily to the police, and they're the ones who may help us find La Poche. We need a man who isn't known, who can infiltrate the gutter groups who only talk in whispers and, I hope, will locate your sneak and a thread to Luzanne and hence, Dalton.'

'He'll need a back-up.'

'He's used to working alone.'

'If there's trouble?'

'He's used to that too.'

'Let's get one thing straight: is he under my command or yours?'

'Yours, of course.'

'Then he has a back-up on stand-by and a line in for communication.'

'In that case, he's still under my command.'

'You're a devious bugger, Lapeyre.'

'Perhaps, but I like to have my own way, I've found it works.'

Closing the door on his two visitors, Pel was thoughtful. It seemed that the tip-off, hinting the armed robbery was only the beginning of something much bigger, was, inadvertently, correct. He now had a drugs dealer, his sidekick, who'd witnessed a gang killing, and a highly dangerous mixture of ordinary medication that turned intelligent human beings into zombies. Did Lapeyre know anything more? He felt it was unlikely; on the other hand, he may suspect something which he didn't want to voice.

Calling Nosjean in, he informed him of the replacement about to unofficially join them and Nosjean nodded, his only comment, 'I hope he's house-trained.'

'For the moment it doesn't really matter whether he is or not,' Pel replied. 'He's going to be sleeping rough and listening to the dope users' grapevine.'

'What name's he using?'

'He hadn't decided.'

'Do we have his photo on record?'

'Not yet.'

'So how will we recognize him in the event of a raid?'

'I think that's the whole point of Lapeyre's plan; you won't.'

Chapter Seven

St David. There was no moon, the sky was as black as ink. A church bell tolled once as Capelle lurched across the pavement. He had a woollen hat pulled down to his eyebrows, a torn anorak flapping open, the broken zip catching on the threadbare jumper. Seeing a fire at the end of the narrow alley, he stopped and leant against the wall, apparently to steady himself. His eyes skimmed over the shadows in the distance: six men, two elderly and small, three younger, taller but thin, and what looked like a woman. The fire glowed orange in the darkness, its flickering light distorting the shapes of the many dustbins and boxes, making the small encampment eerie; it could have been a witches' coven. Behind him the street was empty, he'd already checked; no headlights in sight, no torches, no sound of anyone approaching, all he could hear was the low mumble of conversation and the crackling wood.

Then he'd been seen; one by one the featureless heads rose and turned towards him, someone pointed. Capelle raised a hand in greeting, lost his balance and stumbled forward, tripping and falling headlong into the alley. Lying with his nose pressed into the freezing filthy ground, he wished they'd bloody well hurry up, he could do with a bit of warmth after the empty hours before dawn.

It wasn't long before he was rolled over then hauled to his feet. He listened to the comments.

'Pissed, you can smell it.'

'Think he's still got some on 'im.'

'Try his pockets.'

He felt strangers' hands pawing his clothes, discovering the half-empty rectangular bottle and removing it.

'Good lad.'

'Get 'im over to the fire, he's all wet.'

Hardly surprising, Capelle thought, I emptied the other half of the bottle down my front.

The Misset family had paid for a discreet announcement to be made in the local press about Sandrine's funeral, due to take place that afternoon. An ambitious young journalist, when he saw the copy the night before, recognized the name of the mourning family – Misset was one of the city's detectives – and became interested in Sandrine Da Costa. Having concluded his enquiries at the hospital, where he had no luck, and the morgue, where he was given vague information about a lengthy post-mortem and a carton of clothes going to Forensic for analysis, he went on to the Town Hall, just before it closed at six. There he discovered Da Costa was Madame Misset's maiden name. He had, at last, put two and two together and come up with the right answer: the girl student slain by the police on 26th December was the detective's niece. Much to his disappointment, after all the hours he'd spent on it, the story of the young addict being gunned down was old news now and what he wrote was cut to a short paragraph at the bottom of page two.

The headlines being printed that morning concerned Hicham Bouaouiche, one of the three men suspected of killing a gendarme when he interrupted a robbery on 22nd December at Pont-Saint-Esprit. While his two accomplices had been arrested, Bouaouiche was still at liberty. The large colour photograph showed a young Arab with sad hooded eyes, short black hair, a well-formed mouth and clean white teeth. He was wearing a denim-blue T-shirt. That story was far more important than identifying someone who'd been dead three days.

Rigal stretched and glanced up at the digital clock in the corner of his computer's screen: 0634, finally finished. He'd been there all night, sifting and sorting his way through the millions of documents available. His machine was connected, via a changeable password, to a computer in Paris at the head office of the Centre d'Information et de Documentation. A justification of identity, personal authorization code, numerical address, plus a statement of intent were required before he was allowed access to their site. Once he was in, it had taken twenty-five minutes for his status to be checked and his entry into the archives granted. All known crimes documented in the Republic of France were at last at his disposal, electronically transferred when logged into one of the specific research terminals, such as his own, located in the hundreds of Commissariats throughout the country.

Pel had asked for all information relating to or suspected to relate to the given subjects, which hadn't made it easy for Rigal. The virtual files through which he was searching were catalogued into headings and sub-headings which, under normal circumstances, would short-cut the 'needle in a haystack' syndrome. Although Rigal felt it reasonable to move straight into 'Crimes', ignoring the massive files for 'Violations' and 'Misdemeanours', he groaned as he saw the listing for 'Crimes'. Divided into sub-headings, he was looking at 'Attacks against persons', 'Attacks against property' and 'Attacks against public security.' 'Attacks against persons' was then divided into four further sub-headings – 'intentional homicide', 'intentional violence,' 'non-intentional violence' and 'rape' – which in turn were divided into twelve more groups. 'Attacks against property' included 'theft', 'robbery', 'fraud', 'breach of trust', 'aggravated robberies' and 'vandalism', all having their own listings for variations on a theme. The first heading for 'Attacks against public security' was 'counterfeiting' – it's all he saw at that stage, the rest wouldn't fit on his screen.

Being a methodical man, Rigal started at Group 1, sub-heading I, and worked his way through the whole damn lot. As he worked, he loosened his tie, rolled up his sleeves, drank five paper cups of foul coffee from the machine in the corridor, two paper cups of tea, which wasn't much better, and finally kicked off his shoes, wriggling his toes with tiredness. It was a relief, he thought, smiling vaguely to himself, that 'terrorism' and 'espionage' were not accessible; they were locked away in another terminal to which only men like Lapeyre could acquire the key, the code, or probably both.

Rigal's eyes were heavy with lack of sleep, his skin itched, his back ached. He'd take a shower, slip across the road for a real cup of decent coffee and a freshly baked croissant, then welcome Pel in with the print-outs he'd made.

Placing the thick folder in his briefcase – it didn't do to leave that sort of thing lying around – he clicked it shut and stepped into his shoes with difficulty; his feet seemed to have grown in the night. Then, after running his hands through his hair, he rolled down his sleeves and fastened the cuffs, retied his tie, struggled wearily into his jacket and, taking the briefcase with him, slipped out of the office.

The shower rooms were empty but the water was cold; he decided to skip being clean and settle for breakfast. Unlocking his locker, he removed the briefcase, relocked the locker and headed for the stairs.

The Transvaal was almost empty, one or two taxi drivers complaining as usual at the bar, two members of Klein's team who'd been on surveillance all night, a nurse on her way home – and Pel.

Rigal nodded in his direction. Pel beckoned. He crossed to the table. 'You're an early bird, *patron*.'

'And you're late.'

'*Patron*?'

'I asked for information by midday yesterday, I'm still waiting.'

'I've only just finished.'

'You worked through the night?'

'Yes, *patron*, I thought . . . you said . . .'

'Sit down.' Pel lifted an arm in the direction of the bar. 'Claude, *encore un petit déjeuner!*' The arm dropped; he turned back to Rigal now seated opposite. 'Brought the wife in to catch the early train for Paris, going to see some fashion show. My housekeeper's coffee tastes of iron filings so I thought I'd treat myself to something drinkable, looks like you need one too. Tell me all about yourself, Rigal, haven't seen you for a while.'

'Always busy, you know what it's like.' Rigal wasn't sure what to say, and he wasn't sure of Pel. He'd always been terrified of his commanding officer, although this morning he seemed almost friendly. He cleared his throat. 'The er . . . the computers are the heart of the police station, aren't they? I'm just one of the many elements that make it beat.'

'Very poetic. If you're the heart, what am I?'

'Well, I don't know, one of the fingers, or feet? No, more like one of the eyes, you see and translate information for the brain to understand.'

'Who's the brain then?'

Rigal was beginning regret ever starting his analogy. 'Well, the brain is very complicated, it amasses an enormous amount of facts and figures, reacts to sounds, sights, feelings . . . the brain must be the team,' he said with satisfaction.

'You're not so daft after all, are you?' Pel replied and smiled.

Rigal nearly dropped off his seat with surprise.

The second breakfast arrived, banged down hurriedly. Pel

threw a handful of coins on the table which Claude scooped up – *'Merci, Chef'* – before leaving them in peace again. Both men dunked a corner of croissant and began chewing.

'Are you going to keep me in suspense for much longer?'

Rigal swallowed quickly and reached for his briefcase.

'Give me a verbal account, I'll read it later.'

'There's a great deal of data, a hundred-odd pages.'

'What about specific cases?'

'Girl named Josephine Fendji, seventeen, from Nantes. French mother, father from Camaroun. Left home at sixteen, was found drowned nine months later, January 1999, on the beach at Narbonne; the opposite coastline.'

Pel sipped at his coffee. 'Go on.'

'That's it. She'd been behaving oddly three days prior to her death, friends thought she was drunk, or high – she smoked pot regularly. Suicide was suggested, the autopsy showed she had been using Ecstasy; case closed as a misadventure while under the influence of drugs.'

'So where's the scopolamine?'

'Not scopolamine, *patron*. Traces of benzodiazepine were found in her bloodstream, together with 1.2 grams of alcohol, but it was ignored at the inquest in view of the Ecstasy. That's the only one I remember offhand, but you've got two whole chapters of deaths where benzodiazepines, barbiturates, neuroleptics and narcotics are mentioned. The first lot concerns deaths after a stay of more than forty-eight hours in a mental home or hospital, that's to say the drug was prescribed by a practising doctor to cure an existing disorder. The second is more interesting; the victims, if one can call them that, were between seventeen and thirty-seven. They'd been doping themselves regularly and upped the intake to reinforce the effect.'

'It's a start. What I want you to do now, after you've put your head down for an hour or two of course, is weed out the cases where two or more of the drugs appear; heroin and benzodiazepine, benzodiazepine and a neuroleptic, a barbiturate and something else. I'll need a copy of those autopsy reports, plus transcripts of the questions and answers with family and friends or witnesses.'

Rigal sighed, he was looking at another sleepless night.

'In fact, print out the whole case file, I need the names of the officers who were in charge of the enquiry.'

*　　*　　*

'Who's in charge of the Sandrine Da Costa shooting?'

The duty sergeant put down his pencil and adjusted his mouthpiece. 'Good morning, monsieur. May I have your name, please?'

'Cuquel, Klébert Cuquel.'

'Your address?'

Klébert complied.

'Home phone number?'

He gave it.

'Thank you, monsieur. Do you have information about Sandrine Da Costa?'

'Yes, I ruddy well do.'

'I'll put you through to Commandant Nosjean, he's handling it. Just one moment, please.'

After a series of clicks and two rings, Klébert heard, 'Commissariat, Nosjean speaking.'

'Cuquel here. I'm ringing about my son, Colin, Colin Cuquel. Have you found him yet?'

Nosjean frowned, he'd never heard of Colin Cuquel. He pushed away the file he'd been working on and searched for the missing persons list, hidden somewhere under all the paperwork on his desk.

'Hold the line, please, I'm checking,' he said to the phone, holding it between his shoulder and his cheek. Pulling another file marked '*Personnes Disparues*' towards him and opening it, he asked, 'When was he reported missing?'

'The 26th of this month.'

The terrible 26th December.

'Just three days ago.'

'It may be *just* three days to you, but believe me, it's a ruddy long time when you don't know where your only child's got to.'

'Yes, of course it is.' Nosjean's eyes were running down the first sheet of names; nothing there. He turned to the second: Cuquel, Colin, 20, student. Still missing. 'No, I'm sorry, we've no news for you, we'll be in touch if the situation changes.'

'Well, I've news for you. You know that little girl you shot, Sandrine Da Costa?'

'I didn't shoot her personally, monsieur, but I do know who you're referring to.'

'She was our Colin's girlfriend.'

Nosjean sat up. 'She was?'

'Yes, she damn well was, and now she's dead and my wife's scared out of her wits.'

'I can understand that. Were the two young people very close?'

'I believe so.'

'How long had they been going out together?'

'Since the beginning of October.'

'Just three months.'

'First it was just three days, now it's just three ruddy months. Like I said before, it's a long time to them that's concerned, and I'm *very* concerned. I don't think you're doing anything and my wife's convinced he's going to be the next kid you kill.'

'We don't make a habit of killing kids, monsieur.'

'You shot Sandrine, didn't you?'

'She was resisting arrest after committing armed robbery.'

'With a toy gun. I know, I read me papers and listen to the news, it's just about all I manage at the moment, what with one thing and another. What are you actually *doing* to find our Colin?'

'We're asking questions, monsieur, trying to establish where he was last seen and with whom.' In fact, after the preliminary checks with hospitals, gendarmeries, and their own files, they hadn't done much more – what with one thing and another. Colin was over the age of consent, he could come and go as he pleased. No one could force him to make contact with his parents if he didn't want to, which was usually the case in Nosjean's experience of absent twenty-year-old male students. Now he was connected to Sandrine, however, the missing lad was an important element, they'd have to ask more questions, do the job properly. Trouble was, the university complex was prac-tically empty at the moment, the student digs and dives too, it didn't help. 'I assure you,' he added more honestly, 'we're very anxious to find your son.'

'Not as anxious as I am.'

The morning meeting was snappy, it started at 0800 and finished six minutes later, probably the shortest morning meeting on record. Pel was in a hurry. He crashed through the door marked 'Centre des Enquêtes (I): Inspecteurs', making the collection of cups on the filing cabinet behind it rattle musically, as they did every day of the week when he wanted to make his presence known. Most heads lifted in recognition of their senior officer's appearance, a few looked over their shoulders at him and turned round, one remained locked on to the centre page spread while he scratched an armpit, more out of habit than anything else.

'Bin the tits and bums temporarily, Gilbert, will you? We've got more important things to do.'

The slightly overweight, gently perspiring face finally acknowledged it was being addressed. 'Morning, guv. Hail and hearty as always, nothing like a night with the missus to put a bloke in the pink. How was it?'

'Too short . . .'

'I've got a remedy for that sort of thing, nothing like this Viagra everyone's going on about, just a few quick exercises and –'

'Gilbert!'

'Yes, guv?'

'*Ta gueule!*'

'Yes, guv.'

Pel looked round at the waiting faces. 'As well as the follow-ups you already have to fill your day, I want an intensive search doing into the life of Sandrine Da Costa. We need to know much more about our victim.'

'Why don't you just ask Misset, guv?'

'Because I thought it would keep you busy, Gilbert, and stop you asking bloody silly questions. And I'm not bothering Misset because what we're looking for is precisely the sort of thing a loving uncle and adoptive father wouldn't know. For instance, she was using heroin before she died, who was supplying? She was seen briefly in the company of a dubious character called Luzanne, after which she disappeared for over a week, to do what, and where? Jourdain and Pujol,' he went on, 'you're to work at the university, find out everything from her tutors, friends, acquaintances and her landlady. I know the campus is pretty deserted at the moment but do what you can, the professors at least will be available. I'll get Rigal punching holes in his computer for other sources when he wakes up. Keep your eyes and ears open, add questions to interviews with other witnesses who may have been somewhere near her or her friends since the start of term, and she must have plenty of old school friends in and around town. Nosjean's got a list of her classmates, past and present, don't leave without it. Find them and find out what she was doing before she died. Anything else?'

'Sandrine's boyfriend,' Nosjean said quickly. 'I've just had his father on the phone; Colin Cuquel, he's missing. It was reported on the 26th.'

'Add it to your enquiries, ask questions about both of them. I want anything and everything. Is that all?'

'The Pharmacie Cathala was broken into during the night.'

'Find out exactly what was taken. And request the details of other pharmacy robberies, wherever they were. I want a comprehensive list of all missing medication.'

As he turned to go, Bardolle called him back. 'I had a strange call from our pickpocket last night, *patron*.'

'Follow me. Nosjean, finish off.'

Bardolle followed Pel across the corridor and into his office, closing the door behind him.

'*Accouche.*'

'I went for a beer, as I often do, on my way home last night. The bar was fairly crowded with the usual faces. The phone rang, Claude the barman answered and beckoned to me. It was La Poche in a bad way.'

Pel lit up and said nothing, waiting for the rest.

'He wanted to see me urgently.'

'Why?'

'He wouldn't say any more, asked me to meet him behind a warehouse at the corner of rue des Chaudronniers and rue des Verriers facing the canal. I went, waited, had a poke about; nothing. An hour later, I left. I went back on my way in this morning; still nothing.'

'Why do you say he was in a bad way?'

'Could hardly get his words out.'

'Drunk?'

'No, scared.'

'Give any indication as to why?'

'None, said he couldn't talk on the phone but he needed help from a friend.'

'What's the warehouse used for?'

'It's empty, has been for a couple of years.'

'Who's the owner?'

'A bank, it was seized when the grain merchant who used it went bust. It's up for sale, Immobilier Fourcadel's handling it.'

'Might be worth a visit, have a look around inside . . . Sort it, Bardolle, I'm going out.'

While Bardolle was sorting it – ringing the bank, the estate agents, arranging to collect the keys and persuading Gilbert to stop gawping at either the pretty and rather well-endowed secretary or his ruddy magazine that he insisted on taking along with him, 'It's something to do while you do all the bleeding talking' – Sandrine Da Costa was collected from Misset's house; after the autopsy, her body had been released and delivered to her family's home for mourning, as is the custom in Roman Catholic countries. Now it was locked in a coffin on its way to the city's crematorium on the edge of the city's bypass. Pel and Pujol were standing in the car park when the undertakers arrived.

As the simple wooden coffin emerged from the vehicle and was solemnly carried into the small building, Misset and his wife, driven by one of their three sons, drew up and got out of their car. The other two sons, plus a girlfriend and Misset's wailing mother-in-law, parked alongside. Hands were sadly shaken and the silent crowd, patiently waiting, caps in gloved hands, followed the mourning family inside. The coffin was being laid tenderly on its platform, surrounded by flowers. The four uniformed handlers checked that its positioning was perfect and straightened a wreath before stepping back against the walls, removing their peaked hats and inclining their heads for the service. Pel was sitting directly behind the family at the front. He had a clear view of their faces and it was with enormous surprise, and a little shock, that he recognized Lapeyre. His pale hair was darker, his smooth face grave, older, but there was no doubt, the second coffin bearer on the right was the Colonel.

The tiny modern chapel was overcrowded; mourners spilt out on to the tarmac apron at the entrance and consequently the doors had to be left open. It made Pel realize how well liked Misset must be away from the Commissariat. It also made his nose drip, it was bitterly cold sitting listening to the dull voice of the priest, not that he could hear much of what was being said, the noise of traffic roaring past on the dual carriageway outside drummed and echoed in everyone's ears. It was a miserable little affair and half an hour later it was over, the coffin was removed and taken through a back door to the ovens. The family and friends wandered out through the main entrance and, as Pel's turn came to shake Misset's hand and offer a few inadequate words of sympathy, he noticed the tears glittering in his eyes. It looked as if his brain was plugged in and ticking over dangerously. Whatever Pel did he was going to have to keep Misset away from the case until it was closed for good, and, he sighed unhappily, a long way from Morrison for ever, he didn't want another murder on his hands.

'Well,' Pujol said as he started up the car, 'that was interesting as well as being extremely sad.'

Pel glanced across at the young lieutenant. 'Tell me.'

'Misset asked me where Morrison was, he wants revenge, *patron*.'

'He mustn't be allowed it. What did you tell him?'

'I lied, I said he was still in Paris.'

'Very wise, at least he won't try knocking his teeth out on our patch. The best thing for Misset would be work, it'd keep him busy, get him thinking about something else, but that's going to be difficult while we're still investigating his niece's death.'

'*Patron*?'

'Pujol.'

'If it hadn't been Misset's niece, would we be paying so much attention to her?'

'In view of who killed her, yes, we've got to try and establish that Morrison was only acting within the limits of his duty. Secondly, the pathologists' report revealed a deadly mixture of drugs; naturally we'd follow that up whoever it was.'

'Yes, but . . .'

'I know what you're saying, Pujol, and the honest answer is probably not. Unless of course, it'd been an Arab, in which case we'd be giving it star treatment, you know what race relations are like.'

'That's what I thought.'

Easing the vehicle out into the busy road, Pujol licked his lips. 'Something very strange is going on; that bloody man from Paris was there, you know, Lapeyre, what's he interfering for?'

'How did you recognize him?'

'The signet ring.'

'He gave me a bit of a shock, but I've already had contact with him. Sandrine was seen with a man they've been watching.'

'A terrorist?'

'A pusher.'

'So why's he involved, surely it should be the Brigade des Stupéfiants?'

'I don't think it's just drugs, an arms dealer has been mentioned.'

'Hoped he'd turn up for the funeral?'

'Maybe, Lapeyre can work in mysterious ways. We'll just have to wait and see.'

'*Patron*?'

'Pujol.'

'Remind me to change my will. I always thought being cre-
mated was a good idea, neater if you know what I mean, but
after that, the traffic and so on, I think I'd rather be left to the
worms.'

Pierre La Poche had the worms of fear gnawing at his nerve
ends. He'd been hanging around the warehouse too long. He'd
seen Bardolle and de Troq' arrive in an unmarked car and he'd
watched them open the echoing building and step inside. Once
they were well and truly out of sight, he'd started across the
street from his hiding place. As he approached, he heard a siren
wailing and saw the blue flashing light coming on to the bridge
behind him, cross it and vanish between the buildings. He
ducked out of sight again just in case. Within seconds, the men
he desperately wanted to meet came out at the run. De Troq' had
a mobile to his ear as they exited, shouting to Bardolle to be
quick and lock up, their car thief was on the run at last and he
wanted to nobble him once and for all. The metal door slid to
with a clang, keys rattled, car doors banged and, just so everyone knew exactly who they were, as they drove off at high
speed, Bardolle slapped a blue flashing light on top of the
vehicle and turned on the siren. Pierre La Poche sank further into
the shadows, staring up the street after the disappearing car. He
closed his eyes and wondered what he could do next.
    That was easy. Follow instructions.
    'Okay, Pierrot, on your feet.'
    He knew the game was up.
    The worms of fear made Pierre La Poche sweat and stutter.

While La Poche stuttered out his explanations, Morrison listened
to Juge Jonglez as he was committed for trial. The delay had
been caused by the indecision over what he was to be charged
with. To be fair, Brisard had done all he could for leniency, but
in the end it was still intentional homicide – with Pel implicated
as his commanding officer. As a result, he was present when the
unpleasant interview took place in a small room at the back of
the city courts.
    Unusually, Morrison didn't blush once. He didn't say a word
when he was formally charged and told the trial was set for
Monday, 24th January. He simply nodded in acknowledgement
of the information. When asked if he had a lawyer, he shook his

head and was assured one would be appointed, after which he was allowed to leave, still pale-faced and silent.

Pel caught up with him outside and gently pushed him on to one of the highly polished bench seats lining the wide corridor. They sat for a moment, talking in almost whispers, then, rising together, walked towards the door. 'That's exactly what you told me shortly after it happened, Morrison. Have you really remembered nothing else?'

'I've been over it a million times in my own mind, *patron*. I've told it a million times too, those men from Paris didn't let up once. There's only one thing I didn't tell them and that was how terrified I was. The gun was pointing at my balls, I think I'd've preferred her to keep it aimed at my head.'

Pel stopped to study the miserable, defrocked policeman. 'You need a drink,' he said sympathetically.

'No, thanks, *patron*, I'll be getting off home.'

'It's an order, Morrison.'

The two men went silently out of the court house, across the car park and into the street. They turned right and walked a little further, eventually stopping in front of a bar. Pel opened the door and followed Morrison inside. '*Deux bières*,' he called and went to the far end, well away from the window.

'Say that again.'

'What?'

'About where the gun was pointing.'

'At my . . . you know, my testicles.'

'And you'd've preferred . . .?'

'Her to stay aiming at my head.'

'You didn't get a chance to see into the barrel of the gun?'

'Not long. She took it out of her bag, stuck it under my nose, then smiled . . . cruelly . . . and lowered it to my balls. I should've seen . . . but I didn't . . . *Patron*, I was really scared, I thought she was going to kill me. And instead . . . I killed her.'

'What you've told me may help and if it makes you feel any better, Pujol was just as frightened, he nearly pulled the trigger first.'

'Yes, but he didn't, did he? I did. How's Misset?'

'You don't want to hear it.'

'I won't be a member of your team much longer, will I?'

Pel looked at the young man's miserable expression. He wanted to reassure him and knew in all honesty he couldn't. 'No,' he said simply.

'Will I be on anyone's team?'

'It depends. Don't give up hope yet, son, we're doing all we can.'

Pel returned to the Hôtel de Police deep in thought. He parked his car and as he climbed out, he heard the distant voices of children playing, shrill in the quiet afternoon. Glancing at his watch, he wandered towards the park, his hands shoved deep into the pockets of his overcoat, a wisp of smoke trailing in his wake. Going through the park gates, he dropped the cigarette and crushed it out with his foot, stopping for a moment to sigh. It had been a bright, surprisingly sunny day, now it was growing cold again. The winter sun winked between the gently swaying branches of the trees as it sank in the sky, streaking it with copper and gold. Had he bothered to notice, he'd have said it was going to be a splendid sunset. He didn't. His mind was occupied with uglier things as he walked slowly towards the large pond. There, as he had hoped, he saw the inevitable scattering of children charging around, yelling at the tops of their voices. He found a square of unoccupied bench and sat down to watch, needing something to lift his spirits.

However, it was a disappointing occupation. There seemed no sense to their games: it had all changed since he was a lad. The boys no longer chased the girls with sticks, or insects. The girls no longer sported plaits, told tales, rubbing grubby curled fists into tearful eyes, or shrieking accusations while pointing at the offending little lout. In fact, nowadays it was difficult to tell the difference, the whole lot were wearing colourful tracksuits emblazoned with American slogans and another word he didn't understand – Pokémon, wherever the hell that was.

None of them wore knee-length drooping woollen socks – he'd always wondered why one of his always slipped down round an ankle, he'd never discovered the answer. None of them wore leather shoes, with laces that trailed like spaghetti through the puddles, leaving snail-trails as they skipped off down the path. This lot seemed to be running round and round in circles, carried quietly on their rubber-soled trainers held together with Velcro, shooting imaginary guns.

They weren't playing cowboys and Indians either. The game was much more modern. He studied the stance of a seven-year-old, creeping behind a tree, his hands poised as if holding a pistol, then, as his playmate appeared, both of them took up the cover-and-hold position; legs bent, feet apart, arms rigid, at right angles to their bodies, making a triangle at the point of which their guns were supposed to be. One child simulated fire, his fists jerking upwards as his pointing fingers did the damage and his mouth added remarkable sound effects. The other child spun round, clutching his chest, shouting he'd been hit, fell to the ground, rolled over, lay still. The killer approached warily and, at the last moment, the body on the tarmac path raised his hands and fired. The play-acting had been impressive, it made Pel's blood run cold.

How was it that the human race, apparently the most intelligent life form on earth, allowed small children to play at shooting each other? Didn't their parents bother to explain guns killed people, left great bloody suppurating holes in them, splattered a man's guts and breakfast all over the wall behind, exploded heads in a cascade of scarlet mush, splintered bones, shattered lives?

'Hugo! Say you're sorry to Lucas.'

Pel looked up again; a young woman was chastising the two killers.

'He started it.'

'He kicked me.'

'He pushed me.'

'Both of you say sorry, you mustn't squabble like that.'

Squabbling wasn't allowed, but it was perfectly acceptable to pretend to murder each other.

He watched sadly, lighting a fresh cigarette, inhaling deeply and replacing the *briquet* in his jacket pocket, as the two small boys slouched off to sulk.

And none of these kids had dirty faces.

Or scabby knees painted with iodine.

It's a changing world, he told himself, there must be some sense in it, though God knows where, I don't. These kids won't go home to play hopscotch chalked out on the street, or jump over skipping ropes, or watch Grandad playing *boules*, itching to have a go; no, they'll whizz up to their overheated apartments in the lift and plug themselves into a Playstation until Mum, who's been at work all day, calls them in for a deep-frozen, microwaved supper. What had happened to good wholesome Bœuf Bourgignon? Or home-made soup with whole potatoes, beans and bacon?

Usually too occupied to notice his own bad temper, usually too busy to sit on a park bench, today Pel was feeling depressed and, to add to his troubles, he thought he had another cold coming on.

He sniffed. In six months his team was in tatters; Darcy was dead, Misset was mourning and Morrison charged with man-slaughter. The poor lad wasn't a murderer. But he had made a mistake. He was a policeman, that magnified the mistake, made it public property. Justice wouldn't just be done, it had to be seen to be done. Exit Morrison. Pel's mind was no longer focused on the children. And Lambert, Lambert the Bore, Lambert the Drone, the self-important Snow-Capped Bloody Mountain was still Chief.

'Pel?'

He raised his head slowly, taking in the highly polished shoes, the neat creases in pale grey trousers, a matching waistcoat over a startlingly white shirt, silk tie, smart camel-coloured overcoat sitting squarely on the shoulders, slim gold watch, and a large signet ring on his little finger. He looked up into a smooth handsome face and uncommonly blond hair. 'This isn't a coincidence,' he said, 'is it, Lapeyre?'

'No, I followed you, needed to talk, away from the office.'

'Worried Lambert's bugged it?'

'He doesn't have the authority.'

'I was joking.'

'I wasn't.'

'You'd better sit down then, you're spoiling the view; not that there's much to look at nowadays.'

The elegant clothes shifted to one side and folded on to the bench and the two men sat for a moment side by side, puffing silently. Lapeyre studied the glowing end of the stub he held before flicking it into a puddle and listening to the brief hiss of extinction. 'We've found another one,' he said. '1998, a Portuguese girl in Biarritz who threw herself in front of a train.'

'Funny, Rigal didn't come across her.'

'He wouldn't have, there were eyewitnesses and the inquest returned a verdict of suicide. She was cohabiting with a Basque we were watching after a bomb destroyed the Town Hall at St Jean de Luz. Our pathologist did a very private autopsy; heroin and the zombie cocktail.'

'And I've got a drowning in Narbonne.'

'Plus the army sergeant in London who Capelle mentioned, that was the beginning of 1996.'

'And Sandrine Da Costa in Burgundy.'

'That makes four.'

'In as many years.'

'Not counting the ones who weren't subjected to autopsy. As you are aware, unless foul play is suspected, it's up to the examining medic to make the request. Some don't bother to look too hard, some simply don't think beyond signing the death certificate and hotfooting it home.'

'I've got Rigal digging for others and I've a nasty feeling he's going to come up with several. Scopolamine and phenothiazine isn't the only mixture that can turn a kid into a zombie, the pathologist had a staggering list of possibilities and most of them are currently available, i.e. over the counter with a pre-scription.'

'And chemists are broken into.'

'We're on to that too, collating information about what was stolen and where.'

'I doubt it'll make much difference. The dealers aren't daft enough to buy stolen drugs and sell them on the same patch.'

Pel sighed. 'What were you doing at the crematorium?'

'Taking a look at the mourners.'

'As a coffin bearer. How do you do it, Lapeyre?'

'Simple, I bribed one of them to lend me his uniform and spend the afternoon with his mistress.'

'So who did you see?'

'You and Pujol, Misset and the mourning family, apart from that no one I recognized.'

'So we've still only got four mysterious deaths and a vague connection to Luzanne.'

'And Dalton.'

'The girl who died in Biarritz, where were her parents?'

'Still in Portugal.'

'With the exception of Sandrine, the victims were a long way from home, cut off from their families.'

'They were all under the age of twenty-five,' Lapeyre added. 'Sandrine interests me more and more, she was different; a loving family behind her, well brought up, enough money, a place at university, no real problems. If my thinking is correct, these kids were chosen, and if that is so, why risk whatever they're up to by getting involved with the niece of a *flic*? I told you Luzanne was seen with another girl after Sandrine dis-appeared . . .'

'And the relationship ended quickly.'

'. . . her mother's a secretary at Autun's Town Hall. Well connected, you see. Sandrine must have been a mistake, unless . . . I wonder if being a detective's niece bothered her, a lot of kids shy away from friendship with a policeman's family. What does her father do?'

'Not a lot, he's dead. Her mother died of cancer, her father was killed in a car crash a few years later. Didn't you know she was an orphan?'

Lapeyre looked up abruptly. 'That's what she told her peer group! Now she fits.' He pulled his overcoat closed over his chest. 'It's a pity we can't plant a policewoman on the campus. You wouldn't consider introducing your blonde lieutenant to him, would you, what's her name?'

'Jourdain. Negative, and I insist you don't suggest it to her, or she'll be off to flirt before you've finished explaining. It's precisely that sort of situation she got herself into when she was kidnapped and almost killed. Leave her out of this. What about Capelle?'

Lapeyre smiled. 'I don't think Luzanne would fancy him. Too hairy.'

'He'd make a good terrorist though.'

'With the training he's had, the idea is bloody terrifying.'

'Something's just occurred to me.' Pel frowned deeply. 'The victims are all girls, not a bloke among them. If it's drugs or terrorism, there should be.'

'I wondered when you'd notice.'

'So why are you involved?'

'Dalton, he's the one I want.'

'But what for? You said the idea of him being an arms dealer wasn't convincing.'

'Dalton deals in everything and anything that makes him money, and with men in very high places. La Division keep tabs on him because of the terrorist activity in their homelands.'

'So he could be selling arms.'

'And legs and pretty faces.'

Pel was thinking hard, then he sucked in his breath. 'Christ,' he said quietly. 'No wonder you're involved.'

Chapter Eight

Jeudi, le 30 décembre

St Roger. Four days after Sandrine was shot, twenty-four hours after she was buried, her name had been forgotten by the press. Instead they turned their attention to the passengers of a Boeing 747, en route from London to Nairobi. Wide-eyed with relief, they recounted how a madman had tried to take over the command of the aircraft, wanting to crash it in a crazy suicide attempt. 'A fight broke out in the pilot's cabin and the aircraft made a series of alarming dives. The crew overpowered the man and regained control. One air hostess and four passengers were hurt, the pilot was bitten. The hijacker was taken to a psychiatric hospital for treatment.'

It was about the only article worth reading; the rest of the newspaper was filled with a review of the passing year. Amongst the famous names like Henri Salvador, Vanessa Paradis and of course the entire French soccer team – *les sacrés bleus* – Harry Potter was also mentioned. Pel sniffed; he'd never heard of him.

He smoothed the paper out over his desk then pushed it impatiently away, replacing it with his notepad and, as he stared at the figures he'd just written, the bells of St Bénigne announced one o'clock.

He'd just spent fifty-five tedious minutes listening to the Chief on the year's statistics for his sector of Burgundy – nine murders, two armed hold-ups, thirteen rapes, four bombings of public places resulting in eight deaths. Seventeen lives lost on the public highways. 790 four-wheeled vehicles stolen, 1,001 two-wheeled vehicles. 6,768 robberies ranging from simple bag snatching to emptying a man's flat of everything but his bedroom slippers, plus, of course, the cat burglar who'd finally broken his neck falling down a fire escape, the wave of burglaries in Talant . . . Pel had stopped writing at that point and allowed his mind to wander, but a few moments later his eyes had snapped open – 'Twenty-two threats against civil servants' – surprised that sort of useless statistic was kept. However, he'd carefully noted the drugs seized: 17.5 kilos of hashish, 7.5 kilos of marijuana, 6 kilos of heroin, 10.5 kilos of cocaine, 25 kilos of khat, 171 Ecstasy pills, and 1,604 other pills.

Twisting round, he lifted a thick file off the shelf behind him and, flicking through the plastic-covered pages, he compared the figures with the previous year. The use of drugs listed in Boudet's well-thumbed dictionary of medication, le Vidal, had almost doubled in twelve months.

His stomach rumbled, reminding him he still hadn't eaten and, looking up, he realized the corridor outside was unusually quiet.

Most of the team were either still out on the streets or discreetly eating in the corner of a locker room – Lambert had sent a circular out to all personnel demanding that 'the slovenly consumption of edibles in the offices of this Hôtel de Police will cease immediately'. Unfortunately, unlike Lambert, who often had an important meeting to attend to while filling his stomach at the expense of the city, most of the men and women working under him didn't have the time – or the money – to do more than grab a sandwich and munch on the job.

One of them was Pel, and as he bit into a piece of leathery baguette, someone rapped loudly at his door, startling him. A slice of ripe tomato slipped out and landed on his trousers, adding not only tomato juice and a few pips but also a stripe of good strong Dijon mustard to the fawn corduroy. He cursed eloquently and attempted to mop up with a paper napkin, leaving part of it stuck to the stain. '*Entrez!*'

'*Patron?*'

'Oh, it's you, Gilbert. Have you seen what you made me do, you halfwit?'

Gilbert peered at Pel's thigh. 'Looks like a cat's been sick and you've made a bad job of clearing it up. Either that or a tart's –'

'Thank you, Gilbert. Sit down and belt up.'

'But I wanted to talk to you.'

'What about? The barmaid's bra? Your wife's nocturnal habits? My wife's nocturnal habits? Or was it something trivial?'

'Misset, guv.'

'What about him?'

'I went to see him yesterday evening. To sort of apologize for not being at the funeral.'

'You didn't miss much.'

'He's not coping, guv. And his wife's round the bend, but I think that's normal. She and her mother are a right pair of dragons. *Clope*?'

'Not while I'm eating, you idiot.'

'You've stopped.'

Pel abandoned his unappetizing lunch, accepted the cigarette, offered his lighter and sat back. 'I'm sure you didn't come barging in here just to tell me Misset's wife and mother-in-law are a right pair of dragons.'

'I didn't barge, guv, I knocked.'

'Get to the point.'

Gilbert placed a small notepad on the desk. 'I took Misset for a jar, thought it would cheer him up to get away from the wake. We got talking, well, that's what I took him there for, after you asking for stuff about his niece and me saying why don't we ask him and you saying –'

'Gilbert!'

'Yes, guv. I asked him about his sons first, to ease my way into the subject, you know. Said, did he ever have any trouble with them? He said they were so flaming lazy, a habit such as heroin would be too much like hard work. The only thing they worked at was fondling their girlfriends' tits. I spoke to them, and I think he's right. The one called Christophe was sitting on the sofa with his bird and she had a pair of knockers the size of melons.'

'Gilbert, stick to the point.'

'Sorry, guv. Sandrine – he told me everything he could remember; the clubs she joined, the political meetings she went to, even the address of a party she'd enjoyed, she met a boy at it and was keen on him, I think, must've been that kid Colin, I suppose. It's not much but well, it's better than clutching at straws on the street.'

Pel was turning pages in the notepad. 'And saves your feet, *n'est-ce pas*? What did you tell him to get him to talk?'

'That she'd been set up, we wanted the bloke behind it.'

Pel's eyebrows shot up. 'What made you think of that?'

'I wondered how I'd feel if it'd been my daughter, that's how Misset thought of her . . .'

'Have you got one?'

'Officially or unofficially?'

'Either.'

131

'Well, no, but I tried imagining my lad was a girl, he behaves like one sometimes, nineteen and still not copulating –'

'Gilbert!'

'It would help, though, wouldn't it? To think that your kid's death isn't really his or her fault, therefore not yours as a parent. If you see what I mean.'

'Very perceptive.'

'Yeah, well, he opened up straight away. Told me about her getting a place at university and how excited she was when she went off to sign on. She lived with them for the first year and worked hard. Then in June she announced she was moving into digs, to be closer to the libraries and things, you know, save time on travelling from one side of the city to the other. When term started, she went home every weekend. Then she began making excuses – he hadn't seen her since the beginning of November, she didn't phone either. His wife fussed and called her digs but she was never in, she wanted to go over and see for herself, Misset told her she was an interfering old bat and to leave the girl alone – or words to that effect. Now he's regretting it.'

'And feeling guilty.'

'It's Morrison that's guilty.'

'He hasn't been tried yet.'

'Whatever the verdict, he's guilty as far as Misset's concerned.'

'Get back to the facts. I thought . . . I'm sure I heard his niece had made contact and would be home for the holidays.'

'She rang on the 22nd. He said she sounded different, as if all the joy had been knocked out of her, and all she'd managed at that point was, "Hello, Oncle Jo, how are you?" They chatted for a while about this and that, she said she'd been ill with flu or something but was taking her medicine and should be home soon. He wanted her back for Christmas Day but she said the doctor said she'd be unwise to go out before the 26th, what with the weather and so on. Misset wanted to go and collect her, bring her back to the family to look after her, and she said not to worry, she'd be fine. Misset started saying something else about convalescing at home but she interrupted and said . . . er, sorry, can I have the notebook back? I've forgotten the next bit.'

Pel handed it over.

'She said, "If I don't want to go on with my studies, will you be very disappointed?" Misset said he didn't give a fig what she did as long as she was safe and happy. She burst into tears and hung up. That was the last time he spoke to her.'

'No wonder he's hurting.'

'And he wants to kill Morrison.'

'That, I hope, will pass. Did he try ringing back?'

'His wife did but a girl at her digs said she'd moved out and was living somewhere else, she didn't know where. What's behind it all, guv?'

'I don't know, not yet, but Sandrine wasn't the first youngster to be lured into something very sinister.'

'What?'

'I'm not sure, but there is a vague connection with three other apparently accidental deaths.'

'Sandrine's wasn't accidental, guv, Morrison emptied his fucking gun into her.'

'Had you or I been in his situation, we may have been tempted to do the same. Pujol was. It was the first time Morrison was faced with a supposedly armed and dangerous criminal.'

'That's not the way Misset sees it.'

'The next time you talk to him, you'll make it very clear that we are not the judge and the jury. Morrison will be tried and, if misconduct is proved, sentenced – justice will be done.'

Gilbert sneered. 'If you believe that, guv, you'll believe anything. Justice is a matter of how much you pay your lawyer. And his lawyer was appointed by the state, not paid privately.'

And although Pel dismissed Gilbert, telling him to keep his mouth firmly shut on the subject of justice, he couldn't help but agree to a certain extent. Expensive lawyers sometimes made justice no more than a farce.

The farce in Interview Room 2 wasn't making Bardolle smile. Or de Troq', for that matter. The car thief they'd brought in the previous day was demanding release. 'You've had me in here twenty hours. I know my rights, you can't keep me any longer without allowing me access to a lawyer or letting me go.'

'Unless we charge you.'

'What with? Inadvertently borrowing a stranger's car. I've already told you, mine's at the garage with a split radiator, I rang a mate, Gilles Bousquet, who said he'd lend me his, said it would be parked outside the post office with the keys inside. I went along to the bleeding post office and there it was, a white Citroën Xsara plus keys. I got in and drove off. Next bleeding thing I know, there's a posse of police on my tail and blue lights flashing all over the shop. Ring Bousquet, he'll tell you.'

They had and he did, he'd also obligingly offered to send them a photocopy of his own Citroën Xsara's *carte grise*, just to prove he had one to lend.

'What do you reckon?' Bardolle said as they stepped out into the corridor.

'I think we're going to have to release him. His story checks with Bousquet's.'

'What if he's part of the plan?'

'And just happened to be sitting at his flat window and noticed the other Xsara parked nearby, with its keys conveniently dangling?'

'He hasn't got anything else to do, he's on the dole. He could've been watching for weeks, the Xsara stops every day to buy a Mars bar and a paper next door, it's a diesel so the guy doesn't even switch off the engine.'

'Our thief's certainly not solo,' de Troq' agreed. 'The operation's too efficient, the cars disappear without trace; repainted in another county, sold in a third. And to disappear completely they need log books.'

'From a junk yard? They're supposed to hand them in marked "car destroyed" . . .'

'But one might be making some pocket money by selling them on.'

Bardolle motioned a thumb over his shoulder. 'So what about him?'

'We can't charge him, Brisard wouldn't allow it, not on the slim if not non-existent evidence we have.'

'Bugger it,' Bardolle said quietly but with feeling. 'Just when I thought we'd cracked it.'

'Give it time, give it time.'

'These things take time, Madame Cuquel,' Nosjean said. 'We've had men scouring the university complex as well as the surrounding streets asking questions.'

He had too, they'd been round and round in circles, visiting the digs and dives, the clubs and pubs within walking distance of the university. One or two people knew who Colin was and what he looked like; no one had seen him since the 19th, although he had been heard, it was believed, leaving his room on the 20th. Everyone had heard of Sandrine by now but, similarly, no one had seen her since the 18th. It was possible that the two of them had taken off together, but Luzanne's presence on the

18th when she made a *retrait rapide* at her bank made it look unlikely.

'Is it true Sandrine was a druggie?'

'Yes, madame, it is.'

'What sort of drugs?'

'Heroin among other things.'

'Well, my Colin wouldn't touch drugs, he was brought up right. We told him about the trouble he could get into.'

'Yes, madame.'

Edith Cuquel broke down, 'Well, don't just sit there "yes, madaming" me, go out and find him!'

Nosjean sighed wearily and sadly. 'I'll do my best, I promise you.'

Vendredi, le 31 décembre

St Sylvestre. Morrison wasn't the only policeman to have accidentally killed when faced with a potentially dangerous situation. When Stéphane Beaumont attempted to remove the ignition key from the drugs dealers' car at the tollgate on the A9 motorway at Roquemaure, he was hit in the head by a bullet and died instantly, allowing the two suspects to escape. Ballistics in the Gard had now confirmed it was a stray bullet, emanating from one of his colleagues' automatics. The officer concerned was in police custody.

The weather forecast announced that the last day of the year would be cold and wet.

They'd got it right! It was mean 2 degrees at dawn. And it was raining.

It felt as if it was well below freezing with the wind whistling round their ears. Nosjean's teeth were all but chattering. The woman standing beside him, shivering on the side of the canal, had stopped screaming; she was sobbing loudly. It wasn't much better, he still couldn't understand a word she was saying. Nosjean kindly offered her his handkerchief as a body was lifted out of the water by the frogmen and was hoisted up on to the sodden grass-covered quay.

'I was out walking the dog!' The woman's statement startled him, he turned from the corpse and concentrated on the dripping witness. 'Running the dog actually!' The dog, a large golden Labrador, was sniffing enthusiastically at the mound of drenched rags being manhandled on to a morgue trolley, bouncing and generally being obstructive, enjoying the extra activity.

He'd got the end of a trouser leg between his teeth and was having a go at pulling the body off on to the glistening road for a game.

'Prince is a lively boy! He needs a good run! Prince, don't do that!' She started sobbing again.

'Take your time, madame.' Nosjean sniffed, shrugging himself further inside his anorak.

'*Oh mon Dieu*, you can't imagine! I stopped to catch my breath! And there it was! Floating in the water! *Oh mon Dieu*, I think I'm going to be sick!'

She was.

Nosjean left her to it and wandered over to take a look at the corpse. It was bloated, discoloured and ugly, the stiff darkened hands finishing in fingers that looked like overcooked sausages. They were tattered and fraying thanks to the scavengers in the canal, or living along the edge, and always ready for a convenient snack. He bent closer, asking the attendants to wait before zipping up the body bag, wanting to know if he'd found the unfortunate Madame Cuquel's only child, Colin, and although the hideous disfigured face was unrecognizable, there was something familiar about the twisted features.

Pel met Lapeyre in the Transvaal Bar. He was sitting at the far end nursing a large black coffee and turning a pale blue packet of cigarettes methodically over and over, tapping on the table with each completed movement.

'Sorry to have kept you waiting,' Pel said as he sat down opposite. 'Had a bit of difficulty escaping.'

'Lambert on the warpath?'

'An infuriating man.'

'What's the news?'

'*Un café, s'il vous plait!*' Pel called to Claude, polishing glasses behind the counter. 'Not encouraging, I'm afraid,' he said, turning back to Lapeyre. 'We've got the information we wanted on pharmacy robberies; it's happening more and more often. One place in Paris was held up or broken into six times in the last year; as a result all chemists, from Calais to Carcassonne, are being advised to install surveillance cameras.'

'Some of them already have, that's how we traced Luzanne to Vézelay.'

'*Merci*,' Pel said as his coffee arrived. 'Here in the city, La Pharmacie Cathala was done on 29th December, it was the third in the Côte d'Or for the month. For the whole of Burgundy, fourteen incidents were reported. The amount of barbiturates and narcotics removed is frightening, enough to send an army round the bend. What amazes me is the price users are prepared to pay for pills. Boudet told me that just one could change hands for anything between 100 and 200 francs. Where do they get the money?'

'They steal or harass. Provoking a minor car crash, for instance, and asking for cash compensation to save time with the slothful insurance companies; if you refuse, they finish the job with coshes and clubs. If they haven't got a car, they stand by a cash dispenser, arguing or snogging, and as the notes pop out they swipe them and run. It happened to me last week. It was only when I grabbed the girl and hung on to her that a woman waiting for the bus across the road came over and said it was the third time they'd done it in fifteen minutes. With her help, we identified the boy and picked him up the same afternoon, his pockets were rattling with newly bought pills.'

'Where did he buy them?'

'A bloke at Meudon market. He wouldn't or couldn't give his description.'

'How did he know he was a dealer?'

'Took a chance on a man wearing an Egyptian scarf, black and white, like Arafat's.'

'Easy to wear, easy to discard.'

Lapeyre shook out a cigarette and pushed the packet towards Pel. 'Do the pharmacy robberies pinpoint one area?'

'Not at all. The majority here are small village shops under or alongside the chemist's own home. From what I've seen so far, they wait until the owners leave for an evening elsewhere – fairly easy to hear about at the local bar – discreetly break into the dwelling and enter the shop from there, switching off the alarm from inside.'

'So we're back to working from what we already had on Sandrine and her attack on the tobacconist's with a toy gun. Unless Bardolle's found your sneak?'

'Bardolle didn't find him, but he has turned up.'

'Where?'

'Face down in the canal.'

'Damn. Cause of death?'

'We'll need confirmation but at first glance he drowned. No other apparent wounds.'

'He could have been pushed.'

'Or held under. Or drugged.'

'Comes to the same thing as far as our enquiry is concerned: a dead end.'

'What about Capelle, isn't it time he reported in?'

'He has no firm instructions except to scout, he'll take the time needed and come in when he's ready.'

'Have you any idea where he is? So we don't step on his toes.'

'Three of his toes are plastic, I doubt he'd notice, and no, I've no idea at all.'

Capelle had found a comfortable squat. The tramps had finished his whisky, and tucked him up for the night inside a large cardboard box, kindly packing him with newspaper to keep him warm, then left him to sleep off whatever he'd consumed, which was, in fact, very little; just enough to flavour his breath. He'd spent the rest of the night listening to their disjointed conversation, mostly rambling and complaining, before finally allowing himself to doze off as they left at dawn. He'd slept three hours and had woken feeling very cold and hungry.

At eleven thirty, he was standing in the middle of a short queue of similar men and women of no fixed abode outside the Resto du Cœur kitchens behind the railway station. It was while he dipped his ration of bread into the watery soup that he'd made the acquaintance of Jeff and Pedro, younger than the rest of the crowd and surprisingly well dressed – their clothes were scruffy but adequate for the winter weather. He'd followed them about for a while until they'd told him to piss off.

After another night in a different cardboard box, with a different group of down and outs, he'd returned to the Resto du Cœur. Jeff and Pedro were there again. He told them he needed a squat, to which they replied he'd have to pay. He asked how. Simple, they said, get us some tobacco.

Capelle pulled a face, finished his soup, wiped his beard on the back of his hand and said okay. They said they'd go with him, which seriously reduced his options; men without an address and accepting nourishment from charity kitchens weren't supposed to have money on them or anywhere else besides, and there was no way he could contact headquarters demanding a few coins, nor step into the Banque de Bourgogne to withdraw a similar number of coins from his account – he was going to have to steal.

Pas de problème.

Hunched against the rain, he wandered along the pavement ahead of his new friends. After a few minutes he saw what was needed: a busy tobacconist's. Half a dozen taxi drivers and travellers with suitcases were waiting to be served. He walked in and began leafing through a magazine on the counter.

The man behind the counter observed him for a moment, seeing the dog-eared pages being put back in the pile and another magazine being picked up by grubby hands. 'Read it when you've paid, *d'accord*?' Then turning his attention back to a waiting customer: '*Cinquante-quatre francs, s'il vous plaît, monsieur.*'

Capelle started arguing. 'Got to be sure it's the one I want.'

'Know how to read do you, mate?'

The conversation continued briefly as Fifty-four Francs paid, side-stepped round the tramp and another customer gave his order.

Capelle stretched out a hand, curling his fingers round a Lion bar.

'Here, don't muck about with the edibles!'

His hand withdrew abruptly. 'I'm not mucking about.' He backed towards the door. 'Don't want anything from your fucking snotty shop, mate, stuff you!' He lifted his arm aggressively, his middle finger making a vulgar suggestion, tripped down the step and staggered off.

The shop momentarily breathed a sigh of relief.

'*Dix-neuf soixante, s'il vous plaît.*'

'Sure, when you give me my packet of Gauloises Blondes.'

'I have, I put it on the counter, you picked it up.'

'I don't think I did.' He turned out his pockets and found a handkerchief, a bunch of keys, a wallet and a plastic lighter. No cigarettes.

Capelle handed the red packet to Jeff. 'One do? Or d'you want another?'

Now, with an afternoon of begging in the covered market successfully completed, Jeff and Pedro had bought the wherewithal for an evening's fun and had invited him back to their squat. Considering he'd given them the contents of his woollen hat, it was the least they could do.

The buildings looked derelict, numbers 1–5 boulevard Soult, a wide empty street apparently due for demolition to extend the industrial estate directly behind. Capelle was careful to note his surroundings.

The ground floor was empty; a fierce wind whistled through the gaping holes where the windows had once been, bringing the rain spattering on to their cheeks. There were no doors, the walls were scarred where radiators had been ripped out, plaster was hanging from the ceilings after light fittings had been removed. Upstairs, however, at the end of a series of long echoing corridors, where a passing car wouldn't see the candle-light, three large rooms housed more than a dozen young vagrants. The only remaining door in the whole building was firmly closed and, before it was opened, Pedro knocked four times then twice more.

'It was a school, Collège Jeanne d'Arc, this was the principal's flat,' he explained as they went in. 'She was the last to leave, after the stripping was finished, and the scrap merchants didn't bother to come back.'

Most of the inhabitants sat listlessly one against another, snoozing, one or two were curled up on bare mattresses, and by the open fireplace a colourless girl, well wrapped in a series of shawls, was stirring something that smelt vaguely of beef stew in a cast iron cauldron. She looked up with suspicion as they came in, didn't smile and looked back at the flames flickering round the bottom of the pot, reaching out with a mittened hand for a carton of salt.

'Make yourself comfortable, comrade,' Jeff invited, pecking the girl's cheek. 'Okay, Silver?'

She didn't say anything, simply lifted the lid of her cauldron for him to peer in.

'Here,' Jeff said, 'this'll make the mince go further,' and he handed her the bag of potatoes.

She smiled at last. 'We could do with a bit more to burn.'

'Coming up right now.'

Jeff stood up again and disappeared once more into the corridor.

Capelle found a space by the door and eased himself into the frame, letting the wooden upright massage his back as he lowered himself on to his heels. The cold damp weather was making his shoulder ache but surprisingly his shattered thigh was behaving well.

The room was without furniture, the floor covered only with layers of opened-up cardboard boxes; carton carpet. More were taped on to the windows, keeping out any remaining light, and keeping their world private. He sniffed as another smell joined

140

Silver's cooking: marijuana. It was a good sign, these people may have useful contacts.

A figure stirred on one of the mattresses, groaning, turning over. Capelle stared at the boy then casually looked away.

When the fire was glowing warmly, filling the three rooms with what little heat it could offer, and the cauldron had been bubbling for another hour, Silver seemed satisfied her job was done. She picked up a ladle and tapped on the side of the cast iron pot. Almost immediately there was a rumble of activity. Slowly, one by one or in couples, the young people came forward with a tin cup, a plastic plate, in one case a dog's bowl, and filled them with the ladle. Everyone, that is, except the boy on the mattress and Capelle. Often new arrivals weren't expected to eat the first night in a squat, they would have to earn their keep by working the whole of the following day, so he held back, his stomach turning over sickeningly as he watched the food devoured. But Silver beckoned, polishing a bowl on her skirt, filled it and handed it to him. The bread was rock hard, at least two days old, but dipping his fingers into the greasy juice to retrieve the lumps of soft potato, he felt the warmth spread satisfyingly into his hands. He ate hungrily, softening the bread in the gravy, grateful for the generosity.

Silver took a dish across to the boy on the bed, pulled a torn blanket round his shoulders and started spooning liquid into his mouth. His eyes were glazed, his hands shook.

'Here,' Capelle suggested, 'let me do it. You go and eat.'

She smiled. 'Okay, thanks.' Then she added almost apologetically, 'He's ill, think it's flu. They fished him out of the canal a few days back. Should feel better in a couple of days.'

He fed the boy as best he could, keeping an eye on those around him, and when everyone was busy rolling the after-eating joints, he slipped his fingers under the blanket, fumbling in his clothes, searching for a pocket, hoping to find some sort of identification.

When the joint was passed round, Capelle allowed himself to participate in the smoking, it was expected, if he hadn't he'd have been thrown out, possibly beaten. He preferred not to be, and anyway, there was a small group in the other room that interested him. He wanted to know where they'd got their pills – if they'd be willing to share that information. It would take time to gain their confidence, convince them of his authenticity, and time was the one thing he knew the boy didn't have.

141

Chapter Nine

Samedi, le 1 janvier

Le Jour de l'An. It was raining again. Brittany was flooded, hundreds of people were homeless. *Bonne année.*

Where the weather permitted, the New Year had been cele-brated in the usual traditional – inebriated – way. First thing on the 1st, before first light, still during the night before, so to speak, there were those who staggered out to their cars to go home, and woke up with an almighty headache in hospital – they were the lucky ones, they were at least alive. Five died on the Burgundian roads before dawn.

And there were those who wouldn't remember a bloody thing about it.

And those who didn't give a damn.

Klébert and Edith Cuquel didn't give a damn. They hadn't wished each other a happy new year the night before, they wouldn't this morning. How could it happy when they didn't know where Colin was? They only wished their son would come home safe and sound.

And there were those who would live to regret it.

And those who wouldn't live much longer.

The dying boy was unconscious, lying folded into the corner of the room, partly covered by the ragged blanket, trembling continually, jerking from time to time. Capelle had listened to his breathing half the night, hearing the air rasping in and out of his lungs. From time to time, he touched his forehead, testing his rising temperature, at the same time clasping his wrist with unseen fingers, feeling for a pulse. He guessed it was nearing daybreak, though there was no indication in the black hole they inhabited.

The spasms were coming more frequently, the boy's heartbeat had slowed dramatically, he only had a few hours to live. Capelle couldn't risk waiting any longer.

He struggled to his feet, apologizing as he stepped over other sleeping bodies. '*Faut que je pisse*,' he whispered to an opening eye.

Slipping the single slim Vachette key out of the lock, he dropped it in his pocket and crept into the cold corridor, easing the door quietly closed behind him.

The wind was howling through the ragged cavities, he felt it wriggle under his jumper and creep into his skin. He shivered as he went down the crumbling concrete stairs. Outside, stepping from the shelter of the building, the gusts of freezing rain whipped round the corners, tearing at his clothes, stinging his cheeks. He was glad he'd kept the beard.

The rain was heavy, in seconds he felt it seeping through his worn-out anorak on to his skin and through his hair on to his scalp. His trainers soaked it up, saturating his feet.

He started jogging. His shoulder ached and, with the miserable damp, the strip of metal holding his femur together pulled. Dull and aching.

The first phone box at 900 metres had been vandalized.

He wasn't cold any more though. His thigh was throbbing.

Second phone box, 1,400 metres on, out of service.

He was nice and warm now, but limping. His thigh felt like a boil ready to burst.

He headed further into town.

Another 2 kilometres, beginning to sweat seriously. The knives of pain shot into his knee, reversed and pierced his groin. God, his balls hurt. But he'd found a phone that worked. He tapped in ten numbers, waited for the computer to answer.

In the too small glass cabin, he was steaming gently.

Contact. Introduction, request for personal code. He added ten more numbers.

The windows were beginning to mist. He was asked to identify himself. He did. Three rings.

'Lapeyre, *j'écoute*.'

As Pel's team should have had the Christmas weekend off – hey, it wasn't Klein's fault they got involved in a tip-off for armed robbery – they'd been assigned the New Year weekend. To begin with it was relatively quiet; a drunken bar brawl ending in three people being taken to hospital with superficial wounds, and one person, roaring drunk, being put in the cells downstairs; and an elderly woman, convinced the terrifying stranger outside tapping at her window and shrieking obscenities was about to break in and rape her – it was in fact her married son, well pickled in alcohol, and who didn't dare go home to his argumentative wife. Most of the other emergency calls to '17', which connected directly with the central gendarmerie, were fielded and dealt with reasonably efficiently by the boys in blue.

Instead of drinking champagne at midnight, the remaining members of the team swallowed another mouthful of God-awful coffee and decided they could doze at their desks for a while, anticipating the serious misdemeanours and crimes would get going again half-way to dawn. Pel, although he was *de garde* and had to have his mobile on him at all times, had finally gone home. He retired at 2230, sick and tired of the rubbish on television. He'd slept badly most of the night until at last, around four, he fell into a deep and peaceful slumber. At 0635 his phone broke into an electronic rendering of Beethoven's Fifth and, prising his eyes open – not that it made much difference in the dark – he reached out to answer.

'Nosjean, *patron*. Tip-off for a squat full of Ecstasy, capsules and other tablets.'

Pel heaved himself on to one elbow. 'Another gem from the twisted grapevine?'

'The source is convincing.'

'Who?'

'Lapeyre.'

It took a second for the name to register. 'Capelle! Dawn breaks in less than an hour. I'm on my way, organize the necessary. Give me the address of the rendezvous.'

'Boulevard Soult, 1–5, the derelict school. What about shooters?'

'No! Truncheons. And don't forget the medical back-up.'

By 0715, Nosjean, Pel, de Troq', Jourdain and Cheriff were standing shivering in a broken doorway on the corner of boulevard Soult, studying the street map. Behind them stood two dozen caped uniformed men together with Captain Marteau. And, behind them, two SAMU doctors and the squads from the hospital sat in their ambulances.

'Main entrances; here, here and here. Five possible exits at the back. Three buildings to cover. Do we know which one?'

'The principal's flat.'

'Where's that?'

'No plans of the interior.'

'I know where it is,' Marteau volunteered.

'My men go up with you and six more. Disperse the rest to cover the escape routes. I want the site clearing quietly and calmly.'

Five minutes later, Marteau had his uniforms briefed. 'You, sir?'

Pel hesitated, he couldn't risk eye-to-eye contact with Capelle – if he was still in there. So far, his cover had protected him, he wanted it to stay that way, even if Lapeyre's man spent twenty-four hours in a police cell. 'Radio for reinforcements immediately if you get any trouble. I'll be in the courtyard when you bring them out.'

Nothing went according to plan.

There was little movement in the flat; someone was snoring quietly, a girl turned, sighed and resettled. The boy beside him struggled to breathe. Capelle hoped he wasn't yet in a coma, the last step before death. Then he heard another sound, faint but coming closer, a whispering footstep, treading carefully, avoiding the paper and other rubbish in the corridors.

He felt the boy's pulse again. Hurry up, you buggers!

Turning his head, he listened. The footsteps had stopped.

Silence. Just the pattering of rain on the window panes.

Then the door burst open, wrecking the flimsy lock, and a large Arab staggered in, followed by two plain-clothes policemen and a young woman with short blonde spiky hair. Behind her were the uniforms.

The flat erupted into chaos, like a slow typhoon sweeping through the rooms. Girls screamed, men growled, shouting abuse, and the boy's breath was rattling dangerously in his chest.

Capelle was on his feet. 'Bastards, fucking bastards!'

He threw himself at one of the plain-clothes, pummelling with his fists.

Nosjean brought up his own hands and punched him in the stomach; he buckled. '*Menottes!*'

The Arab bent over Capelle to add the handcuffs, dragging his arms savagely behind his back, pulling the strips of plastic tight.

Capelle struggled, kicking out, catching a uniform on the shins.

'Get him out of here!'

He was pushed roughly into the corridor, stumbling to keep

145

his balance, and started down the stairs, still cursing at the top of his voice. He hooked one foot round the other, tripped and rolled down the last flight, landing in a heap at the bottom. But the uniform was beside him in an instant, nudging him with a boot. 'On your feet, lad, not much further.'

Once they were outside, chilling rain drifting across the courtyard, Capelle at last caught sight of Pel, no more than a dark silhouette on the far side. 'I want to speak to him!'

The uniform grabbed his arm, pushing him in the opposite direction. 'No way, mate, you're for the van.'

Twisting suddenly, Capelle spun round and head-butted the startled policeman. He went down like a felled tree, landing with a dull splash in a puddle.

Pel's eyes moved from the building towards the fuzzy outline of a hurrying tramp, lolloping stiffly across the sodden ground. He moved towards him, a frown on his face, and waited to be informed.

'A kid's dying up there,' Capelle panted. 'Get him out. You need him!'

'Description?'

'Short blond hair, blotchy skin, about twenty, unconscious.'

Pel lifted his radio and spoke to Nosjean.

A second later, they heard a fight break out at the top of the building; shouting, menacing voices could be heard, mixed into a unpleasant cocktail of anger. Both men glanced up.

One of the remaining windows exploded, the rotten wood splintering into sticks, the glass shattered, spraying like confetti, silver and sparkling in the pale daylight. The debris fell, twirling and untidy, and with it came something much larger. Arms and legs flailing, as if it was trying to fly. Long hair trailing like a soiled wedding veil. A blanket fluttered and broke free, following the body, looking like a deflated parachute.

The falling man hit the ground with an unpleasant thud. For a few brief seconds he twitched, then lay motionless in the mud.

Above, de Troq's head appeared through the window then disappeared almost immediately.

Pel radioed for the medics, and as an ambulance splashed its way across the yard, he waved it towards the body.

Capelle was there first, looking down at the limp figure, its head split open like a walnut. 'Pedro,' he said as Pel came alongside.

A young doctor knelt, disregarding the potholes that looked as if they'd been filled with gravy, tugging at clothing, loosening the belt, untying the grubby kerchief round the neck, and pressing two fingers into the dirty flesh to find a pulse.

'He's dead,' he said rather unnecessarily.

'He can wait, get the kid coming out now.'

Cheriff had appeared in one of the jagged doorways, an inert bundle over his shoulder. 'Quickest way down,' he apologized as the medics helped him ease the boy on to a wet stretcher.

'What's he on?' The medics were quick to assess the situation.

'Colourless drops,' Capelle told them. 'Before midnight last night. God knows what went before.'

Pel watched the boy being loaded, the doors slammed closed and the blue lamp ignite just before the siren began wailing and the ambulance disappeared into the street. 'Why's he so important?'

Capelle struggled to retrieve a battered photograph from his pocket, it wasn't easy with his hands still tied. Pel finished pulling it out and stared at it. The inscription on the back was 'For Duduche, love from Gina.'

'Gina? Misset's niece was called Sandrine.'

'But it is her?'

Pel nodded.

'That's what I thought.'

The inhabitants of the flat were appearing now, stumbling into the rain and the light. Capelle resumed his role. 'You bastards, you've killed him!'

Pel pulled out a handkerchief. 'Shut it, Capelle,' he said quietly, dabbing at the back of his neck where rainwater was working its way in. 'Your cover is extremely dubious now.'

'Sod you! Let me go!'

'I said, shut it, you won't be going back on the streets, even if I have to keep you 'cuffed for a month.'

By nine o'clock the rain had mercifully stopped and the site was finally completely cleared. The band of youngsters had been removed, and the building sealed, as far as it could be, taking into account that there was hardly a door or a window remaining. The operation that Pel had hoped would be quiet and calm had turned out to be the opposite.

Sarrazin arrived shortly after Capelle's dying boy had been taken away and as Pedro's broken body was being loaded. He got to work, snapping his camera at the youths who yelled at the tops of their voices. They struggled for all they were worth to break free from the grip of their accompanying officers, making the whole affair look like another case of police brutality. And they'd managed to attract the attention of every single car – of which there were an increasing number as the city's inhabitants made their way to work – every pedestrian and every cyclist, together with a busload of schoolchildren, who cheered and jeered merrily as they passed. The dowdy hotel round the corner provided another couple of dozen spectators, the owners and chambermaids mingling chattily with their customers under colourful umbrellas. In all there were an estimated 130 citizens standing on the pavement, watching the unpleasant end to what should have been a simple dawn raid.

The journalist was delighted.

Pel wasn't.

It wouldn't do the police any good.

It didn't do them much good questioning the kids either.

It took hours to sort through the scruffy sodden group and gently persuade them into the available interview rooms. Even then, most of them refused to give anything more than nicknames. Foot, for instance; so maybe he was keen on soccer? Cutter; of meat, marijuana or something more sinister? Bob; which seemed reasonable until she shook out her long hennaed hair and spat in your face. Mannie, Groupie, Rasta and so on and so forth, they nearly all had a modern American ring to them. And Jeff of course, who hadn't said a word except '*Assassins*,' screamed for everyone to hear as he caught sight of Pedro being lifted carefully into a body bag and zipped up. However, the small amount of information on offer, together with their photographs – which also took hours, thanks to the face pulling and sudden movement just as the camera flashed – was sent down to Rigal and his computer files, the Alias File in particular. His fingers flew across the keyboard, punching in the sparse information they had, mixing and trying to match them to known faces. They hoped he would come up with at least one real identity. A new starting point.

He didn't.

And Lambert called Pel into his office at 1600.

'You didn't salute, Commissaire.'

'No. Sir.'

'You should salute.'

'Yes. Sir.'

'And I didn't tell you to sit!'

148

'No, sir. Permission to sit? Sir.'

'Granted.'

Pel started crossing his legs, thought better of it and pulled out his Gauloises. He had an idea this was going to take a long time – perhaps enough time to smoke the whole ruddy packet. 'What did you want to see me about? Sir.'

'It seems,' Lambert said, wafting away the cloud of approaching smoke, 'you're losing your touch, Commissaire. First the fiasco at the tobacconist's where a defenceless girl was shot dead by one of your own men. Now a simple drugs raid and another innocent person has died. You are becoming a liability to our citizens as well as the force.'

'The deceased was hardly innocent. Sir.'

'You are still responsible for the death. Once again, the police will be accused of unnecessary violence.'

'We weren't even armed. When you read the report of the arrests you'll see he wasn't provoked.'

'When you have delivered it to my office, I'm still waiting.'

'We've only just finished interviewing the buggers!'

'Pel, you really must try and control your vocabulary.'

'Sir, they are an uncooperative bunch of hop-heads, who smoke, swear, hurl insults and, in one case, spit at us whenever approached; she's a charming young lady, I can tell you.'

'Tell your men to take care, we don't want another one throwing himself through a window.'

'They've got bars in this building. And I repeat, the deceased was not provoked.'

'Your presence was apparently enough.'

'I was nowhere near him, if you must know. I was waiting downstairs.'

'Another misjudgement? Perhaps you should have been upstairs where the action was taking place.'

'The only action was a fool trying to fly and discovering he couldn't. I think you'll find the drugs in his system were responsible for that.'

'I, unlike you, Commissaire, shall wait to see the autopsy report before jumping to conclusions that are yet to be justified. In the meantime, Pel, I would be extremely grateful if you would avoid any further mishaps. One mistake is enough, two are intolerable, a third could end your career.'

So that's what this is all about! Pel blinked and leant forward to stub out his half-smoked cigarette, annihilating it slowly and deliberately in the ashtray, watching the thin paper split, the tobacco spread. Lambert the Drone, Lambert the Bore, now Lambert the Disloyal, trying to use two unusually unfortunate and possibly unavoidable events to embarrass Pel.

'Indeed,' he was saying, 'if I were you, I'd watch your step. There can be no cover-ups, you know. The comportment of the police is, always will be, open to public criticism, and there's been rather a lot recently. If necessary, you will be replaced.'

'You're so right, sir,' Pel replied amicably. 'I've been very amiss with my loyalties. In June, for instance, I seem to remember a certain document was withheld, a document that could have saved Darcy's life . . .'

'Pel, I'm warning you . . .'

'. . . I only mention it now because the man concerned, who had the document in his possession, managed to cover his mistake very effectively by the arrests that followed, was indeed congratulated for them, arrests my team made . . .'

'Pel . . .'

'. . . and mistakenly, sir, I said nothing to the press, although I was asked. However, I'd like to make it clear my decision was to protect Darcy's widow, suggesting his death could have been avoided would have been unacceptably cruel. Not, I should stress, to save your skin.'

The Chief opened his mouth but was interrupted again.

'And,' Pel finished with a certain satisfaction, 'it's never too late to talk to a reporter or two.'

'Dismissed!'

Pel didn't move. 'From your office? Or from the police force? Sarrazin would love that story.'

'You are a despicable man, Commissaire. How dare you make accusations and threats.'

'On the accusation and threat front, sir, you are wrong, I am merely stating facts and exploring the eventual possibilities. However,' he gave Lambert the pleasure of an oily smile, 'you may be right about the "despicable".'

Pel was muttering all the way down the corridor to his office. 'Pompous Bloody Snow-Capped Mountain.' He kicked the door closed, lit a fresh cigarette and sucked on it as if it would save his life.

'What's he done now?' Sarrazin was sitting quietly in the corner watching.

'How did you get in!'

150

'My two feet, plus smiling sweetly at the sergeant on duty downstairs.'

'I'll have the bugger sacked!'

'Pel, what's going on?'

He stared hard at the journalist, he couldn't see a tape recorder or microphone anywhere, not that that meant anything, he could have half a dozen up his sleeve, in his pocket or down a trouser leg. 'Let me frisk you first.'

'No need, call the chap at the desk, I left my equipment down there.'

'Why?'

'Because I want you to talk.'

'About what?'

'The weather?' the journalist suggested.

'There's too much of it for my liking, there's always too much bloody weather.'

'Okay, how about Sandrine Da Costa?'

'She's dead,' Pel snapped, 'and buried, God rest her soul.'

'The raid this morning?'

'You got your pictures, why don't you go and print them?'

'I need a story to back them up, my sort of journalism relies on words more than sensational photography.'

'Cut the crap, Sarrazin, we all know what your sort of journalism relies on.'

'It's New Year's Day, it was inhuman to go charging in there and drag all those kids out into the rain. Unless,' the reporter added, 'you were on to something. And the only "something" big enough for that sort of operation is Sandrine Da Costa.'

Pel said nothing.

'She was a good student and well liked. No previous history of drugs, she didn't even smoke. Niece of a decent detective. Difficult to explain, *n'est-ce pas*? I think the raid had something to do with it.'

'Maybe.'

'I've also noticed a certain Parisian about town. The last time he interfered was when we were under siege by a group of terrorists. So, whatever it is, it's big.'

'Typical of a newspaperman. Always exaggerating.'

'Am I? I'll just have to go to press with all the pictures I got this morning and ask my questions publicly to find out. Lapeyre doesn't bother with cat burglars and car thieves, Pel, my readers will want to know why he's involved.'

'You seem to know a hell of a lot about it!'

'That's what I'm paid for. Now give.'

A long sigh accompanied the stream of smoke coming through Pel's clenched teeth. He sat down slowly, thinking hard. 'Do you know a bloke called Dalton? Or Luzanne? Do you know who's supplying our beautiful city with ugly drugs; heroin, cocaine, GBH, Ecstasy? Do you know why an intelligent girl robbed a tobacconist's holding a toy gun? Do you know why the papers were correctly informed and the police were misinformed? That's just for starters. And *our* informant turned up in the canal, drowned. Yes, the raid this morning may give us a lead to some of it. Or it may not. Now get out and leave me to get back to work.'

'Jean-Jacques Luzanne?'

Pel's eyes narrowed. '*Oui, c'est lui.*'

'He's from Paris, Barbès quarter. Surname at birth: Suzanne. He altered it when he was eighteen.'

'I'm not surprised.'

'He hangs about with a chap known as the Black Angel.'

'How do you know?'

'I get about. I have a useful habit of listening in on other people's conversations. I report when it's worth it.'

'Where did you hear about Luzanne?'

'One of the seedier night-clubs.'

'Which one?'

'*Alors là*, no idea, it might come back though.'

'So what's the Black Angel's real name?'

'I don't know that either.'

'Dalton?'

Sarrazin shrugged. 'The only Daltons I know are the dim villains in a Lucky Luke cartoon book.'

'Very interesting but hardly helpful.'

'I could ask around. What's he supposed to have done? If I find him, I could clobber him for an exclusive interview.'

'He's had contact with Luzanne, who in turn was seen with Sandrine Da Costa.'

'Dalton's description?'

'The last photo we have was taken over twenty years ago, so we don't know for sure what he looks like now. He appears to move about freely and the descriptions change.'

'A master of disguises?'

'This is Burgundy, Sarrazin, not Matt Helm in America.'

'How do you know he moves about freely?'

'Credit cards leave traces.' Pel frowned. 'Just a minute, the case we cracked before bringing the Burgundy Butcher in . . . we managed to pin her down when we found out she'd given her credit card to a friend. He left a trail of purchases at precisely the time she was disposing of her husband's mistress.'

'No wonder no one knows what Dalton looks like if he scatters his cards and their codes like confetti.'

'But why?'

'To cover his tracks, like your killer.'

'Or because he doesn't move at all and wants to give the impression he does.'

'Organizing crime from prison?'

'No, he made a phone call . . .'

'Prisons have phones.'

Pel scribbled hurriedly on a notepad. 'Thanks, Sarrazin, one of these days I'll buy you a drink. In the meantime, sod off and let me think.'

'Anything else I should know?'

'Lapeyre wants Dalton either for trafficking drugs or prostitution, or trading arms. So I'd be grateful if you didn't clobber him for an exclusive interview. Keep well away, he's dangerous. If you find anything out about him, just let me know, okay?'

'Do I get the story when you get your pusher?'

'So what's the story, Capelle?'

Capelle had had a shower and changed into clean clothes: khaki corduroy trousers, checked shirt, and a bottle green sleeveless V-necked jumper that was too big. His long hair was tied back behind his head, his beard clipped more neatly. He looked almost human. 'What's the news on the kid?' He rubbed his wrists where the handcuffs had been; there were livid stripes circling both.

'Still alive for the moment. We'll question him if and when his condition stabilizes.'

'What about the photo?'

Pel shuffled papers on his desk and picked up a plastic sleeve containing it. 'We'll get it over to Forensic, but don't hold your breath.'

'For Duduche, love from Gina . . . nicknames?'

'Must be.'

'So who's Duduche? Her supplier?'

'We'll have to keep our fingers crossed he survives long enough to tell us.'

'A supplier dealing on someone else's patch maybe, he was hauled out of the canal.'

'A popular place. That's where La Poche was found.'

'Nosjean told me he drowned. Duduche bought some bad stuff.'

'A self-inflicted overdose?'

'Or someone wanting to stop him selling it on.'

'None of the other junkies were connected to Sandrine then?'

'I don't think so, although I'd like to talk to Silver, Jeff's bird, and Jeff himself, he and Pedro worked together, they seemed to be in charge.'

But Jeff still refused to answer their questions. They tried on and off until the day faded and turned into night again. By 1930 he was visibly trembling and pleading for a needle. Capelle assured him if he talked he'd get what he needed. Finally, and in desperation, he talked and while he talked, shivering uncontrollably in the well-heated cell, Capelle made notes. He was then helped up the stairs to Interview Room 5 where he waited while the notes were put on to paper via one of the computers.

He was asked to read his statement through and sign it if he agreed with what had been written. He seemed incapable of something so simple, holding the paper between trembling fingers, weeping at the effort. When he'd at last added his shaky signature to the bottom of the sheet, he was then charged with resisting arrest and possession of drugs – 63 grams of marijuana resin and 1.5 grams of heroin – and taken to the city's prison medical wing. By the time he got there, he was crying his eyes out and doubled up in pain, which was no help to anyone. His statement wasn't of much help either:

REPUBLIQUE FRANCAISE	L'an deux mille 01
MINISTERE DE L'INTERIEUR	le01 janvier
DIRECTION de la POLICE JUDICIAIRE	à1951
SERVICE :	CAPELLE jean-Claude Officier de Police Judiciaire
DIJON	
PROCES-VERBAL	1. My real name is Geoffrey Lael. My home address is Monsuquet,Les Lormes in Nièvre. Mum and Dad are peasants, they've got a few vines and stuff. I've got one younger sister, Martine.

STATEMENT :
LAEL GEOFFREY

2. I'm studying languages, English and Spanish at the university.

3.My parents send me money to rent aroom, I moved to the squat to save money. I spend the money on dope.   I've got a mailbox in the Students' Union, I told Mum my landlady doesn't want to be bothered with students' letters.   The last time I attended my course was in November.

4.   I don't know who Sandrine Da Costa is.   I don't know who Gina is.I've never heard of her.

5.I don't know who the boy was in the squat.   Someone found him trying to climb out of the canal.   They helped him and took him to the squat, it's not far away.   I gave him stuff, he was sick.   I gave him something I got off Dad when I went home for the weekend , he had a bad shoulder.   He said the drops had bad side effects. They did.   I didn't like them so I gave them to the boy.   He calmed down then. He slept most of the time after that.

6.I know I had a small amount of heroin on me when I was arrested.   I don't use the same supplier all the time, there's always stuff to be bought around.   If you don't buy from one person, you buy it from another.   It depends on the price and what I can afford. It gets difficult at the end of the month.

7.I've been popping pills and stuff since the summer.   I started on heroin at the beginning of December.   I'm not an addict.

Signé L'O.P.J.

'Maybe that's why the canal's so popular,' Capelle suggested. 'There are a lot of squats in the empty buildings along its edge. I came across three squats and two places regularly frequented by tramps. There are probably more.'

'We'll check. I agree it's unlikely we'll find anything interesting but we've got to make sure. Let's hope the kid in hospital stays alive. If he dies we're back to square one with precisely nothing.'

And Rigal turned up precisely nothing in their lists of aliases; Foot, Cutter, Bob, Mannie, Groupie, Rasta, Pedro and the others gave him the remarkable reply of *zéro réponse(s)* from his trusty computer. He'd been through the search process twelve times, now he started on the thirteenth, hoping it might be contradictory and turn out to be lucky. It didn't. The Black Angel wasn't yet known to the police either. Nor was Duduche, they still didn't know who the dying boy was. Dying Boy being their nickname for the kid who was surprisingly still alive and under guard at the hospital. The machinery artificially operating his lungs and giving cardiac stimulation had been disconnected, his organs were at last functioning independently, it was now simply a question of waiting to see if his heart withstood the next few days and, if it did, hoping he wouldn't be a raving lunatic for the rest of his life.

Some drugs do that to you.

Dimanche, le 2 janvier
St Basile. A change was announced in the law. It filled the front page of all the papers:

1. *Possibilité de faire appel en cas de condamnation en cour d'assise.*
2. *Pouvoir de placer une personne en détention provisoire confié à un juge des libertés et de détention.*
3. *Extension du statut de témoin assisté pour limiter le recours à la mise en examen.*
4. *Delais plus stricts dans les enquêtes pour limiter des procédures trop étalées dans le temps.*
5. *Présence d'un avocat des la 1ere heure de la garde à vue (et non plus à la 20e heure).*
6. *Amélioration des conditions de gard à vue (enregistrement des interrogatoires pour les mineurs des June 2001).*

For the police it was one step forward, two steps back. Although a suspect could be temporarily imprisoned while an enquiry was completed, the enquiry would now have a time limit imposed. That same suspect could demand his lawyer's presence the moment he was arrested, instead of after twenty hours in custody. The only exceptions were for *criminalité organisée* and *trafic de stupéfiants*. And from now on, the cross-examination of a suspect, particularly in the case of minors, had to be recorded. Plus, just to add the icing to the cake, sentences from a Court of Assizes could now be appealed. The innocent had to be protected.

There was no change in the weather; it was cold and wet.

In Room 6233 of the General Hospital, logically located in the rue de l'Hôpital, de Troq' took over from Gilbert at 0730. For once he wasn't scratching or picking; he was simply snoozing. The door closed quietly and his eyes opened slowly as the younger man came in. Gilbert had taken his shoes off, and the room, instead of smelling of fading disinfectant, or whatever it is hospitals usually smell of, smelt of feet. De Troq', being well brought up, didn't mention it. While he considered his colleague to be an uncultured slob, he had volunteered for the night watch of Duduche, or whatever his real name was, therefore he deserved some respect this morning. No one had wanted to spend twelve tedious dark hours sitting beside an unconscious drug addict, particularly after putting in an arduous ten-hour day, and everyone was surprised when Gilbert begrudgingly offered, muttering, 'Someone's got to bleeding do it. If he was here, it'd be Misset, wouldn't it? Well, he isn't, poor sod. I reckon I'm the only friend he's got.'

He looked a wreck; his shirt was hanging loose, spilling untidily over his bulging waistline, his brown trousers were crumpled all the way up, and one of his socks had a hole in it, allowing a single plump toe to poke through, doing a good impersonation of a small potato. His eyes had dark pouches under them, his double chin needed a shave and his hair – he looked as if *il s'est peigné avec un pétard* – was a mess. 'Jesus,' he said, tying his laces, 'it's so bleeding hot in here I've been sweating like a pig all night. Look at me, practically swimming in me Y-fronts.'

De Troq' didn't dispute it. There were large damp patches circling his armpits and, as Gilbert moved, the evidence of sweating like a pig was assaulting his nostrils. 'Has our patient come round yet?'

'Sort of.'

'Did he say anything?'

'Oh, bleeding plenty. Nasty little bastard, real aggressive, tried punching one of the nurses. I had to hold him down when she gave him his injection. Got a nice view down her front though. Nice pair of knockers, bit on the small side, not what you'd call a real handful,' he said, turning his own hands over to study their size, 'but firm and pert. Neat little arse too, quite a wiggle when she walked out. Wouldn't mind getting her in a dark corner and giving her a quick bunny –'

'Okay, Gilbert, I'll keep an eye out for her.'

'Don't you bleeding dare! Stuck-up posh sod like you, she'd be eating out of your hand in no time, spoil my chances you would. Anyway, I thought you were poking the Punk?'

De Troq' silently sighed at Gilbert's crude analysis of his relationship with Alex Jourdain but he forced a tight smile.

'I wouldn't have put it exactly like that, but yes, we do have an understanding. I'll leave the nurses to you.'

'Good man and good luck, it's a right hell-hole in here.'

While Gilbert slouched out of the room and into the corridor, satisfying an itch somewhere in the region of his left buttock, de Troq' glanced round the room, noted the green plastic bucket under the bed, the towel hanging alongside, a plastic carafe of water, a cardboard cup. He wandered to the wall where the boy's notes were located and had a look; his condition was stabilizing. After that, he crossed to the window and gazed down into the car park below. Day was breaking, the street lamps glowed only orange now, making large fuzzy-edged balloons in the constant drizzle. There were very few people about. Then, having run out of things to look at, he settled down with the morning paper, wondering how the changes in law would affect the efficiency of the force, before moving on to an article about *La Vache Folle*. Not exactly enthralling, but better than nothing.

The door opened, a woman in white uniform smiled at him, said good morning, came in on cushioned feet and removed the breakfast tray. De Troq' wondered who'd eaten it, Gilbert or the boy? – somehow de Troq' couldn't bring himself to call him Duduche who was a dunce in a story from his childhood. He decided it must've been gawd-help-us Gilbert who'd gobbled the lot, the boy was still sleeping peacefully. He wondered how long he'd have to wait before he surfaced again, and went back to the paper.

At eight thirty, the boy opened his eyes and groaned, rolling over under the thin covers. He caught sight of de Troq' watching him. 'Who the hell are you?' he said, sitting up.

De Troq' told him.

'Another fucking *flic*! What is this? Am I a prisoner?'

'Not really.'

'Then fuck off!'

'I'd like to talk to you.'

'Oh yeah. Well, I don't want to talk to you. Talking's crap. Look, I'm sick, can't you see I'm sick, I need a shot.'

'You've had your early morning medication.'

'They don't know what they're doing here.'

'I think they do.'

'Oh do you? And who cares what you think? They're all pricks and you're the same. That other bastard *flic* tried talking to me too. Tried telling me with his smooth and smarmy voice that he wanted to help.'

De Troq' raised an eyebrow; smooth and smarmy didn't fit with his knowledge of Gilbert.

'The only thing that'll help me is some dope.'

'No dope.'

'I'll talk for days if you get me a bit.'

'The only drug available is the substitute prescribed for your treatment.'

'I don't want that lousy muck. They don't know anything about anything here.'

'What's your name?'

'What's yours?'

'I just told you, Charles de Troquereau.'

'Okay, Charlie, get me a shot, will you?'

'You're an addict, you're here to be cured, the only shots you'll be getting are to ease the pain.'

'I'm not a fucking addict! And you don't know what pain is.'

'I'm witnessing it right now.'

'You're not fucking feeling it. I am. *I'm* the one that's feeling it. Real pain. You . . .' He stopped speaking suddenly and doubled over, clutching his stomach. His face creased, controlling a scream. When he spoke again, his voice was quieter. 'You really want to help cure me?'

'Of course.'

'Then get me some junk. For Christ's sake, get me some junk. Just a bit to tide me over.'

'No junk.'

'You don't want to help me at all, you bastard!'

'What's your name?'

'Anything you fucking want, Pikachou if you like. Look, Charlie, I need a fix.'

'You told me you weren't an addict.'

'I'm not,' he whispered, still hugging himself, rocking back and forth. 'I just need a bit to get me through the crisis. Please . . .' He was wheedling, pleading now. It was pathetic.

'No junk, no dope, you're going to crack it.'

'Charlie . . . I feel really bad.' There were tears trickling on to his cheeks. He was shivering. 'I think . . . I think I'm going puke. Oh shit.'

De Troq' picked up the pale green plastic bucket and held it out.

'I'm not handicapped, I can walk to the toilet.'

'I don't think you can.'

'*Putain. Merde* . . . help me.'

He started retching.

De Troq' held the bucket steady and waited for him to finish. The acid stream of stinking hot vomit splashed into the bucket; the boy's pale face reddened with the effort, beads of perspiration collected and dripped. De Troq' nearly smiled, he'd been wrong about Gilbert: he hadn't eaten the boy's breakfast after all. But he didn't smile; watching a kid do cold turkey didn't even make his lips twitch, it wasn't funny. It was sordid and sad and humiliating. Strangely, he hoped Gilbert had had something to nibble on while the boy ate, or at least a cup of coffee with his usual four lumps of sugar.

The boy's face was ashen now, all the colour had drained away. It was shining wet and his hands were shaking, he looked worse than Gilbert had. Taking the towel from de Troq', he wiped his mouth and fell back on to the pillows exhausted. 'Jesus, I'm ill.'

'You can make it if you want to.'

'I don't want to. I can't.' He was crying, sobbing like a kid, hugging himself again. 'Please get me some dope, Charlie. Please, to ease the pain.'

'Who did this to you?'

'I don't know.'

'What can you tell me about Gina?'

The dull red eyes flashed with fear. 'Gina?'

'Sandrine Da Costa.'

'Oh her.'

'You know her?'

'I knew her.'

'Tell me about it.'

'I don't want to. She's a bitch.'

'Were you friends?'

'Ha! Not fucking likely.'

'Did you do business together?'

'The only business we had . . . oh shit . . . I . . . the bucket!'

This time it was only brown strings of bile that came up from his tortured stomach but he retched just as violently, choking and spitting and sweating, and shaking, and weeping.

Chapter Ten

Ste Geneviève. Pel forgot to wish his wife an especially happy day – it didn't surprise or upset her any more, he always forgot. He did, however, wish his team a good morning when he slammed their door open at precisely eight o'clock. The mugs on the filing cabinet rattled as usual, heads turned or were lifted, the noisy chatter gradually died. A phone rang, big Bardolle answered. He listened and replaced the receiver. 'Gilbert's finished the night shift and is on his way home from the hospital. De Troq's taken over for another twelve hours until Gilbert returns this evening.'

'That man's got more stamina than sense. If he's willing, we'll leave him doing nights. With him and de Troq' stuck with Duduche, we're seriously down on numbers and I need two of you out at the canal. In the meantime, I want to hear what you've got on Sandrine Da Costa.'

Pujol licked his lips. 'First, the Misset family doctor did not prescribe the medication found in her bloodstream. Nor did the university doctor. We contacted the other GPs in the two areas; they hadn't treated her at all.'

'It's what I expected.'

'Jourdain and I traced three old school friends also at the university, the four of them went everywhere together, they all had rooms in the same house. Colin Cuquel was her boyfriend for a while, but she ditched him recently for another guy.'

'Could that be our Duduche?'

'I don't think so, she was infatuated with an older man.'

'What about Colin? Has he turned up yet?'

'No news.'

'Go on, Pujol.'

'Sandrine, or Gina as she was known on campus, ate less and less in the digs – there's a communal kitchen – and stopped

161

putting money in the kitty at the beginning of December, saying as she didn't eat anything in the house, she shouldn't have to pay. There was an argument and the girls told her if she didn't contribute she'd have to leave. She left five days later, around the 18th, they can't remember exactly.'

'Where did she go?'

'Forensic suggested she'd been out in the country, there was duck shit on her shoes.'

'And a pale blue carpet fibre, and city dust.'

'This house where the girls live, is it carpeted?'

'No, *carrelage* downstairs, floorboards upstairs. Some of the rooms have cotton rugs; no thick synthetic and wool pile.'

'So we can assume she walked on pale blue carpet after the duck shit and before the robbery. Anything else?'

Capelle interrupted. 'Have you had the Forensic report on Pedro's brogues?'

'City dust, a bit of mud consistent with the canal, splinters from a cheap wooden crate, fibres of tobacco and, strangely, a particle of potato skin.'

'Someone dropped one in the squat. So he didn't go to the same places as Sandrine?'

'Not wearing the shoes he went flying in. Alex?'

The Punk flipped open her notebook. 'Her character changed during the term, she seemed often unwell, and frequently suffered from colds.'

'Normal in an addict.'

'She became extreme; extremely aggressive or extremely generous, screaming over being disturbed when she was supposedly studying, then lending anything that belonged to her – clothes, shoes, perfume – to anyone that asked. Before the girls had the argument, they tried talking to her, they thought maybe she was in trouble, pregnant for instance. One asked her straight out if she was on drugs, she said she wasn't. She said she was having hassles with her godparents over her allowance and it was upsetting her.'

'Did Misset mention that?'

'Gilbert didn't say so. Misset adored the girl.'

'Teachers?' Pel asked.

Cheriff shrugged. 'Same thing, *patron*. A good student to begin with but her work was tailing off, as if she was losing interest. By the end of term they wondered if she'd be back in January, she seemed obsessed by some other subject.'

'Her new lover and/or her new addiction.'

'Bars and cafés?'

'She'd stopped frequenting the usual ones by the end of November. Instead, she started going to Club 25. Drank a glass of white wine, hung around, crossed and uncrossed her legs, talked to no one. The barman thought at first she was hoping to be picked up, he thought she could be a student prostitute, selling herself to pay for her studies, apparently it happens. She was discreet and he let her be. Around the 10th, not sure of the exact date, a good-looking tall guy with dark shoulder-length hair and dark eyes spoke to her.'

'Dark curly hair?'

'Straight.'

Not Dalton.

'Shall I go on?'

Pel nodded.

'They met once more, the barman hasn't seen her since . . .'

'It all tallies and adds nothing we didn't know, except the tall guy with long dark hair.'

'Not Luzanne, he's got light brown hair and blue/grey eyes.'

'. . . I had the barman in to look at the mug shots; no go.'

'What about the Misset family?'

'We've been through the files and come up with zero. His sons don't smoke, sniff or swallow drugs. They're interested in soccer, the cinema, beer and their girlfriends. One of them drives a delivery van three days a week, the other two, the younger ones, work at anything on offer for AAA Temp agency. At the moment, Christophe's laying paving stones in Commarin, Julien's emptying septic tanks. All three live at home.'

'Misset himself?'

'Professionally there's nothing; his arrests have been of small-timers, most of whom he happened to trip over while they were breaking the law. The longest sentence in the last ten years is eighteen months for unsociable behaviour in a bar, the bloke socked five people on the jaw before Misset socked him. Person-ally there's not much; he's had a few mistresses, one more serious than the others, at the beginning of last year. It didn't last long however, and she's shacked up with a shopkeeper now. There was never any question of him leaving his wife.'

'What about her?'

'Jeannette, she knows nothing about the affairs, may suspect, says she doesn't care, refers to Misset as a fading James Bond with a weight problem. He used to be handsome and romantic, now he's a slob who farts in bed.'

Pel glanced up.

'That's what she said, *patron*, to a neighbour, Madame Lanau. Jeannette had an affair with a driving instructor in 1993 and sometimes regrets not having left Misset but says she stayed for the children who were still young. Madame Lanau thinks it's because she still carries a torch for the dashing newly qualified detective she married.' Pujol took a breath and licked his lips. 'The mother-in-law is just as Misset's always described her, large, bossy, loud, and constantly complaining. She doesn't like him, he doesn't like her.'

Pel sighed, so now he knew. He knew all there was to know about one of his men and his family. He shouldn't have to know all the sordid little details, but now he did. He wondered what they'd turn up if they ever had to investigate him.

'Fine,' he said, 'we can consider the rest of the Missets clean, which is a relief. We're stuck with Sandrine's delinquency and Duduche who had a photo of her. We've been told he was climbing out of the canal when the squatters discovered him. We don't know how or why he was in it. We do know Pierre La Poche drowned in the same canal although not anywhere near the old school. Therefore that area needs to be thoroughly searched. Capelle, you're to keep away, you're known by some of the area's inhabitants to be a police sneak and I don't want you with a knife in your back. Cheriff and Bardolle, spend the day on it, up one side down the other. Start at Chemin de la Noué and work your way along to le Pont de Gorgets, that should be far enough.'

'Er, excuse me . . .'

The team looked towards the doorway where Rigal was hovering. Pel spun round and scowled. 'Don't stand there dithering, man, come in.'

Rigal took one step forward. 'Er, I . . .'

'Count to ten,' Pel suggested, 'then spit it out.'

'You asked for a search to be made on convicted persons possibly organizing crime from prison. Here are the results.'

'Anything interesting?'

'No.'

'Well, that's short and to the point. Are you sure?'

'I've checked and cross-checked. No one using the code name Dalton, Goldstein or Black Angel. No one using names similar or otherwise with activities in our area. The closest I got was Dalbis doing time for a supermarket break-in, and all he's organizing is a watch on his wife.'

Pel sniffed. There had to be another reason for Dalton's distribution of credit cards, leaving a trail, probably a false trail, for Lapeyre to follow. 'D'accord, merci. Right, the rest of you pick up the threads of all our other problems. This may be important but it's not the only case on our books. Lambert's whingeing about last year's statistics. As usual, he's not satisfied.'

Angelo was feeling well satisfied in spite of the rain drumming on the window panes. The replacement bird had successfully been brought home to roost and Gina the Gypsy was now history; the shooting at the Tabac du Centre was last year's news. The over-friendly informant had been dealt with too; just a small paragraph informing the public that Pierre André Stanislav Lacombe had been fished out of the canal. The coroner, having listened to various opinions, and reinforced by the fact that his sister told the police the unfortunate pickpocket couldn't swim, had returned a verdict of drowning; death by misadventure. Things were going very nicely. Just that interfering boy's demise that hadn't been confirmed, but Angelo wasn't really worried, he'd been dumped and wouldn't have survived long alone. He'd probably wandered off and died, curled up in a corner of a vacant building somewhere; he'd be found sooner or later.

Angelo wasn't a cruel man, he didn't consider himself to be a killer. Indeed, he'd never handled a gun in his life and the only knife he'd touched was the one he ate with. Unfortunately, his childhood and adolescence had taught him to look after number one, he'd learnt no one else would do it for him. When he went into business, selling the favours of the girls who begged his attention to the other boys on the street, he insisted on payment, in money or marijuana, before setting up the meet. The marijuana he sold on, at a large profit, and very soon he had a healthy account at the post office.

Like any truly successful businessman, which is how he liked to think of himself, sometimes he had to be ruthless with those standing in his way. If the Gypsy got shot, it wasn't his fault, he'd tried hard to make her understand and, in the end, Dalton had taken over. It wasn't his fault she'd died. He hadn't killed her. It was the same with that La Poche. A stupid man to have talked to the police in person. Angelo had told Luzanne to teach him a lesson. It wasn't his fault he couldn't swim, it wasn't his fault Luzanne had been heavy-handed holding him under. And the boy, Duduche, well, he'd been a real nuisance asking questions. It wasn't his fault he'd been looking for Gina. Luzanne had very kindly brought him to see her, and equally as kindly taken him back to town. It wasn't his fault the kid didn't know what day it was. Well, perhaps that was his fault, but it certainly wasn't his fault he'd been so desperate to get away that when the car stopped at the first traffic lights, he'd leapt out, staggered off and fallen in the same canal Luzanne had put the pickpocket. Perhaps he'd never got out? Perhaps they should take another route into town for a while?

It naturally didn't occur to Angelo that the rising death rate in Burgundy due to drugs was his fault. He reckoned it wasn't his fault the kids of today were stupid enough to get themselves hooked. He never thought about the agony those kids suffered before finally being released by the black wings of death. He didn't think about the bereft parents left behind and the shock of knowing their child had been an addict, or that the infant they'd given birth to, adored and lovingly guided through primary school into adolescence and adulthood had, in terms of the law, committed suicide. He didn't know how difficult it was for loving families to live with that. Had he known, he'd have very probably shrugged his shoulders and said, 'What the hell, that's life. I can't be responsible for other people's mistakes.'

The news that evening mostly concerned Jean-Christophe Mitterand, the son of the republic's ex-President, suspected of selling arms to Angola. He had at last been granted bail but, not being able to pay the 5 million francs demanded, had remained in prison.

The news Cheriff and Bardolle gave Pel was no more cheerful.

No leads on the banks of the canal, just empty warehouses, a few fishermen, people taking their dogs for walks – and to leave small coils of steaming excreta on the tow path, one of which Bardolle had stepped in – and, as darkness blanketed the area, hiding the dirt and dust and mud and muck, the bands of tramps who crawled out of the woodwork, setting up home in the sheltered corners, lighting their fires and sorting out their cardboard box beds.

The news Nosjean gave him was even worse.

While climbing about in the attic of a house in Talant, trying to establish if the burglars had come through the roof as its owners suggested, Pujol had tripped and put his foot through the ceiling of the room below. His foot was followed by the rest of his leg, his other leg, his body, his arms and finally his head, all landing in an untidy tangle on the floor 3 metres below. He was now in hospital with an open fracture to his tibia and would be completely out of action for a fortnight at the very least, off the streets for a great deal longer. Plus the owners of the house were, of course, pleasantly but firmly making an insurance claim against the Police Judiciaire for damage done by one of their officers.

Pel lit up savagely. With de Troq' and Gilbert watching Duduche, it left him with only five active men: Nosjean, Cheriff, Bardolle, Jourdain and Capelle. Actually, to be more exact, it was four men and one woman, but Pel couldn't get out of the habit of thinking of the team as his men. He'd have been had up by the sex discrimination board – or whatever it's called – if he'd lived in the United States. Fortunately for him, this was France, where feminism had finally been heard of but only in the big cities. As far as he was concerned, Alex Jourdain did the same hours as everyone else and was prepared to risk her life just like the rest of them. She spoke two extra languages, English and Spanish, almost as well as de Troq', and had, innocently at the time, stopped him making a disastrous marriage and moving into manufacturing rivets for a living, for which Pel and de Troq' himself were very grateful. And apart from all that, she managed to smile a lot under her extraordinary spiky blonde hair – which helped a sometimes flagging morale. He hadn't intended to, but Pel liked her a lot, therefore she was definitely one of his men and to hell with the Americans!

Mardi, le 4 janvier
St Odilon. It was four o'clock in the morning. Gilbert was slumped in a chair in the corner of Room 6233, snoring loudly. His shoes were off, so were his jacket and tie. He'd remained awake until after 3 a.m, forcing his eyes to stay open, blinking hard. Then as the fatigue deepened, and the boredom became unbearable, he'd allowed one to close, just one and just for a second, that's what he'd told himself. He'd had problems dragging it open again, but open it he did. He closed the other one, briefly. Then the first one drooped. He'd tried to resist, he'd battled against the waves of bliss when he blacked out the night

light and the sleeping form, lying comfortably on its side in that delicious bed. He'd had imaginary and suggestive conversations with the nice little nurse, proud owner of the pert protuberances. He'd had arguments with men at the Hôtel de Police who teased; the buggers that thought they were so bloody clever. He'd willed himself to stay awake. He'd even put his fingers to his eyelids once and physically pulled them apart. Now he was snoring, his flabby chin, covered in stubble, folded on to his chest, his hands looped round his stomach, his legs outstretched. Gilbert was out.

The boy opened his eyes. He was frightened. Suddenly, clearly, frightened. 'Where the hell am I?' It was only a whisper but it sounded loud in the silence of the empty hours in the hospital.

Gilbert went on snoring.

The boy sat bolt upright and saw the overweight figure slumped in the chair by the window. 'Oh Jesus . . . I've got to get away . . . so tired . . . where've they taken her?' He frowned. 'Gina . . . I've got to find her . . .'

Gilbert's chest rose and fell, peacefully engaged in slumber.

'Sandrine . . . ' He dragged back the covers and put his feet to the ground. He felt sick. 'I've got to get out of here.' Steadying himself, one arm stretched out to the wall, propping himself up, he breathed deeply, straightening, his eyes squeezed together with the effort. Taking step after slow step across the polished plastic flooring, he stumbled towards the open bathroom door to splash water on his face, and, as he went, he noticed a pile of clothes, folded neatly on a wooden chair; underneath was a pair of trainers. He looked down at himself for the first time: he was wearing a white smock! As he bent over, his head swam and the sickening nausea welled up inside, but finally, after three attempts, he managed to gather up the clothes and shoes with trembling hands.

The water was refreshing on his hot skin and, putting his mouth down to the tap, he drank thirstily, trying to wash the thick coating from his woollen tongue. Picking up a towel, he looked in the mirror. A stranger stared back at him . . . I don't understand . . . The only thing he understood was that he had to get out of the building and run for it. Shakily, he started to dress.

Coming out of the bathroom, he tiptoed unsteadily to the door on bare feet, the canvas shoes dangling from his left hand, his panic subsiding slightly – the guard was still asleep. His right hand stretched out to the handle, his weak fingers closed round it, and twisted.

A gruff voice made him turn abruptly. He lost his balance, nearly fell.

'It's locked.' Gilbert was on his feet, shaking himself like a dog from his basket.

'You can't keep me here! My parents'll come looking for me! They'll report me missing to the police. You've got to let me go!'

'Hey, whoa, lad, being here's for your own good. You're in hospital.'

'Hospital?'

'That's right, son. Where did you think you were?'

'In that house . . . I can't get away . . . the fences . . . and those dogs.'

'Now where would this house be?'

'I . . . I don't remember. I just remember the fences and all the dogs prowling and barking and howling like wolves. Who are you!'

'Jean-Louis Gilbert, lad, Brigade Criminelle, the police if you prefer. Now don't get excited.' He scratched his crutch and shuffled towards him. 'Do you know who you are?'

The boy's face creased with anxiety, he propped himself against the locked door and studied the floor. 'I . . . I'm Colin. Yes, that's right, my name's Colin Cuquel. Why am I here!'

'And we thought you were called Duduche.'

'Well, I am, sort of, it's a nickname. Duduche's a cartoon character or something and . . . it doesn't matter! Why am I here?'

'You've been ill, lad. Come on, come and sit down. Stop worrying, you're safe now.'

Colin allowed himself to be coaxed back to the bed and sat down obediently.

Gilbert eased his rump on to the crumpled covers beside him. 'How do you feel?'

'Terrified.'

'Well now, that's a good sign. Tell me about it.'

'I . . . I don't know. I just feel frightened.'

'Of what exactly?'

'Monsters, demons, devils.' Colin hid his face in his hands. 'I don't know!'

'Do you remember how you got here?'

'I don't remember anything.'

169

'Except the house with the fence and the dogs.'

Colin nodded.

'Someone stuck you with heroin, son, you've been sweating it out for a couple of days.'

'Heroin! I wouldn't touch that stuff.'

'Possibly, but you were addicted. Looks like you cracked it though. Congratulations.'

'But . . . who? Why?'

'I think it was something to do with Gina, you had a photo of her in your pocket.'

'Gina . . . yes, that's right, Sandrine. But . . . how do you know?'

'I work with her uncle.'

Colin looked up abruptly. 'She didn't want him involved . . . Oh, God, does he know I'm in here? And about the heroin?'

'No,' Gilbert replied, thinking quickly, 'he's not on this investigation.' He straightened a leg and fished in his hip pocket for a dog-eared piece of paper.

The boy slowly unfolded the photocopy of Sandrine's smiling face. 'She dumped me,' he said sadly. 'That's why I went to the house with the fence . . . and the dogs . . . to try and find her, talk to her.'

'And did you?'

'I . . . I think I saw her once, from a window, she was coming across the yard. But she didn't see me. She looked awful. I . . . I have a feeling she's in trouble. Will you help me get her out?'

Gilbert ignored the question. 'There was a yard, in front of the house?'

'I think so, yes, a muddy yard and other buildings, farm buildings on the other side.'

'Good lad, anything else?'

'There were poultry . . . guinea fowl! I remember the awful noise they made, like a rusty chain being wound up from a well.' Colin looked up with frightened eyes. 'Will you help me get her out?'

Again Gilbert ignored the question. 'You say she looked awful; what sort of awful?'

'I don't know . . . She didn't look well . . . sort of weird. I know it sounds silly, but she looked, well, spaced out, you know, hypnotized.'

'It doesn't sound silly at all, son. How did you get to the house?'

'Someone took me.'

'Who?'

'I can't remember. It was a man I met in a bar somewhere. I was looking for her and he said he knew where she was.'

'What did this man look like?'

'I don't know, he was ordinary-looking but big.'

'Short hair? Long hair?'

'Short, it was blond, bleached blond, the roots were darker.'

'Good lad. Was he wearing anything special? You know, snazzy shoes, tight jeans, flashy jacket?'

Colin shook his head.

'A signet ring then? A moustache? Any piercings?'

'An ear-ring! He had a diamond ear-ring.'

'Great stuff. Know where he lives?'

'No, I didn't ask. I didn't care. He was going to take me to her, out in the country, lots of fields and trees and space, he said it was really peaceful, the perfect place for making up.'

'So the bloke, the big blond one with dark roots and an ear-ring, took you to the house.'

'Yes. After we had a drink to celebrate. I said I'd already got one. He said beer wasn't a drink, it was *pissette* and he bought me a whisky. I drank the whisky.' Colin frowned deeply. 'And that's the last thing I remember – except the fence and the dogs and Sandrine, but that was all like a dream, you know, fuzzy and disjointed, sort of floating – until I came round here with you snoring in that chair. You were making a hell of a racket!'

They looked at each other and smiled.

'Sorry about that.'

'No harm done.'

'Do you know what day it is, Colin?'

'Not really, but it must be getting pretty close to Christmas.'

'Prepare yourself for a shock, lad, it's 4th January.'

'I don't believe it!'

Gilbert rose stiffly and went to the table where de Troq' always left his newspaper for him. He came back and held it out for Colin. 'And that's yesterday's.'

'Jesus, that means . . .' he counted on his fingers, 'I just lost a whole two weeks! I missed Christmas and the New Year! My poor parents . . . do they know I'm here? I must phone them. Jesus . . . and Sandrine. Is she all right? Did she go home, the way she was supposed to? I must talk to her. It doesn't matter about the other man, not if she'll have me back.' Colin looked down at his fingers in embarrassment. 'I love her, you see.' Then his eyes flicked up. 'Will you help me find her? Please?'

For a moment, Gilbert – vulgar, overweight and flabby, sex-obsessed scratcher and picker, who spent all his spare time drooling over lewd magazines and making even lewder comments; Gilbert, the rude, the ill-mannered, uncouth cop; Gilbert with his extensive vocabulary of swear words and coarse expressions, who managed to put policemen off their food by just being in the same room and upset every female member of the force without even trying – *that* Gilbert didn't know what to say. He just sat looking at Colin's young anxious face and truly didn't know what to say. 'I can't, lad. I'm sorry . . .'

'Why can't you? You're a policeman, you said you were! Hey, what's the matter? Where is she?'

Very gently, Gilbert put an arm round Colin's shoulder. 'She's dead, lad. They buried her on the 29th.'

While Colin wept, Gilbert shuffled into the corridor where he pulled the mobile from his pocket and tapped in a well-known number – well-known to Gilbert and the rest of the team. It was only 5.15 a.m.; too bad, Pel had to be told.

'*Oui. Merde . . . pardon. J'écoute.*'

'Sorry to disturb you and your dear lady wife, guv, I hope I'm not interrupting anything intimate . . .'

'Only the few hours' sleep that were allotted to me. What do you want, Gilbert?'

'The boy in hospital, guv, he's talking. I thought you'd like to listen, with perhaps a recorder plugged in. He's been pretty interesting so far.'

'What's he been talking about, Gilbert? Tits and bums?'

'Sandrine Da Costa, and where she was just before she attempted her armed robbery.'

'You'll never cease to amaze me. I'll be there shortly. By the way, who is he?'

'Colin Cuquel. Funny isn't it, with a name like that you'd have expected his nickname to be Cul-cul or something, not Duduche. I mean, for crying out loud, what's Duduche got to do with –'

'Gilbert!'

'But guv, he was her boyfriend, he's been missing for a fortnight, see? He's worried about his parents, perhaps you'd let them know?'

'As soon as I've got a statement from him. Why didn't we recognize him?'

'I don't think he'd recognize himself at the moment, he doesn't look anything like the photo we've got on file.'

'What's he like? Still aggressive? Do we need Bardolle to act as bodyguard?'

'No, guv. He's confused and bereft. I just told him Sandrine's dead. He loved her, you see, poor lad.'

Pel disconnected and stared at the phone in his hand, frowning. He thought – although it was hard to believe – he'd heard a hint of tenderness in God-awful Gilbert's voice. Then, dismissing the idea as absurd, and blinking quickly to warn his brain of impending action, he slipped out of bed. He fumbled his way towards the bathroom, banging his knee on his wife's dressing-table stool and swearing quietly, very quietly, hoping not to wake her, shuffled round the furniture, muttering expletives.

'Switch the light on Pel,' Geneviève said cosily from the pillows. 'I don't want to have to call an ambulance.'

As Pel left the hospital, having given Gilbert permission to inform Monsieur and Madame Cuquel their only child was safe and, if not sound, certainly alive and recovering, it was well and truly light. The city's workers were streaming in for the eight o'clock start, and traffic jams were temporarily building up in the centre. He lit up impatiently, and listened to the news on a crackling radio. 'In Spain, twelve men died after a collision between a train and a minibus. The minibus, transporting agricultural workers, tried to cross the railway line after the train's approach was signalled.' Pel switched off – wasn't there ever any good news?

Someone punched at a car horn. The lights had changed, he was holding everyone up. Pel shoved the car – still the one borrowed from his garage – into gear and released the handbrake. As he brought his hand back to the steering wheel, he caught the end of his Gauloise on it and a small ball of burning cinders dropped between his legs. In fear of his life, or worse, he swung the car over, two wheels on the pavement, and started swatting the smouldering upholstery.

Once the fire was extinguished, and the large black hole in the seat well and truly inspected – *oh con*, what would the garage say? – he eased his way back into the traffic. While he drove, his mind wandered back to more important things: what he'd just heard at the hospital.

Lapeyre's suspicions had been confirmed, Luzanne was definitely involved with Sandrine Da Costa, and they knew he'd bleached his hair. They had a vague but useful description of where he'd taken her, although how useful, he wondered. It could be any one of the hundreds of farmhouses dotted around the 8,763 square kilometres of his own patch, the Côte d'Or. Or it could be any one of those dotted around the 6,817 square kilometres of Nièvre, the 8,575 of Saône-et-Loire or, come to that, 7,242 of Yonne, all of which were the *départements* that made up the *région* he'd loved since birth, la Bourgogne. He hoped he wouldn't have to bother the police in Yonne, however; they had enough to do with Emile Louis, and the sordid remains of the seven handicapped kids he'd killed. But they all had to be alerted.

On the other hand, if the man they were after *knew* they were after him, he may make a move, or go to ground. If he went to ground, he might try getting out of Burgundy which amounted to making a move; Pierre La Poche had gone to ground but not in any of his normal hiding places, he'd moved around because he'd been scared. And if Luzanne *was* working for the mysterious Dalton, he too might get scared that Dalton would deal with him before the police got to him, which meant he'd definitely be on the move. With road blocks and Luzanne's description in everyone's pockets, the possibility of nabbing him was high.

It was unlikely, in the event of press coverage, that Luzanne would sit tight and do nothing – criminals couldn't, they liked to think they were clever devils who outwitted the idiot police easily. In fact, most criminals weren't particularly clever at all, which is why they were criminals and not surgeons, stockbrokers, engineers or, come to that, Commissaires in the Police Judiciaire. And knowing that, it wasn't too difficult to work out the sort of reaction Luzanne would have if he knew the idiot police were after him: he'd run for it. It was worth a try.

Pel stepped on the brakes, received a loud blast from the car behind, indicated right and pulled over. The vehicles that had been following accelerated away, one or two drivers shaking their fists. When the coast was clear, Pel indicated left, executed an illegal U-turn and headed back the way he'd come. Sarrazin's office was a short 2 kilometres away.

'I thought I saw a light on,' Pel said as he walked in.

'Like to see my word as it comes off the press,' the journalist replied, holding out his hand to be shaken. 'You don't usually visit me, what's up?'

'I don't *ever* visit you,' Pel corrected. 'However, under the circumstances, I thought we might be of mutual use to one another. I've got information that you might like to print . . .'

'In return for?'

Pel shrugged. 'In return for nothing, actually. I just want to shake someone into action, that's all.'

'Take a seat and tell me all. Do I switch on my recorder? Or not?'

'Plug this one in, if you like.' Pel placed a small appliance on Sarrazin's desk. 'It's all on that.'

'Story time! Coffee or cognac?'

'Both?'

'Coming up.'

They listened to the first official interview with Colin Cuquel – at that precise moment talking to his tearful but ever so relieved Mum on the phone – and sipped alternately at the good strong coffee and the even better aromatic cognac. When Pel clicked the machine off, Sarrazin sat back, stretching.

'What do you think?' Pel asked.

'Well, I can't print it the way it is, it wouldn't make good reading. I suggest something more along the lines of "Slain Student Held in Drug House".'

'Is that grammatically correct?'

'Who cares? It's the dubious art of headlines – my editor will probably come up with something even worse. It's the copy I'm concerned with; I'll have to reiterate, briefly, what happened on the 26th, but I think I'll put that at the end, after I've stated that the police now have information about a certain drugs dealer and his whereabouts . . . Do you want his description included?'

'Not yet. If he knows we know what he looks like, he'll change his appearance again and we'll lose our advantage. Plus of course the general public will block our phone lines reporting sightings all over the bloody republic. No, it's the whereabouts that are important.'

'Okay, so I'll emphasize the whereabouts and keep the description to a minimum. Would "man with blond hair" be okay?'

'Just "man" would be better.'

'I'm hardly going to put "donkey", Pel. Give me a break.'

'"Man with blond hair" then. I suppose it's ambiguous enough.'

'Right, then I'll insinuate his involvement, or even better, his responsibility for Sandrine's death.'

'You'll be done for libel.'

Sarrazin smiled confidently. 'I said insinuate. That's what modern journalism is all about, making people believe something's true without actually stating it as a fact.'

'I'm glad you're on our side.'

Again Sarrazin smiled. 'Not on your life, I'm on my side, but you don't owe me that drink any more, *mon brave, le contraire.* Thanks, Pel, and I hope it has the reaction you anticipate. The story should be in the evening editions.'

'If I have to cancel?'

'1600 or it'll be too late, and Pel, if you do cancel, you'll owe me again – and much more than a drink.'

When Nosjean arrived at the top of the stairs, having taken them two at a time, he almost collided with Pel, who was standing at the top waiting for him.

'In my office, we've got developments, and do it quietly, Sir's got his door open.'

'Capelle called late last night, he wants to see you.'

'Just because he's been transferred from Paris doesn't mean he gets special treatment. Tell him to be at the morning meeting, he'll see me there.'

As they tiptoed into Pel's office, however, they found Capelle standing by the window. He turned, participated in the inevitable hand-shaking, and waited to be spoken to.

'What've you got, Capelle?'

'Precisely nothing, sir.'

'Don't call me sir. Why did you want to see me?'

'To give you a message from Lapeyre. He'll be in the park at midday.'

'I hope he enjoys himself.'

'I think, sir, he was expecting –'

'Yes, yes, it's noted, I'll be there. Now, as you're here, sit down, shut up and listen to this.' For the second time that morning, he pulled the small tape recorder from his pocket and switched it on.

While the description of the farmhouse, such as it was, was sent out throughout the four relevant *départements*, with the added note, 'If you or your men – meaning women as well – do suspect you recognize this place, do not attempt entry or enquiry, inform sender immediately,' and with the morning's urgent appointments and phone calls completed, Pel crept from the Hôtel de Police and made his way to the park. He'd just endured an hour and a half 'in conference' – that's what Chief Lambert called it, Pel called it a bloody bore, he called Lambert a bloody bore as well, but not to his face, to his face he called him 'Sir' adding as much sarcasm to the word as possible – and he was in dire need of a breath of fresh air. It wasn't enough that he'd lost Morrison, Misset and now Pujol, that his team was in tatters; it wasn't enough to know that's the way it would probably stay for weeks, everyone walking their legs down to stumps and doing double hours; it wasn't enough to know the pushers and junkies of his beautiful county were causing heartbreak and mayhem, no, all that wasn't enough; Lambert, with Brisard to back him up, just had to add salt to the wound and rub it in laboriously for one and a half hours. Damn Pujol for falling through the ceiling, it really was the icing on the proverbial cake.

He stopped and removed his glasses to polish them, thinking hard, then, lighting a Gauloise, breathed deeply, inhaling the smoke right down to his socks. A couple of kids came streaking past on their *trottinettes*, shrieking at him, '*Eh, le vieux! Attention!*', but before he could reply, they'd disappeared up the path, the rubber wheels of their scooters hissing quietly on the damp tarmac. Pel walked on thoughtfully.

Lapeyre was sitting on the same bench as before. He stood up as Pel approached. 'We've got to stop meeting like this,' he said humourlessly.

'Oh, I don't know, counting the minutes off to midday saved me from falling asleep and possibly doing myself grievous bodily harm as I crashed to the floor on Lambert's carpet.'

'How did he ever get the job?'

'He knows a lot of important people.'

'So do I.'

'You didn't apply. Did you?'

'What I'm saying is, if he's hampering our operation –'

'I don't think he's got a clue what's going on. His grasp of the situation is hardly comprehensive. He thinks we're after a pusher to cover up for Morrison's mistake.'

'But it wouldn't.'

'Precisely. Look, you didn't get me here to discuss Sir. Clope?'

'No thanks, I brought my own.'

Both men puffed silently for a moment, sorting their thoughts into coherent order, ready for exchange.

'So,' Pel said at last, 'what's new?'

'I was rather hoping you were going to tell me. Rigal's busy sending a description of a farmhouse to all Burgundy's gendarmeries, why?'

'How do you know?'

'He works on a research terminal. All external messages received and sent are automatically copied through to Paris.'

'But you're here.'

'Paris sifts and sorts, then communicates the relevant stuff to la Division. Rigal's request was relayed to me by phone.'

'Capelle was quicker, he told me you wanted to see me first thing this morning.'

'Because he told me the boy from the squat was talking. What did he say?'

Pel pulled a small cassette from his pocket. 'The transcript's being typed, this is a copy. I thought you'd expect it.'

'*Bien*, so what have we got?'

'A big blond man, dyed blond he thinks, with diamond earring, taking Colin Cuquel to a farm, where he saw Sandrine. After that, he doesn't remember a thing, except the sensation of being wet and cold, then waking up in hospital and believing he was still being held against his will.'

'Does he remember anything about the room in which he was held?'

'He thinks he went temporarily blind.'

'In a cellar?'

'Possible.'

'That's all?'

'So far. I've still got Colin guarded twenty-four hours a day. If he says anything else, I'll let you know.'

'If it concerns Luzanne or Dalton, do it by phone. I'd rather Lambert knew as little as possible.'

'He's my Chief of Police, he has to be informed.'

'It's not that I don't trust him, but he has, as you just told me, a lot of important friends, and he can be boastful. You never know who he may talk to. I'd rather keep my involvement off the record, let him go on thinking I'm trying to trace a dealer of drugs and arms.'

'Which is, in a way, true.'

'In a way.'

'I don't like this, Lapeyre.'

'Neither do I. The men at the end of the line are abusing our hospitality and we can't touch them. If we even bent the laws in their countries we'd probably be hanged, shot or at least chucked in a rat-infested cell and forgotten for ever.'

'You should've picked up Luzanne when you had him in your sights.'

'We only saw him on two security videos and, anyway, Luzanne's just a common thug taking orders. It's Dalton I want. He's the one running the supply and demand. If we get him we'll stop the flow.'

'Of one of the veins.'

'It's a start.'

'It makes my blood boil to think of these girls being used in this way.'

'You're fortunate not to have a daughter.'

'Do you?'

'Two; fifteen and seventeen.'

'I don't know why, but I didn't think you were married.'

'It can happen to anyone, Pel. Look at you.'

'Mm, eleven and a half years – something like that. A long time anyway. I don't honestly know why my wife puts up with me, I wouldn't. She must be a saint.'

'She is. Mine divorced me five years ago, my daughters live with their mother.'

'I see.' Pel flicked his glowing stub out on to the path in front of them, thankful he didn't have children to lose sleep over. He sat up abruptly. 'We're getting off the point, you poncy Parisian, stick to the subject.'

Lapeyre took a last drag at his cigarette and dropped it, grinding it out with his shoe. 'What else are you doing to find this farmhouse?'

'Everything and more.'

'Your friend the journalist?'

'He's not my friend, but he is printing an abridged version of Colin Cuquel's statement.'

'I'd like to move in on the subsequent panic.'

'So would I, but we need the subsequent panic first.'

'Sitting waiting makes me nervous.'

'I thought your nerves were made of steel?'

'It's about the only part of me that hasn't been medically interfered with or replaced.'

'It must be fun working for the anti-terrorist division.'

'The damage was done in the army, special regiment.'
'Ah,' Pel said.

When the evening papers appeared on the stands, only Sarrazin had the full story. The other journalists had padded with what they'd managed to get from the hospital and statistics:

Colin Cuquel, removed from 1 bld Soult during a drugs raid at the empty building of Jeanne d'Arc College, was in a critical condition. He was taken to l'Hospitalier Générale where, after three days in a drug-induced coma, he has at last regained consciousness and is helping the police with their enquiries. The drugs problem is on the increase in our city, particularly around the university area, and the police are anxious to control the epidemic of related accidents and deaths. Since the beginning of December, 15 people either took their own lives whilst under the influence of drugs, or died from overdoses. This represents a shocking increase of 10% on previous years.

Pel looked up from the newsprint. An increase of ten per cent? 'Nosjean, what's ten per cent of fifteen?'
'One point five.'
'That's what I thought. Apparently, during December there were one and a half more deaths due to drugs.'
Nosjean chuckled. 'Maybe Colin accounts for the half. He was half dead when Capelle found him.'
'Who's with him now?'
'Gilbert and de Troq' should be changing over any minute.'
'Contact them, speak to them both personally. They must check everything administered to him, food, drink and medication. I wouldn't put it past Luzanne to try and poison him, or at least cloud his memory. Perhaps it would be wise to fetch consumables from the canteen from now on.'
'Leaving Colin alone in his room. We need another man, *patron.*'
'We can't spare one. Damn it, you'll have to get on to Marteau, he'll supply us with a uniform but make sure he's properly briefed.'

Mercredi, le 5 janvier

St Edouard. 'To those of you who've just joined us, good morning. It is nine o'clock, Wednesday, 5th January. Here is the news. Yvan Colonna, wanted since May 1999 for the assassination of Préfet Erignac, Corsica, has been arrested after being denounced by two militant nationalists. He stated, "I didn't kill the Préfet."

'After Italy, Portugal and Belgium, it's France's turn to be affected by the Balkans Syndrome. Four soldiers, having served in ex-Yugoslavia, are being treated for leukaemia.

'Police in Burgundy have now confirmed that Sandrine Da Costa, shot on 26th December by one of their officers, was the victim of a vicious drugs ring. Police are looking for a large blond man to help them with their enquiries.

'There will be scattered showers throughout the country, some sun in the south.'

Goldstein wasn't listening, he preferred to read the news, and what he'd read didn't please him. He picked up the phone and dialled. After five rings his call was answered. He didn't introduce himself. 'Have you seen *La Dépêche*?' That's all he said. Angelo knew who the voice belonged to.

'Luzanne's only just brought them in.'

'Take a look. You'll see what's upsetting me.' He heard paper rustling as it was unfolded and opened out.

SLAIN POLICE OFFICER'S NIECE HELD IN DRUG HOUSE – the witness wakes up. Yesterday, Colin Cuquel told the police in Dijon (Burgundy) how he'd been taken to a farmhouse on 20th December where he saw Sandrine Da Costa, known as Gina, the niece of Lt. Josephe Misset (Police Judiciare). She died after an attempted 'armed' robbery at the Tabac du Centre on the 26th. 'She seemed to be hypnotized,' Cuquel said. Details are now coming to light of a dangerous drug ring . . .

Angelo skimmed through the article, his heart beating more quickly. When he looked up from the papers, there was a fuzz of perspiration on his upper lip. Colin Cuquel; that bloody boy!

'Not good,' he said. 'Very unexpected.'

'I agree. You told me the outlet had been taken care of. I don't like liars, Angelo.'

'Luzanne said –'

'And I don't give a damn what your idiot employee said! I want you to straighten out our little problem, okay? You're in

181

charge of the operation there, therefore you are responsible for anything that goes wrong. The girl was the niece of a *flic*, you know what that means, they're tracking you and won't stop until they've got you. You have until tomorrow morning which is when I expect to see a positive result printed in place of this monstrosity. If not, my little Angel, you'll be appearing in the papers too, but not on the front page, in the obituaries. And Angelo, a word of advice: don't go tearing out of the front gate in your flashy car, there's police activity all over the countryside. Use the jeep and the back track, okay, nice and quiet. Public transport when you reach the city limits.'

Angelo stared at the now silent phone. 'Luzanne! Get in here.'

Luzanne zipped up his flies again, he'd been on the point of attending to the housemaid in the kitchen. As he left the room, she looked round from where she was bent over the table, shrugged and stood up, smoothing her skirt down over her buttocks and thighs.

'Look at that!'

Luzanne's eyes laboured back and forth, trying to understand the article's implications. In the end, he managed, 'But he should've died.'

'Well, he didn't. What are you going to do about it?'

'Finish the job, I suppose.'

'We'll have to think up something rather special, he's under police guard. It's got to be quick and neat, if that kid starts remembering any more, we're looking at either life imprisonment or Goldy's bullet in the back of our skulls.'

'How about if we make a run for it?'

'Don't even think about it, he says the fuzz are out in force, probably road blocks and stuff. He's bound to be right, he always is, and they've already got your description.'

'You'd better go then.'

'You're the one who let the fucking kid escape! You shut him up.'

'First we've got to find the little blighter. Does it say which ward he's in?'

'Of course it doesn't! We'll have to work it out.'

'Angelo . . . what if we left the country?'

Angelo thought about this for a moment, weighing up the possibilities, then, slowly, he shook his head. 'Where do you propose we go, Outer Mongolia? If we hop it, Goldy'll supply the fuzz with photographs, plus all our personal details, down to the size of our dicks, faster than you can pack an overnight bag. He'll tell them to watch the airports and everything. We'd never make it. And *you're* already on the wanted list, remember that little incident a few months back – Abeddaa?'

'He was an Arab.'

'You still slit his throat.'

Luzanne, with newly dyed dark brown hair, a pair of steel-rimmed glasses – bought at a village chemist's on the way to the station – and a box of chocolates under his arm – bought as an afterthought when he stopped at the chemist's – jumped down from the train and marched towards the ticket barrier, swinging his free arm. Outside the station, after a few minutes' wait, he stepped up into a bus, paid for the short journey to the hospital, and settled himself into a seat. Ten minutes later, he walked through the main entrance, crossed the wide hall and stopped by the lifts to study the signboards. He had a long morning ahead of him; he had to find Cuquel. He couldn't ask at *Acceuil* – the police, Angelo said, would have given the receptionist a list of visitors to be allowed through, and there was probably a plain-clothes watching the desk – so he'd have to do it the hard way: ward by ward, walking the long corridors, politely saying good morning, and telling anyone that asked he was going to see his brother, Edouard Urbita, who'd had an accident. Luzanne didn't have any brothers, but Angelo said he had to say something if a nurse did her 'Can I help you?' act on him. So it was Edouard Urbita. He'd picked the name out of the telephone directory, from the Soulutre section, and he hoped like hell the guy hadn't had an accident. Not because he wished him well, simply because it would bugger up his plans and he'd have to think up a new name, and Luzanne wasn't very good at thinking, he left that to Angelo and Goldy.

He pulled out the list Angelo had written and looked again at the destinations on offer. 'Maternity.' He chuckled, not very likely. 'Paediatric.' He frowned, that was something to do with feet, wasn't it? – *pied* = foot, stupid but logical to a not very bright Frenchman. In any case it wasn't on his list. 'Gynaeco-logy.' Tarts' arses – not quite right but near enough. 'Geriatric.' Old codgers. 'Pneumonology' he couldn't pronounce. 'Radi-ology.' He knew what that was, he'd had his chest X-rayed as a kid – but none of them would fit with a boy who'd been drugged up to the eyeballs. 'Casualty.' Okay! 'Neurology.' Bingo! 'Psychiatry.' Right! He'd found the departments he wanted.

Neurology was closest. He started walking.

By midday, he was feeling hungry and fed up. The hospital was vast, like a city within a city, and no policemen sitting outside any of the hundreds of rooms he'd passed on the four floors of the first building. Exceptionally, an intelligent thought occurred to him. Maybe the fuzz was sitting inside? *Merde*. He'd have to start all over again.

Taking the lift down to the ground floor again, he wandered into the canteen, collected a tray of chicken and chips and sat down to eat, trying to work out how to avoid another three hours traipsing about the collection of buildings looking for Colin Cuquel, alias Edouard Urbita.

Half an hour later, feeling satisfied with his mental arithmetic and the solution he'd come up with, he made his way to *Urgences* and rang the bell.

'Monsieur?'

'Yeah, er, hi. I'm lost.'

'You're not the first person to tell me that.' The woman smiled sympathetically. 'Where do you want to go?'

'Well, that's just the trouble, I'm not sure. My kid brother, see, he, well, he had a bit of trouble last night and was brought here.'

'I don't have the admissions listings, I'm afraid. You need to ask at *Acceuil*.'

'I've just spent an hour trying to find it, I came in through one of the side entrances, you see. If I spend much more time in this maze, I reckon I'll just give up and eat these chocs myself. Can't you point me in the right direction?'

'Well, I don't know. What sort of trouble did your brother have?'

'Er, it was drugs. He was unconscious, but your guys saved him.'

'Have you tried Psychiatry? Third floor, Bâtiment B, it's on the other side of the car park, there's a ward on the third floor for drug-related problems up there. If not, ask in Cardiology, Bâtiment E, ground floor, he may have spent the night there.'

'Well, thank you.'

'My pleasure.'

Not bad for someone who wasn't very good at thinking.

Across the car park, into Bâtiment B, up to the third floor, turn right, push open the swing doors, and hey presto! A blue uniform sitting snoozing on a chair. He shifted the colourful box under his arm and held it carefully in his hands as he walked down the long corridor. Nurses bustled, patients shuffled and the blue uniform just sat there staring at the wall opposite. At each door, Luzanne stopped and pretended to peep in, shrugged and set off again. As he approached, the gendarme, whose name was Cédric Maupou, looked up and watched him.

'*Bonjour*,' Luzanne said in a friendly way.

'Monsieur.' Maupou stood up and saluted. 'Looking for someone?'

'My kid brother, they said he was up here. He's not the guy you're guarding, is he?' Luzanne joked and glanced over the blue shoulder in through the door's small glass panel.

'What's his name?'

'Urbita, Edouard Urbita.'

'Nope, it's not him in there.'

'Oh well, I'll just have to keep looking, thanks anyway.'

'Don't mention it.'

Luzanne continued his walk, still stopping at each door to look in, although he'd already found what he was searching for. Over the gendarme's shoulder, he'd caught a glimpse of a youngish plain-clothes detective – he knew he was a detective by the red, white and blue stripe on the plastic lapel label he was wearing on his shirt pocket. He'd been peacefully reading the newspaper at the end of the bed where a bump in the sheet indicated the feet of someone otherwise unseen. It wasn't much, but it was enough. It was all he needed to know. When he reached the end of the corridor, he exited through a second pair of swing doors and turned towards the stairs and the public phone booths.

Coming back an hour later, having dumped the chocolates in a dustbin, he walked back past the gendarme and raised his hand in greeting. 'Still here?'

'Until six. Find your kid brother?'

'Sure, he's doing fine. Going to buy a toothbrush for him. See you later.'

And sure enough, he walked past the other way shortly afterwards, clutching a magazine and a toothbrush he'd bought in the hospital's small supermarket downstairs. They nodded at each other. This time however, having gone through the second pair of swing doors and down the three flights of stairs, he went out into the street. He had some shopping to do.

At six he was back. Now there were two uniforms. 'Hey, shouldn't you be on your way home now?'

'Just being relieved.'

'I'm going down for another magazine, I left our Eddie gawping at the telly. Goodnight then.'

'*Bonsoir, monsieur.*'

Both gendarmes watched him disappear. 'Who the hell's that?'

'Just a bloke visiting his kid brother.'

On his way back, Luzanne stopped to introduce himself to the new uniform. 'Christian Urbita, I'm taking care of my kid brother.'

'That's good of you, monsieur.'

'Have they changed the man inside too?'

'Not yet.'

'Well, I'll be getting back to Eddie, he wants me to stay the night.'

It was 1900 hours. Pel leafed through the replies faxed from the gendarmeries in Auxerre, Côte d'Or, Nièvre and L'Yonne. They'd been coming in slowly since mid-afternoon; now the last one completed the pile. There were thirty-nine suggestions for the location of the mysterious farmhouse; Burgundy was a large region, 31,397 square kilometres to be precise. Thirty-nine farmhouses with high fences, well back from the road, poultry in a central yard, and dogs that barked – well, it narrowed it down slightly. Trouble was, not one of those gendarmeries could report suspicious behaviour in any of them. Not one of them reported unusual movement, or cars leaving in a hurry. Or cars arriving in a hurry. Or unidentified vans, arriving or leaving. Or motorbikes. Or limousines. Or any bloody thing out of the ordinary, just quiet country houses with poultry in the yard and dogs that barked. Tomorrow, each one of those thirty-nine farmhouses dotted all over Burgundy would have to be visited by two officers from the gendarmeries concerned. And he didn't like the idea. He'd have preferred the visit to be made by his own men, but that was impossible; three of them were out of action, two were doing hospital duty, and there were still dozens of cases needing their attention while they worked on the Da Costa killing. He had to let the boys in blue deal with the possibly dangerous task of interviewing the occupants.

And the road blocks around the city centre had so far produced nothing but thousands of irate and impatient motorists. They'd stay in place, in case. Luzanne had to make his move soon, both Pel and Lapeyre were sure he wouldn't ignore the press coverage he'd had.

Closing the file, he scribbled a note for the following morning, and climbed inside his overcoat. Then, gathering up the two open packets of Gauloises, he stepped out into the corridor. Klein was catching calls during the coming night; he'd been informed and knew where to find him if Luzanne did turn up. Marteau and his boys in blue also had strict instructions to make contact immediately if they sighted their prey. Mentally checking once more he'd done everything he could, Pel turned towards the stairs and a few hours at home.

Klébert and Edith Cuquel were already home. They'd spent the previous afternoon at their son's bedside, tearfully thanking God he was still alive. They'd come back that morning, sitting with him while the doctors did their examinations, and were reassured repeatedly that Colin would be all right, he'd been very lucky. They'd watched him eat a little lunch, brought up from the canteen by the detective on duty, Inspecteur de Troquereau, then finally left at four, kissing Colin goodbye and wishing him a restful night. That evening, sitting opposite each other in the kitchen, a game show flickering on the television set at one end, Edith smiled for the first time since Christmas. 'At last, Klébert,' she said, 'for the first time in weeks, I'm not frightened. Thank God it's over. Our Colin is going to be fine. He'll be home soon.'

Klébert looked up from his plate and the wedge of home-made pâté he was wrestling with and smiled back. His wife had grown older, her hair seemed even greyer than ever, her face more lined; she looked tired, very tired, but she was smiling. 'That's what they say,' he agreed happily. 'Tell you what, how about opening the bottle of champagne we bought.'

Edith sighed deeply. 'I think that's a very good idea, we'll have a glass and celebrate Colin being given back to us.' And suddenly she was crying again. 'I'm sorry,' she wept as her husband rose to comfort her, 'but . . . I can't explain . . . it's just . . . well, it's just such a relief he's alive. He's all we've got.'

'We've got each other, love.'

'I know,' she said, kissing his cheek, 'but you understand what

I mean; he's the only child we'll ever have. Do you remember when we first brought him home from the foster family?'

'How could I forget? You know, at the time, I wasn't sure we'd done the right thing adopting.'

'You never said.'

'Well, no, I couldn't, could I? And anyway, you were sure enough for both of us.'

'I loved that little bundle the first time I held him in my arms.'

'It took me a bit longer.'

'When?'

'The first time he smiled at me.'

'Oh Klébert. And to think after all those years of praying for a baby, and finally being blessed with one . . . he was such a dear little boy.' Fresh tears sprang into her eyes and as they over-flowed, her husband wiped them gently away.

'He's grown up a bit since then. Our Colin's turned into a brave and bright young man, he'll make a success of his life.'

'He very nearly lost it.'

Klébert smoothed his fingertips over Edith's damp cheek. 'Come on, love,' he said kindly, 'stop your sniffing and tell me where you've hidden that bottle. We know our son is safe, the police are making sure of that; a man on the door, another inside the room. Colin's well looked after.'

Jeudi, le 6 janvier

St Mélaine. Gilbert stood up and stretched, glancing at his watch as he did so. 2.30 a.m. The worst bit of the night had just begun and he'd almost dropped off once already.

He checked Colin was sleeping peacefully, picked up his thermos and slipped out into the corridor. The gendarme jerked his head up.

'I'm off to get some more coffee, Jeanjean, I won't be long.'

'Yes, sir, I'll take over while you're gone.' He picked up his wooden chair and settled himself just inside the room, closing the door behind him.

Thirty seconds after Gilbert disappeared through the swing doors at one end of the corridor, Luzanne pushed his way through the swing doors at the other end, and strolled casually towards Room 6233; no gendarme. He must be inside like the last time.

Looking through the window, he tapped on the door and

watched Sergeant Jeanjean stand up and turn towards him. The door opened a crack. 'Evening, sergeant. All alone again?'

'Only for a minute.'

'Brought you a cup of coffee, thought you looked like you needed it the last time I passed.'

Jeanjean saw the cardboard cup full of steaming black coffee and smelt the rich aroma. He thought about Gilbert chatting up the nurses downstairs, drinking his. His nostrils twitched, his mouth watered. He was tired and bored out of his skull; guarding a sleeping kid in an overheated hospital was the pits. He was sorely tempted. 'Well, thanks . . .' Then he remembered Gilbert's warning and the explicit threat that went with it – if he left his post inside Colin's room, even for a second, he'd thump him hard enough to push his teeth so far down his throat he'd be eating through his arse for the next month – and hesitated. Gilbert was a big bloke and looked capable of doing just that. 'Well, thanks,' he said again, 'but I'd better not, I've got strict orders not to leave the room until the other man's back.'

'Oh well, never mind, I was hoping we might have a chat. You know, pass the time, it's still hours till breakfast.' Luzanne turned to go, and, as the door started closing, he turned back. 'Take the coffee anyway.' He shrugged, 'I've drunk enough to keep me awake all flaming night.'

Gilbert walked towards the lift, a cup of coffee in his hand, the refilled green thermos in the other, a collection of wrapped chocolate biscuits rustling in his pocket. He was proud of himself; the little nurse with the nice knockers had given him the eye, swaggered over, knowing her hips were swaying provocatively, smiling as she saw him watching her lightly bouncing brassiere, oh yes, Gilbert was really proud of himself. She'd swaggered over, leant across the table where he was sorting out his purchases – nice view, *ma poule*, right down to your navel, pretty lacy panties, *chérie*, I love your loose-fitting uniform – and she said, 'Hey, don't I know you?'

Corny maybe, but it works. It worked with medical students, it worked with young housemen just afforded official duty, so it must work with cops, *non*?

No. It didn't.

Gilbert smiled apologetically at her, stubbed out his half-smoked cigarette, and said, 'Not tonight, Josephine, I'm on duty,'

189

and left that swaggering, pouting, ready-for-it nurse, sulking in the canteen.

Boy, he was pleased with himself. Pel would be pleased with him if he knew. A right old bugger, Pel. He could, if he wanted to, bring you right down to rock bottom with a single word, but, and it was a big 'but', he was okay. He shouted and bellowed at him, but then he shouted and bellowed at everyone – that was the difference; Gilbert for once in his life didn't feel singled out for the animosity on offer. Even Nosjean felt the sharp side of Pel's tongue once in a while, and Nosjean was, after all, second-in-command, Pel's confidant, Pel's favourite. He rather wished he'd known Darcy, the one who'd been killed – they still talked about him, he was badly missed. He'd been second-in-command before Nosjean. Darcy was supposed to have been a right play-boy; tall, dark and hellishly handsome, a pro at horizontal jogging, bed-hopping from one beautiful girl to another – until he'd met Kate. She was supposed to be more beautiful than any of them; mellow, sophisticated, fucking gorgeous. Maybe he'd like to meet Darcy's widow. No, hold on there, Gilbert, that wasn't cricket, or rugger or any other real man's sport. We're talking about a deceased detective's widow here. *Pas touche, mon vieux. Pas touche.* Don't even think about it. Fantasies ain't made from a dead colleague's lady.

It was with these admirable thoughts in his mind that Gilbert made his way to the lift, stepped into it, pressed 3 and watched the doors whisper to a close. He stared at Sergeant Jeanjean's coffee, at the thermos in the other hand. Not daft the old Gilbert, thought of everything, something for them both to munch to get the old digestive juices going, and coffee to keep them awake – strong, sweet, black and hot – all through the bleeding night. And he'd remembered to bring plenty of change for the rotten ruddy dispensing machine.

The lift doors whispered open again. He stepped out into the corridor, pushed his way through the swing doors and started on the long slow trek to the other end.

All was quiet, all was calm. He nodded at a nurse coming out of a room where someone was moaning, and continued towards Room 6233. The smells were familiar; hospitals, he hated them. They reminded him of his dear old mum dying of cancer a few years back. So he hated hospitals. Big deal. He was doing a job, that was all.

He hoped like hell Colin would be okay, he was a nice kid, and ever so apologetic for the trouble he'd caused. It wasn't his fault for sod's sake, just another victim of the filthy bastards pushing drugs. Still, thanks to Capelle's quick thinking, he'd been saved. Capelle was a funny bugger, looked like a right royal yoghurt weaver, *un hippie*, the sort Gilbert used to take great pleasure in whacking with his CRS truncheon and trampling all over with his CRS boots while fighting his way forward during a demonstration. But his career in the Compagnie Républicaine de Securité was behind him now. Now he had to work with wets like Capelle. On the other hand, he argued privately as he juggled the thermos and the spare cup of coffee, trying to turn the door handle of Room 6233, Capelle's brain was in the right gear under all that hair. He'd found Colin and got him out. Just in time, according to what everyone was saying. Gilbert was pleased about that.

He got his back to the door and pushed it open.

After all, he allowed himself a satisfied smile, Colin was an only child, very precious to his parents, and for a moment he wondered how he'd feel if it was his own son in Room 6233.

As he went in, Jeanjean was sitting, as he should have been, on the chair propped against the bathroom wall, his head tilted gently on to his chest and breathing quietly.

'Poor bastard, couldn't keep awake, doesn't have my stamina or my foresight.' He shoved at his shoulder with an elbow, taking care not to spill the contents of the cardboard cup. 'Here, mate, I've brought you a coffee and something to chew.'

The gendarme went on sleeping peacefully.

Transferring the cup into the same hand as the thermos, Gilbert shoved him again. A good hard shove this time. 'On your feet, sergeant!'

Jeanjean rocked and fell forward on to his face, sprawling inelegantly on the floor.

For a split second Gilbert stared at him kissing the deck, then leaping over him, dropping coffee, thermos, the lot, he came to a sudden stop by Colin's bed.

'Jesus,' he said quietly, 'oh Jesus. Oh no. Jesus, no.'

Jesus wasn't listening.

Chapter Eleven

'I was away from my post for a maximum of ten minutes, guv. Just enough time to go downstairs, fill the thermos, grab a cup of coffee for Jeanjean, pay for the edibles and catch the lift back. He was keeping guard, as arranged, inside the bleeding room.'

'I don't know what happened!' Jeanjean was on the verge of tears. He'd finally come round, having slept for an hour and a half, to be faced with Pel's urgent questions. He'd seen the boy's body as it was being transferred to the path lab bag. 'One minute I was wide awake drinking my coffee, the next I was out like a light.'

Forensic had gathered up the broken thermos and the two empty cardboard cups and taken them away for analysis; they'd also hoovered the floor of Colin's room. Fingerprints were still working on the door and the furniture, and the clingfilm. The pathologist was now working on Colin. The scientific reports would take at least twenty-four hours to complete and Pel wasn't waiting. He was sure of the results; they'd find traces of a strong tranquillizer in one of the cups. If they found anything unusual on the floor, it would indicate a person who'd been on a farm recently, one with poultry. They would find no fingerprints other than the medical staff, the assisting policemen and Colin's parents. Everyone knew about latex gloves, specially in a hospital; an association of ideas would guarantee the murderer was wearing a pair. Colin would be declared as 'death by suffocation'.

While he was sleeping deeply, helped by the prescribed sedative, his hands had been tied to the metal bed by strips of locking plastic, the sort that hold fragile objects in place during transport, and his head had been tightly wrapped in plastic. When Pel had seen the body, he'd been revolted by the horror of it, it would've taken a number of long minutes to die. The boy's eyes were wide open and bulging, stuck to the inside of the plastic wrap. In his last desperate attempt to draw air into his lungs, he'd managed to suck the thin transparent film part way into his nostrils, but for some reason, it was his tongue Pel had noticed first; swollen and purple, it looked like an enormous piece of liver, wrapped and ready for sale in the supermarket. And while he struggled to free himself, the plastic strips had cut livid wounds into his wrists; the blood had dripped into small crimson puddles on the floor. He understood exactly why Jeanjean was crying.

After all their precautions of bringing food and drinks up from the canteen for Colin, of checking the medical staff's identities before allowing any medication to be administered, after the tedious night and day watches, the result was still the same: their witness, their one and only valuable witness, was dead.

And someone had to tell his parents.

He sighed unhappily and concentrated on Jeanjean. 'Okay, sergeant, I understand that you're still suffering from the effects of a tranquillizer as well as shock. But please try and tell me exactly what happened from the moment Gilbert said he was leaving.'

Jeanjean tried, but he couldn't get the image of the kid's bound face out of his mind, and the more it throbbed in his brain, the sicker he felt. Pel turned back to Gilbert.

'Who else did you talk to besides Jeanjean?'

Gilbert scratched his head. 'De Troq', when I took over from him. The nurse who came to settle Colin down for the night. The bird getting a cappuccino from the machine; she couldn't work out how to get it to work so I showed her.'

'And?'

'And she picked up her cup full of froth and hotfooted it back to her hubby.'

'After that?'

'A nurse who wanted a chat.'

'Which nurse?'

'The one with big knockers –'

'Gilbert!'

'But she did, guv. She came over to the table where I was sorting what I'd bought, stuffing what I could in my pockets, there were no trays for carrying it all back and I'd got double rations for me and Jeanjean. She leant over and I saw right down her front. I reckon she did it deliberately, you know, on night duty and bored out of her brain, after a bit of illicit slap and

tickle round the back of the ruddy coffee machine . . . sorry, guv
. . . but they were a lovely pair.'

'So you stopped for a chat?'

'No I didn't, I told her I was on duty and left her to find
another fool for a quick –'

'You surprise me.'

'I swear it, it's the truth!'

'*D'accord*, who else?'

'No one else, guv. Well, I might have said good evening to a
couple of people, but I didn't stop and I didn't talk to anyone
else.'

'Okay. Look, I think Jeanjean could do with a breath of fresh
air to clear his head. Take him outside and try to get him talking.
Get him talking about anything, you're good at that. Tell him
about the nurse's knockers or something. Then work your way
round to who he spoke to. Someone doped the poor sod, we've
got to know what the killer looked like.'

Wearily, Pel made his way back through the constant drizzle to
the Hôtel de Police and wasn't surprised to find a message
waiting for him: Lambert wanting to know what had gone
wrong this time. He had a nasty feeling he was looking at
enforced early retirement and, for once, he didn't give a shit. He
clicked on the message and deleted it from the screen. He was
bloody angry and bloody tired. Lambert was the last person he
wanted to discuss Colin's death with. 'Nosjean!'

His second-in-command appeared through the door.

'What's happening about these farmhouses? Have they started
yet?'

'They've been on it since daybreak. No news yet.'

'Fax them all again, stress it's urgent. I want all reports in by
six tonight.'

'Shall I put our men on to it as well?'

'What are they doing?'

'De Troq's following up a new lead on the car thefts with
Bardolle. Cheriff and Jourdain are out in Talant, another chemist's shop was broken into.' He fell silent.

'And?'

'And I was holding the fort until you came back.'

'Jesus bleeding Christ! Is that all I've got left?'

''Fraid so, *patron*.'

'If I'd had my full quota of men, that poor bloody boy might

194

still be alive! If it had been one of you sitting inside that room instead of an outsider who didn't know what he was up against . . . *Putain, quelle merde!*' He snatched up a packet of Gauloises from the desk and tapped it violently on the palm of his hand. The contents cascaded out, three fell on the floor. He stared at them furiously before kicking them out of sight. Picking another off the paperwork, he lit it aggressively, his frustration bubbling just below the surface. 'Where the hell's Capelle!'

'He was in when the news broke about the suffocation. Then he took off saying he was going to see a girl.'

'I'll have him sacked, now is not the time to go chasing skirt! Find him and make it snappy. Bring him in, bring them all in, send them all out again. Get them working their way into the country from the west side of town from the roads crossing the canal.' He exhaled noisily, shaking his head. 'You never know, we might just get fucking lucky for once.'

They didn't.

By midday, however, Pel did have Jeanjean's description of the man who'd fed him the doped coffee: 'One metre eighty-three, heavily built, short dark brown hair, I reckon it was dyed, it was that sort of brown, the same brown all over, almost like a cheap wig, steel-rimmed glasses, softly spoken, very friendly. Wearing a diamond in his ear.'

Luzanne.

By 1830, all the gendarmerie reports were in. The farmhouses had been visited. The only unusual comments were from the daughter of a farm labourer who couldn't open up because she didn't have the keys to the gate and the owner was 'way down the field on the other side of the river'; plus an obstreperous and very smelly peasant who addressed them as *les cons de flics*, and demanded to know if they hadn't anything better to do than pester people with work to do, finishing with, 'I ain't done no wrong, piss off.'

'These two,' Pel said, handing Nosjean the faxes, 'will have to be visited again,' he glanced at his watch, nearly 1900, 'tomorrow morning. If that gives us nothing, we'll get a ruddy helicopter on the job. That way at least we'll be able to see the set-up of a couple of dozen places in a day. One of them's got to have a second entrance . . . Capelle! Where the hell have you been? We're seriously undermanned and you go swanning off chasing girls. If you want to stay on my team, you'll bloody well take orders, not make them up as you go along. It that clear? And in future, don't interrupt a private meeting!'

'I knocked, sir.'

'I didn't hear you.'

'I did, *patron*.'

Pel scowled at Nosjean and flicked his attention back to Capelle. 'I repeat, where have you been?'

'Talking to Silver, sir.'

'I beg your pardon?'

'The girl who did the cooking in the squat.'

'She was released, she had nothing on her and no useful information to give us.'

'She contacted me.'

'How does she know your name?'

'She doesn't, she asked to speak to the hairy one.'

'Get your hair cut, Capelle, you're too easily identified.'

'Yes, sir. Do you want to know what she said?'

'If it'll help the enquiry.'

'She'd remembered something that may be important. As she was the one who nursed the boy, I thought it would be worth following up. I insisted we met.'

'And?'

'It took a long time to persuade her but finally she agreed to a cup of coffee in the Transvaal.'

'Oh jolly good, she sounds just the sort of young woman you need, homely, kind and a good cook. I hope you'll be very happy together.'

Capelle persisted. 'When Colin arrived in the squat, he was delirious. She sat with him while Jeff found the drops to calm him down.'

'Bully for her.'

'He kept screaming, *chiens*, call off the dogs . . .'

'He confirmed there were dogs at the farm, we already know that.'

'. . . and *blaireaux*, sir.'

'Wonderful, the lad was a badger fan!'

'Among the sites visited today,' Capelle went on, 'were houses near a *plan d'eau*, another just outside Blerard, and a third near Plériot. He may have been trying to indicate one of them.'

Pel shuffled through the pile of faxes. 'It's possible,' he said slowly. 'We'll have to take a closer look. Get back out there, Capelle, and bring the girl in, I want to speak to her myself. Apart from anything else, she'll be safer inside than out.'

'Sir –'

'Don't just stand there, man, get going! Congratulations on

finding her, congratulations on the information, will that do? More congratulations will be coming your way when you've got her safely off the streets.'

'Sir –'

'And don't call me sir!'

'*Patron*, she's already in.'

'*Quoi!*'

'I left her in Interview Room 2.'

'Alone?'

'No, I had to arrest her, she wouldn't come in willingly. Sir?'

'I'm *not* sir, how many bloody times –'

'Does it really matter what I call you? Surely it's what I find out that counts.'

Pel sighed, detesting the man momentarily, fighting to control his acute anger at having too few men at his disposal, at the tragic consequences: Colin Cuquel's death. The hospital surveillance had proved to be a waste of time, ending in a terrible and pointless waste of the young man's life. 'Point taken,' he said more calmly. 'What have you found out?'

'It's Silver; there's something funny about her.'

'Brilliant, a female comedian. What do you mean?'

'She's clean.'

'So am I.'

'But you're not living in a squat. All the other kids had black fingernails, if they weren't bitten down to the quick. Hers are clipped and clean, and her skin's clear, I had a good look at her today, not a spot in sight.'

'What are you driving at?'

'That's unusual in an undernourished junkie.'

'A useful observation, Capelle. Whether she's genuine or not, we can't ignore what she said. Nosjean, get that helicopter organized, we'll double-check her story and be ready to move in. And for that we need Lapeyre. Where the hell's he got to? Pissed off back to Paris, I suppose? Dining, no doubt, in his luxury apartment.'

'He lives in a château, sir.'

'He would!'

'It's only a small one.'

'I don't give a damn! Phone him and tell him to get his arse down here and quick.'

'No need to phone, sir.'

'Why? Is he telepathic as well as everything else?'

'No, sir, he's downstairs.'

'He is? What the hell's he doing downstairs?'

'Interrogating Silver, sir.'

Lapeyre lit up and pushed the packet across the table, watching Silver closely. She picked out a cigarette and leant over the offered flame, her long pale hair closing like flimsy curtains, hiding most of her perfectly oval face. She inhaled, sat back and smiled timidly, twitching the remaining mesh of hair over a shoulder. With a bit of make-up and money she could have been splendid.

'And that's all you can remember?' Lapeyre said quietly.

'I think so. He was jabbering about dogs, and *blaireaux*, ghosts, Gina, and . . . and,' she frowned, 'I almost forgot . . . not that it makes sense . . . something about wires singing to him.'

'Singing wires?'

'Well, yes. You don't suppose he meant electricity cables, do you? Sometimes, when the wind . . . I mean, well . . . it was just an idea.'

'Tell me, love, why did you decide to talk to us now?'

'He's been murdered, hasn't he?'

'Who told you?'

She crossed her legs under the long skirt. 'I went to the hospital to find out how he was. I know it sounds daft but I was worried about him. I didn't dare go before because . . . well, I just didn't dare because of the raid on the squat . . . I thought maybe the police would be there and . . . and I didn't want . . . well, you know.'

'So you went to the hospital and they told you he'd been murdered.'

'Not exactly. No one would tell me anything at first. I went up to the ward . . .'

'How did you know which ward he was in?'

'I didn't. I guessed.' She shrugged. 'He's not the first guy I've known to be treated for drugs. When I saw all the uniforms, I knew I'd guessed right. A gendarme outside told me he was dead, that someone had killed him.'

Pel knocked and pushed the door open. Silver looked calm and, as Capelle had described her, clean, although her clothes were colourless and worn.

Lapeyre's expression was bland as he stood up, thanked Silver and, taking Pel's elbow, guided him back into the corridor, closing the door gently behind him.

'A farmhouse near electricity pylons.'

'Plériot and Blerard, there are overhead lines there.'

'Who are the owners?'

'Rigal's working on three possible sites, he should have what we need shortly.' Pel frowned. 'Look, Lapeyre, I know this is probably the break we've been waiting for but Capelle seems to think there's something suspicious about the girl turning up so conveniently.'

'He may be right. Colin's murder hasn't been made public yet, has it?'

'No announcement's been made to the press.'

'She knows.'

'How?'

'A gendarme at the hospital.'

'It's not impossible.'

'Either she's telling the truth or she's a bloody good actress. Whichever is the case, we've got to act on the information she's given us, it's too good to ignore.'

'We've got a 'copter on stand-by for first light.'

'No time for that. I'm sending Capelle in to take a look. Don't forget, it's not just the men inside I'm after. I want their employer, wherever he is. For that we need to be quick.'

'What's Capelle going to be this time? A meter reader from the EDF?'

'Something like that.'

'He'll have a proper back-up; two armed officers in a car, the gendarmerie and constant radio contact.'

'He's used to working alone.'

'My men work as a team. He's a good officer, I want him protected as far as is possible.'

'He's still under my command.'

'I see.' Pel's eyes narrowed. 'When all this started,' he said quietly, 'you asked for my co-operation and I agreed. At his own request, I also accepted Capelle. However, one thing I do not agree with is risking a human being's life unnecessarily. Either you take over officially and use your reserves from Paris, plus Capelle if you insist on withdrawing him, or you let me handle it my way. Personally, I don't want him to be the next body found in the canal with his head stuffed in a plastic bag.'

'He's trained for –'

'Lapeyre, I don't give a damn!'

Lapeyre abruptly changed the subject. 'What do you intend doing with Silver?'

'Hold her for the permitted twenty-four hours, although on what charges . . . I'll think of something.'

'Has she asked for a lawyer yet?'

'I don't think she's aware of the juridical changes.'

'Okay, Pel, I'll agree to your terms; Capelle has a proper back-up but he goes in tonight.'

'Tomorrow.'

'Tonight.' Lapeyre turned his wrist over and stared at his Rolex. 'It's only 2100 hours.'

'My team is exhausted, we've been on our feet since the small hours this morning.'

'Capelle doesn't need much sleep.'

'Lapeyre –'

'Look, Pel, we've come to a compromise on the handling of the operation, let's try and agree on when. It's got to be tonight.'

'Why?'

'If it turns out to be a hoax, I'll need to speak to Silver again. She's not stupid by any means; keep her in overnight and she'll be bellowing for a lawyer at dawn. I must know who's in the house while she's still in custody. Now Colin's dead, she may be our only link to Dalton. When the news of the boy's death is made public tomorrow morning, the occupants are almost bound to make some comment, proving their innocence or otherwise. Our equipment must be in place by then, I want their voices recorded.'

'I can't authorize that!'

'I can. Let me use Silver's twenty-four hours to tap their private conversations. If I haven't got a lead on Dalton by then, I'll concentrate on her and you can take whatever action you see fit. Pimps and pushers are ten a penny, putting them away might help your list of statistics for this year but it won't stop the oldest profession in the world, or kids killing themselves with heroin, and what Dalton is doing is much worse.'

'Mixing the two into a tragic cocktail.'

'That's right.'

'It's not just drugs and prostitution though, is it, Lapeyre?'

Lapeyre shook his head. 'No, unfortunately it's not.'

'I need you to explain to the team, they must understand what we're dealing with.'

'You've worked it out, haven't you?'

'I think so.'

'And you've discussed it with no one?'

'Correct.'

'I'm going to have to insist on your continuing discretion. Letting your men in on the whole truth makes us vulnerable. If something, just a whisper, is leaked, the shop'll shut up tight, we won't even get our fingers in the door. The fewer people who know the better. Don't forget, Silver found out about Colin somehow.'

'If she didn't know already.'

'For the moment, I have to presume she didn't.'

'Lapeyre, I refuse to work with my men only half in the know. Remember what happened last June; Lambert kept certain information to himself and Darcy died.'

Lapeyre sighed. 'I know, but this is different. It's not terrorists this time, the men involved are clever and protected. Just for the record, if we make a mistake, you and I may find ourselves out of a job.'

'If we make a mistake, I'll definitely be on the dole, Lambert's already said so. But until I am sacked, I intend doing my duty properly and that means without putting my men, any of them, unnecessarily at risk.'

'I'll give you the goods, everything I know. I need a research terminal to do it, and after that, I hope you'll understand my caution. In the meantime, you need to cover yourself. La Police de la Police are investigating Morrison, and indirectly you. Lambert must sign before you move a muscle. Request radio and visual surveillance until 1800 tomorrow, and eventual entry to seize contraband – something along those lines. I'll countersign it, that way he won't raise any objections.'

As a car set off for Lambert's home, where he was waiting to autograph the carefully worded paperwork, Lapeyre followed Pel to the room Rigal occupied during normal working hours – and which he was still occupying at 2235 that night. Pel didn't knock, just walked straight in. 'What have you on the three "*blaireaux*" sites?'

Rigal scanned up his screen. 'Blerard: La Garrigue, owner, Jean-Paul Robert; 19 hectares of vineyards; wife, Paulette; two children, five and seven; local councillor; no convictions. *Plan d'eau*: Les Barthes, owned by Englishman, David Pugh; wife, Nicola; three children, eleven, sixteen, seventeen; he works for an insurance company, commutes between France and London;

she speaks good French, he doesn't; no criminal record. Plériot: Le Bourg, owner Angelo Dinero, no wife, no children; inherited the farm from his uncle, Mario Dinero; house was on the market, but was withdrawn after three weeks, still raising pigs on the property; no convictions.'

'How old is Dinero?'

'Thirty-three, born illegitimately, adopted by Pierre Malfaite when he married his mother, changed his name back to Dinero when his mother died.'

'Dinero,' Lapeyre repeated. 'Means nothing to me but "black" in Italian.'

Pel looked up, his face creased in concentration. 'What did you say?'

'Nero, it means black –'

'Just a minute . . . something Sarrazin, the journalist said . . . He told me Luzanne hangs out with a man known as the Black Angel. Loosely translated Angelo Dinero means . . . This has to be the one. What else have you got on him, Rigal?'

'Six-month-old BMW 320 coupé, registered in his name, plus a 1981 Land Rover, still registered in his uncle's name, bought from a *vignoble*, Lescarret, in 1996.'

'Who lives on the farm with him?'

'According to the mayor of the village, he lives alone, which doesn't tally with the report from the local gendarmerie who, when they visited, were told by a farm labourer's daughter that she couldn't open the gate, she didn't have the key and the boss was out working in the fields.'

'One of his trainees sent out to see them off?'

'Could be. Phone numbers?'

'A land line: 04 34 59 12 15. Plus a monthly payment to SFR for a mobile: 06 64 43 80 02.'

'Good work, Rigal,' Lapeyre said immediately. 'Get on to them, we need to intercept from their satellite. All calls, in and out, immediately. Capelle will deal with the land line. Go up to Pel's office, give them your instructions from his terminal, they'll agree without question if it comes from a Commissaire's address.'

'I've got a direct contact from here, sir. They know me.'

'I'm delighted,' Lapeyre replied, 'but I need to use your machine, in private.'

As Rigal closed the office door, Lapeyre sat down, closed the program operating on the computer and opened another, punching numbers into the keyboard.

As the screen came to life again, Pel pulled a second chair across and sat alongside Lapeyre, now tapping code words in. After five minutes' manipulation, during which the lighted information in front of them changed a dozen times – none of which meant anything to Pel – a young coloured girl came clear. She was holding up her hand to hide part of her face.

'That's Sofia,' Lapeyre said. 'She's twenty-two, from Somalia and spent four years working in Paris for a Djiboutien diplomat.' He clicked on *'Suivant'*; the screen changed. Another young girl. 'Solange, nineteen, from the Ivory Coast. This one: more than ten years unpaid "employment", the Secours Catholique found her, undernourished and unconscious. Here's another one: Ismah, Indonesian, sixteen months working for the Sultanat d'Oman. And she,' he clicked on a title, 'started her nightmare at the age of fourteen. Have you seen enough, or shall I continue?'

Pel sighed. 'You've made your point. Tell me, those cases were here in France, does it happen elsewhere?'

'Name a country, any country; it's going on all over the world.'

'So how can we expose the bastards using these girls?'

'Le Comité Européan Contre l'Esclavage Moderne was set up on 4th December 1999, it does what it can, it's made a good start. Statutes are written and adopted by various governments, society is being made aware, but the trouble is, as you've seen, the men interested in buying are often visiting dignitaries. Then the problem multiplies; it's not just a question of morality, there are the political implications to consider as well.'

'But they're breaking the law!'

'Once you cross the threshold of a foreign embassy, the laws of its own country apply, not the country in which the building stands. They'd have to be practising outside the embassy – which they don't.'

'For God's sake, we must be able to do something.'

Lapeyre reached for Pel's packet of cigarettes and took one out. 'Stop the supply,' he said and lit up. 'The trade of nubile young bodies is making fortunes. First the girls pay for a European work permit and the passage into a host country. If they can't pay, they carry dope. This one,' the screen flickered and reignited to show a corpse, curled into the foetal position, thin legs poking out from a long skirt, 'Istrah, just twenty, was found at Charles de Gaulle airport. She'd swallowed ten plastic sachets of heroin. She died of a massive overdose when one of the bags burst in her stomach.'

'Jesus.'

'At the time, the enquiry was dealt with by the drugs squad. Automatically, the details came to us, in case the funds from drug trafficking were going into terrorism. But it was only recently I made the connection with Burgundy. Traces of benzo-diazepine were found in the suicide, Théodora Roussillon, then Sandrine Da Costa died. Between us we came up with a number of other mixed drug deaths. That's when I began wondering if one of the men selling slaves – let's face it, that's what they are – had cut his costs down to a minimum and was recruiting here in France, using ordinary medication to persuade the girls into co-operating. My research made me look more closely at a report on a house in Bordeaux. When it was closed down, the young prostitutes were treated and rehabilitated, their sponsor escaped. I discovered Dalton had been withdrawing money from a central cash machine for two weeks; the day before the Brigade des Mœurs made their raid, he stopped.'

'If it was him and not just his card in someone else's hands.'

'Indeed. I think, in view of the fact he was supposed to be crippled after his Porsche crashed twenty-three years ago, your idea of him establishing a false trail is more than credible. However, even cripples move around, it's possible he can still drive, and he must be somewhere, working from a base, another supposedly "safe" house. I'm hoping he moved from Bordeaux to the farm at Plériot, or at least near it; the timing is right. The situation too, as we saw on the *cadastre* map; it's isolated, well away from the village, surrounded by trees and fields, with a good view of the approaching road. It may be only a terminal where girls are prepared before being sold on to their new owners, but I'm sure he's involved.'

'Slavery in Burgundy,' Pel muttered, shaking his head. '*Mon dieu*, whatever next?'

'Unscrupulous men have always found a way round the law, camouflaging their illegal operations with an innocent-looking front. Running an international matrimonial agency, for instance; desperate to avoid the arranged marriages and sometimes cruel husbands in their homelands, the girls are promised a new nationality and a new name. An employment agency, offering bona fide work permits with "well-placed" employers and free lodging. We've even come across a charity for misplaced persons which claims to find jobs and housing for kids who've managed to get themselves into Europe but now find themselves destitute and desperate. They've all been closed down.'

'Here in France?'

'Europe, Pel. The epicentre of Earth's civilization.'

'*Quelle honte.* We're worse than animals; their justification for killing and copulating is survival. *Homo sapiens'* is greed.'

'And self satisfaction.'

Pel sighed tiredly. 'Lapeyre, I'm getting too old for this game. There was a time when life held few surprises for me, you get used to man's inhumanity to man in the police force, but, if what you say is true, I'm prepared to listen to suggestions – whatever they are.'

'Corner Dalton.'

'But apparently he doesn't even bother with a front. He simply sends Luzanne out to pick up pretty girls. Do you think he's calling himself Dinero now?'

'I doubt it, but he may be. A pimp in Bordeaux referred to a man known as Goldilocks, presumably a bastardization of Goldstein; his given name at birth. Goldilocks, Black Angel, why not?'

'He was a medical student, wasn't he?'

'For five years.'

'Which would explain his knowledge of pharmaceutical drugs and their side effects. And which also indicates a man of keen intelligence. My next-door neighbour's son was doing medicine, he's a very bright youngster, and he failed the first year, twice.'

'You're beginning to understand what we're up against; Dalton is no ordinary criminal.'

'So why pick on Sandrine?'

'You said yourself, it's Luzanne who makes the first contact, he wasn't careful enough. Until Sandrine, he'd chosen girls that were a long way from home, cut off from their families; when they disappeared, no one noticed, no one kicked up a fuss. Sandrine was thought to be the orphan Gina Da Costa; they didn't know she was also the niece of a policeman. Had Dalton been aware of that, he would've probably sent Luzanne out with her to be shot at the tobacconist's.'

'Poor kid. She must have resisted her treatment, a mixture of medication to make her co-operate with his plans for unpaid prostitution . . .'

'Plus her imposed addiction to heroin.'

'. . . and as a result, she was conned into committing armed robbery, with a gun that didn't go bang, in the hope that she'd be conveniently disposed of.' Pel paused to light up. 'Perhaps Dalton did find out who she was.'

'I don't think so. Had that been the case, she'd've been dealt with more quietly; a simple overdose somewhere in a university building. No, I believe they wanted her violent death made public, perhaps as a lesson to other obstinate girls. Which would mean they all speak and read French.'

The two men studied each other's serious face. It was Lapeyre who broke the silence. 'Now you know why I want Dalton so badly.'

'*D'accord*, but the secrecy still seems excessive.'

Lapeyre turned back to the computer and tapped in a new series of figures, followed by a further code word. 'Because, as you pointed out, Dalton is clever, exceptionally clever. And because most of the men using the girls are protected by diplomatic immunity' – six male figures appeared on the screen, all handsome, neatly groomed, expensively dressed and well nourished, one of them a well known French politician – 'and,' Lapeyre finished, 'because of him.'

'He can't be implicated.'

'He is.'

'I don't believe it.'

'If I'd told you last year that the son of our well-loved and highly respected – now dead, fortunately for him – ex-President Mitterand would be accused of selling arms to Angola, would you have believed that?'

Chapter Twelve

St Cédric. At one minute past midnight, an unmarked Citroën Xantia moved out of the Hôtel de Police's forecourt and turned left into the quiet tree-lined avenue. The street was almost empty, just one car trailing its tail lights, heading out of town. Cheriff was driving, Nosjean was studying a map in the passenger seat. Capelle was stretched out on the seat behind, hands behind his head, knees slightly bent; his attitude suggested someone relaxing in the afternoon sun. He was dressed from head to foot in black; in his hand he held a commando's balaclava, also black. Following the Xantia were Pel and Lapeyre in the borrowed Peugeot.

Once they were out of the city, Capelle sat up and watched the dark countryside slip silently by. There were few lights still showing from the dwellings dotted across the hillsides; an occasional bedroom window shone yellow in the distance; a huge modern cow shed glowed between the trees in the valley. There were hardly any cars. After Christmas and the New Year, Burgundy's inhabitants were behaving surprisingly well for a Friday night. The clubs and discos would empty as dawn approached but they hoped to be at home in their own beds by then.

Pel yawned, shivering involuntarily as he shut his mouth, wishing the operation was over, and looked across at Lapeyre. He seemed totally untouched by the danger Capelle faced. If the dogs' interest was roused at the farmhouse, if the fence was wired with an alarm, if he happened to break a tile on the roof as he climbed towards the chimney to lower his bug into the cavity and hence into the main room of the house, if he slipped and fell . . . if something went wrong he'd have to send Nosjean and Cheriff in, plus Marteau's men waiting just outside Plériot.

If something went wrong, there'd most likely be shooting and wounded.

If something went wrong – again.

Cheriff slowed to a stop, doused his lights, and reversed back into the cover of the small copse they'd chosen. The reversing light turned the overhanging trees behind momentarily red, ominous and sinister.

Nosjean climbed out as Pel parked the Peugeot alongside. 'That's as close as we can get, *patron*, without going into the private track, and there's no cover there.'

'Not even a bush for a quick leak. I'd better take one now.' Capelle moved towards the trees and turned his back.

Opposite, in the patchy moonlight, they could just make out the black ribbon snaking its way over the fields on through the well-spaced pig pens, leading to the gate, and behind that, the farmhouse with its single external lamp. Three other lights were lit, one at the back of the house, two upstairs.

'How far?'

'According to the map, 978 metres. Contact Marteau?'

Pel nodded. 'Check his men are in position.'

Lapeyre said, 'We'll have to wait for all the house lights to extinguish.'

They waited.

Nosjean, Cheriff, Capelle, Marteau's men, Pel and Lapeyre. They waited and watched impatiently as the minutes ticked slowly away.

One by one the lights went out.

It was 0215.

'The yard's still illuminated, that's all.'

'Wait half an hour more, I want them well and truly asleep.'

Pel rubbed his red-rimmed eyes and lit the thousandth cigarette.

At two forty-five, a tall dark figure pulled the balaclava over his head, eased his hands into two pairs of gloves – one no more than a second skin to prevent fingerprints being left, the second thicker for protection, while climbing for instance – checked his pockets, and walked away.

There was little moonlight now, the slim crescent that helped him find his way disappeared from time to time behind thick clouds promising more rain. He would have preferred no moon at all. Capelle felt secure in a shadowless world of darkness. His eyes gradually adjusted, shapes became clearer as he made his way down the track, trotting steadily along the grassy ridge in the middle, avoiding the unseen potholes and puddles, and keeping noise to a minimum.

As he advanced, he glanced to either side, looking for a possible escape route. His thigh was doing fine, he hoped it wouldn't let him down if he had to scale the perimeter fence in a hurry and run for it. To the left and right were ploughed fields. Running uphill across soggy ploughed fields was hard work in daylight, the mud clogging thickly to the soles of shoes, but at night it was dangerous, stumbling and falling lost precious minutes when being pursued, making you a sitting target for aiming night sights. Sprinting back up the track would be suicide, like a three-legged rat limping up a drainpipe with a shotgun shoved in the other end. He'd just have to be careful and not get caught, that way he would walk out.

A noise overhead halted him abruptly. He crouched low, holding his breath, and saw an owl coming shrieking through the silence, its face pale, its eyes bright, like a ghost. Then it was gone.

So was the farmhouse, hidden behind the brow of a gentle hill. He'd been working his way down into a shallow valley.

Then the track began to rise, not much, but enough for his thigh to start aching. He slowed to a walk, keeping low as he came closer to the top of the slope. His feet made little sound, padding quietly beneath him. His ears pricked for anything else.

As the farm came into sight again, he sank to the ground, blending himself into the contours, eyes wide, watching, listening, for movement ahead. There was none. There should have been dogs prowling.

Below, the hillside evened out into the blanket of night, the distant rolling landscape relieved only by the dull silhouette of trees, grouped together, looking like dinosaurs, hunched in the hollows. And to either side, the moon occasionally illuminated the pigs' corrugated metal shelters. The enclosures seemed empty but, after a few seconds, he heard a sleepy grunt; the animals were there, sleeping and dreaming of whatever pigs dream of. If pigs dream at all. He smiled to himself, amused by the stupidity of his train of thought, and set off down the remaining 400 metres of track.

He could see the barns and house more clearly, the fuzzy

orange spot over the front door made the corners of the building sharp there. Nothing was moving. Where were the dogs?

It started to rain. Lightly at first. Growing heavier. It was an advantage, raindrops pattering on roof tiles would be an adequate cover for any accidental sound.

At 50 metres, he stopped again. The gates ahead were brand new, riveted sections of smooth aluminium, a heavy looping chain holding them together, secured no doubt with a stout padlock. Too noisy to risk, not only would it set the dogs off – wherever they were – but the tinny echo might alert an inhabitant. From their constant use, people recognized the sound of their own front gates.

The fence looked flimsy in the insipid light; like a spider's web strung between the slim concrete posts that stuck up like candles on a cake. Possibly electrified or attached to an alarm. Possibly not. He thought not, that's what the dogs were for – if they existed. Could Colin have been mistaken about the prowling hounds? Were they part of his drugged nightmare, along with the dragons and demons? No, the gendarmerie had confirmed canine agitation. They could be inside. Or chained up. He had to be sure. Nothing worse than getting your arse eaten just as you're tiptoeing through the tulips. It hurt too. Capelle didn't enjoy pain. He'd put up with plenty in his career with Lapeyre, he didn't want any more.

Picking up a pebble, he hurled it at the wire. As it hit, the chain link rattled, the sudden sound amplified by the silence, and immediately he heard barking. Two Alsatians came bounding into sight. They stopped, sniffed, one cocked his leg on the wheel of an elderly Land Rover, then, having circled several times, they turned and trotted off, presumably to the comfort of their kennels. Two dogs; affirmative.

To gain access to the final perimeter fence, he had to climb in and out of a pig enclosure. Going in was no real problem. He backed up the track to a safe distance, scaled the shoulder-high chain link, keeping vibrations to a minimum, leaning into the post to swing his legs over, twisted, jumped and landed in thick mud. Messy buggers, pigs. It occurred to him that they too used their teeth if their emotions were roused, and he moved as quickly as possible down the field, keeping to the edge where the ground was firmer.

The final fence – the one that could be electrified – surrounding the house was higher, 2m 50 maybe 3 metres, smaller gauge, too small to get a grip with his feet. He'd need a helping hand over that. There was no cover on the far side, just 200 metres of flat ground. It too looked muddy. Footsteps in squelching mud that close to home could reawaken the dogs. He didn't want to bring them back. He skirted round to the west, the single light disappearing behind the building as he stumbled on through the dark, almost total at that moment, temporarily dazzled by staring into the spotlit yard. The moon was completely covered by storm clouds. His toe caught on an unseen object and, involuntarily, he reached out to save himself, caught the wire between his fingers. No electric current. No noisy alarms. He breathed in slowly and deeply, allowing his eyes to finish adjusting, studying the scene. On the other side, another flat area. Paler. Seeing the rain rebound, he thought it must be concrete, for pig lorries to turn. It would have to do.

Pulling two hooked loops of nylon webbing from his back pockets, he reached up to insert one hook into the mesh suitably close to the stout concrete post, where the chink of the chain links would be barely audible. Bringing up his right foot, he inserted it in the loop. Bouncing gently, he took his weight on that leg and stepped up into the loop, already 60 centimetres off the ground. Lifting the left hook level with his shoulder, he positioned it on the other side of the post, letting the loop dangle, and inserted his left foot. Holding the webbing with his left hand, he stepped up again and moved his whole body weight to that side in order to reposition the right-hand loop. Hardly a sound and he was 1m 20 above ground level; thigh giving warning signs but taking the weight. Right hand hook up, foot in loop, relief as his weight shifted away from the bolted femur. Only a 30 centimetre rise; too hurried, a wasted lift. Once more he shifted his weight to the left, rising correctly this time. His thigh was screaming stop. He was sweating. Rapidly up on to right leg, pain subsiding. Breathing returning to normal. On to left, daggers digging at his groin. Taking some of the weight with his arms, level out with right loop. Time to go over the top. Leaning into the post, pivoting his body on taut stomach muscles, he carefully unhooked each of the two loops, twisted round and placed them on the other side of the fence, both high. One leg went over, then the second. Stop, check, take a breath. He started down the other side. Weight to the right; right. Weight to the left; double-bladed scissors working their way into his nervous system. Weight to the right; fine. Weight to the left; knives, darts, hacksaws . . . He looked down, low enough to jump, sod being a handicapped Spiderman. Unhooked the higher of the two loops – might need it later – and dropped quietly to the ground. And nearly fell as sharp arrows of pain shot from his weakened femur, making him gasp. Balls on fire. Bugger the weather. He stood motionless for a moment, then, retrieving the second strip of nylon webbing, packing it away, zipping the pocket, he made his way to the shadows of a wall.

Crouching under the overhang of the house, he took thirty seconds' recovery time, letting the perspiration grow cold, making him shiver. He pulled off the first layer of gloves and rubbed his damaged thigh, tight and hot under his fingers. As his heartbeat calmed, he assessed the situation. The roof was out of the question, it was much higher than it had seemed from the car on the hill. The dripping trees, which had appeared to be growing against the building, were 5 metres away. He wished there'd been time for a helicopter recce. Too bad. He'd have to improvise. Throwing a grappling hook would wake the dead – he smiled, he didn't have one.

He knew this was where the operation became seriously illegal; he had to break in. He'd had the usual warning: 'If you physically enter the house and are caught, you'll be denied, and Pel's back-up, no more than a taxi service really, will be withdrawn.' Before leaving the Hôtel de Police, Lapeyre had also removed his identity card, wallet and house keys, saying, 'Rather like old times, *n'est-ce pas?*'

Three windows on the wall he was leaning against. All closed with shutters. The back door with two panels of glass was locked. He picked the pen light out of a breast pocket and swept the interior with its powerful beam. Oval table, wooden chairs, fridge, sink. He was looking at a kitchen. He was listening to his heart thud, constant and heavy in his chest. Two and a half minutes later, with the help of a roll of tape, a vacuum pad and a glass cutter, his hand was inside, spraying the locks with lubricant from a small plastic bottle. He turned the key, slipped back the bolts. Removing his shoes, to avoid leaving unsightly footprints – not through respect for the housekeeper – he twisted the handle and insinuated himself through the aperture, putting his feet gently on to the floor, pushing the door closed behind him. Open doors create draughts. Draughts create problems; rattling a folded newspaper, making a candle flicker, slamming shut something that was left ajar – another door for instance – or touching a sleeping cheek, opening an eye.

In spite of the small rubber friction pads on the soles of his socks, he felt the coolness of the smooth stone floor under his feet as he made his way towards the table. He knelt, peered under it and pressed a tiny microphone, 1.5 centimetres in diameter, into the angle made by one of the legs, and stood up.

One down, three to go.

Heart thumping good time.

Rain tapping on the window pane.

He went to an internal door and eased it open.

Utility room.

Closed it carefully and crossed to a second.

The old-fashioned catch snapped up, metal on metal, the sound loud in his ears. He waited, heard nothing, and moved into the room. A fireplace with easy chairs, low table, two empty glasses, a bottle of Armagnac. He moved to the fireplace, lifted his hand and fingered the old oak of the beam above, searching for a small cavity out of sight.

Second microphone in place.

Two down, two to go.

His heart was going like a sledgehammer.

Thunder rumbled overhead, distant, still a long way off, and, although it was muffled by the shutters, he could hear the rain falling outside.

Rain was a good sound cover.

Storms were bad, storms disturbed.

The fire, now just glowing embers, still threw out a comforting warmth. When it was relit, the crackling and hissing logs would interfere with reception. He wondered if Lapeyre had thought of that when giving his instructions. It occurred to him Lapeyre had known all along that physical entrance would be an obligation.

He swung the pen light round, padding silently after it as it lit the silent walls.

Sideboard; a pair of candelabras, a bowl of fruit, a base with portable on charge. He picked up the cordless phone. A Matra Soléa 200; easy. He unscrewed the aerial, unclipped the coloured cover, and prised the phone apart. Behind the sealed battery was plenty of space for number three. Having pushed the tiny microphone into its new home, he reassembled the phone and put it back on charge.

Three down, one to go, then exit.

Perspiring freely. Pulse pounding.

Another roll of thunder, closer now, a heavy squall hit the

shutters, the raindrops like impatient fingers drumming on the wood.

Had to hurry.

Pictures. One at the base of the stairs with a heavy gilt frame.

Swinging it gently on its hook . . .

A crack of lightning, a short explosion, sharp in the silence, flickering through a woodpecker's work, a small beam of sudden light, piercing the room like a javelin.

He froze. Getting fear under control.

And above him someone turned over in bed, moaning at the effort . . .

The base of his spine tingled unpleasantly.

Exit. Exit!

He let the picture fall back into place, checked it was straight.

For a moment, he remained rigid, ears straining, the hair on the back of his neck rising, prickling his skin in warning, then, touching his still throbbing thigh, his senses twitching, he moved back towards the fireplace. As he went, he picked up a silver candelabra.

He thought he heard a floorboard creak; the moaner, woken by the storm, needing the bathroom?

Still tuned to the whisper of movement, adrenaline pumping, he dropped the remaining microphone into the embers and padded silently towards the kitchen and his way out.

The rain was pounding on the car's roof as Nosjean twisted in his seat. 'He's been gone a hell of a long time.'

Lapeyre clicked on his torch and looked at his watch. 'Ten minutes to penetrate the property, ten minutes inside, ten minutes back, maximum; he should've been back by now. Try the receiver.'

Nosjean pulled up his collar and climbed out to slap the magnetic aerial into place. Dropping rapidly back into his seat, he slammed the door closed. 'It's still pissing down,' he said as he caught the hanging wire, drew it inside, and shut the window on it. Then switching on the dim internal light, he connected the jack plug to a small grey apparatus he now had on his knees. It was no larger than a Walkman but inside it contained the technology to translate the *ondes* received into audible noise, and record it on a tiny cassette. He fingered the controls on either side of the plastic casing, watching the needle quiver uncertainly as he tried to pick up a signal. 'Nothing but static. We'll have to wait for the storm to pass.'

Another knife of lightning split the sky in two, illuminating the undulating countryside below, turning night briefly into day, and four pairs of eyes stared anxiously through the sheeting rain, straining to see the familiar silhouette jogging back up the track. But all they saw were the pig pens, an empty path, closed gates, a deserted farmyard and an apparently silent house. Then it was dark again, pitch black, and their shocked retinas readjusted to focus on the single dull and distant light, winking erratically through the rain.

'He's nowhere in sight.'

'Another light's come on,' Cheriff pointed, 'at the back.'

'You think they've heard Capelle clambering about on the roof?'

Lapeyre cleared his throat and passed a packet of cigarettes round. 'I doubt it,' he said.

'Or falling off?'

'Very unlikely.'

'The dogs savaging him?'

'A possibility,' Lapeyre replied nonchalantly.

'It's gone out again.'

'What's going on?'

'Probably nothing more than someone needing a pee or a glass of water.' Lapeyre clicked his lighter into action then handed it on.

'A light upstairs.'

'Going back to bed.'

'That's gone out now.'

'What do we do?'

'We wait and listen.'

They waited, smoking and, from time to time, listening to the decreasing interference.

At three forty-five, the storm was over. It was still raining hard, hammering on the roof of the car, but the static had stopped. No noise at all from the receiver.

And no Capelle.

Fifteen more minutes passed. As their ears became tuned to the silence, they realized there was a faint sound coming from Nosjean's little box. It took them a while to work it out but, in the end, they all agreed it was the chink of a bottle on a glass, someone was getting slowly drunk. It wasn't much.

A door creaked open, and clicked closed again.

Cheriff sat up, pointing. 'What's that?'

'A torch?'

'Bugger this rain.'

'Keep watching.'

'I can't see a thing.'

'It looks like a torch, the way it's moving. Someone's out there.'

'Looks like two torches now.'

'Switched off.'

'If only we could get in closer.'

'If it stopped ruddy raining for a minute.'

'There they are again.'

'They've gone.'

'Now it's just one again.'

'Gone.'

'Must be looking for an intruder.'

'Let's hope they don't find him.'

Dawn crept pale and grey over the horizon like a hesitant bride tiptoeing from her bed with a headache, not wanting to wake her lover. The sun's watery rays gradually spread across the colourless countryside, flowering slowly into the saturated valleys, tingeing the swaying trees with gold, cautiously lighting the shadows, showing the shapes that had been hidden by night.

A bitter wind, as sharp as knives, whistled up the bleak hillside, the grass bent flat along the verge; it was as if the weather was at last taking its revenge for the mild days of December. The four men in the car stretched wearily and yawned, cursing the cold, rubbing their hands and blowing on their fingers.

'Capelle won't be coming out now, not in broad daylight. Where the hell is he?'

'If he disturbed them, Pel, he'll be hiding,' Lapeyre replied. 'Don't worry, he knows how to behave.'

'I'm bloody freezing.'

'So am I but I'm not satisfied. I must find out who's in there. Be patient.'

'For how long, until the summer comes?'

Nosjean suddenly lifted his binoculars. 'Someone's out in the yard.'

Lapeyre lifted his. 'Can't make out who it is.'

'It can't be Capelle.'

'He's gone behind an outbuilding.'

'No, there he is again.'

'He's going back to the house.'

'Listen!'

A door groaned open and slammed shut. There were footsteps, growing louder as they came into range, then they had the pleasure of hearing one side of a telephone conversation:

'Goldstein, this is Luzanne. Angel's done a bunk . . . Last night I reckon. After I cornered the burglar . . . Yeah, that's right . . . No problem, I let him have it, you know the gun you gave me, always keep it loaded . . . Angelo seemed upset, in a right panic. I went to bed after, he stayed up to calm his nerves with another Armagnac. When I went out this morning to feed and lock up the dogs, he'd gone, so's the jeep . . . Through the back gate . . . Of course I'm sure it was a burglar, I caught the bugger with the silver in his hands. I frisked him and everything, there was nothing else, not even his papers, but I found his tools and stuff by the back door . . . Tall and hairy bastard, wearing a hood, soon had that off him . . . Bury him? But I . . . Look, Goldy, I don't like it. What with Angel gone and everything. It's giving me the creeps. I can't run this place on my own . . . No, it's just that . . . Well, this isn't the way it was supposed to be. You said . . . No, no, it's okay, but what about Angel? . . . Honest? . . . What time? . . . Any time's fine by me . . . About eleven, how's that? . . . Yeah, sure, I'll get one of the girls to rustle something up . . . Thanks, see you later . . .'

'Well,' Pel growled viciously. 'Are you satisfied now?'

Lapeyre frowned, muttering to himself. 'Capelle shot? He can't have been. In and out of the house, nothing simpler.'

'*In* the house! He was supposed to be –'

'That's not important . . . Goldstein is. How did the Angel slip through?'

'In the old Land Rover?'

'Why didn't we see him?'

'The rain reduced our vision to almost zero.'

'We did see what looked like two torches, they were only lit briefly, so Luzanne wouldn't notice, I would imagine, the shutters are open upstairs.'

'But they didn't go anywhere.'

'The single one did. He must've been hanging out of a window with the torch, to light his way through the woods, then away across the fields.'

'The cunning bastard –'

'For heaven's sake!' Pel cut in irritably. 'Who cares how he did it? The point is he did. Nosjean, call Rigal, he's got all the details; *avis de recherche*, immediately.'

'And find out if SFR recorded Luzanne's call, it would help to have the other half. They might be able to give us Goldstein's location.'

'And Capelle?'

Lapeyre's eyes glittered hard and cold. 'There's no point worrying about him any more, is there?' he replied angrily.

Pel picked out a Gauloise and lit it. 'Luzanne called his boss Goldy.'

'Short for Goldstein.'

Pel paused, puffing thoughtfully on his cigarette. 'It goes well with Silver.'

The car was filled with an unpleasant hush.

'You think this *is* a set-up? It can't be. If that's the case, why kill Capelle?'

'Because Luzanne's a murdering thug.'

Nosjean turned in his seat. 'SFR didn't get the conversation; their instructions were to intercept everything passing on Dinero's number, for which there's been nothing so far. Luzanne must have his own mobile.'

'*Merde!*'

'If Luzanne's getting one of the girls to rustle something up, Goldstein must be coming for lunch.'

'What time did he say?'

'About eleven.'

Pel pushed his jacket cuff up and looked at his watch. 'I suggest we go down there now, arrest Luzanne, bring Capelle out, and wait for Goldstein inside, out of sight.'

'Too risky. Luzanne's already nervous, possibly ready to panic. If he sees two unknown cars approaching, he will. We don't know how many people are in there; men, or,' he added ominously, 'girls. We could provoke a massacre.'

'For God's sake, all we've heard so far is Luzanne's voice –'

The receiver sprang into life, interrupting Pel. 'Get yourselves smartened up, we've got an important visitor arriving at eleven and I want the place looking good.'

Pel sighed. 'That's buggered that idea.'

'And tell Marteau to move the road blocks. If Goldstein's coming in, I don't want him frightened off. We don't know what he looks like, we don't know what car he has. We're going to have to let him drive right up to the door.'

Plériot police station wasn't used to visiting dignitaries. It was almost as good as the annual gathering for 14th July. The nearest they'd come to dealing with a dangerous criminal in the last twelve months was when a pair of peasants were involved in a hunting accident. The accident didn't merit their intervention, just one man's hat holed by shot and rolled in the mud, until, that is, they started fighting and bloodying each other's noses – that's when a witness pulled his phone out of his pocket and called for help. By the time the navy blue gendarmerie break arrived, the two stocky and extremely muddy old men were back to back, preparing for a full scale duel. Only a few more weeks and the locals' hunting rifles would be cleaned and polished and put back in their racks for another year, it was a relief. In the meantime, Adjutant-Chef Moustrous was wondering what today's excitement was all about. The *caserne*'s small forecourt seemed crowded with cars. Doors were being slammed, heads put together confidentially, and mobiles clasped in earnest hands.

Sergeant Boyout nudged him. 'The little one with specs, that's Commissaire Pel.'

'Will he be coming in? Or does he want to hold his party out there?'

His question was answered as the men outside turned towards the building. A moment later, when Pel introduced himself, Moustrous executed his best salute.

'Yes, jolly good,' Pel replied absently, holding out his hand to be shaken. 'We need your support in a small operation we're planning.'

'Yes sir! Certainly sir!'

'No need to shout, where can we talk?'

Pel calmly briefed Moustrous who, having clarified various points, volunteered every one of his men.

'Eight will be enough, spread out behind the house along the edge of the woodland, here.' Pel moved his finger across the map. 'Colonel Lapeyre and Nosjean are hidden here, watching the site and listening for any further conversation which may help. The road blocks we'd set up have been removed temporarily, to let the wanted man through. Once our target is in, you will move into position. Two of Marteau's men will take over from

Lapeyre and Nosjean, the others will be coming with us to the farmhouse. The medics and ambulances will approach and wait here. Any questions?'

'Not at the moment, sir.'

Glancing up at the wall clock, Pel sighed unhappily. 'You've got an hour and a half to organize it. Be ready by ten thirty.' He replied to Moustrous' smart salute with a nod as the Adjutant-Chef left, then looked up at the remaining faces, one of which shouldn't have been present.

'What are you doing here? You're supposed to be resting.'

Gilbert relieved an itch in his armpit. 'Can't sleep a wink, guv. It's Colin . . . I want the bastard that killed him.'

'No heroics, no unnecessary violence. We're going in to arrest and remove, d'accord?'

'D'accord, guv.'

Alex Jourdain's spiky blonde hair turned towards Pel. 'Where's Capelle, patron?'

'He didn't come out.'

The Punk's eyebrows rose abruptly. 'He was caught?'

'Something like that.'

'What do you mean, patron?'

'Ask Lapeyre!'

Alex frowned but she said no more.

'De Troq', did you see Silver?'

'She'd gone, before I had a chance to speak to her.'

'Gone?'

'She was allowed her phone call late last night. First thing this morning, a big shot lawyer came in with all the appropriate papers and demanded her release. I checked with Lambert and Maître Brisard, and it was agreed the lawyer was within his rights, she was only being held on suspicion of criminal complicity and/or intent. There was no proof and no specific charges to be brought, we had to let her go.'

'Lapeyre will be delighted.'

'Patron?'

'Have you got the handguns?'

'Enough for the team. Marteau's supplying for his men.'

'Bullet-proof vests?'

'We'll all be wearing one.'

Ten thirty came and went. The groups of men, uniformed and plain-clothes police, medics and ambulance drivers, fidgeted and shuffled round one another in the gendarmerie offices. Outside, the vehicles were lined up in order, ready to move out.

Eleven o'clock.

Eleven fifteen; Pel's stomach rumbled. They'd been offered breakfast by Moustrous' wife but he hadn't been hungry at nine, too much to do and worry about, just a cup of coffee to wake him up. Now his stomach felt as if it might cave in any minute. His eyes were itching with tiredness, his head ached and his mouth felt like the bottom of a bird cage with all the cigarettes he'd smoked. And the end was still a long way off.

His mobile trilled, making him jump. He wrenched it out of his pocket and listened to the whispered words. 'Lapeyre *à l'appareil*. Metallic grey Renault Saffrane just turned into the track. One man inside. Black curly hair flecked with grey. Wearing glasses. Get moving.'

'Affirmative.' Pel cut the communication. 'Everybody out!'

It started raining again as they moved out of the forecourt. The windscreen wipers flipped back and forth, rhythmically, hypnotically. Pel allowed his heavy eyelids to sag, he'd been on his feet for nearly thirty-three hours non-stop. For what seemed like a second, the whole world and all his problems faded into delicious oblivion, then he woke, startled, as Lapeyre climbed in behind him. Nosjean slipped in behind Cheriff and closed the door.

'Dalton's been inside for ten minutes now,' Lapeyre said. 'They should be sipping their first drink. Take it nice and easy, Cheriff, the ground's slippery.'

The line of slow-moving cars looked like a train coming into a siding as they halted one behind the other on the waterlogged track. Nosjean walked to the aluminium gates, carrying a large pair of wire cutters. A moment later the heavy padlock was in his hands. The chain separated and slid to the ground. He pushed both the gates open.

The cars surged through, splashing across puddles, halting haphazardly in the yard, spraying mud as they stopped. Doors flew open, policemen poured out, to the left, to the right, fanning out along the perimeter fence. Dogs started barking from unseen kennels, the police could hear them leaping at the walls of their cage, growling and howling with savage excitement.

Pel and Lapeyre went rapidly towards the front door. Nosjean, de Troq', Cheriff, Bardolle, Jourdain and Gilbert followed, forming a semicircle, three facing in, the others facing out, keeping their backs covered.

Lapeyre put his ear to the weather-worn wood and listened. Silence.

He lifted the large metal knocker, glanced over his shoulder, and let it drop.

It echoed inside. The place seemed empty.

Then they heard footsteps, a lock being turned, and the door opened.

When he saw the police, the man behind the door turned and fled through the house.

He didn't get far. Lapeyre shot him in the foot.

He fell shrieking to the floor, blood dripping from a hole in his shoe. Without hesitating, Lapeyre holstered his gun, took five short steps and tugged the man's arms behind his back, clipping on the plastic handcuffs.

Three young women came from the kitchen and stood looking terrified. One shuffled forward and knelt by the bleeding man. *'Mais Monsieur Dalton, qu'est-ce qu'il y a?'*

Pel beckoned to the waiting team. 'Search the house,' he said. 'Take care with the girls, we don't know who they are yet.'

Luzanne, having just dug a nice deep hole in which to bury the burglar, began whistling as he walked back from the woods. He hesitated by the open five-bar gate when he heard the dogs' ferocious barking. When he heard the shot, he started to run.

As Pel's team broke their semicircle, Luzanne came round the corner, a garden spade in his hands. And slithered to a stop.

A uniform appeared behind him, placed a hand on his shoulder, opened his mouth to caution his prisoner.

Luzanne side-stepped, swung the spade and caught the unfortunate gendarme on the side of his head, sent him flying. Luzanne dropped the spade, turned and took off, back towards the woods.

Jourdain was the nearest. Slipping as she accelerated away, rapidly regaining her balance, she sprinted across the yard.

De Troq', 75 metres further back, set off after both of them.

As Luzanne reached the beginning of the trees, Jourdain, an efficient sportswoman, had closed the gap. Then she was hurling herself at his back.

The collision knocked Luzanne off balance and the pair of them went down, arms and legs flailing like a great ugly octopus. For a moment, Jourdain's blonde spiky hair disappeared from sight as she tried to maintain control of the much larger man. He was struggling violently, kicking and swearing. They were rolling in the mud, both of them filthy and cursing.

Jourdain had to land a punch, finish the argument for good.

One fist pinned under her, the other, twisted into Luzanne's clothes.

She was losing her grip.

De Troq', where are you!

Then, abruptly, Luzanne was on his feet, pulling something out of his pocket.

Jourdain was spluttering, shaking her head, swiping mud from her eyes, opening them.

Staring into the barrel of a Smith & Wesson.

This one was loaded with real bullets.

Shifted her gaze to Luzanne's cruel face.

Saw his eyes narrow.

Knew he intended killing her.

As he squeezed the trigger, a series of sharp explosions, one following immediately after the other, almost merging, like a powerful firecracker, filled the yard.

Anticipating the impact, involuntarily she'd closed her eyes. Felt nothing. Snapped them open again. Luzanne's arms flew up, he toppled over backwards, folding up as he dropped.

De Troq' lowered his gun.

He started running again, feet pounding, plastering his neatly creased trousers. As he took off, from the corner of his eye, he saw someone else go down.

Nosjean threw himself into the nearest car, snatched up a microphone and screamed, 'Get the medics in – fast!'

When de Troq' fired, he hit Luzanne in the chest; the bullet pierced the right pectoral muscle, penetrating between the fourth and fifth ribs, it glanced off the sternum, which deflected it through the pleura, and punctured a lung before slicing through his heart and exiting beneath his left shoulder blade. Blood bubbled from his mouth and nose. He was dead when de Troq' arrived at his side, but he hadn't died immediately.

The muzzle velocity of de Troq's handgun was 411 metres per second, faster than the speed of sound, and the impact of a bullet travelling at nearly 1,500 kilometres an hour is enormous. It doesn't just make a hole.

As it punched its way into Luzanne, the shock knocked him off his feet, throwing him over backwards, felling him like a tree and, as he fell, the barrel of his Smith & Wesson lifted, away from Jourdain's head. As it rose, another member of the police force came into its sights.

Whether Luzanne saw the man he hit, no one knew, but before his short criminal career was terminated, he too fired, twice.

As de Troq' crouched beside Luzanne's body, smiling reassuringly at Jourdain, congratulating her on her speed and courage, she didn't smile back. Her eyes, wide with surprise, were fixed on something coming across the yard.

He spun round, raising the MAS-G1 once more, taking aim, and relaxed.

It was only God-awful Gilbert galloping towards them. His legs going like pistons, boots spraying grimy water, the jowls of his cheeks bouncing off his jaw. He had an evil look on his flabby face.

Before de Troq' could stop him, he'd seized Luzanne by the hair and was smashing his fist into his face, breaking his nose, loosening teeth.

De Troq' had great difficulty hauling him off. 'For Christ's sake, Gilbert . . .!'

'*Putain d'enculé*!' he shrieked, fighting to get free. 'I'm going to mash his fucking head!'

But the energy had drained out of him.

He stood limply, staring at de Troq'.

He had tears in his eyes as he spoke. 'He just topped the governor.'

224

Chapter Thirteen

Pel lay in an ugly heap, his raincoat twisted uncomfortably round his body, rucked up across his throat. His specs were at an odd angle, bent and broken, one lens splintered, a shard piercing his eyelid, a thin crimson dribble trickling from the tiny wound; it looked as if he was crying his own blood.

As the ambulance sirens wailed from the hillside, coming down the track, growing louder as they approached at high speed, Nosjean lifted the edge of Pel's lapel and replaced it gently. The pale blue shirt collar was already drenched and changing colour. A small but ghastly river of red flowed into the muddy puddle beneath the motionless head. It looked as if someone had spilt a saucepan of badly mixed tomato soup. Nosjean swallowed hard, he knew only too well what it meant; something vital had been ruptured. Pel's chances of survival were very slim.

The first van slewed to a stop. Reversed. Doors were thrown open.

'Over here! *Vite!*'

The *médecin d'urgences* jumped down and hurried towards the body, squatted beside it. Another white uniform joined him, opening a folded thermal blanket as he approached, spreading it over Pel's legs and chest. Calm latex-covered hands explored, searched for a pulse, eased open the raincoat. Qualified eyes calculated the damage. A medical case was snapped open, a large pair of scissors extracted to cut through the outer clothes. Then the confident fingers fumbled and hesitated, struggling to remove the useless bullet-proof vest. Taking precious seconds to undo the heavy garment, Nosjean at last lifted it off and dragged it away, leaving a wide crimson stripe in the dirt. The drenched shirt was sliced into strips and, as the final flap of fabric was peeled away, blood spurted rhythmically on to gloved hands; Pel's life juices were being pumped from a severed artery. Imme-

225

diately, the medic punched the palm of his hand into the cavity. *'Rupture de la carotide.* Guy,' he said to his assistant, 'be ready to replace the pressure.'

Guy's clean cotton trousers knelt in the bloody puddle. The doctor's eyes flicked up briefly to give instructions. 'When I remove my fist, replace it with yours immediately and push like hell. If you don't, he'll bleed to death in a matter of minutes. Don't release the pressure until you're told to. You'll get cramp after a while, you'll want to weep, but you mustn't let go. Do you understand?'

A concentrated head nodded.

'Ready?'

'Ready.'

'Now.' The medic's hand rose. The hideous scarlet fountain sprang up like a small geyser and, for a split second, it seemed Guy wasn't going to react. It seemed he was too horrified, totally unable to help. Then, at last, his fist came down.

The blood bubbled through his fingers.

'Push, man! More pressure!'

'I'll fucking kill him.'

'He's dying anyway.'

A second strong hand slipped under the neck, biceps flexed, tightening visibly under the sleeve of his splattered jacket as he squeezed, and abruptly the pulsing stream stopped.

The doctor straightened up, grabbed his bag and dragged it towards Pel's exploded shoulder.

'Aren't you going to clamp the artery?' Nosjean demanded, startled by their basic, almost barbaric methods.

'To clamp it, I've got to see it,' came the succinct reply as the larger wound was probed. 'Can't afford to waste time on that now, muscle is the safest bet.' As the medic swabbed and began plugging the bleeding crater with cotton wadding, tossing torn and emptied sterile envelopes away as he worked on the fleshy pulp, Nosjean glimpsed fragments of splintered bone, sharp and white, and he wondered where the missing bullet was. One of them hadn't exited. If it had been deflected by the shattered shoulder blade towards his heart, then manipulating him the way he had – the way he'd had to – to get the bullet-proof vest off, could be enough to shift the lethal missile closer to a fatal contact, could be enough to kill the *patron* during the dangerous and unavoidable journey to hospital.

'Well?' Lapeyre snapped, coming to a halt beside them.

The doctor didn't look up. 'He's not dead yet.'

Nosjean turned slowly away. The squalid farmyard was strangely quiet, just a hint of birdsong somewhere far away. And oddly, the hysterical dogs had at last stopped shrieking, someone must have shut them up. He gazed blindly at the wide-eyed, unbelieving faces of what was left of the team; his team – Pel's team. Then for some reason, as Gilbert came into focus, dabbing at his eyes with a grubby handkerchief, his brain clicked into gear.

'We're not finished yet,' he said. 'A thorough search is to be made of the premises. Any and all inhabitants are to be removed. And softly does it, *d'accord*? There may be other youngsters being held here who haven't a clue what's going on, they'll need immediate medical attention and a great deal of understanding.'

Gilbert blew his nose then pushed his handkerchief out of sight.

'Okay, move out.'

As they started the search, Pel's inert form was being inserted through open ambulance doors. Guy, splashed with mud and blood, was shuffling along beside him, lips stretched back over his teeth as he struggled to maintain the pressure. The medic climbed in after him, the doors closed with a click and the van began to move very slowly towards the gates. It stopped twice on the track leading to the road, then gradually disappeared as it made its way carefully along the winding country lanes towards the city.

Nosjean sighed miserably, pulled a packet of Gauloises from his jacket and lit up, then, reaching inside a patrol car, asked to be patched through to the Chief.

There were no other girls, just the three still looking lost in the sitting room, not understanding, not able to answer any questions, holding Lapeyre's smouldering cigarettes between trembling fingers. They were helped gently out to the second ambulance, together with the gendarme Luzanne had concussed, and were taken away for treatment.

Dalton had his foot bound before also being taken under police escort to hospital. He was crying as the car drove him away.

And just before the whole messy affair was wrapped up for the morning, Jourdain kicked in the only remaining locked door. Behind it, she found stone steps leading down to a cellar, and gingerly, calling to de Troq' to bring a torch, she started down into the darkness. It was cold and damp down there, and in the corner, on a worn-out mattress, under a threadbare blanket, they finally found Capelle.

He was curled into a ball, his knees to his chest.

His skin was as white as paper.

Jourdain crouched beside the body, reaching out a shaky hand; she had to make sure.

'About flaming time, Gorgeous. I thought you'd never get here.'

He was extremely weak and, as they helped him to his feet, he yelled with pain, doubling over, clutching at his thighs. As he straightened up, his eyes were fixed on Jourdain, half closed in concentration.

'The bastard got me in the leg, the good one! I've got a lifetime of limping to look forward to.'

De Troq' frowned thoughtfully as they hobbled a little further.

'Me crippled and you don't give a damn.'

Jourdain glanced at him. 'Pel was hit in the neck.'

'Is it bad?'

'Very.'

'So I shut up and limp. Right?'

At twelve thirty, Lambert met Brisard for lunch at the well-known and very expensive restaurant, La Marmite. While they studied the menu, they ordered drinks: a beer for Brisard, tonic water for Lambert.

When Lambert had tasted his tonic water, he looked up and tried to smile, but the satisfaction he wanted to show didn't quite make it to his mouth. 'Sorry I'm late,' he said dully. 'Un-expected developments. Pel was being transported to hospital.'

'Oh, how delightful. Nothing trivial, I hope.'

'He stopped a couple of bullets.'

Brisard's eyes flicked up.

'It was sheer bad luck the vest didn't save him.'

Brisard put his beer down with a click. 'He's dead?'

'Not yet.'

The *juge d'instruction* pushed his glass away. There was an unpleasant silence. Then, 'Will he die?'

'It's a strong possibility.'

Brisard's small eyes hardened. 'He'd better not, Lambert.'

'I beg your pardon?'

'He'd better not,' Brisard repeated coldly.

'I thought you hated his guts.'

'Not enough to want them spread all over the pavement. Where did it happen?'

'Place called Plériot. He was keeping tabs on a dealer. When they had confirmation of his presence, Pel went in to make the arrests.'

'You'll be held responsible, you know.'

'I had nothing to do with it.'

'You're his Chief of Police, you signed the authorization. Or was he out of order again?'

Lambert sighed. 'For once the paperwork was perfect.'

'It doesn't really make any difference, you're still his senior officer and as such –'

'I can't be held responsible for his mistakes!'

'You can and you will, just the way we held Pel responsible for Morrison's. You can't pass the buck this time, Lambert.'

'I'm shocked by your reaction, I thought we'd agreed –'

'You're forgetting, Lambert,' Brisard interrupted, refolding the serviette he'd had on his knees. 'Pel's a difficult little bugger, I wanted him put in his place, not in his coffin; this city needs him.' He stood up slowly. 'And,' he went on, pushing his chair under the table, 'he was here first. I hope you enjoy your lunch. Personally, I just lost my appetite.'

Sarrazin found out early that afternoon.

He verified the facts with the Commissariat and wrote a short article for the evening edition. Having checked it through, he printed it on to clean paper, underlined his instructions in thick red crayon and went out to his car. He dropped his copy in to *La Dépêche*'s offices just before four and didn't wait to speak to the editor. Instead, he drove to the hospital and asked to see the Commissaire. He was told Pel was still in the *bloc opératoire* undergoing further surgery.

'What's his condition?'

'I don't know, monsieur, I'm sorry, I can't tell you any more for the moment.'

As he walked back towards the exit, he noticed Pel's wife, sitting beside her weeping housekeeper in a small waiting room, and changed direction.

Geneviève smiled bravely as he came in. 'There's no news yet.'

'I know,' Sarrazin replied quietly. He dug deep into his mackintosh pocket. 'Here,' he said, pulling out a hip-flask, 'you look as if you might need a drop.'

She took the small silver bottle and thanked him, turning it round in her hands, studying it, lost in thought.

'It's strange, isn't it?' she said at last. 'You and he argued over everything, but now he's . . .' Her whispering voice trailed off as her eyes filled. 'Oh dear, I'm sorry.'

Sarrazin sat down beside her.

'He's a difficult little bugger, madame, and I'm sure he can't be easy to live with, but I'm beginning to understand why you married him. He's one of life's contradictions, isn't he? A bully but kind, bad-tempered but fair, obstinate but open-minded.'

'He's a *very* difficult little bugger, Monsieur Sarrazin, a very difficult but a very intelligent little bugger.'

Madame Routy looked up from her saturated handkerchief. 'Madame! How can you say such things? He's an absolute darling!'

Geneviève stared at her employee – the one Pel called a wicked old witch, or fire-eating dragon, whom he accused of making his coffee with iron-filings, and cooking bats' wings and toads' tails in her cauldron, the woman he sacked several times a day – and started laughing, tears spilling out on to her cheeks.

Still weary, Lapeyre lifted his head from the campbed and wondered what the strange noise was. It had filtered into his dreamless sleep, irritating and niggling.

The borrowed interview room was grey in the fading light; chilly and cheerless, it was the best they'd been able to offer him.

He'd been exhausted when he'd finally finished tying up the loose ends of that morning's tragic operation.

The bleeping continued and, stretching out an arm, he picked his phone off the floor, made the connection, and put it to his ear. '*Oui.*'

'Rigal here, sir.'

'What time is it?'

'1755.'

'Don't you ever go home?'

'Not often at the moment.'

'Any news of Pel?'

'No, sir, no change.'

'Capelle?'

'Luzanne's bullet has been successfully recovered from the vastus lateralis.'

'I beg your pardon?'

'It's the muscle that extends the knee joint.'

'Ah, good. The second femur wasn't fractured then?'

'It was chipped, not broken. He'll heal. He's been moved from *Réanimation* to Room 119.'

'Fine. What did you want?'

'A call was intercepted to Dinero's number. It was answered and music was heard. When the music stopped, after a little more than two minutes, the communication was cut. A second call was answered five minutes later; the same thing. A third has just been made; still nothing but the receiver saying "Hello" and the music. SFR traced the phone to the outskirts of Nîmes. The second time it was 7.5 kilometres to the west. The third, 7.5 kilometres further on, still travelling west. Taking into account the movement of the mobile, I've calculated that he's travelling at a constant 90 kilometres an hour heading in the direction of Montpellier, very probably on the A9 motorway which divides at Narbonne for Perpignan and Spain, or Toulouse where it divides again. Shall I alert the motorway patrols and have him picked up?'

'Yes, and warn them he may be armed and dangerous. What about the caller, is there no clue as to who it was?'

'The calls originated from one of four apartments at 15 rue Rivière, on the outskirts of Auxonne. We've pinpointed the location but don't know which floor.'

'Where's Nosjean?'

'Asleep, sir.'

'Who's awake?'

'De Troq', Bardolle, Jourdain and Gilbert.'

'Okay. Thanks, Rigal. They'll be fine for the search.' He coughed, rubbing his eyes with his free hand. 'Where's Lambert?'

'As far as I know, he's still in his office.'

Lambert clicked the door closed, crossed to his desk and sat down, placing the newly bought newspaper in front of him.

BLOODY SHOOT OUT AT PLERIOT: SANDRINE DA COSTA'S EPITAPH

Acting on evidence of prostitution and misuse of potentially dangerous medication, the police surrounded and cleared a Plériot farmhouse. One man was arrested. A second, Jean-Jacques Luzanne, defended himself with a garden spade, wounding a police officer, then attempted to escape. He was shot dead after firing his Smith & Wesson twice, wounding a second police officer. Three girls between 17 and 21 were removed from the house. Two of them will need psychiatric help once their enforced addiction has been treated. The third is expected to be repatriated with her family in Amsterdam (Holland) during the next few days. E.C.D. Pel (Commissaire, Brigade Criminelle), hit in the neck and shoulder by Luzanne's bullets, is in a critical condition. A hospital spokesman said earlier today he's not expected to survive. J.-L. Lambert (Commissaire Principale) commented, 'Being a criminal detective is a dangerous profession and worsens every year. You only have to look at the statistics to see what I mean. It will be a sad loss for us all if Pel dies.'

If Pel doesn't survive, it will be the second funeral for Lambert's command. In June last year, Cmdt Daniel Darcy was assassinated by a terrorist. Lambert took up his post here 9 tragic months ago.

Uneasily, Lambert passed a hand through his snow white hair. The article implied it was his own command that was at fault; he *was* being blamed – and for more than just Pel.

Strategically placed beside Sarrazin's text, a second headline caught his eye:

DIPLOMATS GO HOME
An Embassy official stated that the unexpected repatriation of five of their staff and families was due to fatigue. 'Living in a foreign country can be very tiring,' a spokesman said. The diplomats . . .

Lambert looked up as someone knocked at the door. He resisted pressing the button on his desk to change the lights in the corridor from red to green. Instead, he shouted, '*Entrez!*'

The *procureur* was already pushing the door to behind him. Lambert shot to his feet and saluted smartly.

It was 2100. Nosjean was on his feet and feeling exhausted. He and Cheriff had snatched a few hours' rest before completing their reports, dictated in desperation to Rigal when their fumbling fingers insisted on hitting the wrong keys. Then, when they'd signed and distributed them to the correct filing trays, as well as mailing copies to various terminals, they went across the road for a beer.

Lapeyre was already there, looking glum, turning a large bowl of cognac round and round on the table.

Nosjean yawned, apologized, gave their order and went to join him.

'What's Dalton saying now?' he asked, easing himself into the booth.

'That his foot still hurts and he isn't who we think he is. He claims he's an actor, paid to hire a car and make the trip to Plériot, introducing himself as John Dalton. He was playing the role of a businessman with problems, keeping his answers to any questions ambiguous. He was to have lunch and leave. He says he was told the whole thing was being recorded by hidden cameras and it was an audition for a film.'

'So why did he react so suspiciously when he opened the door?'

'Frightened out of his wits by all the guns pointing in at him.'

'Do you believe his story?'

'I'm going to have to; his X-rays show no evidence of broken bones – apart from the metatarsal that I demolished.'

Nosjean smiled wearily. 'Had you hoped to do more?'

'Goldstein smashed up his Carrera and himself in 1980.'

'Before he started using the name Dalton.'

'Our man isn't him. The hire car was legitimate, the identity card he produced too; André Matthieu Marsot, born 14th February 1957. He's too young; he was set up, as we were.'

'What about the apartments? *Merci.*' Nosjean picked up his newly delivered beer and drank thirstily.

'One of them was probably Goldstein's, the chaps from SPST are doing their stuff but I'm not expecting much. It was the third we searched and all we found was a bloke who'd been instructed to phone Dinero's number every five minutes and wasn't sure what to do when he stopped answering.'

'To make tracing him easier?'

'You've got it; Goldstein giving us a helping hand.'

'Have the motorway police picked him up yet?'

'Yup. They scraped him off the windscreen. Dinero panicked

and hit the upright of a bridge head on. He wasn't wearing a safety belt.'

'Goldstein couldn't have arranged that.'

'It's been a right fuck up,' Lapeyre said with feeling. 'Luzanne's dead, Dinero's dead, and bloody Goldstein got away, again.'

'Plus Misset's niece.'

'And Capelle's other leg, although in a way, that was a bit of good news. Until Jourdain helped him out of that cellar, I thought he was dead too.' Lapeyre downed a mouthful of cognac. 'And of course, there's Pel. What's the latest?'

'The hospital is horribly reticent to say anything any more, they expected him to die hours ago.'

Chapter Fourteen

St Lucien. Lapeyre turned over on the campbed and set it squeaking again. It'd been like that all night.

He could have gone to a five star hotel and slept in a five star bed. He could have gone back to Paris and slept in his own bed. He'd preferred to doss down in the interview room again. Somehow, luxury or home comforts didn't fit his mood. And every time he turned over, the ruddy campbed's legs squeaked.

Just before six, he finally gave it up as a bad job and went to shower and shave. After breakfast in the Transvaal, he set off for the hospital, stopping en route to buy a handful of *Daims* for Capelle – a chocolate bar he craved like a pregnant teenager – and a packet of Gauloises for Pel.

If he was alive.

Now it was 0700. It was still dark, the hospital car park was almost empty. Pulling on the handbrake, he snatched the cigarette from his mouth and ground it out as he stepped on to the glistening tarmac. It wasn't raining yet, but the forecast was depressing.

Locking the car, he walked slowly towards the main entrance.

Pel couldn't bloody die, not now he'd got Capelle under his command, not now he'd managed to infiltrate the Police Judiciaire in Burgundy. Pel was a good contact and colleague to have, they worked well together, he'd been very useful to la Division Nationale Anti-Terroriste. Apart from the professional respect Lapeyre felt for Pel, he had to admit that, although he could be difficult, he damn well liked the little bugger.

Room 119. He knocked and pushed the door open and, as he entered, was surprised to find Alex Jourdain sitting by Capelle's bed.

She stood up, smiling, and shook his hand. 'Please will you

tell this daft sod, sir, he will not be back at work in a fort-night.'

Capelle looked pale but extremely pleased with himself.

'I wouldn't dare. How are you feeling?'

'Bloody angry.'

'You've recovered from worse.'

'Not about the leg, that's an occupational hazard working with you. I'm angry about Pel. It shouldn't have happened. He was a difficult little bugger but his team is an acceptable replacement for la Division. And I'm not working for that puffed-up ponce, Lambert, or the Belgian called Klein.'

Lapeyre sat down on a spare chair. '*Was* a difficult little bugger?'

'Well, he was, wasn't he?'

'Should I be ordering a wreath?'

'Not as far as I know.'

'So what's the news?'

'Alex here keeps checking. The medics aren't saying much. It doesn't look good.'

'What are they saying about you?'

'If I had someone to look after me at home, I'll probably be allowed out at the end of next week. I'm prospecting for volunteers.'

'Count me out, I'm going back to Paris today. Have you got a home?'

'Not really. Since I arrived in Burgundy I've been living in cardboard boxes and squats. Had a couple of nights in a cheap hotel but most of my kit's in my van. Perhaps I'll have time to look for a base now. I've got nothing much else I can do.'

'Do you want to know what's happened since you were whisked away from the farmhouse?'

'Alex filled me in. We failed, didn't we?'

'Not altogether, we effectively closed down the operation, and one embassy is embarrassed enough to have sent its users home. It's a step in the right direction and the newspapers are making more people aware of the dangers. It could be worse,' Lapeyre sighed, 'although not much. Dalton's still on the loose, or Goldstein, or whatever he's calling himself now, and we've got an *avis de recherche* out for your friend Silver but she appears to have vanished.'

'You reckon she was working for him then?'

'It's a possibility.'

'Maybe she's his mistress.'

'That also is a possibility.'

'Shame, she could've been quite a good-looker.' He winked at Alex. 'Although not really my type.'

Relieved by Capelle's apparent high spirits, Lapeyre dropped the *Daim* bars on the bed and left him and Jourdain, both munching relatively contentedly.

Thoughtfully, he made his way to Intensive Care.

As he was admitted to the specialist block, a small woman came charging out. She collided with Lapeyre and stopped to glare aggressively at him. Her eyes were swollen with crying and, recognizing Pel's belligerent housekeeper, he opened his mouth to speak but got no further, Madame Routy burst into new tears and fled.

Lapeyre walked cautiously down the corridor.

Geneviève was sitting outside Pel's room, her fingers twisting a lace handkerchief, dabbing at her eyes as she stared at the floor.

It was obvious she'd been weeping – was still weeping.

Lapeyre came to a halt, anticipating the worst.

She looked up at him, her eyes brimming, lips trembling, trying to get herself under control. She stood up slowly, took two paces forward and, as he opened his hands in silent question, she collapsed against his chest. His arms went carefully round her and, as she sobbed, his throat thickened. He swallowed hard, let his eyes close momentarily, preparing himself for confirmation of Pel's death. He didn't want to hear it. Then, as he pushed her gently away, held her at arm's length, she smiled.

'Watch out,' she said shakily, 'he's worse than ever.'

Pel was propped up on two stark white pillows, attached by tubes and wires to drips and machinery. He was wearing a white smock that didn't suit him, and a very deep scowl. 'Ruddy nurses,' he said faintly, 'say I can't smoke.'

With his spare pair of specs, he looked like an ancient and very battered Buddy Holly. Lapeyre couldn't help laughing.

'And if you mention my appearance I'll call Matron and have you injected . . . *merde*, ejected.'

'Feeling better, huh?'

'Feeling like death warmed up. Still,' he grinned feebly, 'it's a damn sight better than death itself. My wife tells me I came close.'

'Too close, but I don't think our good Lord is ready to receive a difficult little bugger like you yet. You'd mess up the harmony of His heaven.'

'Even God doesn't want me. Can't say I blame Him.' He paused, either considering the enormity of what he'd said or searching for the strength to continue. 'You know, when I opened my eyes and spoke to Geneviève, she started crying uncontrollably. She says with joy, but I'm not so sure.'

'We're all very relieved you made it.'

'And that silly old witch, Routy, had hysterics.'

'No doubt you sacked her. '

'That made her even worse. Wife had to send her off. What's the score?'

Lapeyre frowned. 'Which match?'

'La Division versus Dalton. Did you get him?'

'We got a man calling himself Dalton, but it wasn't.'

'You've lost me already.'

'He wasn't the real Dalton, he was an actor. It was a set-up. I've been trying to work it out and the only explanation I can come up with is that Silver and Dalton were connected in some way. He must've sent her out to check Colin had been properly dispatched and she ended up in the squat watching him die. But we got him out and she passed on the information that Capelle was an undercover policeman. Dalton presumably started getting worried Colin would talk and, I think, decided to close Dinero down, sending in Silver again to nudge us into doing his dirty work. She asked to speak to the "hairy one", hence when Luzanne gave his burglar's description over the phone, Goldstein knew it was Capelle again. And if the police had sent in a burglar, it was to place bugs, so the conversation he was having with Luzanne was very probably being listened to. That's when he played his ace, deliberately getting Luzanne to announce the time of his arrival, for us to hear, knowing we'd make our arrests shortly afterwards, giving him, the real Dalton, plenty of time to disappear.'

'I'll take your word for it, Lapeyre.'

'Are you all right?'

'Got brain ache. I think they removed half of it when they operated, I can't seem to concentrate for more than a matter of seconds.'

'The effects of anaesthetic.'

'I hope it'll wear off soon, I can't remember where I parked my car.'

'You were brought in by ambulance.'

'See what I mean? What about the other one? Robert Dinero, the Hell's Angel.'

'He's dead, crashed the Land Rover into a motorway bridge.'

'Nasty. Anything else before I fall asleep?'

'We traced what I think was Goldstein's flat and found a man sitting by the phone. Another actor, paid to call Angelo every five minutes and play him the music of his choice.'

Pel blinked slowly and closed his eyes. 'Why?'

'Why what?'

'Why serenade Angelo?'

'He'd done a bunk. Goldstein wanted us chasing him, it was his way of indicating where he was, saving Goldstein the trouble of . . .'

The heavy eyelids lifted a crack. 'How?'

'The SFR satellite picked up the calls and pinpointed his position.'

'Dalton's crafty, isn't he?'

'And the worst of it is, I still don't know what the bastard looks like.'

'He made fools out of us.'

'There'll be a next time.'

'God help you. How's Lambert?'

'Unusually quiet.'

'Goodnight, Lapeyre.'

Et finalement, just for the record, *lundi, le 24 janvier*.
Jean-Philippe Gaffié stood trial for unintentionally causing the death of Sister Agathe. After three hours, he walked out of the courtroom at midday, a free man.

The lawyer acting for the Republic – working on instructions from Maître Brisard and, indirectly, the police – couldn't *prove* he'd caused the nun to topple from her bike and fall over the bridge's parapet into the swirling river below. He couldn't *prove* Gaffié had been drinking; a blood test wasn't taken; Gaffié was identified and picked up seventy-eight hours after the event – too late. His friends, called as witnesses for the defence, swore he wasn't drunk. His wife, under oath when she made her statement, insisted they had seen no nun.

In a final attempt to prove Gaffié's involvement, if not his guilt, Forensic were called in and assured the court that the paint on the lamppost was the same as that used on Renault Kangoos, the car Gaffié had been driving. But Leguyder had to admit, when asked by the defence, that it was also the same paint as used on many other models manufactured in Renault's factories

– therefore it wasn't necessarily a Kangoo that had clipped the lamppost. The fact that Gaffié had lied about the reason for repainting his vehicle was ignored.

No fine, no time; Gaffié walked away scot-free.

Morrison also walked away scot-free.

Apart from the humiliation, demoralizing slander and constant accusations that he'd been subject to since 26th December, he was – at last – revindicated as having simply carried out his duty, while under orders from Commissaire Pel, to arrest the armed robber or robbers expected at the Tabac du Centre. Sandrine Da Costa *had* robbed the tobacconist's, she *had* produced a gun, albeit a toy. Although the court watched the incident replayed from the recorded video, the Republic's representative, a slick Parisian appointed by la Police de la Police, still insisted the girl was defenceless. However, it was finally accepted to be a very convincing replica after Morrison's lawyer suddenly produced a similar one and stuck it under the slick Parisian's nose. His arms went up immediately and he shrieked, 'Have you gone mad! For crying out loud, don't shoot!'

After that, the defence presented the judge with Pujol's and Misset's written statements – Pujol was in court, Misset wasn't – confirming that Sandrine had used threatening behaviour, shouting, 'Get out of the fucking way, or I'll shoot the lot of you.'

Gaffié acquitted.

Morrison acquitted.

The difference between the two men leaving the courts was that Gaffié looked cocky and damn pleased with himself, Morrison looked completely beaten.

Lambert had turned up in person to assist at Morrison's hearing and, uncharacteristically, he offered him a lift home. As the driver waited to draw out of the car park into the heavy traffic, Lambert glanced at the young officer sitting miserably beside him. 'Misset is back on duty,' he said. 'Having considered the situation, the *procureur* believes, and I am in full agreement with him, that it would be wise for you to take some leave, as long as is needed for the formalities of your transfer to be completed. We are both sorry to see you go.'

'*La justice est la liberté en action.*' (Joubert)

'*La justice est le respect de la dignité humaine.*' (Proudhon)

'*La justice est en fonction du prix auquel tu paye ton avocat.*' (Lt J.L. Gilbert to Commissaire E.C.D. Pel, *30 décembre*)